IN HER SHADOW

KRISTIN MILLER

IN HER SHADOW

A NOVEL

BALLANTINE BOOKS
NEW YORK

A Ballantine Books Trade Paperback Original

Published in the United States by Ballantine Books, an imprint of Random House, a division of Penguin Random House LLC, New York.

BALLANTINE and the HOUSE colophon are registered trademarks of Penguin Random House LLC.

This book contains an excerpt from the forthcoming book *The Sinful Lives of Trophy Wives* by Kristin Miller. This excerpt has been set for this edition only and may not reflect the final content of the forthcoming edition.

ISBN 978-1-524-79949-6
Ebook ISBN 978-1-524-79948-9

Printed in the United States of America on acid-free paper

randomhousebooks.com

9 8 7 6 5 4 3 2 1

Book design by Jen Valero

For Justin, forever.

Desire, when it has conceived, gives birth to sin, and sin, when it is fully grown, brings forth death.

JAMES 1:15

IN HER SHADOW

PROLOGUE

COLLEEN

"Help." My voice is hoarse. Fading fast. *Someone help me.*

But no one's coming. No one knows I'm down here. My head pounds. My vision blurs. A stream of blood leaks from my nose, tickling my lips before dripping onto the wine-cellar floor. Pain splinters through my legs, which are crumpled beneath me. Out of instinct and sheer terror, I haul myself across the tile, first one arm and then the other. I shift my weight from side to side, careful not to smash my pregnant belly.

A cracking sound draws my attention to the stairs.

At the top, the dark silhouette of a man blocks the doorway, obstructing the glow that'd spilled into the cellar moments before.

He's not finished with me.

I have to get out of here. He's insane. Not in his right mind. He staggers down the stairs, crying out my name. Behind him, a flash of orange illuminates the kitchen. Smoke billows, dark and thick, clinging to the ceiling as it rolls toward the living room. Something has gone terribly wrong.

Ravenwood is burning.

"Please, for the love of God," I pray. My stomach throbs from where I landed during the final tumble. "Take me if you have to, if it's my time, but—oh, please, God, don't—please don't take our baby."

I don't know what I would do if we lost our baby now. We are so close to having everything, to being blissfully happy with our little family.

"Please . . ." I can't move another inch, and I don't have the energy to fight back. "Please, you don't have to do this. . . ."

He descends further.

Breathless, heart racing, I roll onto my back. I can't escape him. There's nothing more I can do. My vision swims. The acrid scent of smoke burns my nostrils, and I realize if he doesn't kill me, the fire will. Darkness closes in.

Oh, please, God, no . . .

I'm going to die. And it will have all been for nothing.

SUNDAY

One Week Until Colleen's Murder

COLLEEN

"Home sweet home," Michael says, turning in to his driveway at the corner of Beach and Cypress Street. "Impressed?"

I can't breathe, let alone gather my thoughts. I haven't even set foot on his property and I'm already stunned into silence by a throttling mixture of shock and fear.

Stacked boulders guard the entrance like a barricade, and towering eucalyptuses line the narrow, winding drive, shrouding his home. Overhead, tree branches arch like the ceiling of some magnificent cathedral, twisting and tangling, allowing only slivers of morning light to pierce the fog. When we finally emerge from that tunnel of shade, Michael makes a wide, sweeping turn around the circular driveway, passing a six-bay garage before coming to a stop in front of a flight of dark limestone stairs.

He shoves his Maserati into park and races around the front of the car to open my door. Cradling my belly, I step out of the car and brace myself. A thick blanket of mist covers everything in a gray haze. Blasts of frigid air hurtle over the garage and whip through the drive, and I reach up to push the hair out of my eyes. Even the weather has conspired against me. I'm wearing capris and a sweater too thin to stave off the cold; I wasn't prepared for any part of today. He closes the car door behind me with a thud, momentarily drowning out the banging of my heart. The sound echoes off the stone facing of his house and garage and the archway of watchful trees.

"No reason to be nervous," Michael says, patting my hand. "You're going to love it here."

"I'm sure I will," I say, hesitant. "It's a lot to take in, that's all."

Deep down, I know it's more than that. I don't belong here. Not in a home as magnificent as this. Michael and I come from such starkly different backgrounds; the chasm has never felt more profound than it does now, as I stare up at the towering walls of his home. It feels as if I've walked into a designer shoe store, knowing I can't afford a single pair of heels on the shelf. Pretending to be something I'm not, I've tried on my favorite pair and fallen in love, damn the consequences. I'm trying hard to fit into this lifestyle that's so foreign, but I'm already faltering, before I've taken a single step.

On the drive here, Michael said his home was a sanctuary, the only place in the world where he felt he could let his guard down. He told me the house was south of San Francisco, a short drive along the coast, in a private neighborhood off the beaten path. He'd left out the fact that it's prime real estate on a huge corner lot, across the street from a Monterey cypress grove with a stunning view of the sea. He'd forgotten to mention how it was built to look like a gothic castle, with black arched doors and wrought iron accents. How the circular driveway was painted a silvery shade of gray, with a starburst pattern in the center made of some kind of crushed shell. Couldn't he have explained how the fenced-in yard stretched around back, consuming the block?

Or how the house was so close to the sea, I could taste the salty sea air on my tongue?

But until an hour ago, when we were sitting in the car, his hand on my knee, Michael hadn't said much about his home at all. For all he'd revealed, it could've been an apartment in Oakland or a three-bedroom, two-bath house in Pleasanton. He never, not once, let on to the fact that he lived in a mansion plucked from *Luxury Living* magazine.

Michael hadn't ever let me *visit* his home, let alone move in. I would've thought, after five months of dating and frequenting my tiny apartment in the city, he would've wanted to invite me over if for no other reason than to show off this place. A few times I'd asked why it seemed as if he was hiding his home from me. He assured me he wasn't concealing anything; he simply needed more time to open up. How could I be mad? He was an intensely private person, and that was one of the reasons I loved him so much. He was quiet and strong, confident without being confrontational. I liked to believe that he wanted to keep his home private because that was just the way he was, that it had nothing to do with me personally.

Now I try not to think about the obvious truth: he didn't want to bring me here, into his world, because he knew I wouldn't fit in. He'd be right in his assessment, and that hurts above all.

"Come on," he says, grabbing my hand and leading me up the limestone steps. "Grand tour starts this way."

I would laugh, but I fear he'll hear the tremble in my voice, betraying my anxiety. The stone-covered walls are impossibly tall, with details that can't be taken in all at once. The carvings and decorations must've taken years to design. High above, on the eastern side of the house, pointed-arch windows are closed tight with thick swags of dark fabric. A curtain moves suddenly as if touched by a draft, and balloons inward.

I'm being watched.

Breath frozen in my throat, I follow Michael through the massive front door and into the entryway, and gape at the enormousness of it all. Colossal vaulted ceilings. Sparkling multi-tiered chandeliers. Ornate, gold-rimmed mirrors. Paintings—original and renowned, I'm sure—color the walls. On the left, a dark wood staircase wide enough for Michael and me to traipse upstairs hand in hand coils like a serpent to the second floor. I can't help but compare it to the grand staircase of the *Titanic* shown in the film—the only thing missing is the gold cupid smirking in the foreground. At my feet, a mosaic of colored marble stretches to a room that's paneled in pale maple and furnished sparsely with black leather couches. Ahead, glimpsed through an oversize window and a set of glass double doors, an emerald lawn rolls toward Cypress Street and the Monterey cypress grove beyond.

That must be the public entry, I realize, as the crisp ocean air wafts through the open windows. And we'd just come in through the back door, the servants' entrance.

Servants.

This place is too large for Michael to keep up himself. Will there be people cleaning up after us, cooking our meals, and caring for the landscaping? Never in a million years would I have dreamed I could have anyone seeing to my needs, let alone the staff of a grand house.

To think, if I hadn't gotten a job at Harris Financial, Michael's company in the city, we would never have met. Under different circumstances, I might have visited the cypress grove one Sunday afternoon and walked right past this place. I would have wondered what kind of people could afford to live this way, so close to California's coastline, and fantasized about what went on inside these walls.

"This way," Michael says, leading the way past two powder rooms. "I've been wanting to show you this since the first time I saw you burying your face in a mystery novel."

We enter the library through a set of heavy double doors. The air is staler in here, as though the windows looking out on the lawn haven't been open in some time. A Persian rug in rich shades of brown and red stretches out beneath our feet, worn in the center from years of padding across the knotted silk and wool. Shelves crowded with books cover three walls, and on the fourth, a marble fireplace promises to radiate warmth through the room. Plump chairs face the hearth, and I wonder if this is Michael's personal space. Will I sit beside him here, reading one of my favorite novels? Or will we spend our time in the living room with its breathtaking view overlooking the grove?

"It's grand," I say, because I'm feeling smaller by the minute. "Is this where you unwind at the end of the day?"

"Sometimes."

But he doesn't offer any more than that.

If I want to belong here, I'll have to learn the routines Michael already has in place. I'll need to fit seamlessly into the day-to-day.

It'll take a long time to adjust.

"So?" Michael asks, when we've returned to the sun-flooded brilliance of the living room. "You love it, right?"

"It's . . ." *Intimidating.* ". . . beautiful."

"We call it Ravenwood."

We.

The word stings, burrowing deep in me with a poison that makes me ashamed of myself. He doesn't mean him and me, and we both know it. This is the home he occupied with his wife—his *missing* wife. Joanna isn't missing in the sense that someone kidnapped her, only that she moved back to Los Angeles to live with her sister, and hasn't been heard from since last July. Six months without a single word.

At least that's what Michael tells me.

He hasn't filed for divorce yet, and the thought bothers me more than I'll ever admit aloud. He doesn't say much about their marriage or its demise, and I don't ask about either. Don't want him to think I'm meddling. Adding my two cents where they don't belong. The last thing I want is to push him away or have him close down completely. So I've given him time and space to figure things out on his own. Eventually though, we'll have to address it, and I assume the time is coming soon.

They were married five years, Michael and Joanna, and before she vanished Ravenwood was their home. When my heart starts to ache with the fear that he didn't truly want to invite me here, I remind myself Joanna is his past. I am his future. Michael wouldn't have invited me to move into this gorgeous estate, he wouldn't be starting a family with me, if he didn't believe we have what it takes to make a relationship last.

All that matters is the health of our baby.

Last month, after I awoke to find spots of blood on my sheets, I was terrified of hearing the worst, of losing the baby. *Rest,* the doctor insisted. He said the spotting was probably caused by overexertion at work. Nothing to be too concerned about, but I'm desperate to give our baby as much of a chance as possible.

Stay off your feet, no stress or strain.

I soared with relief, knowing our baby was still growing inside me, but I had no idea how much my life would change in order to meet this prescription of rest and relaxation. When I told Michael, he immediately insisted I quit my job. He said he'd provide for us and suggested we live at his home in Point Reina until the baby was born. Sometimes I wonder: If the pregnancy had been smooth sailing, and the baby had been fine, would we have continued sleeping at my place? Would I be moving in? Or would Ravenwood still be a giant secret between us?

It kills me that I know the answers to those questions without even asking them.

"The people before us must've named the place," Michael goes on. "They engraved its name into the exposed beam above the front door. See? Didn't feel right changing it."

Letting my gaze wander over the letters gouged into the wood, I stroke my hands over my growing belly—something I've caught myself doing a lot lately.

Ravenwood.

I wonder who named this home, who walked across this gleaming floor before Michael and Joanna, what secrets are still hiding here. Moving to the wide span of living room windows, I stare at the twisted branches of the cypress grove across the street. After our baby is born, we'll take long walks at sunset, I promise myself. Follow the winding dirt path into the dark, past that first row of trees, and then deeper, where the cool ocean breeze will filter through the green canopy, filling us with a sense of peace.

It'll be heavenly.

A flat-screen television is mounted above a fireplace so clean I'd eat off the stones. On the mantel, a carving of a raven perches proudly, keeping watch over everything. Wings tucked against its narrow wooden body. Head tilted upward. The leather couches are flanked by matching armchairs, and when I slide my hand over the cushions, I don't leave a single imprint. Definitely can't see cuddling up to watch my late-night shows on that thing. I don't even know if we'd both fit side by side. Spooning is going to be near impossible. The books on the coffee table are all hardbound, stacked in a gradient scale from dark to light. Someone had too much time on his hands.

"Because this area is off the main highway and hidden behind the grove, it's quiet," Michael says, his tone direct. As if he's on a business call, hammering out the details of a new deal. "Not many people know about it. It's our private sanctuary. Perfect for what you and the baby need right now."

The baby.

Not *his* baby. Not yet. Funny how such a small word can kill you inside. Just once, couldn't it be *our* baby?

He leads me to the dining room. It features a grand table that easily seats twenty, a cabinet full of china, and a stocked mahogany bar.

"The ceiling was modeled after a cathedral we visited in England," he says dryly, pointing upward without so much as a glance. "It's called a rib-vault. Every room on this level has a fireplace. You won't feel a chill the rest of the winter."

My mouth hangs open in awe as I glance up. The ceiling is nothing less than magnificent. Painted in starkly contrasting dark and light, the rib-like beams branch out overhead like a spiderweb.

"That sounds nice," I say, but I'm still trying to picture our dinners here, at this table, beneath this regal ceiling.

I don't belong here.

The kitchen is situated beyond the dining room, through a large arched doorway. From what I've seen so far, it's the most modern room in the house, though no less striking than the rest. Stainless steel appliances. Two gas ranges with six burners each and elaborate hoods. White-and-gray speckled quartz counters. Dark wood cabinetry with intricate carvings across the top. Six barstools have been arranged around a sizeable square island—the perfect place to have breakfast when it's only the two of us. A door against the back wall most likely leads to the side yard, though I can't quite tell from where I'm standing.

Instead of continuing the tour outside, Michael opens the door to our immediate left, beside a set of stairs much narrower than the one in the foyer.

"I know you can't enjoy this now," he says, clicking on the light, "but in a year or so, you're going to think this is the best feature in the house."

We descend a steep flight of stairs into a tiled entry that smells like cleaning solution and old wood. Wall-to-wall glass enclosures catch my eye first. Hundreds of wine bottles fill the pigeonholes, each one backlit to showcase its labels.

Michael stands in the center of the space like a king, spreading his arms wide. "Great, right? There's a self-contained cooling system in here that keeps the temperature at fifty-nine degrees."

I've never known Michael to drink wine. When we go out, he orders whiskey. Every time. He doesn't even check the wine list. Why would he act as if the wine cellar is the highlight of the house when he doesn't drink, and I can't either?

Could this have been—it kills me to think it—Joanna's vault? Were these her bottles, and her favorite part of Ravenwood?

A shiver creeps up my spine. I fold my arms over my chest to ward off the chill. "It's amazing."

"Look up," he says proudly. "Italian tile, vaulted like a barrel. Cost a fortune, but worth every penny. Come on, there's more I want to show you."

As we return to the main level, I realize Michael's home is immaculate from corner to corner. Not a single piece of clutter. No dishes in the sink needing to be washed. Not a speck of dust on the windowsills framing the sea. It's pristine.

"Everything you need should be within walking distance." Michael's gaze flickers to my belly, but it doesn't linger there. It never does. "It shouldn't be a problem that you don't have a car."

Living in the city, I never needed one. Parking near my building was a nightmare, and public transit was top notch. Now, though, I'm not sure what the future holds, and it's frightening. If I want to go farther than the small town of Point Reina, I'm completely dependent upon Michael to get me there. If I really think about it, I'm trapped.

"There's a small store," he goes on, as if reading my mind, "and a doctor's office, bank, you name it, so you won't need to go far."

Nodding, listening, I take in everything around me. Something is off, though I can't pinpoint what it is. It's not the house—it's gorgeous and more than I could've ever hoped for. But no cars pass on the street beyond the living room windows. No garbage trucks honk at cars parked in their way. No drunks stumble home after a long night partying. It's peaceful and serene. Everything San Francisco is not, and precisely what my doctor told me I needed. But that doesn't mean it's going to be easy to fit into Michael's world.

Even if I wanted to protest this new living arrangement, there's no turning back. The lease was up on my tiny apartment in the China Basin district. Everything I own is already on its way over in the moving van. It isn't much, but it's all I have.

Now that I think of it, I know exactly what's missing from Ravenwood.

Joanna's things.

Where are the candles and fuzzy blankets? The romantic, whimsical artwork, potted flowers, and feminine scents? Joanna must've had at least a few of those things, and they're noticeably missing. Everything in Ravenwood is glossy, cold, and expensive. Simple and starkly beautiful. Missing a woman's touch.

"Come on, there's more to see," Michael urges, heading up the main staircase. At the landing, the hallway veers east and west. Straight ahead, out the giant windows to the south, is the grove. He makes a hard turn toward the east wing, as if he's climbed the stairs and headed that way a thousand times before, but at the last second, he pivots suddenly on his heel and turns left. "You'll love the view from the master."

"What's that way?" I ask, ghosting my hand over the wrought iron banister.

The east wing is cloaked in shadow. Every door is shut.

Michael doesn't slow his pace and doesn't turn around as he answers, "The east wing houses a billiards room, gym, screening room, two bathrooms. If you want to get into any of those rooms, you'll have to let me know."

"Why's that?"

"I keep them locked."

"All the time?"

At that, he turns, his mouth in a hard line. "You know how much work takes out of me, Colleen. I don't have as much time for recreation as I used to. It didn't make sense to have Samara clean the rooms in both wings, if I was only going to be using one side."

"Samara?"

"My housekeeper."

"I can't wait to meet her," I say, glancing back at the doors once more. Was Samara the one watching from the window when we first pulled up? No, couldn't be. It's Sunday. Surely Michael wouldn't have staff here on the weekends. But if not her, then who? "It's only the three larger rooms on that side, then?"

What had he said? *Billiards, screening room, and gym.*

"There's an office, and two bathrooms as well. Oh, and a smaller bedroom and second master." His pace slows, only a beat, as he glances at me out of the corner of his eye. "But you shouldn't have any reason to go in there."

What an odd thing to say.

"Is it for guests?"

"No."

"Extra storage?"

"I guess you could say that." He pauses. "This way."

But I wonder what he'd been about to say, and what he keeps in those two other rooms in the east wing. They're not for guests or storage, that much is certain. I can always tell when he's lying—his voice lifts. It's slight, but I've come to know it well. He lies at work. Not about serious things, of course, but tiny white lies about how long a certain meeting lasted or when he'll be able to finish paperwork.

I don't like the fact that he's lying to me now. Especially about something as ridiculous as what he keeps behind those doors. What could he possibly have to hide?

We pass half a dozen bedrooms decorated in dark, masculine tones, and just as many bathrooms, before reaching the master. These doors are left open, I realize, because these are the rooms I'm allowed to go in freely.

When I reach the entry to the master, I swallow a gasp. Minimally decorated, it has a king-size bed with a nightstand on either side. White lampshades. White duvet, fluffy and inviting, piled with a dozen white pillows. Over the lower quarter of the bed, a sapphire blanket has been perfectly folded, adding a tiny splash of color to the immaculately decorated space.

Is this the bed where *they* slept together? Did she sleep with her head on that pillow, right next to his, tangled in those white sheets? My stomach sours at the image.

As my attention shifts from the bed to the windows, I approach Michael and follow his line of sight. Beyond the glass is an unobstructed view of the sea. Waves tumble and crest before crashing onto the sand. The weather's churning kelp in the surf and tossing it around. Wind gusts over mounds of sand and dense shrubbery, bending the gnarly branches of the cypresses in the distance. It'll rain tonight, I'm sure of it.

I must've made a shocked sound, because Michael says, "I know, right? It's a twenty-million-dollar view."

I can't fathom that number, and once again, I'm reminded how surreal it is that I'll be living here, with my former boss, on his beach estate.

He wraps his arms around my belly and rests his chin on my shoulder. He smells clean and fresh, like the air after a good rain. "Everything is going to work out, Coll. It'll be perfect. You'll see."

Leaning against him, I let out a sigh and weave my fingers

through his. And then, slowly, I guide his hands in small circles over my belly. "I hope so."

"You're good here, aren't you?" He drops his hands from mine and fishes for the keys in his pocket as he turns away. "I've got to get back to the city before ten."

"Now?" I can't keep the disappointment from my tone. "It's Sunday."

"I have a big meeting with the Lennox Group first thing tomorrow morning, and the team isn't ready to present the new development yet."

"Can't someone else take over? Just for today?"

"Honey, you know this won't wait. Lennox is important. Besides, you can handle the moving guys. It's your stuff anyway. I wouldn't know where anything goes." He hands me a single key. "Check out the place. Make yourself at home. I'll be back by seven. Still early enough to spend time together tonight, right?"

"Sure," I manage, though my voice wobbles. "Sounds great."

"Hey, are you feeling all right?" He brushes the back of his hand down my cheek. "You went pale just then."

"Now that you mention it, I am feeling a little queasy. I'm sure it's simply the excitement of today."

"Why don't you lie down?" He motions toward that pristine bed. "The movers won't be here for a while. A twenty-minute nap might do you good."

"Yeah. Maybe."

"The doctor did tell you to take it easy."

I let him guide me toward the bed, and as I lie down on top of the covers, I can't help but wonder if this is his side or—God, I hate to think it—*hers*. A fresh linen scent wafts from the duvet and pillow, giving nothing away. Fishing my phone out of the back pocket of my capris, I set it on the bedside table, along with the key to his home.

Michael shoots me one of his classic smiles—the kind that usually gets him anything he wants—and when I finally rest on the pillow, he says, "I knew you'd love it here."

And then, before I can say goodbye, he's gone, shutting the bedroom door softly behind him.

His words replay in my head as I focus on my breathing and try to relax. *I knew you'd love it here.*

How could I not? The views of the Monterey cypress trees and the ocean are stunning. The air is pure, and I feel like I can breathe here. And this house—Ravenwood—is perfect. Everything I could've dreamed of and more.

But . . .

There always seems to be a *but* where Michael is concerned. He wants to be with me, *but* thinks we shouldn't let too many people know yet. He must be worried about how it'll look to his employees, my former co-workers. Sleeping with the boss is hardly professional. If he's not ready, I respect that. I'd wait forever for him to come around. After all, he's the perfect guy—kind and witty, handsome and sophisticated, warmhearted and financially stable—and he wants a big family. Lots of kids running around. A few dogs. Summers spent running on the beach below the house.

But when two tiny blue lines showed up on that stick, the first step toward a future he said he'd always dreamed of, he seemed removed from it all. Distant and almost melancholy. We hadn't planned on getting pregnant—after all, we'd only been dating for a month—and had used a condom every time we were together. One of them must've broken; it was the only explanation I could give when I'd missed my period.

It was both the most shocking and the most satisfying moment in my entire life. I know this baby will be the greatest thing to happen to either of us, but I want *him* to want it, too. I ache for the joy to be *ours,* not solely mine.

And now, while he works, I'm going to have to occupy

myself, alone in this giant house he shared with the wife who left him.

....

Even before I open my eyes, the smell of crisp bacon and freshly brewed coffee hits me, urging me to get out of bed. Bacon *and* coffee? Michael must've decided to stay home after all.

As I slide out from beneath the covers, a smile on my face and one hand brushing my stomach, a draft sweeps through the room, chilling me. Across the room, floor-to-ceiling drapes are drawn, but sunlight slashes through the crack at the center, cutting the floor in half.

How long have I slept? Couldn't have been more than an hour. Reaching for my phone on the bedside table, I check the time: ten-thirty. I've slept almost two hours in this bed that's not mine, in this home where I'm a complete stranger.

I must've been more tired than I thought.

Running my fingers through my hair, I notice boxes stacked near the closet. Strange, but I didn't hear the movers arrive. I should've stirred at the beeping of a truck reversing down the long drive, the slamming sound of the front door, or Michael's footsteps. *Something.* I don't normally sleep that soundly, especially in a place that isn't mine. Head aching, I shuffle toward the closet.

If Michael kept to one side when Joanna lived here, it isn't the case now. His things spread across both sides, and it's impossible for me to tell where *she* could have fit. Where did Joanna hang her clothes? On the right, or the left?

There must be traces of her somewhere in this house. I wish I knew more, but Michael and Joanna's life together is as much of a mystery as what separated them.

All I know is this: One day, Michael and Joanna were living their picture-perfect life. Gorgeous home. Travels through the Mediterranean, Africa, and Eastern Europe. After trying and failing to get pregnant for years, they were finally going to be parents. She was five months along and the baby was healthy. Then, out of the blue, she was gone. Office rumor has it she left him for someone else. Some think she lost the baby and her grief drove her away from him.

I'm currently twenty weeks along. At the same point in the pregnancy Joanna was when she left him. Odd, but I hadn't realized that until now.

Michael won't tell me what really happened between them, and the last thing I want is to make him think I'm prying into his past. It must bother him to know there could be a child out there that he'll have nothing to do with. I'm sure he tried to get Joanna back, or at least confirm her whereabouts, but came up empty-handed.

I can't wait to see him. Thank him for staying home, when he could've ditched me for his stuffy Lennox Group team. Snatching my phone and the lone key off the nightstand, I head into the hall. Barefoot at the top of the stairs, I stop. My eyes go to the doors in the east wing.

What's the reason he keeps those doors locked? *It didn't make sense to have Samara clean the rooms in both wings.* I'm not buying it. He could easily keep the doors closed. Why locked? Why the secrecy? I wonder if my key will work. . . .

It'd be easy to check. It'd only take a few seconds. He's so busy making breakfast, he wouldn't even know. On the tiptoe trek over, I glance over the rail, down to the span below. Music wafts from somewhere. I recognize Hozier's "Work Song" immediately. Funny, I've never known Michael to enjoy listening to music. On the weekends, when we're together in the mornings, he prefers to watch the news.

Checking over my shoulder, I try to shove my key into the lock of the nearest door, but it won't fit. Not even close. Out of sheer curiosity, I press my ear against the door.

Silence.

From somewhere below, Hozier wails.

Moving to the next door, and the next, I test the key in each lock and finally round the corner. The hall is long, mirroring the layout of the west wing. At the end, where I'd find the master suite on the opposite side, an oversize set of double doors calls me closer.

The second master bedroom.

You shouldn't have any reason to go in there.

Still aware of the music drifting from the kitchen, I tiptoe over the plush carpet, eyeing the tapestries—beautifully woven images of the sea in soft blue and gray hues—as I approach the other master. Grasping the handle, I begin to turn it.

"Miss Roper?"

I spin, screeching in terror as the stranger's dark eyes widen in horror.

"Jesus, don't scream," he pleads, covering his ears. "I'm Dean Lewis, the Harrises' chef. I heard you wandering around up here, and thought I could direct you to the kitchen."

"Michael?" I call out.

"Shh." He squints in pain. "Mr. Harris isn't here. He left for work hours ago."

"Michael didn't mention a chef," I stutter, hands up in pathetic defense. Surely Michael would've told me if someone else was going to be here, and this man isn't wearing an apron, or anything to identify him. My heart is pounding. "Don't come any closer."

He sighs, canting his head to one side. "I'm not going to hurt you, Miss Roper. Didn't you get a text from Mr. Harris?"

I hadn't noticed a message alert.

Heart in my throat, I try to make mental notes in case I need to describe the intruder to the police. He's a few inches taller than Michael—six foot two, maybe. Black hair cut short on the sides, longer on top. No facial hair, but he's got an ugly scar on the right side of his neck. Probably from another home invasion gone wrong. White shirt. Blue linen pants. No shoes.

He folds his arms over his chest. "He should've told you how things are normally run around here," he says primly. "There's a routine we keep to, and this isn't it."

I'm listening, gripping the door handle at my back. If I could get into this suite, I could slam the door behind me and call the police.

"I usually come in at eight o'clock." The stranger's mouth pinches as he eyes the key I'm still gripping. "I cook the meals for the day, and—oh damn—your bacon's burning."

He spins and darts down the stairs, sliding his hand along the rail as he goes. *Here's my chance.* Releasing the door handle, I sprint across the bridge overlooking the living room, back into the west wing. I dart inside and lock the master bedroom door behind me, breathe a sigh of relief, and dial the number for Michael's cell. He picks up on the first ring.

"Hey, sweetheart. Rest well?"

"Tell me you have a chef," I blurt without thinking.

"Yeah, I probably should've mentioned him, but I thought a hot, home-cooked breakfast would be a nice surprise. Everything all right? You sound winded."

"He scared me half to death." Flopping onto the edge of the bed, I rub a protective hand over my belly. "He caught me in the—in the middle of the hall, and said something about a schedule, and bacon and—well, I thought a crazy ax-murderer had broken in or something."

Michael laughs. "Ax-murderers don't kill you with breakfast."

"How would *you* know?"

"Don't be ridiculous, sweetheart." His tone is flat. "Dean Lewis is harmless. Best chef in the area."

My heartbeat finally slows, now that I'm confident I won't be hacked to pieces. "Any other help I should know about before I let you get back to work?"

"Someone comes by on Tuesdays and Thursdays to do landscaping. Dean and Samara, our housekeeper, are the only help we use daily, with the exception of Saturdays. I thought we'd like to keep that day quiet."

We. Does he mean the two of us this time? I bet he and *Joanna* decided to keep Saturdays to themselves. I try to push away thoughts of how they'd spend their days together.

"So there are always people here," I say.

"No, not *always.* Not if we don't want them to be. We can always adjust the days they work. Do you have a problem with something?"

"No." But it's only Sunday, and I'm afraid to stare down the long barrel of the week. "I just wasn't expecting such a large . . . operation."

"I couldn't keep Ravenwood up by myself." More voices join the conversation in his office. I wish I was there with him all day, the way I used to be. "It takes a team of people to keep the house running so I can be here. Listen, Coll, I have to run. Love you."

He ends the call. I sit for a moment, then pull myself together. Unlocking the door, I traipse downstairs into the kitchen.

"Let's try this again," I say sheepishly as I slide onto a stool at the massive island. "Good morning. I'm sorry about before, I didn't know that you—"

"It's fine." Dean's tone is clipped as he feverishly shifts from the stove to the counter and back again. "As long as you enjoy your bacon burned to a crisp."

Folding my hands over the quartz, I take another look at him. I notice the seams on his linen pants are crisp, and he's wearing a thick gold-chain bracelet. Not exactly daytime ax-murderer wear. He's young too. Thirty, maybe.

"Bacon's bacon," I assure him. "I don't think it's possible to ruin it."

"Coffee?" he asks, after removing the charred bacon from the grill. "I made you decaf."

Before I can answer, he pulls a delicate china cup from a cabinet and adds two spoonfuls of sugar and a heap of vanilla creamer before passing it over. It's not the way I like my coffee. Not even close—I prefer mine black with a shake of cinnamon. He didn't even ask.

"Thank you." I'm not about to correct him. Not when I'm pretty sure he's still pissed over my freak-out that ruined his precious bacon. Who knew chefs could be so touchy? How did he expect me to react anyway, when I wake to find a strange man has been *cooking* while I slept upstairs? "When did you get here? I didn't even hear you come in."

"I told you, Miss Roper. I'm here every morning at eight."

"But you weren't here earlier, were you? When Michael was here? He didn't leave until almost nine."

"This morning was an exception, thanks to you. Every day—except for Saturdays, which are my days off—I'm here at eight. This morning, Mr. Harris requested I make you something special since you weren't feeling well. That called for a late trip to the market." He glances at the strips of burned bacon and makes a disgruntled sound. "Anyhow, I have a key. I always let myself in so I don't wake Jo—anyone."

"You can call me Colleen." I pretend I didn't hear the slip. "Miss Roper sounds way too formal. If you're here every morning, we're going to be seeing a lot of each other."

"I prefer formality." *He's still annoyed with me.* Spinning to the sink, he scrubs his hands and gets back to work. "There's nothing wrong with boundaries. They keep the water clear."

Yet if I'm not mistaken, he was about to call Joanna by her first name a moment earlier.

The coffee he poured is so sweet it zings my teeth. Did he make it this way because this is how he used to make it for Joanna? Am I sitting where Joanna used to sit?

"Eat up," he orders, sliding a plate in front of me.

It's a tower of eggs sprinkled with something red on top—maybe bell pepper—and parsley for decoration. The only time I've seen meals this artistic is when I've gone out in the city with Michael. If he employed a chef in his home who could cook the same way, why didn't we save the money and come here instead?

There's only one answer: he didn't want me here, in his personal space. In *Joanna's* space, I correct, feeling tears sting. And Chef Dean doesn't seem too happy to see me here, either.

"What is this?" I ask, stabbing a chunk of egg.

"Artichoke-scrambled eggs Benedict on an overturned English muffin. It's one of her favorites."

The ache in my chest grows stronger. *One of her favorites*. Joanna might as well be sitting on the stool beside me.

Dean's breakfast is fit for a king—or, I suppose, a queen. Joanna, the former Queen of Ravenwood, with her perfect home and personal gourmet chef.

"You can leave the plate there when you're through with it," he says. "I usually cook all the meals for the day first, pack them in the fridge, and then wash the dishes before leaving. I'm out by eleven most days, unless Mr. Harris requests something really special."

Mr. Harris. So he's not on an informal first-name basis with Michael either. Only Joanna. I don't know whether to be offended or curious. Maybe I'm both. I push the coffee aside and dive into breakfast as he removes duck from the refrigerator and begins prepping a second meal.

"How long have you worked for Michael?" I ask, picking out the artichokes and pushing them to the side of my plate.

"I've been employed at Ravenwood for the last two years." He frowns. "Do you not like artichokes?"

"They're fine, it's just—I don't think they'd go the best with eggs."

His left eye twitches, as if I've tried to stab him in the face with a fork.

"It's the pregnancy," I cover up hastily. "My tastes are out of whack. It's delicious." And then I shove a heap into my mouth and choke down the artichoke before it makes me gag.

"You're one of those picky ones, aren't you?" he remarks, spinning on his heel and burying his head back in the fridge. "This is going to be a harder transition than I thought."

Had he meant to say that more softly so I didn't hear?

"Do you have any food allergies?" he demands.

"Not that I know of." I bite off the end of a charred piece of bacon, simply to prove I won't make a fuss if something isn't perfection. "What are you making now?"

He slams a bunch of endive on the cutting board and slowly slides a butcher knife out of the block. "Miss Roper, I know you're new here, and unaccustomed to the way this household is run, but allow me to enlighten you."

I feel slapped. As if I'm a child being scolded for not finishing my dinner. "I was only trying to make small talk," I grumble, setting down my fork.

Raising an eyebrow in distaste, he lifts the butcher knife high. Then he slams it down, severing the leafy vegetable in half.

"Most days Mr. Harris has left for work by the time I show up. I let myself in and start on breakfast. You stay in your room, asleep, until the coffee finishes brewing. When you make your way out, I serve you wherever you choose to sit, and then you eat in silence. This allows me to finish my work. Lunch today is a summer citrus salad with red Belgian endive, microgreens, candied walnuts, and raspberry vinaigrette. Dinner will be a baby arugula salad with dried figs and duck prosciutto, paired with rack of lamb, haricot verts, and fresh figs. Unless Mr. Harris changes his mind and wants something simpler, like seared Alaskan halibut over stir-fry vegetables. Do those sound suitable for your delicate pregnancy tastes?"

I stay in my room until the coffee's done?

I eat in silence?

That was *their* routine, and how Joanna started her mornings. He expects me to slip right into her shoes—designer, I'm sure—and dance the same step.

Rather than wait for me to answer, he dives back into the fridge for more ingredients. How do I respond? I couldn't understand most of what he said. He was speaking a foreign language. Culinary-ese. Did he say 'verts'? What on earth are those?

"That all sounds wonderful." I force a smile. "But I'd hate to see you overwork. Food from a can is good enough for me."

He rises from his crouched position and stares, his jaw dropping in horror.

"I'm kidding." My smile falters. "I'm sure whatever you cook will be fine."

"*Fine,*" he whispers, parroting me. "I'm sure."

I eat in silence as I was told to and listen to the music filling Ravenwood. I try to focus on the emotion in Hozier's voice, but I can't stop thinking about Joanna in this immaculate space, eating his food.

"How are the menus decided?" I wonder aloud when the silence becomes unbearable.

"When Joanna and Mr. Harris lived here together, she and I would pick the menu every morning. I shopped and prepped based on what she preferred. After she—well, when Mr. Harris found himself alone, I'd email the menu to his offices. Since August, he's been dining out most of the time—I'm assuming that has something to do with you—so the food would rot in the containers. Awful waste of time."

"I'm sure he appreciated your work," I offer, stabbing a chunk of artichoke. "And he had to have eaten *some* of the food you cooked. I mean, we didn't eat every meal together."

"I wasn't talking about the food."

My mind reels. What was an awful waste of time then, if not the hours spent cooking?

The realization trickles in, dark and cold.

"Me," I think aloud, the tremble in my voice giving away my nerves. "You meant Michael's time spent on *me*."

Dean huffs deeply and turns his attention back to his masterpiece. "I'm teasing, obviously. One thing you'll learn about me is I have a dreadful sense of humor, and the timing that goes along with it. But I *can* cook. What do you think?"

"It's great." I smile again, pushing my food around the plate. "Really."

"It was Joanna's favorite breakfast. All of the meals I cook are her favorites, actually. Tailored to her tastes. Her requests. Right down to the seasoning. None of those will be changing, of course. Mr. Harris has specifically requested all meals remain the same."

"Has he?" I feel the color drain from my face. "Well, if that's the way he wants it, I'm sure it'll be lovely." I bet Joanna loved every bite of his meals. I'm sure they talked about fancy flavors and tastes and recipes to try for Michael when he had a long week at work. I look up at Dean. He's standing still as stone, unmoving for the first time in the huge kitchen, a hand on his hip, the other clutching a dish towel. He eyes me carefully, waiting. I get the sensation that I'm being baited, analyzed for signs of weakness. I feel two inches tall. As if I'm an incompetent child who can't appreciate the glorious food he's prepared.

Suddenly I feel like I'm going to be sick.

"I'm sorry," I mumble as I rise to my feet, steadying myself on the counter. "If you don't mind, I'm going to head upstairs for a while. Start unpacking a few things."

Taking the stairs slowly, I hear Dean turn up the radio. He sings along over the racket of clanging pots and pans. He knows he got under my skin—he has to know. And he's doing it on purpose. He must've been friends with Joanna. They must've been close. Here I am, replacing her, an unworthy imposter. It can't be easy to lose a friend and gain a stranger.

Does Michael feel the same?

He wants me to live here, walk where Joanna walked, rest my head where she did, eat what she ate. But in time, he'll get over her. Soon, the meals will be to *my* taste.

"Everything's going to be perfect," I say aloud, remembering Michael's words as I rummage through the first box. "Perfect."

....

After Dean leaves, I pad downstairs and nearly collide with a squat woman with short, mousy-brown hair. She's wearing a midnight-blue polo, khakis, and a pair of blue Nikes that match the color of her shirt. This time, I'm better prepared for the unexpected intrusion on my privacy.

"Good morning," I say, stopping with a smile. "I'm Colleen Roper, Michael's—"

"I know who you are," she interjects with a nod. "I'm Samara Graves, the housekeeper. Pleasure to finally meet you. We've been prepped for your arrival."

"How so?"

She begins digging through her pockets. "We were instructed you were to have no stress and do nothing that will cause physical strain on your body. Here." She hands over a ring with two silver keys attached. "Mr. Harris also asked that I give these to you. The keys to the castle. The one he gave you earlier opens every outer door. That one," she says, pointing to the more jagged key, "opens most of the doors on the inside—at least to the rooms you'll be using."

She doesn't mention what the second key on the ring opens, though I think I already know.

"Thank you," I say. "That was sweet of Michael to make copies so quickly."

"Those aren't copies, miss." She strides past me. "They were Joanna's."

"Oh, I—I don't know what to say." The key ring seems to burn into my palm. "Thanks."

Why wouldn't Michael have made me another set—one of my own? It's not like it would've been incredibly difficult or expensive.

Samara turns back, a strange smirk lifting the corners of her thin lips. "Would you like me to give you a tour around Ravenwood? Or can you find your own way?"

I pocket the keys before replying. "A tour isn't necessary. I'll find my own way. Thank you, Samara."

Without an acknowledgment, she continues her trek up the stairs. But when I hit the bottom, I swear I can hear her laughing from the top.

I perch on the edge of a black leather couch in the living room, amid rows of taped boxes, and strain to hear where Samara heads first. *West wing*. I wonder—no, I shouldn't even be paying attention to such things. I should be focused on my own workload. There's still so much I have to do to prepare for our baby. Shopping and decorating the nursery top the list. Unpacking. Hiding out every morning until Dean leaves isn't going to work. Not if I want to be productive.

Outside, curtains of mist roll in over the waves, sweeping over the garden and right up to the house. The sunshine won't last long at this rate, and from the look of the flat gray horizon, another storm is moving in on the heels of the last. Whether it's the excitement of the morning, the decaf, or the earlier exchange with Dean, I'm bushed, and the day hasn't even really begun.

Through the spotless glass of the living room window, I watch the parade of Point Reina's royalty with morbid curiosity. The sidewalks are busy this morning. A forty-something brunette steers a stroller around a puddle and over a curb. Another, a blonde, strides across the street holding a bulging bag of groceries. I imagine them to be mothers and wives, nannies and mistresses. They're late to yoga. Book club. Private tennis lessons. On their way to secret midday rendezvous in a dark corner of Starbucks. All important appointments that can't be missed, of course.

A hatchback BMW passes slowly, curving around the bend leading toward the cypress grove. The woman inside waves at the others, and they all smile.

Michael didn't tell me he lived in Stepford.

One woman in particular catches my eye. Waving enthusiastically at someone on the opposite side of the street, she's strutting over the sidewalk as if it's a catwalk, hips swaying, blond curls bouncing. To my surprise, she turns into Michael's yard. I slide to the edge of the couch, watching her glide through the garden toward the entrance.

Oh God, no.

I'm not ready to meet anyone else. I'm barely keeping my head above water as it is.

She's decked in workout gear—Nikes, leggings, white tank top peeking from beneath a purple sweater—but one glance at her flawlessly curled hair and fully made-up face, and I know she's not headed to a gym. Her eyes are outlined, her lipstick too glossy and perfect.

She gracefully skips up the front steps and raps on the door. Two sharp bangs.

I hold my breath and wait for movement from upstairs. Am I supposed to answer? Is that what Joanna did? Or did she wait for Samara to greet guests?

More knocking.

No steps overhead.

Joanna's not here anymore. I'm the woman of the house now. *I* should be the one to welcome people to Ravenwood. It's my job to make them feel comfortable in this place, even if I'm not.

"Who is it?" I call out, rising.

"Rachael Martin." The voice is kind. "I'm Travis's wife. I—Travis and I—live next door. I wanted to stop by and introduce myself."

Oh, thank *God*. She's normal. A thoughtful neighbor from right next door. Although the Point Reina vicinity boasts multimillion-dollar homes, each one impossibly lovelier than the one beside it, I can't quite pull the Martins' home from memory. I'd been so preoccupied with the scale of Ravenwood, I hadn't taken time to scope out its neighbors.

As I catch a glimpse of my face in the reflection of the window beside the door, I nearly jump. "Just a minute," I call out.

My face is gaunt and my color is off. I'm too pale, nearly translucent, and my cheeks look sunken. Our baby might be quite literally sucking the life out of me. I pinch my cheeks, smooth back my frizzy, chestnut-dyed hair, and adjust my sweater.

As good as I'm going to get.

"Good morning," Rachael says when I open the door. She's smiling brightly, expectantly. "You're Michael's new woman, right? Colleen?"

New woman? "That's me."

"It's great to finally meet you." She leans around me to peek inside. "Is Dean still around? I've been craving his apple cider beignets for ages. Don't mind if I come in for a few, do you?"

"I'm afraid you've missed Dean, but . . ."

"Oh, that's all right. We'll have plenty to talk about without him. I live over there." She waits for me to take a step onto the porch, and then points to the spectacle of architecture to the right of Ravenwood. "That's us, Travis and me, just next door."

"The see-through one?"

"That's it."

It's ultra-contemporary, built with more windows than walls. It's one of those houses featured in magazines, where the residents give up their privacy for drop-dead-glorious views. Transparent architecture, that's what they're calling it, I think. I could never live somewhere like that, where every-one knows what's happening inside my home.

I'm still gawking when she walks into the house as if she's been welcomed inside a thousand times before.

"Did Michael mention I'd be coming by this morning?" she asks, circling the couch.

"You know, I remember him saying something about it," I lie. "My memory hasn't been the best lately. I think the high doses of vitamins are getting to me."

"Oh, right."

She decides on a proper spot, plops down, and instantly arranges herself as if she's posing for a photo shoot. Long legs tucked beneath her. Arm draped over the sofa back. Other hand placed delicately on her knee. Now *this* is the type of woman who belongs in this space.

"I heard there were congratulations in order. A new rela-tionship, *and* a new baby. *Whew*." She blows out a soft stream of air between her bright red lips. "You're biting off quite a lot."

She's graceful and self-confident, one of those women who seem to effortlessly have everything together, and I hate her already.

"Thank you." *I think*. "Can I get you something? Coffee, tea, or—"

"Espresso would be amazing."

"Sure."

Espresso? I haven't the faintest idea what kind of coffee machines Michael owns. I'd wanted to explore more of the house this morning, but Dean put a damper on that agenda. Walking into the kitchen, I scan the counters.

"If I were an espresso maker," I mumble, "where would I be?"

I open the cabinet to the left of the sink. Glasses and mugs. I pull one down for Rachael, open the next cabinet door and the one below that. Plates. Bowls. Spices and wine glasses. Beer steins. Salad sets. Pots and pans.

"Here," Rachael says, and I gasp. I hadn't even realized she'd come up behind me. She opens the pantry door—a sliver of an opening compared to the wine cellar—leans inside, and emerges with a bulky machine. She goes to work plugging it in and setting it up next to the sink. "This kitchen is so well organized. Joanna had a hand in it, of course."

Joanna's name rings through my brain and stiffens my spine. "I would've found it eventually."

"I'm sure you're going to reorganize this home in your own way, in your own time." She strides to the bar in the dining room, returns with a bottle of Irish cream, and sloshes a heavy drop into the bottom of her mug. Then she winks. "Though I do hope you keep some things in the same place."

After filling her cup, Rachael returns to the living room and strikes the same pose as before. I get the feeling this isn't the first time she's made her own spiked espresso and curled up on the couch this way. Unease tingles through me as I slouch into the chair across from her and start sifting through the box closest to me. It's filled with knickknacks from my old apartment. I pull out a few of my favorite books by Agatha Christie and Stephen King and stack them on top of the other books decorating the center of the table.

Rachael stares at the books for so long, I restack them,

this time taking care to make sure the spines line up correctly. "Have you read all of those?" she asks.

I brush my hand over the cover of *Rebecca,* my favorite Daphne du Maurier. "Most of them a few times over."

She chuckles tightly. "I'll never understand why people keep books they've already read. If you know what's going to happen, why would you want to read it again? Seems like an incredible waste of time and shelf space."

If she doesn't understand it by now, she never will. Books are my oasis, my home, and always have been. I didn't have the best childhood. My parents died in a car accident when I was fifteen, and I bounced around from one foster home to another for the next few years. When most kids were playing Barbie, I was curled up somewhere, lost in a novel, using the characters to keep me company. Deep in the pages of *Rebecca,* I strolled through Manderley's magnificent halls and breathed in the sweet hydrangeas that lined its drive. These books were my friends, my refuge, and the first thing I packed for my new adventure with Michael.

"Have you met Samara yet?" Rachael asks. "Oh, duh, she comes today, right? How'd you take to her?"

How'd I take to her? Like I'm some sort of fungus. "Good, I guess. I only ran into her this morning."

Rachael makes a humming sound of acknowledgment. "She loves Joanna, you know. Dean loves her, too. They simply *adore* her."

No wonder my welcome has been frosty. I'm the second-tier replacement.

"How far along are you, if you don't mind me asking?" Rachael asks cheerfully. "You're so slim, I can barely tell you're pregnant at all."

"Five months," I say, pulling out a few candles and setting them on the table.

"Past the halfway mark. Good for you." Leaning back,

she dismisses me with a wave of her hand. "Did you have morning sickness?"

"Only once."

"Lucky." She eyes me over the rim of her mug. "Your first, I'm assuming?"

"It is."

"Such a blessed time for you both, I'm sure."

"Do you have any children?" I fire back.

She chokes on her drink, and then covers her lips with her hand before going on. "Do you know how you look at some couples and you just *know* they're going to be amazing parents? They're going to travel the world with their kids, provide everything they could possibly want and need? And you know unequivocally, from their demeanor alone, that they'll be patient and loving and selfless in the way that children deserve?" She drops her hand and grins wickedly. "No one looks at me and Travis that way. And if they do, they're delusional."

I can't help but laugh, too. "I'm sure that's not true."

"Oh, it is, believe me. *Know thyself,* right? Isn't that what they say? We're happy, Travis and I, just the way we are. Not everyone is cut out to be a parent," she says definitively, twisting her wedding ring around her finger.

Maybe, if I'm lucky, I'll be sporting a big freaking rock on my finger just like Rachael's. That thing's huge—a solitaire, three-carat minimum. Michael and I haven't talked about marriage yet. I don't want to push him to file for divorce so he can marry me, but we are having a child together, and wouldn't it be wonderful if I had the same last name as our baby? After we've been here a few months and the timing feels right, I'll drop the hint.

"What does Travis do?" I ask, dragging my gaze from the sparkling diamond on her left hand. Instead, I focus on unpacking the next box, pulling out more books, journals, a few framed black-and-white photographs of the city.

"You don't know?" Rachael leans back, relaxing as she sips her spiked espresso. "I thought for sure you would, working there yourself and all. He's the head of marketing for Michael's company."

A deep red blush heats my cheeks. I should've at least recognized his name. And now I've insulted her.

"I started at the end of July, and I worked as Michael's personal assistant for most of that time. I didn't get to meet everyone."

"Whoa, back up." She arches a thinly plucked eyebrow. "You said you're five months along."

"That's right."

And I know exactly where this is going.

"Didn't take you long working at the company to land the boss. Talk about climbing the ladder."

My jaw tightens as I digest her tone. It's playful, without a hint of maliciousness, and when she buries her smile with another sip, I repress the urge to ask her to leave. *Rachael and her husband are Michael's neighbors,* I remind myself. *Our neighbors.* I need to be on my best behavior.

"That wasn't my plan," I offer, watching her carefully. "It just happened."

"That's what they all say. Didn't you feel bad about sleeping with the boss so soon after his wife dumped him? You don't have to answer—no pressure or anything—I'm just curious. You'd have to feel bad, wouldn't you? Even a little bit?"

"Umm . . . I guess." How do I answer? If I say I felt bad, I'll be showing weakness. If I say I didn't, that makes me callous. "I was cautious, but when I'm with Michael it feels natural. Like I've known him for years."

"Have you?"

"Have I what?"

"Known him for years?"

"No, I'd never met him before he hired me. What about

you?" I ask, determined to refocus the questioning on her. "Do you work outside the home?"

Footsteps sound from somewhere upstairs, followed by the slamming of a door. Samara is on the move.

"I'm a real estate agent for a firm in the Marina district. I handle business space, mostly. I enjoy it, though sometimes the hours are long, which means I don't have much time for charity work. Joanna volunteered at a healthcare foundation and served on the board for so many charities. I would be doing that too, if my career weren't so demanding. She used to say it was the most rewarding job in the world. Do you volunteer anywhere?"

"Not yet." I shake my head. "But maybe someday."

"Everyone I know pushes it off to 'someday.' Everyone except Joanna." Rachael takes another long sip, then turns her attention to a twenty-something dog walker struggling with four boxers across the street. "Anyway, Point Reina is our little gem, hidden away from the rest of the world. The pace is slower here because no one really knows about it. It's the perfect place to raise a family, or at least that's what I hear. Travis mentioned you needed rest and relaxation for the pregnancy, so I can understand why Michael suggested it, but honestly—and I hope you don't mind my saying so, Colleen—I'm surprised you agreed to it."

"Why do you say that?"

She leans forward as if she's divulging a juicy secret. "Aren't you afraid, even just a little, that everyone's going to compare you to *her*? If you're living in a different space, it's not a big deal, but Ravenwood was *their* home. You know Joanna's still here, even if her things aren't."

To keep Rachael from seeing my hands tremble, I empty the box at my feet. "I think it's going to be a transition for all of us. It'll take time to feel natural." I reach for another box, laying everything out on the coffee table so it can be sorted later. "But Michael and I are a team. If he thinks this is best, I'm all in, no matter what that means."

"Michael is the most thoughtful partner, isn't he?"

It's not until Rachael's blabbering on about her husband's position and late nights in the city that the realization sets in. She's never known Michael and me as a couple, never once seen us together. She couldn't possibly know how he treats me, whether he's thoughtful or rude.

But that's just it.

He *was* a thoughtful partner. Not with me, but with *her*.

The mistress of this immaculate home.

"He's amazing." I go still, my fingers clutching a framed picture of a selfie Michael took of us on our first date at the Rose Garden in Oakland. Shifting my weight carefully, I slide to the edge of the chair and lean on the armrests to help myself up. The bookshelf nearest the hallway has an empty space, and I suddenly feel the need to place the photo there. I can feel Rachael's eyes on my back as I arrange the picture of Michael and me. "I couldn't ask for anything more."

"Oh, I bet you could think of something."

At that, I turn around, but I can't read her expression. It's flat, almost blank, but there's a steeliness in her eyes that surely wasn't there before. Her gaze flickers to my stomach.

"I hope you don't mind my asking, but . . ." She pauses, a tight smile drawing the corners of her mouth up. "How'd you do it?"

I'm confused. "How'd I do what, exactly?"

There she goes again, twirling that giant rock around her finger with her thumb. "Get Michael to snap out of his funk? He was torn up after Joanna for weeks, threw himself into his work—it wasn't healthy, let me tell you, and we were all terribly worried that he was depressed—but then suddenly there you were, like a light in the dark, saving him. How'd you do it?"

Like a light in the dark.

I like that, though I never knew about his depression.

"I don't know," I answer honestly, flashing back to the time spent in his office, working beside him through the night, "but he must've been ready for another relationship. Because he approached me, not the other way around."

"Really? I can't see it." She yelps. "Oh, why can't I just keep my trap shut? That was rude. I shouldn't have brought up anything about them in the first place—"

"No, it's fine." *Now's my chance.* "I know about Joanna and the way she left him."

"He told you?"

I nod and push the empty boxes aside. "Are you and Joanna close?"

"For years, we were the best of friends," Rachael says, rising to her feet and crossing to the wall of windows. "With our husbands working so closely, it was hard not to be drawn together. When they moved here, we were pretty much inseparable, but then I started working, and things . . . changed. To be perfectly honest, we suddenly had different ideas, Joanna and I, and different priorities that led to a few arguments. And then she was gone. We were never as close as I thought we were."

She pauses, staring beyond the garden to the cypress grove across the street, and I get the feeling there's more to the story than Rachael is letting on.

"Have you kept in touch with Joanna since she left?" There I go, pushing too far, asking one too many questions. "Never mind. Forget I asked. It's none of my business."

"No, it's fine," she says, picking at something beneath her glossy thumbnail. "I haven't talked to her since last summer. I'm glad she dropped off the face of the earth, to be honest." She shrugs, and then flicks whatever she found beneath her nail onto the floor. I crouch to open another box; this one's full of dishware. Before I can decide where to unpack it, Rachael points toward the dining room. "You'll probably want to store them in there. That's where she used to keep her dishes."

Biting my tongue, I excuse myself to the dining room, and open the china cabinet. Every shelf is bare. I can't help but wonder what Joanna's dishes looked like, and how they compared to mine.

"She had the most exquisite china set," Rachael says over my shoulder, startling me again. Her voice seems even more insistent in here than in the living room. Must be the acoustics of the cathedral-like ceiling. "It was gorgeous. The pattern was simple and dainty, and I'm sure each dish cost a small fortune. Looks like she took everything with her. I don't blame her though, do you? One day, we come over, Travis and I, and—poof. We didn't even see the moving van."

"What's she like?" I retreat into the living room, trying to keep my voice casual. "I've been curious, but haven't wanted to ask Michael."

"Oh, Joanna is poised and graceful and unbelievably beautiful. You can't stop staring, no matter how hard you try. Without doing it on purpose, your eyes naturally search for any kind of flaw in her, because you simply can't believe you're standing there, talking with someone so *perfect*. You look for an indention in her chin, maybe, an unseemly mole, or one ear that's higher than the other, but there's not one part of her that's blemished. Everyone loves her, naturally, and because of that, some part of you hates her." She turns toward me suddenly, setting down her espresso, a smile fixed on her face, though it doesn't reach her eyes. "I'm glad you're with Michael now." And then she's turning on her heel, heading for the door. "Thanks for the drink, Colleen. See you tomorrow."

"Thanks for coming by," I say, taking the mug and setting it on the coffee table. "Wait—what's tomorrow?"

"Didn't Michael tell you? You'll be coming over for dinner. The guys can talk business, and we can get acquainted."

As she waves goodbye and heads down the sidewalk toward the cypress grove, I stand at the spot in front of the windows where she stood moments before. I can't shake the feeling that she was probing me for answers, trying to get a feel for me, to see if I was some kind of threat. But that's ridiculous. Isn't it? All I know is, whatever our meeting was, it wasn't innocent.

I spend the next few hours unpacking and filling Joanna's china cabinet with my own dishes. When Samara makes her way downstairs, she insists I leave the empty boxes near the back door for her to pack away in the garage, since I shouldn't be carrying heavy loads. For some reason, unpacking my things makes me feel better. Like I've finally made my imprint on this place, no matter how faint. Rachael's comments spin through my head: *I'm glad you're with Michael now.* Because I'm not a threat to this neighborhood. I'm far from glamorous and at times uncomfortable in my skin, and won't make Rachael feel intimidated. *How'd you do it?* As if landing Michael was a trick, because he couldn't possibly like me for the woman I am, not after the perfection of Joanna.

If I want to be in Michael's life for the long haul, I need to become the kind of woman deserving of his love and attention. I'm going to have to make Ravenwood my home, so I don't feel like an invader, squatting here in Joanna's space.

Rachael may be gone, but her words are lingering, ringing in my heart.

I don't think they'll be leaving anytime soon.

MICHAEL

By the time I wind my way up the drive and pull into the garage, it's six-fifteen and I'm burned out. Meetings all morning. Development paperwork all afternoon. Conference calls on the way home. I haven't heard from Colleen since the morning and I want nothing more than to see her. Judging from the way she crashed this morning, she's probably spent the day recuperating.

If I know Colleen, no matter how tired she is, she'll greet me at the door with a kiss and a smile. I don't know how it's possible, but she has a talent for making the madness of my day melt away. She hates the fact that she's not more of a Betty Homemaker type—she's mentioned her lack of housekeeping skills a time or two—but with Samara on staff, she won't have to worry about that anymore. She'll be able to relax and enjoy her days. I don't mind that she can't cook anything edible, either; it's the reason I kept Dean on staff after Joanna left. What woman wouldn't enjoy having a personal chef who does the grocery shopping and cooking?

For the first time since Joanna ended our marriage via text message, I think I'm finally ready to file for divorce. My past with her will stay buried. With Colleen there is a new start. I turn up my collar to brace against a frigid blast of wind and eagerly jog up the steps. I don't think I've ever been happier to walk through the front door.

"Hey, Coll, I'm home!" Pushing inside, I hang up my jacket, set down my briefcase, and stop in my tracks. "What the hell?"

The house is eerily quiet, cold, and dark, as if the life has been sucked right out of it. A few dim overhead fixtures trickle light, but shadows claim every corner. The boxes I'd stepped over this morning are gone. The couch is now covered in fuzzy blankets and throw pillows. Framed pictures of us have been hung on the walls.

Colleen's been busy today, but where is she?

"Colleen?" I pad through the living room. "Sweetheart?"

In the study, the air is stagnant and chilly—the fire hasn't been lit—and the curtains are closed tight. At first glance, it doesn't seem as if Colleen has been in the room at all. Then, I catch sight of something on the bookshelf across from my desk. A romance novel. Next to it, a thriller.

Those definitely aren't mine.

On closer inspection, an entire row of my financial books has been replaced with genre fiction. Mysteries, romances, thrillers, and sci-fi.

"You've made yourself at home," I whisper, and then shut the door behind me. "As long as you haven't . . ." I glance at the ceiling, beyond the headers and beams, and imagine the second story over our heads. "Colleen? Baby, where are you?"

Slightly panicked, I search through the house with renewed purpose. Dining room and kitchen are empty. The counters look different, as if something's been moved. Wait— the Keurig that had rested in the corner has been replaced with the espresso machine. Bizarre, since Colleen can't have caffeine until the baby's born. I dart into the wine cellar. No trace of her. Charging to the second story, I call her name over and over again.

I stop at the top of the stairs. Right or left?

Please, God, don't let her have ventured too far. . . .

I'm not ready to have that conversation yet.

"Colleen? I'm starting to get worried. Where are you, sweetheart?"

If something were really wrong, if something had happened to Colleen or the baby, I would've gotten a call from the doctor. Or an emergency room. So where could she have gone? Having lived in the city for the last six years of her life, she doesn't own a car. And she doesn't know anyone in Point Reina.

She has to be here.

I listen intently for any sound, anything that might give away where she might be, and then dart to the right. I have to make sure she hasn't discovered what I'm keeping in those rooms. The doors leading to the screening room, billiards room, and gym are all locked. At the end of the long, dark hall, the door leading to the second master makes me stop. Perhaps it's the way shadows slant over its ornate wood carvings, revealing angles and lines that strangely resemble a face. Or maybe it's what I fear is waiting for me inside.

"Colleen?" I call out, my voice harsher than it'd been before. "Enough games. Where are you?"

I don't want to go in there. Nights hit the hardest, and I won't be able to take it. How would she have gotten in, anyway? The room at the end of the hall is always locked, and there are only two keys. One is always on me. Last summer, right after Joanna left, I found myself spending more time in that room than my own. It was easiest to keep the key on me at all times. I suppose it's still a habit to shove it into my pocket each morning. The other key is with Samara, so she can keep the space fresh. She wouldn't have . . .

"Colleen!"

Storming down the hall, I pull the key from my pocket and reach for the lock. I pause, listening. I know what lies beyond the door, what dark secrets the past holds, and if Colleen's in there, I know what I have to do. Fear cements my feet to the floor.

I can't do this. I can't face her.

"Michael?" she calls from somewhere on the other side of the house. "Is that you?"

I pocket the key with a ragged, relieved breath and race down the hall, over the bridge stretching across the living room, and into the safety of the west wing.

"Colleen? Where are you?"

"Getting out of the bath," she calls back. I hear water sloshing.

I turn the corner and stride into the master. The bed's

made, and she's lit candles on the bedside tables. She hasn't been in the other rooms. She hasn't seen anything to upset her.

"I couldn't find you," I say, unbuttoning my top button and slinging off my tie. "I was getting worried. I must've called your name half a dozen times."

"I had my headphones in. Didn't hear a thing." Water drips, and then her footfalls echo through the bathroom. "I'll be out in a second."

Shrugging out of my jacket, I step into the closet. Colleen's unpacked her boxes. Unloaded her purses, shoes, and clothes, and reorganized them on the right side of the space. Joanna's things were there last year. Her endless stacks of heels were exactly where Colleen's few shoes are now. Her coats were in the back, clothes in the front, organized by length and color. It's like I've stepped back in time. Only difference is the sheer volume of clothes Joanna possessed. Even with every outfit Colleen owns, the closet still looks barren. Joanna moved her stuff out of our bedroom and into her own private space last May, when things started to go sour between us, yet I remember her wardrobe filling the closet like it was yesterday.

Maybe it's too soon, too fast. Maybe Colleen and I should have slowed down. Maybe I should have made sure I was over Joanna before inviting another woman into our home. I shouldn't be looking at Colleen's wardrobe and thinking of Joanna.

Or maybe I'm reading too much into it. Does every woman choose the right over the left side? Who gives a damn, anyway? It's only clothes.

Colleen is *not* Joanna.

I think about the gorgeous woman stepping out of the bath in the next room. Suddenly I can't wait to get her into my arms.

"How was your day?" I ask, finally feeling normal again. But when I turn, Colleen is standing in the doorway, and I don't remember what I'd asked. Light from the bathroom spills around her dark hair, her narrow shoulders, and—*God help me*—the blood freezes in my veins. Colleen's wearing *her* robe. The one I bought Joanna for our first Christmas together. It's cashmere, white as snow, with the emblem of a blood-red rose etched over the right breast.

For one horrifying moment, I think . . . *no*.

I shake my head fiercely as I struggle to piece together my thoughts.

"What's the matter?" Colleen smoothes wet hair back from her face, frowning. "You look like you've seen a ghost."

Something in my chest shifts, and my mouth goes dry as the Sahara. "Just not used to seeing you here." I cross the room and kiss her on the cheek. Her skin is still damp. "Where'd you find this?"

I reach out to touch the fabric of the robe, to brush it against my fingers, but pull back my hand at the last second.

"I spent a lot of time going through boxes today," she replies, tightening the robe around her, "and Samara was a huge help. When I mentioned I was beat, she said I should take a bath, and it sounded like a wonderful idea. Right before she left she brought me this. She said it was reserved for guests. Wasn't that nice?"

Reserved for guests.

I'll have to talk to Samara about her gesture, and her lie, later.

Colleen retreats into the bathroom, and I follow, tugged along by the cord of torturous memory.

She gazes up at me in the mirror as I lean against the towel rack to steady myself. "Michael—what's the matter?"

"Nothing." *The robe.* "I'm sorry, I'm not—"

"Is it the closet? I was worried about how you'd react. Samara said you take the left, so I thought my stuff could go on the right, but if not . . ."

"Oh, that. Yeah, Coll, it's fine."

She spreads lotion over her face in tiny circles, and I feel like I've dreamed this before. "After talking with Rachael, I—"

"You met Rachael?" I ask.

"She came by this morning." She swipes her hand over the fogged mirror, leaving two streaks wide enough to reveal her face. "Michael, are you sure everything's all right?"

Her reflection blurs as water drops scatter down the mirror, and I swear Joanna is staring back at me. I wish I could forget her. Wish I could forget the finger-smudge marks Colleen just made over the mirror, too. In the morning, Samara will have to wipe everything down.

"Michael?"

"Yeah. Sorry." I swallow hard. "Zoned out for a second. What'd Rachael have to say?"

"That she thinks the world of you."

I'm her husband's boss. She's not going to tell the new woman in my life that I'm a monster. Even if it could be the truth. "Rachael likes everybody."

She looks up at me in the reflection as she runs a brush through her hair. "She said you're a thoughtful husband."

"I hope you didn't waste your morning gossiping about me the whole time. I think you two might have a lot in common."

"Really?" She pouts her lips and applies a glossy touch of lip balm. "Like what?"

"Travis and I both work at the company." In the mirror, she levels a stare at me that says I shouldn't be finished talking, so I continue. "Rachael's career-oriented, just like you were before we made the decision for you to stay here. She's health-conscious and attends those sweaty yoga classes, or whatever they are."

She giggles at that, lowering my defenses.

"Don't laugh. You know you used to go to those things too. You used to tell me all about them." I steal behind her and wrap my arms around her shoulders. The scent of her hair is familiar too. It's soft and subtle, teasing my senses with something long forgotten. "I'll never understand why anyone would want to work out in a sauna."

"It's good for you," she says, leaning back against me. "Detoxifies your muscles. Relieves stress."

"I know another way you can relieve stress."

I turn her around to face me. She laughs, covering her mouth with her hand as I wedge her knees gently between my legs. She tips her head back and smiles, and it's times like this that she takes my breath away.

"What do you say we get you out of this robe and into bed? I'd love to show you how much I appreciate everything you've done."

"Sounds perfect." She turns back to the vanity and opens her bag. "Let me do a few more things first. I want tonight to be special."

"All right," I say with a wink. "Don't keep me waiting too long."

In the bedroom, I strip down to my boxers and pull back the covers of the bed. The rush of the wind whipping through the grove across the street is strangely hypnotic. Like white noise. Outside, the temperature is dropping fast. It'll be bone-chillingly cold tonight, I can feel it. Another storm is sweeping through.

"Okay," she says, behind me. "I'm ready."

I turn. She's still wearing Joanna's robe, and she's drawn her silky black hair over both shoulders. From the way the cashmere clings to her body, I can see the faintest pooch of her belly, and a zinging feeling of happiness streaks through me. I know she's bare beneath the cashmere. Maybe when Colleen's in my arms, I'll be able to close my eyes and forget Joanna existed at all.

She approaches me with a smile, but when I reach out for her, a familiar scent strikes me. It's not the scent of her shampoo. It's something else. Something *intimate*. Colleen is swathed in it.

"Are you wearing something?" I ask, hands trembling as I tug her against me. "Did you try on a new perfume?"

She gazes up at me, blinking slowly. "It's Joy. By Jean Patou. I absolutely *love* the scent."

Joy was Joanna's favorite fragrance—I'd buy it for her every year for her birthday. Over six hundred dollars for a single ounce. Damn Samara if she gave Colleen that, too. She'll be perusing the classifieds by noon tomorrow.

"Nice." I force a flat tone. Nonchalant. "Where'd you get it?"

"I found it tucked in the back corner of the vanity," she says, untying the robe to expose her naked body.

But I can't focus on her curves, or the gleam of the bedside lamps bathing her skin in a golden glow. Because I'd cleaned out the vanity months ago. She's lying. Where could Colleen have found Joanna's perfume?

"Did you know ten thousand jasmine flowers and something like twenty-eight dozen roses are used to make one ounce?" She presses her breasts against my chest. "I looked it up."

Closing my eyes, I draw her against me tighter and stroke my hands up and down her back. The robe is soft in my fingers—the luxurious texture is the reason I bought it for her—and her scent is just the way I remember. Flowery and musky, so sweet it makes me dizzy.

With a hiss, I shove Colleen out of my arms.

I didn't buy the robe for *her,* but for Joanna. Colleen stands before me, arms hanging limp at her sides, her lips parted.

How easy it'd been to forget, to think about Joanna, to wish even for a moment that she were the one in my arms. Colleen's expression fades from happiness to confusion as she backs away from me, cinching the robe's belt around her waist.

"What the hell's gotten into you? If you don't want to sleep with me tonight, that's fine, but you don't have to push me away. I was just trying to—"

Damn it. "Colleen, that's not it."

"I hear what you're saying, but I'm throwing myself at you, and there's disgust in your eyes right now. *Disgust,* Michael. That's not exactly the emotion I was hoping to see tonight."

"Colleen . . ."

"Don't," she bites out. I think she's crying. And now she won't even look at me. "Today has been the longest day I can remember. I just want it to be over."

When she slips into bed beside me minutes later, she faces the opposite direction. She has to say *something* or I'm not going to get a minute of sleep tonight.

"Penny for your thoughts?" I ask finally, keeping my voice low.

She sighs. "Is that all you think they're worth?"

MONDAY

Six Days Until Colleen's Murder

RACHAEL

My phone buzzes against the bedside table, dragging me from the deepest sleep I've had in, God, I don't know how long. Fumbling, I put on my glasses, hold the phone over my face, and read a series of texts from Lora that I must've missed while I was out.

> OMG, Rachael, wake up.
> I heard it's a woman. Wake up!!

Sitting upright and swinging my legs over the side of the bed, I rub the sleep out of my eyes and struggle to piece together what she's talking about. Lora regularly starts texts with OMG. She's probably about to spoil the ending to *The Walking Dead*.

> Look outside. A circus! Dead body in the grove!

Fear jolts through me as I reread the words. It's a good thing Travis has already left for work. He hates it when I hop on the phone first thing in the morning. When Lora picks up, she's out of breath. Borderline hysterical.

"About time, Sleeping Beauty," she shouts. "Get to your front window. You're not going to believe it. Nothing ever happens here. Nothing! Now this. It's like a *CSI* episode, and we have a front row seat—*look*!"

Clutching the sheet to cover my breasts, I race down the hall and stare at the grove of gnarled cypress trees not a hundred feet away. On any given day, Cypress Street is quiet, the sidewalk often empty—save for a few dog walkers, stay-at-home mothers strolling with their infants, or tide poolers using the Bluff Trail to trek to the beach below. Today though, Lora's right: it is a circus. Neighbors cluster on each side of the street, whispering and pointing. Yellow police tape flutters from a tree near the cliff to one on the opposite side of the trail. Police buzz like bees circling a hive, talking to reporters and neighbors and waving traffic along.

The pavement is still wet from last night's rainstorm, and the forest floor across the street has turned to mud. The sky is still flat gray—which is not a surprise for the coast. Looks like it might rain again.

Traffic—there's something I've never seen in Point Reina. Everyone in the area is desperate to see what's going on. A line of Mercedes and BMWs weaves along the narrow road, and—oh, look, there's Amanda Patel, turning the corner in her brand-new, fire-engine-red Jaguar. I try to duck out of sight, but she spots me in the window, flashes a smile, and waves. I return the gesture and quickly escape back into my room. Damn, I can't stand that woman. Thinks she's better than everyone else in the neighborhood just because she went to medical school and married a detective. How do they afford a home in this neighborhood on his salary?

"What happened?" I ask into the phone, clearing my throat to get rid of the morning rasp.

"I don't know *all* the details." Lora huffs, as if she's walking fast. "And no one knows *exactly* what happened yet, but around seven this morning, Sarah was walking a couple dogs, and one of them came unleashed. She said it pulled and jerked free and headed straight toward a tree near the bluff."

"Oh my God." Taking a chance at being spotted again, I peek around the doorjamb as a news van pulls up and parks across the street. Behind the van, half a dozen police cruisers are parked, one after another. "You weren't kidding. It's madness."

"You haven't heard the worst of it," Lora babbles on. "When Sarah finally caught up to her pup—remember, she's still not up to full speed, not since her knee surgery—she discovered that he'd dug up a bone. A partially decomposed *human* femur. Sarah was totally grossed out, and showed it to Amanda, who called her husband and the sheriff right away."

"Oh, how terrible! Look, here comes another news van. Where do they think they're going to park? There's no more room."

"I bet they're going to try to park in your driveway."

"That's not happening." I race downstairs and press my face against the glass, watching as the second van squeezes between two police cars. "Do they know anything else?" How did I sleep through all this?

"Well, from what I hear, the police have already started interviewing people in the area. Really informal, you know, but Sarah overheard Don from the distillery saying it's a woman, though you know how reliable *he* is. They've already started digging, and from what Sarah says, they're going deep."

"God, please stop." Nausea cramps my stomach. "I can't hear any more."

"I have to take off. I'm already late for my massage. Rachael, all I know is this: if you ever wanted to be on television," she goes on, and I can tell from her tone she's smiling, "now's your chance."

"Exactly how shallow do you think I am?"

Nineteen minutes later, after I'm dressed in my cutest hoodie, a pair of black leggings, and my new Nikes, I set the security system and head out. For the first time in my life, I wish I had a dog, so this would look natural. As if I went out every day for a run with hyperactive Spot or floppy-eared Fudge. But when I step outside into the plumes of ocean mist and start stretching, my muscles scream in protest. I zigzag over puddles and weave around splotches of mud as if this is part of my normal routine. No way these Nikes are stamping my carpet again.

I'm not a runner. I don't do this. But I'm itching to know what people are hearing and saying. Do the cops know who the victim is? I wish I'd spent more time with the people in this sleepy town. Wish I'd made more friends, or gone to more Bunco nights. That'd make it easy to walk up to any of the people gathering on the street and start asking questions. Although I see many familiar faces, I'm not comfortable enough with any of them to strike up a conversation.

And then I see her.

Colleen, talking with a bright-eyed news reporter near the start of the Bluff Trail, all dewy-faced and pretty in a tight maternity outfit. I recognize the woman she's conversing with instantly: Melissa Mendes from the six o'clock news. I've watched her for years.

There's my way in.

"Morning, Sunshine," I say, jogging to Colleen's side. I'm winded. My chest is tight, my legs screaming. But Colleen and Melissa Mendes turn my way and smile, oblivious to the fact that I haven't run that far since I was in high school and forced to take physical education classes. "What's going on?"

Colleen's gaze lowers to my shoes before she meets my

eyes again. "I was going for a walk when she approached me." She motions to Melissa Mendes, who seems to be feverishly taking notes on a pad of paper crammed in her palm. "This is Rachael Martin. She lives next door to us, right over there."

"Nice to meet you, Rachael." Melissa shakes my hand limply before diving back to her notes. In person, she's not nearly as smiley as on TV. Or maybe it's the corpse that's putting a damper on her normally bubbly mood. "How far do you usually go?"

"Excuse me?"

She points to my shoes with her pen. "When you run. How far?"

"Oh." I flip my hair over my shoulder. And realize I'd forgotten to tie it back. Rookie mistake. "About a mile. Just enough to get my blood pumping."

Sounds like something a runner would say, doesn't it?

"Do you run along the Bluff Trail?" Melissa just won't let this go.

How do I answer? If I say I usually run through the grove, it'll put me running through the area where a body was just found. The next question would inevitably be, "When was the last time you ran through?" One untruth would lead to another.

"No, I'm a street runner," I say quickly, drawing my ankle up behind me in a stretch. "The grove gives me the creeps."

Not totally a lie. Once the sun dips below the horizon, the grove is shrouded in shadows. The trail gets treacherous, and even if you've walked it a million times before, it's easy to get lost. You'll find your way out—it's not *that* large—but you might have to stumble or climb over a couple fallen branches to get there.

I lose my balance, topple a bit, and catch myself on Colleen's shoulder. "Do they know anything yet?" I ask her.

"They're in the early stages of the investigation," the reporter answers for her. "So the police will keep everything on lockdown until identification is established."

"And then what?"

"They'll notify next of kin before they make any public announcements."

"It's terrible," Colleen says, her hands on her stomach. "Just terrible. I can't believe it. Right across the street. And you said this place is quiet."

I can't help but laugh. "It is—or, it was."

For the next fifteen minutes or so, Melissa asks a ton of questions about where we're from, how long we've lived here, and how busy the grove might be on any given day. They're harmless, getting-to-know-you questions, and I can't help but wonder when she's going to pull out the camera.

She never does.

Maybe there's another crew out here who'll want to record my interview. As my gaze tracks around the grassy area in front of the grove, two men in white coats catch my eye. One is over six feet tall, lean, with glasses and slicked-back hair. The other is shorter and stockier, with reddish hair cut short, military-style. Both duck beneath the stretch of yellow tape and talk for a moment.

"Who are they?" I ask, pointing.

Melissa and Colleen both turn.

"Detectives," Melissa says bluntly, watching them step into the shadows. "There'll be more where those came from. I need to run, but it was really great talking with you two."

"That was disappointing," I say, thinking aloud, as Melissa hurries back to her van.

Colleen is watching the grove. "What was?"

"Nothing." But I'd been hoping for some kind of excitement. It would've been fun to record myself on television and show it back to Travis. We could've drunk wine and laughed at how foolish I looked in my workout gear. "Are you headed back home?"

"I probably should," Colleen says, finally turning toward me. "We still on for dinner tonight?"

"Of course. Won't let a murder keep us from living it up. Oh, by the way, be a doll and tell Dean I'm still waiting for that beignet recipe. I know he's already gone for the day, but he won't mind if you call and ask him to make something special, especially if he knows it's for me. I'd simply *die* if he could whip up those beignets for you to bring tonight."

"Sure, I'll give him a call. Wait, *murder*?" Colleen's voice kicks up a notch as she clutches the scarf around her neck. "You really think someone was killed out there?" She's gone very pale. Poor kid. *Welcome to the neighborhood.*

"I'm no detective, but people committing suicide or dying by natural causes generally have problems burying themselves."

DETECTIVE SHAW

"You've been working on that thing for months," Patel says, unfastening his seat belt before the car rolls to a stop. "You're never going to get it."

Spinning the sides of the Rubik's Cube in my fingers, I stare at the scene unfolding out the windshield. A narrow street winds between a row of houses and the cypress grove. The crime scene has been taped off, with a crew swarming around it. The coroner's already here, along with two paramedics and a cluster of news rats.

"Want to put money on it?" I toss the unsolved cube in my bag and exit the car as soon as it stops.

"Fifty bucks you don't solve it by Valentine's Day."

"Done."

"I'll tell Amanda to make reservations somewhere nice. We'll drink to your loss," Patel says, following on my heels.

He doesn't mean the comment to be an insult; Patel doesn't

have a malicious bone in his body. Working with him for the last five years has solidified my early conclusions about his character. But he doesn't know how badly I wish I could be making reservations with *my* wife. How I ache to pop open a bottle of champagne and celebrate our most recent birthday, anniversary, or promotion. For the rest of my life I'll have to settle for a toast with a concrete headstone, and something inside me dies a little more every time I think about it.

The sound of Patel's boots plodding through the muddy grass shakes me from thinking about Karen, and I'm thankful for the shift of focus.

Back to the crime.

We're not going to walk down the trail. It's closed off so we can take photographs of footprints. If early reports of the body's decomposition are correct, it's been buried for months, so I doubt any footprints we find will be of much use. But we have to unearth every secret of this place, look under every rock, to lock down the crime scene before we leave.

Thick ocean air rolls over the bluff, ruffling my coat, chilling me to the bone, and dragging with it the smell of sea and salt. Before disappearing into the cover of the grove, I take note of the trail up ahead. Wooden stairs zigzag down to the beach and the Williamson Wildlife Reserve. The dirt trail, muddy and potholed, is like a tongue lolling out onto the grass. We duck beneath caution tape and enter between two towering trees.

The trail is wide, clean, and well maintained, and the spindly branches of the trees arch overhead, creating the sensation of being in a cave. It's surprisingly peaceful, like a cemetery at twilight.

"Still don't know why you just don't look up the formula on YouTube," Patel says as we approach the crime scene. "You'd solve it much faster, and you'd be fifty dollars richer."

Since I first decided to tackle the Rubik's Cube—as a way to tolerate the eternal stretch of the late-night hours—I've come to realize that there are two kinds of people in this world. Those who want to solve it for the sake of saying they've done it, and the ones who want to understand how and why the advanced algorithms work. At first, when I held the multicolored square in my hands, I fell into the former category. I wanted to solve it as fast as I could. It was a challenge. Although I haven't told Patel, I *did* look up the videos on YouTube. I solved it, but only by learning an existing solution. I didn't find an answer to the problem myself.

I'd stared at that damn cube for hours. Its sides matched up perfectly. Blue with blue. Red with red. But I couldn't shake the feeling that it'd gotten the better of me. I hadn't conquered it, hadn't figured out how it worked. Not really.

So I'd gotten up in the middle of the night, scrambled the sucker up, and gone for it again.

"Guess I'm a glutton for punishment," I say, giving Patel an answer he'll accept.

But I know the truth, deep down in my gut: I won't let it beat me, and I won't stop until I figure it out for myself. Some questions in this world can't be answered. Problems won't be solved. Cures won't be found. I've learned that lesson the hard way. But this six-sided puzzle has a solution, and I'll find it.

As we approach the scene, the uniformed deputy calls everyone over, away from the body. He's just completed an initial full-body examination and is prepared to give us the rundown. Patel is on the bubble, which means he's the lead detective on this one. I mentally log the details as the deputy talks fast. Female body found at approximately seven this morning by Sarah Rhys, a local dog walker. Four feet deep. Back of her skull bashed in. No weapon found yet. No wallet or keys. No cellphone. Time of death is estimated to be six months ago, judging by an early assessment of the tissues, but the coroner will nail it down. The moistness of the soil in the grove will affect the rate of decomposition, so he'll take that into account.

Another deputy approaches holding an evidence bag. There's a dirty gold medallion inside. "This was found on her chest," he says, handing it over. Rolling the grains of dirt around, the deputy eyes the gold necklace. "Looks like the Virgin Mary. No other jewelry found on her."

I nod. "There's some kind of stone on it. It's a start for ID."

When he's finished giving the briefing, Patel goes to work assigning tasks to the officers on scene. Within two hours, a pop-up tent is erected over the grave to protect it from rain. And then, for most of the day, soil is shoveled and sifted to ensure not a single thing is missed. Everyone who has tramped through the scene has the bottom of their shoes photographed.

Hands on his hips, Patel circles the shallow grave, shouting orders to the deputies on scene.

"I want every license plate on that street photographed."

"Everyone who comes in and out of this grove uses this path right here, the one we just trampled on."

"I want identification and I want it fast."

As he goes on, barking orders and processing the scene, I move toward the edge of the cliff, to where the dog walker stands talking with a young deputy. She's clutching a shawl around her shoulders, staring at the ground over the rim of her glasses. She can't be more than forty, though her hair is so gray it's almost silver.

"Good morning," I say when I reach them. "I'm Detective Shaw. Were you the one who discovered the body?" Though I already know the truth.

She looks up at me, worry plaguing her eyes. "Yes, that's me. Sarah Rhys."

"Can I talk to you for a minute?"

"He said I'd be taken to the station to give my formal statement." She gestures to the deputy at her side.

"Right," I say, moving beside her so I can face the scene. "But I'd like to talk to you informally, if you wouldn't mind."

"All right."

The deputy nods in my direction, as if to tell me to keep my eye on the witness, before he heads back to the scene.

"What happened to your dogs?" I ask Ms. Rhys.

"My husband came and took them home. One of the deputies said he didn't want them messing up the scene."

"What kind are they?"

Her thin eyebrows arch. "Today I was walking a Chihuahua and a beagle. The Chihuahua is mine, the beagle, Rufus, belongs to my neighbor. Rufus is the one who pulled the bone out of the mud."

I clear my throat as memories of my wife begin to flicker through my head. Karen had a Chihuahua named Cookie—the damn dog didn't want me near her. Especially at the very end, when it sensed she was sick. The pup died a month after Karen, probably of a broken heart, and I was left to pick up the pieces alone. Guess I can't hate Cookie for loving her as much as I did. "Do you live on this street?"

"No, the next one over." Ms. Rhys points through the trees, though from here, the street is hidden from view. "Terrace Avenue."

I log every detail of our conversation in my head. I don't take notes, but as long as I'm focused on the details, my mind won't slip back to Karen, and I won't feel like the world has gone dark. Wind picks up behind us, slamming into the cliff and gusting between the trees. It's cold, even for January. Fishing my phone from my pocket, I check the weather app. Forty-six degrees. With the wind howling at my back, it feels like thirty. I left my gloves in the car.

"Lived there long?" I ask, returning my phone to my pocket.

"Ten years."

"And you walk dogs through the grove every morning?"

"Usually." Sighing, her gaze shifts mournfully from one deputy to another as they sift through the mud. "It's a woman, isn't it?"

"What makes you think that?"

"When one of the deputies was talking to me earlier, I saw—well, they brought up a hand. She—or I suppose it could be a he—was wearing red nail polish."

I eye her carefully and realize she's much younger than I thought. Her eyes are bright blue and sharp, her skin smooth. "What do you do for a living, Ms. Rhys?"

"I run a daycare out of my home Monday through Friday, mostly in the afternoons when parents can't pick up their children from school."

"For families in this area?"

She nods. "A few, though most of my parents live in Half Moon Bay."

I let my gaze wander through the grove, lingering on a few low-hanging boughs and the shadows darkening around turns in the path ahead. In the distance, fat waves crash against the shore with muted booms. I can count the time between the swells. One . . . two . . . three . . . *boom.*

"Ms. Rhys, have you ever noticed any suspicious activity in the grove?"

She shakes her head. "No, never. Well, besides the body Rufus discovered, of course."

"Just one more question, Ms. Rhys, and then I'll have someone drive you down to the station."

She watches me unhappily.

"Did you walk through the grove yesterday with the same dogs?"

"I did."

"On the same route?"

"Yes."

"Did you see anyone else walking around at the same time?"

Lips twisting, she chews over my question. "There are always people walking around here, Detective. It's a beautiful path."

"Yes, but I'd like to know specifics. Can you offer the names of anyone in the neighborhood who frequents the grove?"

"Well yes, I suppose. Don from the distillery was sitting on that bench over there yesterday, the one overlooking the ocean. He's always there before work, having his coffee with a view. The new woman staying with Michael Harris—he lives right over there"—she points through the trees—"came through yesterday too. She had a book in her hand, so I assume she spent the morning reading on the beach."

"Anyone else?"

She shakes her head.

"That'll be all for now." I extend my hand. "Thank you for your time, Ms. Rhys, it was a pleasure talking with you."

After ensuring Sarah Rhys receives a proper escort to the station to record her official statement, I shove my hands into my pockets and turn back to the scene. Bones, partially decomposed flesh, and thick clumps of mud consume what's left of my day.

It's six o'clock in the evening by the time we're finished.

The scent of dirt and decay stings my nose, and I know I'm not going to be able to eat for days. There are times I don't know why I do this, why I chose to go into homicide. But then I get handed a case like this one, where there's a body with no identification, and a killer on the loose somewhere smugly assuming he or she has gotten away with murder, and the thought of it won't leave me alone. My palms start to itch. The hair on the back of my neck stands up.

Toxicology and the coroner's report should be back in about a week. Identification sometime in there as well. Then, the real work begins, hunting the hunter.

When Patel and I get back into the cruiser, I pick up the cube and shift a few squares into place.

COLLEEN

"You feeling all right?" Michael asks as we walk through the garden and over the stepping-stones leading from Ravenwood to the Martins' glass monstrosity. "You haven't said much since I came home from work."

"I'm fine."

I can't stop thinking about the body pulled out of the ground across the street. I'd told Michael about it, but he didn't seem shocked or interested in talking about it at all. In fact, the only thing he'd offered was some mumbled response about keeping our noses out of it so the police could do their job. His nonchalance struck me as strange, but maybe I'm reading too much into it. Once I find my footing in a daily routine, things will feel more normal, and I won't have to overthink anything.

Tonight the air is bitter cold, especially when the wind picks up, but buttery-warm lights illuminate the Martin home like a beacon.

"How'd you sleep last night?" Michael asks.

"Fine."

"Didn't seem like it. You tossed and turned for hours."

"I didn't mean to keep you up."

"It's more than last night," he goes on. "I don't think you've been sleeping well since you found out you were pregnant."

"That's not true. Remember how I crashed for hours yesterday morning, after you left for work?"

He kinks an eyebrow. "So you've slept well *once* in the last five months. That's your defense?"

"I've been worried about things—the pregnancy—going smoothly. You know that." And now, I'm in his wife's home. It hasn't helped my anxiety. "I'll sleep normally again eventually."

Last night, shadows in corners seemed to move and shift as if someone was hiding in them. And sometimes, out of the corner of my eye, I caught a flurry of movement. A flash of something dark darting across the hallway from one bedroom to another. When I looked, nothing was there. The more the night wore on, the more I started to hallucinate. Michael and I didn't make love, either. First night in the house, and he didn't even try to touch me.

"I think being in Ravenwood will take some getting used to, that's all," I go on. "You know how it is, when you sleep in a new place." I don't know if I'll ever get used to sleeping in a bed Michael slept in with Joanna. "It should start to feel like home soon."

"I hope so. Insomnia could affect the baby."

Lowering my gaze, I curl my fingers around the appetizer tray. Apple cider beignets. When I returned from my walk this morning, I didn't think Dean would have taken on the headache of shopping and cooking at the last minute for Rachael's special request. I was wrong. Apparently all it took was Michael calling him to make the request, and Dean was all too happy to make one of Joanna's favorite treats.

"Maybe we should talk to Dr. Souza," Michael suggests, "to see if exhaustion and mood changes are normal for this stage of the pregnancy."

"Every pregnancy is different. There is no normal."

"I'm concerned, that's all. The last time—"

And then he stops. Just like that. Mid-sentence, moments before he compares this pregnancy to the last one, with her. He clears his throat as if he'd meant to stop, as if some random piece of sand flew off the beach and lodged in his throat at the opportune moment. I know better, and it burns me inside.

Joanna's here, even now, on our way to a dinner party next door.

She might as well still be living in Ravenwood. If I'm curled up on the couch, staring out the window at the cypress grove, a whisper in the back of my head says this was her view, and she had it first. When I'm taking a bath and slipping underwater, I close my eyes and get the feeling she's looming over the tub. Late at night, when I'm lying in bed, I think I hear footsteps creeping down the hall, softly scuffing the floorboards. Ravenwood creaks when the wind howls through it, and I can swear it's calling her name. Even it knows I'm an imposter. I thought moving my things into Ravenwood would've solved everything. It was supposed to fill the void in Michael's world that Joanna left. When I curl up on the couch, *my* blanket is the one we now use to warm our bodies. *My* clothes are the ones filling the empty rods. And late at night, *I'm* the one he draws close.

But, according to Samara, Michael insisted everything else in Ravenwood remain the same. Exactly as Joanna had wanted it. Same meals. Same cleaning schedule. "Minimal change," he'd told her.

I'm already eating her favorite meals, bathing in her tub, and making love to her husband. Do I have to sleep in her sheets too?

I find myself exhausted from the stress of it all. It's no wonder I can't sleep.

"What I meant to say was, it wouldn't hurt to call the doctor," Michael corrects himself, much too late.

"I'll call in the morning."

"I think that's best. Can never be too careful."

As we cross the driveway, I peer through the glass, into the privacy of the Martin home. A streak of wickedness rushes through me as I drink in the details, feeling like a voyeur, but in an acceptable way. Because if they didn't want anyone peeking inside, they'd invest in curtains.

The house is spacious and immaculately clean, light bouncing off the bright white cabinets in the kitchen. Rachael is curled up on the white couch, a glass of red wine in her right hand, a magazine open on her lap. I can't see Travis, but Lord knows it's not for lack of light. It's as if God kept every inch of the earth dark at night except for 200 Cypress Street. That house and the creatures inside, He must've decided, were so glorious they deserved to be permanently bathed in light.

Michael's finger hovers over the doorbell. "You ready?"

"Mm-hmm," I say, but my stomach aches.

I thought I could handle Rachael's snide remarks and her references to Michael and Joanna's relationship. But now, standing on her doorstep, I just don't think I can keep up the charade.

Every time I look at Rachael, I see what I should be, and what I'm not. I see Joanna's friend, not mine.

I suppose I could always stay for dinner and then say I'm not feeling well. No one is going to question a pregnant woman's motives for heading home and crawling into bed. On second thought, if I chickened out, I'd be going back alone, to stare at the ceiling. Michael would probably stay with them. And I'd inevitably drive myself crazy wondering what was going on next door.

"Have you met Travis?" Michael asks, jabbing the doorbell.

"Maybe in passing at the office, but not formally. I wouldn't be able to pick him out of a lineup or anything."

He laughs tightly. "That's an odd thing to say."

"It's the truth." I pause, listening for footsteps on the other side of the door. "Hey, I think we should come up with something to say that alerts the other we're ready to leave. Something discreet."

"We haven't even walked in the door, and you're already planning our exit?" He turns to me then, his skin ghostly white in the glare of the porch light. "Is there a problem?"

"No, nothing's wrong, I was—"

The door swings open, cutting our conversation short. I force a smile, though my insides are eating at themselves. Rachael is standing in the doorway, one hand clutching the delicate stem of the wine glass, the other on the door handle. She's wearing black slacks, a white sweater that scoops down deep in front, and a shade of blood-red lipstick that accentuates the plumpness of her mouth.

"Welcome," she says, backing into the room, extending her hand. "Come in, come in. Colleen, you look gorgeous, as always." She wrangles me into an embrace, kissing one cheek and then the other, and I suddenly feel sicker than before. "Michael, darling, always good to see you."

She hugs and kisses him on both cheeks too, as I suppose is customary. But I don't like it. She lingers too long. Squeezes his shoulders a little tighter than she did mine. Once inside, I take in the grandeur of their home and struggle to keep my jaw closed. The entry is endless and tiled, pure white with a glossy finish. A grand piano is in the office off to the right of the entry. On the wall in front of us, an ornate wrought iron cross and an oversized abstract painting splotched with crimson and orange command attention. Directly ahead, a staircase zigzags up to the second floor. I step down a single stair to a sunken living room with a deep mahogany hardwood floor and a sea of snow-white furniture.

"Here, let me take that for you," Rachael says, stealing the tray from my hands. "Are they the beignets I asked for?"

"Dean came back for another hour this morning to make them for you."

"That's wonderful. I'm pleasantly surprised he agreed to it." A wry smile turns up the corner of her mouth as she glances at Michael. "Travis is upstairs, but he should be down in a minute. Here, let me take your coats."

She's only gone for a moment before she returns as bubbly as ever. "Drinks?"

"I'll help myself," Michael says, and heads straight for the bar separating the living space from the kitchen. It's stunning, with a hanging rack for glasses, shelves of liquor along the wall, and droplights that illuminate it all. "I can't believe he bought it," Michael says. "I told him not to."

"Bought what?" I'm at his side, one hand resting on his shoulder, the other on my belly. "The scotch?" I press, when he doesn't answer.

He holds it up, ogling its label, stroking its sides as if it's a baby who's just been born. "It's the King George V Edition of Johnnie Walker Blue Label. It's six hundred dollars a bottle."

I exhale heavily because I know what this means. They're going to break the bottle open, drink until it's dry, and I'll only have two choices: go home early alone, or stay and baby-sit a drunk.

Neither of those sound particularly pleasant.

"You have a beautiful home, Rachael," I say, joining her in the kitchen as she refills her glass. "Did you decorate it your-self?"

"Heavens, no." She slides a glass of ice water over the is-land toward me. "Travis did. He's got an incredible eye."

Before I can process what she's said, and the image of Tra-vis that's taking form in my head, I hear footfalls above.

"Sorry to keep you waiting so long," a raspy voice calls. "I was cleaning my new toy."

Michael turns, then freezes. And then I turn and gasp. A man clad entirely in black is bounding down the stairs.

He's holding a gun.

I stagger back against the bar. No one else seems to notice

the air go cold. My heart hammers in my ears as he reaches the bottom, clutching the gun to his chest. His eyes meet mine.

"Can't believe you got it," Michael says. "No wonder we're celebrating. Cheers to the new Glock."

He holds up his glass and takes a drink as the stranger who must be Travis drops the gun to his side and extends his hand toward mine.

"You must be Colleen. I'm Travis. Pleasure to finally meet you."

It's only then that I get a good look at him. His clothes are expensively simple, much like his home. But his skin is a different story. A display of colorful tattoos wraps around both arms from biceps to wrist. I can't exactly make out the shapes, and I don't want to stare too long, though splashes of blue catch my eye. His hair is black as night, wild, and toppled over the buzzed-short sides.

A spark of recognition burns through me. Yes, I'd seen Travis pass by my desk on the way to Michael's office a dozen or more times. He never stopped to ask if Michael was in. Never gave me a second look, actually. He was always dressed in suits, his hair tamed, tattoos covered. A far cry from the guy standing in front of me now.

"I'm so sorry," I say, shaking his hand. "You scared me. With the gun, I thought—God, I don't know what I thought."

"That I was coming downstairs to kill everyone?" he says, his tone going flat. "Not today."

After a long, awkward silence, he laughs, and Michael joins in.

As my smile falters, Rachael comes into the room and smacks him on the shoulder with the back of her hand. "Would you quit scaring our guests? It's poor timing, isn't it? The events of this morning have everyone on edge."

I'm glad that I'm not the only one anxious about the corpse being found across the street. Local channels were flooded with stories about the discovery all day. Normally, I would have switched off the television and gone for a walk, but those detectives were marching around the scene like ants.

"Have you heard anything else about the murder?" Rachael asks. "I wonder who the woman is. I don't remember there being any missing persons in the area."

"How do you know it's a woman?" Travis probes.

"Sarah Rhys says one of the detectives confirmed it."

"And you think she's local simply because the killer decided to stash her body across the street?" Travis kinks his head, glaring. "That's kind of a leap, don't you think?"

She rolls her eyes. "Well, she could be anyone then. Someone in the wrong place at the wrong time. Maybe she was a marathon runner training in the city, and ran through a rough neighborhood. Or maybe—and wouldn't this be perfect—it was someone who had it coming. Oh!" She bounces up and down on her toes. "What about that young nanny who worked for the Pinkertons down the street? Kira, that was her name. She was sleeping with Paul for months, right beneath Bernadette's nose, and quit out of the blue last summer. Bernadette might've snapped. Could've been her."

"We could be speculating all night," Michael says. "And it won't get us any closer to figuring it out, so what's the point?"

"I have to agree with Rachael," I offer with a shrug. "I bet it's going to be a criminal, or someone really evil. Someone who deserved to die. I hate to imagine someone innocent would be buried out there."

"Can't we leave it?" Travis snaps in exasperation. He's looking at his wife. "It's been on the news all day. I'd rather use this time with our friends to talk about other things."

"I agree. That's one wicked gun." Michael pushes the beignets aside to make room for the weapon. "Put it here, I've got to get a better look at it. You taken it to the range yet?"

"That's not going to happen. Take a look at this."

Travis goes to work dismantling the back part of the gun—hell if I know what its proper name is—and then clicks a silver knob-thing out of place.

"See that?" he asks, pushing the tiny knob from side to side. "Slide this over, and the Glock becomes fully automatic."

"No shit," Michael says, gawking, stroking the barrel. "Isn't messing with that thing illegal?"

"Hell yeah it is." Travis beams. "But I know a guy who hooked me up."

"May I?" After getting the go-ahead, Michael holds up the gun, pointing toward the door, closing one eye as if practicing his aim. "It's lighter than I thought it'd be. Man, I really need a concealed carry permit. How long did it take you to get yours?"

As Travis goes on about the permit process, which I now understand doesn't include the carrying of a modified weapon like his new "toy," I watch Michael pull back on the top of the Glock. I've never seen him handle a gun, but he looks natural, as if he's done it before. He's not hesitant or twitchy, not like I would be. Actually, I never knew he was interested in guns at all. I've never even thought to ask. Michael might own an arsenal I don't know about. Maybe that's what he keeps in the locked rooms in the east wing. It's not a far-fetched thought considering I still haven't figured out what's behind those doors. I haven't even been on that side of the house since my encounter with Dean.

"If the gun is illegal," I ask, sheepishly, "why would you want it?"

"Because it's fucking awesome," Michael blurts, shaking his head in disbelief as he replaces the gun tenderly on the bar. "Why *wouldn't* you want it?"

"It's for home defense," Travis answers. "Can never be too careful, especially after that dead woman was discovered today. If there's a killer on the loose in our neighborhood, and he tries to break into *my* house, he's not leaving in one piece."

I search Travis's expression for signs of humor. But there is none. And then he winks, chilling me to the core.

"Come on, Colleen." Rachael drapes an arm around my shoulder and leads me into the kitchen. "I could use some help with dinner."

Twenty minutes later, we're seated in the formal dining room. Ravioli and salad cover our plates as candles flicker from glass cylinders in the center of the table. Helping Rachael in the kitchen turned out to be removing foil lids from catering pans and tossing prepackaged salad. I don't mind. Since arriving at Ravenwood yesterday morning, I've eaten every breakfast and lunch there. I'm grateful to have a meal where I'm not eating from a menu handpicked by Joanna.

"What do you say we play a game?" Rachael asks, stabbing a cherry tomato with her fork. A reddish glow has bloomed over her nose, and her fourth glass of wine sits in front of her—not including the one she had in her hand when we arrived. "Remember when we used to play games, Michael? Before Joanna left? Oh, they were so much fun. Would You Rather was always my favorite—what a riot."

The mention of Joanna's name has me sitting up straighter and listening harder.

"I'd rather not," Michael counters. He squeezes my knee reassuringly beneath the table. "No offense, Rachael, but some of those parties were a drag. Pass the salad, would you?"

"Come on." Shooting him a slanted glare, Rachael hands over the chilled bowl. "Loosen up. Have another scotch. Colleen, I know you'll play. Would you rather travel back in time, or to the future?"

"The future," I answer immediately, and meet Michael's eyes in a way that tells him I can roll with the punches and handle myself. "I can't wait to meet our little one, so I'd travel to the day he or she is born."

"God." Rachael drops her fork and claps her palms together. "Isn't that the cutest?"

"I'd go back in time." Travis shovels a second helping of ravioli onto his plate. "Lord knows I've made mistakes in my life that I wish I could take back. I'd definitely rethink a few of my poorer choices."

"Only a few?" Rachael hiccups into a laugh, then directs her attention to Michael. "Your turn."

"I said I'd rather not." He takes a long drink, emptying his glass. "You guys know I've never been into these games. Can't we just eat, drink, and argue about politics and religion like normal people?"

"Who's normal these days? No one I know," Rachael snaps. "Looks like it's just the three of us playing, then. Colleen, your turn to come up with a question."

"Would you rather," I say slowly, letting my thoughts simmer, "live in the house of your dreams, but it was haunted by ghosts? Or live in a run-down apartment that wasn't haunted?"

"Oh, that's a great one," Rachael croons, stuffing a ravioli into her mouth. For the first time, she looks sloppy, waving her fork in the air in front of her face, smacking her lips together. "Let me think. Think, think, think."

I like drunken Rachael.

"Got it," she cries out, lifting her fork as if it were a scepter. "I'd live in the haunted house, but hire an exorcist before moving in. Voilà. Ghost problem solved."

"You can't do that." Travis shakes his head. "That's going against the rules."

"This is my game. I make the rules."

She laughs for no obvious reason at all, and I can't help but giggle along with her. Her laughter is infectious and melodic, a string of sweet, high-pitched sounds that I wouldn't have expected to come from her.

"Do you always have to manipulate things in order to get what you want?" Travis asks.

"We've been together nine years, and you're still asking me that question? Sometimes I wonder if you know me at all." She beams, revealing perfectly straight teeth stained a disgusting shade of purple. And then she laughs harder, smacking the table with the palm of her hand. But she misjudges the distance, hits her long, manicured nails instead, and pulls them back with a squeal. At that, everyone laughs hysterically.

"We don't even have to ask *you*," she says to Travis, clutching her hand against her chest as she nurses her nails. "You'd live in the house of your dreams. You don't believe in ghosts."

"Why would I? I've never seen a ghost. Have you?" Travis glowers at his wife as if he's waiting for a challenge. "What about you, Colleen?"

"I'd go wherever Michael goes," I say, probably too quickly. I've had more than enough time living in this scenario to make up my mind. "He's worth the haunting."

Rachael stares at Michael. "Is she always so gaggingly sweet?" she demands.

He nods. "Every single day."

"It's lovely." She presses her lips together, but a chuckle bubbles out of them. "Your turn, Travis. Ask away."

He finishes his salad and his drink. Wipes his mouth. Sets down his napkin. "Would you rather," he says, drawing out the words, "kill or be killed?"

"Oh, give me a break," Rachael grumbles as she pushes back from the table and disappears into the kitchen. When she reappears seconds later, she's carrying the platter of beignets. Dropping it in the middle of the table, she steals the one closest to her and takes a generous bite, even though she hasn't finished her dinner. "Oh God, these are as good as I remember. Colleen, be a dear and thank Dean for me. He both sabotaged my diet and salvaged my night in one eight-hundred-calorie swoop. Anyway," she says, dabbing powdered sugar from the corners of her mouth with a napkin, "why are you bringing up death at the dinner table?"

Travis shrugs. "Thought you'd be all for it, considering how obsessed you are with that body dragged out of the mud this morning. What would you rather, honey? Kill? Or be killed?"

Rachael makes a satisfied sound as she sucks sugar off her fingers. "I would have to be killed. . . . I think."

"You think?" Travis mimics, nastily. She ignores him.

Michael finishes his dinner with a sigh and pushes his plate aside. He's been silent the whole time, except for those few times he's laughed at Rachael's drunken expense, and his silence hasn't gone unnoticed. He hasn't touched me through dinner either, now that I think of it. Not since the one time he put his hand on my knee. Is it the game that's bothering him? Or something else?

"If I killed someone," Rachael prattles, "I'd go to jail, and have to leave all of this behind. I might as well be dead. Besides, can you imagine me in an orange jumpsuit?" She gives a visible shudder and laughs, tipping her glass back to down the very last drop. "That's not a way to live."

"That's if you get caught," Travis counters, straight-faced. "What if you kill and get away with it?"

"If they don't catch you right away, you wouldn't be able to think about anything else until they did. You'd drive yourself crazy, wondering when someone was going to beat down your door and haul you away." She shakes her head, flinging her blond hair about her face. "I'd rather die than be a prisoner in my own hell."

She hasn't mentioned a single thing about committing the actual crime, or the guilt of taking another life, only the ramifications it'd have on hers. I'm not surprised, but a part of me hoped she'd have higher morals.

"What about you, Colleen?" Travis says, twisting in his

seat to face me. "I'm *dying* to hear your thoughts on this. Kill or be killed?"

"Or more importantly," Rachael presses, leaning over the table and lifting the dessert tray. "To beignet or not to beignet?"

I can't bear to eat more of Dean's food. No matter how delicious, I inevitably think of Joanna with every bite. If Dean made these beignets, Joanna must've approved the recipe. She must've chosen which nights she and Michael would indulge in the treat. And one or more of those nights, Rachael and Travis must've come to visit and fallen in love with the dessert as well.

"No, thank you." Placing a guarded hand over my stomach, I shake my head. "Not this time, anyway. Desserts haven't been sitting right with me lately."

"Seems like nothing has," Michael interjects under his breath.

I shoot him a sideways glance that goes unnoticed.

"I'm not letting you off the hook that easily, Colleen. You still haven't answered." Resting his elbows on the table, Travis temples his fingers together and stares me down. "What say you? Kill or be killed?"

My cheeks heat as the table goes quiet waiting for my answer. "I think it would probably depend on who was trying to kill me—I mean, if it was self-defense, well, I suppose it would—I don't know, but I guess—"

"I'd kill," Michael blurts, his voice dark as the night. "Without a thought."

The table goes quiet as all eyes turn toward him.

"Well, of course you would, Michael," Rachael says with a smirk as she slides another beignet off the tray. "Travis may own guns, but you're the one with a history of violence."

This time, when she laughs, nearly falling out of her chair, no one laughs with her.

MICHAEL

"What'd she mean?"

"Who?"

"Rachael."

It's well after midnight, and I'm so exhausted, I can barely hold myself upright. Probably has to do with the amount of alcohol I consumed tonight, but how could I resist? It's not every day someone buys a bottle like that.

Staggering, I heel off my shoes, then shelve them in the closet. When I emerge, Colleen is dressed in a pale blue satin nightgown, her dark hair falling over her shoulders, and my breath catches. Removing the throw pillows from the bed, she gently pulls back the covers, adjusting them so they're perfectly folded back.

Tonight's the night. Finally, after a week of taking care of my own needs, I'm going to have sex with my girlfriend. It's been so long, anticipation makes my movements twitchy.

"When she said you have a history of violence," Colleen goes on without meeting my eyes, "what did she mean?"

There goes any hope I had of sleeping with her tonight. It's not happening, not now. The air is suddenly full of tension, and I can tell she's upset. I love her so damn much, and I want to tell her everything.

But I can't.

I can't tell her about Joanna, about the fights we had near the end of our relationship, about the time she ran to Rachael's house and called the police. I did things I'm not proud of. Pushed boundaries. Lost my temper and my mind. I've never been an aggressive person, but my marriage had deteriorated to a point where I hardly recognized myself when I looked in the mirror. It's not an excuse—there's absolutely no justification for what I did and said to her—but we were both to blame. I wasn't innocent, but neither was she.

With Colleen, I'm not even a shadow of that man any-more. I'm the man I used to be, the one I want to be.

I'd never hurt her.

Dredging up the past will only bring that negativity into *our* relationship. Once I tell Colleen the truth, she'll look at me differently, with regret in her eyes instead of adoration. And there might be fear there, too. Fear that I'd do the same thing to her.

I couldn't bear it.

"Last summer a guy came into the office," I lie as I strip to my boxers. "He was irate, screaming, causing a scene about a deal gone wrong, and when I went to escort him out, he swung. I reacted fast, dodged his punch, and took him to the ground. Everything happened so fast. It was blur, really."

She looks up at me for the first time, skepticism darkening her eyes. "What happened?"

"I let my anger get the best of me. He ended up with a cut over his eye and a bloody lip. Thank God he didn't press charges." I toss the pillows on my side of the bed to the floor and yank back the covers. "I was never arrested."

The story's not entirely fabricated. A man did come in, upset by one of his investments. He had made a scene in the lobby of my building. When I went down to confront him, he screamed until a crowd gathered around us. From there, se-curity escorted him out. I didn't lay a finger on him. Doesn't mean I didn't want to.

But the violence Rachael mentioned is much worse than beating up a stranger in the lobby of my building.

"Do you . . ." She stops as she kneels on the edge of the bed.

"Do I what?" I press, knowing I shouldn't.

"Do you own any guns?" She pauses, tension ballooning between us. "I'm just curious."

"No," I say. "I don't own any. Never have."

Doesn't mean I've never wanted to, but I leave that part out.

"That's good." She slips beneath the covers and draws them up to her chin. "I don't care for guns. I wouldn't want any in the home. Especially with children running around."

"I agree." I lie back, folding my hands behind my head. "Now let's try to get some sleep. You're not the only one exhausted by what's going on."

She crosses her arms over her stomach and sighs. A few moments later, she rolls onto her side, facing me. I can almost feel her gaze burning into the side of my face. A stark change from the way Joanna would sleep, turned away from me all night.

"Michael, do you . . . Never mind."

"What?"

"Well, it's just that we—you and I have never talked about your wife."

Not what I was expecting. She pronounces Joanna's title hard and clipped as if it's cursed. Forbidden. Perhaps it should be.

Wife.

Outside, the wind howls, slamming against the bedroom windows. We're in for another bad storm. "We haven't talked about her because there's no reason to. She's not my future. You are."

There. Cut and dried. Conversation finished before it could begin.

"Good night," I go on, hopeful.

"But . . ."

"What, Colleen?" I snap. "Why would you want to know anything about my wife? Our marriage is *over.*" Only it isn't. Not legally, anyway. But in every other sense of the term, Joanna is dead to me. "I thought we agreed to leave the past in the past and focus on our future."

"I know, I know that's what you said, but—"

"But what?" Anger scrapes away at my insides. "You suddenly want to know everything about her? All the juicy details of our marriage? Why? What good would that do either of us?"

She looks away as if I've struck her. "I guess I'm just curious," she whispers.

"Curiosity killed the cat, remember?" I scrub my hands through my hair as if that'll help me understand how this evening unraveled so quickly. "You want to know? Fine. We met at a charity function in the city, we were married five years—only truly happy for a fraction of that time—and then she left me."

Silence seems to stretch for minutes, and I breathe deeply, thankful she's finally dropped the subject.

"If you weren't happy," she asks, "why didn't you get a divorce?"

"For the love of *God,* Colleen, drop it," I holler. "I don't want to talk about my wife again. I don't even want to hear her name. Not tonight, not ever." I'm shaking with rage. Why wouldn't she just leave it alone?

As I turn over, dragging the covers over my chin, I feel the weight of her body turn on the bed, away from me. *This* was how I remembered the long winter nights with Joanna. Guilt-filled silence. A bare shoulder trembling in the moonlight. I don't want to upset Colleen, but why can't she understand? I don't want to talk about Joanna. To relive those memories. I want to move on. And before tonight, I thought we had an unspoken pact: no discussion of former loved ones. With Colleen, I'd found a unique sense of freedom I hadn't felt with anyone else. Because she didn't ask pestering questions about Joanna and our marriage, I could be a new man—one deserving of her love, living with a clean slate.

I won't let Joanna's memory ruin what I have with Colleen.

When she sighs heavily, I reach over and switch off the light.

"I didn't mean to upset you," she says in the dark. "I only

want to make sure I'm doing everything right, the way it's supposed to be. I'm trying to be the perfect girlfriend."

"Try harder."

Damn it.

I should've kept that last part to myself.

I don't know how we've come to this place, a stalemate. We used to be unable to keep our hands off each other. Now, although there are only a few inches between us, the distance is a canyon, and I can't cross it without knowing if she wants me to.

"Colleen," I say after a few quiet minutes. "Are you still awake?"

She never answers.

I close my eyes and pray for sleep to hit fast, but the recurring nightmare is already taking form, blurring the line between memory and dream. I can hear the jingle of Joanna's keys as she walks up the drive. And in that split second before sleep sucks me back in time, I can almost feel the anger lashing through my body as I slam Joanna against the wall.

JULY FIFTEENTH OF LAST YEAR

MICHAEL

When the clock over the bar strikes ten, I finish off the last of my Jack and Coke and order another. Normally at this hour I'd be on my way home to Joanna. But tonight, as usual for the second Friday of every month, she's out with Rachael.

On a typical night, they walk to the distillery for dinner and the first round of drinks. Now that Joanna's pregnant, Rachael drinks her share. Afterward, they catch an Uber into the city, and then Christ knows what. They used to like to use their girls' night to paint hideous cityscapes on canvases while drinking obscene amounts of wine. Really just an excuse to get plastered, which was fine by me. How they entertain themselves is none of my business. Since Joanna hasn't been able to drink for the last six months, I'm sure she simply enjoys the time apart—I know I do.

Her nights with Rachael give me alone time to do whatever the hell I want.

And tonight, I want to drink without feeling like I'm doing something wrong. If my gaze lingers on a beautiful woman, I won't have to explain myself. I want to be able to order a third, or a fourth, drink if the urge strikes me, without feeling as if I'm being monitored.

It's not like I drove. I stopped off at home to change clothes, walked the two blocks over, and plan to stagger home.

Every table at the Point Reina Distillery is packed, especially the ones near the windows overlooking the sand and surf. A full moon looms over the black sea, illuminating the waves with a rippling white ribbon.

With a view like that, it was a miracle my seat at the end of the bar was open.

"Bad day?" Don remarks as he slides my glass of Jack and Coke across the bar. It stops right in front of me. "That should help."

I've always liked Don. He's a hipster in his late thirties with a thin mustache, sharp eyes, and a dirty sense of humor. He'll go shot for shot with anyone who challenges him, and never falters on an order.

"Bless you," I say, burying my nose in the drink. "It's been the day from hell."

I was late to work that morning, thanks to an accident on the bridge. The meeting I'd scheduled first thing had to be pushed back, which in turn ruined the scheduling for the rest of the day. I slammed down a sandwich for lunch and haven't eaten since. It shows in the shake of my hands.

"Tonight it's me and you, and that bottle of Jack." I drink up. "Joanna's out with Rachael."

"Sounds like she's feeling better." He shakes a martini, pours, then hands it to the waitress waiting at the end of the bar. "That's good to hear."

"What do you mean?"

Joanna's not sick. I was just home, and she wasn't there. Her car was parked in its usual stall next to mine. And I talked to her on my way home from work. She was fine. Going out with Rachael, she'd said, as usual.

"Rachael was in earlier. Sat right over there." Don points to a table tucked in the corner with an ocean view on two sides. "When she showed up alone, I asked where Joanna was. Said she was sick as a dog. Holed up at home in bed."

"Joanna wasn't here? Are you sure?"

"Positive. Rachael came in alone," he says, drying a tall glass with a dish towel. "She stayed for a while, ate clam chowder and fish and chips, and drank two glasses of wine. I picked up the table since Monica wasn't on the clock yet. It was before the dinner rush."

"Odd," I say.

Because when I'd called, Joanna told me she left home *hours* ago.

Don takes another drink order from the waitress leaning over the bar and goes to work mixing. "Maybe she caught up with Rachael later, once she was feeling better."

"I doubt it," I mutter, because Don just shined a spotlight on one of my worst fears.

She's sneaking around behind my back.

I toss cash onto the bar and push out the distillery door, charge down the steps, and round the corner of the block before my thoughts come together. If Joanna's not home sick in bed, I'm going to lose my mind.

The lights in Ravenwood are on, but it's empty and cold inside. She's not in our room or the second master. She moved out of our bedroom in May—nearly two months ago—because she claimed she needed space. She'd secluded herself in that new room of hers for at least a week when she first moved in, and I'd thought for sure it was over. Since then, she's remained aloof about resolving the issues in our relationship.

Hey, honey, I text. *Just got home. Still out with Rachael?*

I keep my phone in my hand as I pace through the house like a caged lion. I shouldn't get worked up, not until I hear what she has to say, but I can't keep the bitterness at bay. I call Joanna, leave an urgent voicemail, and then search through my phone contacts, stopping at *M* for Martin. I punch the call button for Rachael's cell.

No answer.

I call Travis and also get voicemail.

Furious, I pitch my phone across the kitchen. It hits the wall and drops to the floor with the expensive sound of glass meeting tile. I feel like tearing the house apart. I want to track Joanna down and demand to know where she's been. I want to hear the truth from her lips.

When the lights of a car sweep through the living room at two o'clock in the morning, I tip back my glass and down the remains of my Jack. At this point it tastes like water. That's what usually happens after the fifth—or was it sixth?—drink. I'm no longer on the verge of bursting through my skin. I've moved beyond the wild, irrational state of anger. The fury inside me has boiled down to contempt.

Joanna strides through the front garden as the purr of a motor pulls away from the house and rumbles down Cypress Street. I hear keys jingling in the lock, and the handle turns. She appears in the foyer, smiling to herself, her eyes downcast as if she's lost in thought. She glances into the kitchen and spots me sitting at the island in the dark. Her smile drops.

Sick, my ass.

Ditching Rachael freed up Joanna's night to see whomever she wanted.

"Michael?" Clicking on the light, she closes the door behind her. "You scared me. What are you still doing up?"

Even in my drunken haze, I can see she looks stunning tonight. She's dressed in a low-cut pink top, dark blue jeans, and spiky heels. Her stomach appears flat. Her black hair is pinned on top of her head except for a few tendrils tickling her neck. Silver earrings dangle from each ear. She's made up her face with smoky eyes and red cheeks, but her lips are bare. Not a hint of lipstick. She's probably kissed it off.

"How was paint night?" My words drag, slowed by the liquor chugging through my system and the numbness tingling my mouth. I'm probably slurring, but I can't tell.

"What do you care?" she says. "You've never asked before."

"I'm asking now."

"I'm nearly a Monet. A few more classes and I think I'll best him. Is that what you want to hear? That my time away from you isn't wasted on something frivolous?" Scoffing, she shakes her head. "I made it home safely. You can go to bed now."

She avoids my eyes as she takes down her hair and disappears into the living room. I hear her footsteps on the stairs and then, moments later, a faucet. She's showering to wash away the scent of another man, I know it.

I charge upstairs and into her master. Her room smells so different from mine—floral and sweet mixed with something else I can't place. A new perfume, maybe? Or the scent of *him*.

"Where's your painting?" I holler.

"Can't hear you," she calls from the bathroom.

"Where is your painting? The one you made tonight. I want to see it."

"Oh," she calls out. "Gave it to Rachael. She liked mine better than hers, so I told her she could keep it."

Liar.

I'm stumbling into her bathroom, clutching the doorjamb to steady me. "Where'd you go for dinner?"

She's nude, staring into the mirror with her back to me. Five months pregnant, her figure is gorgeous, her skin smooth as porcelain, which makes me wonder when she'll really start showing. I haven't seen her naked since she moved into this damn second master. And we haven't had sex since then, either. Hell, we've barely been looking at each other.

But now that Joanna is carrying my child, she's more beautiful to me than she has ever been. The possibility that someone else has been thinking the same thing, and touching her body with the same kind of reverence, kills me.

"We ate at the distillery," she says flatly, testing the water, "and then we went for dessert after painting. We worked up an appetite."

"I bet," I spit.

At that, she turns, frowning, and she doesn't bother to cover up. She stands like a soldier, hands at her sides, holding strong to the lies she's just told. Her body seems strange and foreign. A piece of art I can admire, but can't touch.

"What's the matter with you?" she says.

I swallow down a vile taste that's lodged in the back of my mouth. "I went to the distillery tonight."

"That's not a surprise." Stepping into the shower, she drops her head back to allow hot streams of water to sluice down the curves of her body. "From the glazed look in your eyes, I can tell you drank yourself stupid again."

"I texted you when I got home."

"You did?" She turns beneath the spray. "I must not have heard it. It was loud. You can't expect me to check my phone every ten seconds."

"How about every six hours?"

Swiping her hands over her eyes, she levels a stare at me through the dimpled glass. "You're turning into a control freak, you know that? I moved into this room to get away from you. I can finally *breathe* in here. It's refreshing."

I open the shower door and grab her by the arm. Water sprays everywhere, drenching me. "We need to talk."

"Can I finish?" Her eyes flick over my fingers biting into her forearm. "Is that okay with you?"

Her face blurs, and for a split second I see two Joannas, and then three, before they merge together once more.

"Don from the distillery said you never came in tonight," I manage, pinching my eyes closed as a wave of nausea rolls through me. "He said Rachael came alone and told him you were too sick to go out."

"Really? That's bizarre." She nudges my arm off as the color drains from her face. Then, as if to cover her shaking hands, she reaches for the soap. "He must've mistaken another woman at the bar for Rachael. It was packed. You should've seen that place during the dinner rush. It's no wonder he was confused."

"Seriously? You're going to tell me Don can't recognize Rachael?" I can't do this anymore. "Where the hell were you?"

Water spills onto the floor as steam fills the bathroom and fogs the mirrors, but I don't care if the whole damn house floods. We're not brushing this off. Not tonight. Gripping her elbow tight, I wrench her out of the shower.

"Where were you?" I demand once more.

She shivers and covers her breasts with her hands. "Michael . . . I don't want to hurt you."

"Then tell me the truth. Where'd you go tonight?" I glare down at her as my head pounds. And then, because I can't bear to see her play the victim, I yank the towel off the rack and toss it at her. "Who were you with?"

"Jesus, Michael, I'm so tired of answering to your demands every time I go out." She dries off angrily and then shoves her arms into the white cashmere robe I bought her last Christmas. "When I married you, I didn't sign up to have a watchdog hounding my every move. You're the most suspicious man I've ever known."

She steps past me out of the bathroom, shoving me in the shoulder as she goes, and I follow.

"Then leave," I taunt. She's so close. With one move, I could grip her hair in my fist and yank her to the floor. "But we both know you're not going anywhere, don't we? Because you love the life I've given you. You get off on the clothes, and the cars, and the staff waiting on you hand and foot. You love Ravenwood, and you *especially* love the way that people look at you when they realize you live here."

She rounds on me then, eyes narrowing, lips pinching in disgust. "Oh, yeah, you nailed it. I love that my home is practically a prison, and that I can't go anywhere or do anything without hearing an earful from you when I come home." Whirling around at her bedroom door, she swings her arm toward the hall. "Get out of my room."

A laugh erupts from my chest as I charge at her, eliminating the space between us. "You've lost your mind. Who do you think you're talking to? This is *my* house, and I'm not going anywhere until you tell me who you were with tonight."

"Get out!" she shrills, lurching forward so that our noses nearly brush. "Goddamn it, Michael, leave me the hell alone!"

"Tell me who you're fucking, honey, and I will."

She clenches her jaw tight.

"Is it Dean Lewis? Distillery Don? All of the above?"

She swipes wet strands of hair out of her face. "Yes, Michael, I'm fucking *everyone*. Our chef, the bartender, and the skinny guy who delivers the mail, too. Would you really like a list of all the men I've slept with? Because boy, it's a long one!"

"Maybe." There's a sharp pain in my forehead, making me dizzy again. "If that's the truth."

She meets my gaze now, and there's no anger in her eyes. Just gut-wrenching indifference. "Just get out. Seriously, just go."

"How long has it been going on?"

"A few months. But stop being ridiculous. It's just sex. It means nothing."

I'm furious that she thinks she can write this off so nonchalantly.

"At least I don't have to hide it anymore," she adds with a shrug. "No more sneaking around, no more lies. If you could accept this, it could work. We could all be happy."

"We could *all* be happy? You're going to keep seeing this bastard?"

Frowning, she crosses her arms over her chest. "Well, that would be ideal. We're in a traditional marriage in a modern world, Michael. Let's catch up to the times. You could have someone on the side too. It could be fun. Think about it."

"Absolutely not." I can't believe she's being serious. "I didn't get married to have my wife spread her legs for anyone who asks."

She smirks. "Don't be so closed-minded. There are couples in open relationships everywhere. Why can't we be that way?"

"Name one couple we know in an open relationship." I square up to her, though I get the feeling I'm swaying. I'm having trouble focusing. "One couple who's happy to see their spouse screw other people."

"Rachael and Travis," she says triumphantly. "And Rachael says they're doing well."

"Fuck." I scrub my hands through my hair and steady myself on the doorjamb. "That's your example of a *happy* couple? They're delusional. *You're* delusional."

"Why should we have to choose between a boring monogamous marriage and living the exciting single life? Why can't we have both?"

I step forward and peer down over her. The natural scent of her skin, sweet and fresh, wafts over me. "Because that'd make you a whore."

"A *whore*?" she seethes. "Is that what you think I am?"

My head pounds. "Don't ask questions you're not prepared to hear the answers to."

"You're impossible to talk to when you're drunk. And I'm done being insulted by a man who can barely get it up. If you don't think I'll leave you, you can stand there like an idiot and watch me go."

"Get your ass back here." I clutch her shoulders as she strides away, and pin her against the wall. "Does he know you're married?"

Her eyes flare with anger. "This conversation is over."

"This conversation is over when I say it is. I'm going to ask you again, and this time you're going to answer me." I speak as coldly as possible. I won't let her off the hook. "Does he know you're married?"

"Of course."

"And he doesn't care?"

"He's married, too."

"Goddamn it."

"Michael," she starts, her tone pleading, but I won't hear any of it.

"Don't you dare say my name." I have the feeling that something inside me is about to snap like a rubber band. *Breathe. Just breathe.* "Not from your lying, cheating *whore* mouth."

I pinch her lips between my fingers and squeeze.

She jerks away. "Don't touch me, *Michael.*"

At her defiance, adrenaline spikes through me. My hands fly up to her neck. I want to shut her up. I want her to barely be able to breathe. My fingers crush her windpipe. I've got her fully in my grasp, under my control.

"Let me go." She struggles to form the words. Finally, I see horror in her eyes.

"Do I know him? What's his name?"

She shakes her head, wet hair thrashing. "Get off me."

I press my thumbs harder into the groove at the base of her throat. Her face distorts, twisting and turning as my stomach churns. Somewhere in the back of my brain, I hear a whisper of caution, but I cast it aside. I'm too far gone. She deserves this.

"I gave you everything, every piece of clothing in your closet, the car you drive, the bed you sleep in—but *he's* the one you let put hands on you? I bet you let him touch you any way he wants. Because that's what whores do." The thing that'd been coiling inside my gut moments before finally breaks free, releasing a tidal wave of hatred that threatens to drown me. "And you really thought you could have both? Your husband to *love* and other guys to *fuck*. Our goddamn anniversary is tomorrow, Joanna."

Tears drip down my cheeks, but I don't soften. Nothing will diminish my rage. She lifts her chin defiantly, as if she's done nothing wrong, as if she hasn't just ripped out my heart and stomped on the pieces.

"Five years, and this is what you give me? You're not the woman I thought you were. You're nothing but a dirty *slut*."

The words fall from my lips, vile and toxic, but once they're out there, I feel instantly relieved. It's as if I've purged the venom from my veins. I don't loosen my grip on her neck.

"You're a demon," she croaks. Her voice is strained, but rebelliousness blazes in her narrowed eyes. "I don't know why I ever wanted to have a child with you."

I jolt back and let my fist fly. She screams and cowers as my hand hits the wall over her shoulder, bursting through the drywall with a sharp crack. Eyes pinched shut, Joanna sinks to the floor and covers her head with her arms, but I can't stop now.

The world falls into darkness, and I can't feel my body, can't think a single rational thought. But I can hear everything. Shrieks of pain. Cries for help. The creak of the back door. Footsteps pounding through the living room and into the front yard. And then, finally, an eternity later, the wail of a siren.

TUESDAY

Five Days Until Colleen's Murder

COLLEEN

Rousing from my broken slumber slowly, achingly, I instinctively search for the warmth of Michael's body. Reaching out, I claw at nothing but cold sheets, and grip them in my fists.

A peck on the cheek before he got out of bed would've been nice. Or, seeing that I'd kicked off the covers, it would've been thoughtful if he'd replaced them at my chin. He could've whispered a few choice words in my ear to inspire an amazing dream. Any one of those loving things would've started my day off right. We could forget about dinner at the Martins' and how we went to sleep angry last night. We could start fresh.

Instead, I wake exhausted and searching for him.

Rolling over with a groan, I check the time on my cell.

Eight-fifteen.

A text alert darts across the screen. It's from Michael, thirty minutes ago:

> Morning luv. Going into work late today so we can spend some time together. Went for a walk in the grove to kill time until you wake up. Back in about an hr. xo

Excitement bubbles through me at the prospect of spending time together this morning. Michael must be bothered by how we went to bed angry. I'm sure he too wants to put last night behind us and move forward. But why would he venture into the grove? The police probably still have the search perimeter up. The last thing he needs is to be entangled in their investigation.

What are the chances someone would find a corpse across the street the day after I move in to Ravenwood? I'd say it's perfect timing, but nothing is perfect about this. This time with Michael was supposed to be quiet and relaxing. *Bonding* time. Now it could be ruined.

Slipping into my new favorite cashmere robe, I pad down the hall, swiping my finger over my phone. Yawning, using the banister to steady myself, I reread Michael's text.

> Back in about an hr.

For no reason at all, my gaze flickers to the east wing. It'd be wrong to try the doors, to check one more time if they're unlocked, wouldn't it? It'd definitely be a violation of Michael's privacy. Especially since he explicitly told me *not* to go in there. I can't help but be curious, though. It's kind of weird to block off a large part of one's home, to leave it unlived-in, isn't it?

Even though I know I shouldn't be, I'm drawn to those rooms.

I only want to see what he keeps in there. One peek, and then I'll forget all about that dark hall. Racing back to the master bedroom, I head toward the nightstand where I'd set my purse after coming home last night. I dig through the pockets, find Joanna's keys—*my keys*—and clutch them as I dart back into the forbidden wing.

Listening, getting a read on activity in the house, I hear something sizzling downstairs in the kitchen. Dean's hard at work cooking God-knows-what. Probably something Joanna gobbled up with a smile. Behind me, down the hall I'd just come from, there's a rush of water. The clank of something banging around in the dryer. The sound of a woman humming. Samara is busy with laundry.

There's not going to be a better time.

Nothing wrong with exploring my *new house,* I think, though deep down I know better.

Walking barefoot over the tile, I'm hyper-aware of the sound of my footsteps, which echoes my heartbeat. *Thump-thump-thump* as I rush over the bridge linking the safety of the west wing to the mystery of the east. *Thump-thump-thump* as I turn the handle on the closest door. The first key doesn't work. It must unlock most of the other doors in the house, as Samara had said. I try the second key. It turns easily. With my heart in my throat, I push the door open.

The room is still and clean, sunlight flooding through the uncovered windows. It's a billiards room, with a massive mahogany table in the center and a rack of poles hanging on the wall. I confess I'm a little disappointed.

The second locked door swings open to reveal a home movie theater, dark, with stale air. All the windows here are hidden by thick swags of rich purple velvet. Not a glimmer of sunlight comes through. Three slightly elevated rows of black leather seats are situated in the middle, and the largest movie screen I've ever seen in a private home is mounted on the wall.

I move quickly on, from one room to the next, unlocking Ravenwood's secrets. A gym, an office, and two bathrooms, just as Michael had mentioned. Still, I'm drawn to the door at the end of the hall. Even the ornate wood carvings set it apart from the rest.

Will I be able to unlock it like the others?

"The second master," I whisper, as though it's sacred.

I move closer, heart in my throat, listening for the soft beeping of the alarm to alert me to Michael's return.

Gripping the key I'd used to unlock the other rooms, I slide it into the lock and turn the handle downward.

It releases.

The door opens a sliver, and a draft of perfumed air escapes the room.

I gasp softly, covering my mouth with my hand. I know that smell. . . .

It's familiar, tantalizingly so, and yet I can't place it. Shadows cloak everything beyond the threshold, but when I pocket the key and push the door open wide, light from the hall spills into the room.

The layout is identical to the other master, only flipped. The windows here face the Martins' rather than the sea. The walls are painted soothing shades of cream, matching the mohair rug. It's fully furnished, with a bedroom set identical to the one we've been sharing. Four-poster bed. White duvet folded back. Row upon row of fluffed pillows resting against the headboard. Two nightstands, each with a tall lamp. A crystal chandelier hangs from the center of the vaulted ceiling, splashing rainbows of splintered light onto the walls.

It's beautiful. I'm breathless, the tension finally catching up with me. *So this was what Joanna wanted. All the trappings of her marriage, but with her husband subtracted.*

The bathroom is spotlessly clean, as if Michael's expecting a guest. Hand towels are folded and draped over the edge of the sink. I brush my hands over them and let my fingers sink into their softness. Bottles of body oil and lotion and perfume line the vanity.

"Why couldn't we open up this room to guests?" I wonder aloud.

Row upon row of the most gorgeous dresses I've ever seen hang in the closet, perfectly organized by color and length, dark to light. I wander inside, caressing sequins and silk and fur before spotting shelves lined with purses and clutches, all in their proper place. Feeling a little like Cinderella, I peruse the wall of shoes—Louboutins and Guccis and Manolo Blahniks and Jimmy Choos, arranged by style, and probably dollar amount. Every single pair looks to be the same size.

My insides go ice-cold, and my vision swims. *This is someone's room.*

The weight of the realization crashes down on me. I can't let the truth seep in, can't believe what I've walked into. My stomach twists, and I swear I'm going to be sick.

"Joanna . . ."

These are her designer shoes, her purses, her clothes. Her immaculately arranged, everything-in-its-place master bedroom. I back out of the closet, nearly stumbling over the rug. Dizzy with a bizarre mixture of confusion and envy, I reach for something to hold on to, something to steady myself. I strike the dresser with the back of my hand. A single framed picture wobbles, and I grab at it to keep it from falling. My fingers curl around an image of Michael and Joanna locked in a passionate embrace in front of the Eiffel Tower.

I hungrily swallow the details.

Rachael was right: Joanna's flawless. I notice the radiance of her smile first. It's the beam of a woman deliriously in love with the man who holds her in his arms. Her tilted face is heart-shaped, her lips pouty and lush. I can tell how perfect her body is from the gentle slope of her narrow shoulders. She's petite, but not weak. Defended by wealth, she glows with unblemished confidence, like the other women who parade across the sidewalk each morning.

I've been comparing myself to her, to women like her, my whole adult life. I'm not an extrovert who commands the attention of other people. I'm not what one would call "naturally beautiful." I'm not voluptuous. I've never been told my smile lights up the room, and I know why. There's nothing "special" about me. And now, standing in the middle of Joanna's room, surrounded by her things, in her home that's supposed to be mine, I slam into the one depressing conclusion I've feared most: I don't measure up.

Not by a long shot.

Everything here is still set up the way she must have left it. That means Michael's been waiting for her to come back. . . . But if that were the case, why would he invite me here in the first place? What was his plan if Joanna were to walk in the door, ready to pick up their life together right where she left off?

Trembling, I replace the picture where it'd been, right beside a vanilla-scented candle and a small gilt lamp. She's staring right at me. She's grinning because she's certain she has a hold on Michael, even now that he's mine.

She knows she's won.

I turn for the door. But nestled on the opposite side of the entry to the bathroom, another closed door catches my eye. The other master doesn't have a door that matches this one.

Downstairs, a door slams.

"Colleen? Honey? I'm back!"

Heart hammering against my ribs, I stare at the door as Michael calls my name again. I'm not going to get another chance like this one. I grab the handle and swing the door open wide.

Oh, he kept a—he couldn't have—but why would he have—*oh my God, no.*

It's a nursery.

Complete with mahogany furniture set, bright yellow rug, a crib—Lord help me—decorated with a patchwork quilt, and a carousel whose tiny stuffed animals dance in midair. The only thing missing is a baby.

Their baby.

MICHAEL

Any other day, I'd be up at six-thirty, scrolling through incoming emails on my phone, even as I stumble into the kitchen. Then it's downing my coffee while I turn on the television and watch the news. I have a lot riding on my investments, and although I have people monitoring them for me, I like to be in the know. Then, it's the drive into the city, which is hellacious if there's traffic.

Today, though, I decided it'd be best to slow things down, and take some time to clear our heads before we start to do and say things we don't mean.

I was up well before dawn. I couldn't bear to wake Colleen. She was deeply asleep, fists gripping the pillow, fierce as a child. Rather than interrupt what might've been the first solid night of sleep she's had in months, I snuck out of bed, threw on some clothes, and went for a walk. I needed fresh air to think, to clear my head. To remind myself that while things may be difficult now, we're in the middle of a giant transition. And transitions are always difficult.

Things will get easier.

At first, I thought I'd head to the beach, but my feet had other plans. Call it morbid curiosity, but I wanted to know what the grove looked like now that the police had swarmed through it.

The police tape and tents were gone, but the scent of fresh, wet earth hung in the air. Fog lingered beneath the canopy too, blanketing the ground. I stood at the place where they'd dragged the body from the mud.

No one is in the grove at this hour, so I'm not worried

about anyone seeing me near the grave. No one in this neighborhood gets moving before six. No one except for Distillery Don, who sits at the cliff's edge drinking his morning mug of coffee and Baileys. He's usually working off a hangover, and mostly keeps to himself.

As usual, he doesn't notice when I walk by. Doesn't turn around, not even when I greet him by name. Someone who didn't know him better might think he's deaf. But I know he just prefers to keep his mornings sacred and quiet.

I skirt the burial site and head straight through the grove, beneath the web of tangled branches, to the northern edge and back again. The earth is uneven and still muddy, but I'm not worried about losing my footing. I've gotten to know the grove trails well. I could maneuver through them blindfolded. I sidestep fallen logs. Duck beneath low branches. Stop for a few minutes at the northern lookout point and stare out to sea. As dawn breaks, I check my watch.

It's happened again.

I've lost track of time. It's like the grove shares the same mysterious magnetism as the Bermuda Triangle. It's not the first time I've misplaced a few hours while hiking through these trees.

I cut through rows of cypresses to head back the quickest way possible. Distillery Don has left his post for the day, and the sea lions have begun to bark.

Colleen has to be awake by now.

I approach Ravenwood from the front—the shortest route coming from the grove—and cut through the garden up to the front door. Have to tell the groundskeeper to trim those hedges. They're overgrown and crowding the path. I'm shocked to see the roses dying. They were Joanna's favorite flower, but they didn't even last through the first part of winter. Pity they were too weak.

Once inside, I throw a greeting to Dean, who's busy crafting the menus for the day, and call out to Colleen. It takes her a while to answer, and as I'm taking off my jacket, I swear I hear footsteps upstairs.

But that can't be right, because that would mean she's in the east wing.

"Colleen?" I call out again. "Where are you?"

"On my way down," she answers. "Be there in a minute."

I don't want to make something out of nothing, so I smile as she shuffles down the stairs. She's wearing Joanna's cashmere robe. Why can't she find something else to wear? Something that's *hers*.

"Hey," I say. "Been up long?"

She shrugs. "About twenty minutes."

"That's good." I give her a hug and kiss her forehead. I almost wish I'd woken her this morning. The walk might have done her good. She looks a little pale and distracted. "That means you slept well."

She goes stiff in my arms, and pulls away. "I was up through the night, but this morning I finally slept a few solid hours. I got your text."

I watch her pad to the living room window, and I wonder if she saw me walking through the grove. Would she think it was strange, considering a dead woman was discovered there yesterday?

"I needed fresh air to clear my head," I offer.

"It's dreary today," she says, not turning. "Do you think it'll burn off?"

"It should."

At that, I join her at the window, watching plumes of mist tumble over the cliff. After yesterday's chaos, when the street was packed with news vans and police cars, today promises to be peaceful. Back to normal.

I kiss her cheek. "You should call the doctor this morning. See if he can get you in sometime this week."

She sighs again, revealing how deeply tired she is. What little sleep she's getting isn't enough. "I will."

I know Colleen doesn't want to hear it, but Joanna was exhausted at this stage too. She suffered from morning sickness from the moment she found out about the pregnancy—at about week four—until the time she moved into the second master at about week ten. Throughout that period, she was miserable. She went to the doctor in the middle of May, and he must've prescribed her something to help. After that, her spirits lifted considerably.

Two months later, she left.

I can't think about the baby, not without feeling like I've been punched in the gut. The only things I'd ever wanted were to be a successful businessman, a loving husband, and a better father than the absent one I had.

I was going to have it all.

But that was before . . .

"I wish today were Saturday," Colleen whispers, turning to me. "So we could be alone. It would be nice not to have Dean and Samara hovering over us."

This is the first negative mention of the staff I've ever heard. Shocked, I pull back. "I thought you liked having Dean around to cook for us. And Samara is a lifesaver. Don't they take some pressure off?"

"I do. They do." She pauses mid-breath, as if she's trying to decide what's really on her mind. "But I think—I'm not sure Dean likes me, that's all. It's like he's always watching me, waiting for me to mess up."

From the kitchen, pots and pans shift in the sink. I don't get the feeling Dean's listening—never have—but I suppose if he's making Colleen uncomfortable, that's something I should take into consideration.

"How could you possibly mess up?" I ask, kissing her again.

She shrugs, and leans into me. "I don't know. It's like he's comparing me. To Joanna."

"Oh, don't be ridiculous. He just needs to get used to you and the way you do things."

It was this way with Joanna too. Soon after we moved to Ravenwood, Joanna suggested we staff the place—it was too large for her to keep up on her own, she pointed out. Dean came highly recommended by an old colleague, so I hired him on the spot. He worked in sullen silence for months until he finally warmed up to her, and then they became great friends. For a while, though I hate to admit it, I was jealous of their connection. Especially near the end, I suspected they were having an affair. I never discovered *whom* she was having an affair with. Honestly, it could've been anyone. I would much rather Colleen's feelings toward Dean be wary and cold than loving, the way Joanna's were.

But I'm done thinking about Joanna.

Behind us, Dean starts singing, but I can't make out the song.

"Do you want to get out of here today?" I ask, weaving my fingers through hers and drawing her hand to my lips.

She glances up at me, hopeful. "Really?"

"You haven't been to Half Moon Bay yet. There are all kinds of stores downtown." Although I hate shopping, I'd do anything to see her face light up the way it is now. "We could pick up something for the baby's room and then grab lunch at the distillery after. There's even a bookstore you might like. Getting out of Ravenwood for a few hours might do us both some good."

Her eyes glisten as if she's tearing up. "Michael, I would— That'd be—I'd love that, but about the baby's room, I—"

I squeeze her against me, cutting her protest short. "Go get ready."

"But . . ."

I shush her with a kiss. "We can talk on the way."

She smiles meekly and heads upstairs.

She really is the brightest part of my day, and has been from the first moment she came into my office for her interview. As awful as it sounds, I don't notice everyone who walks in and out of my building. But from the moment I saw Colleen that hot afternoon in late July, she caught my eye— and not just because she was trapped between the elevator doors as they clamped shut. It was her laugh that really got me. She sounded carefree and lighthearted, reminding me of a time when things weren't so serious, so stressful.

She hasn't smiled the way she used to for a while now. Maybe today I can change that.

I head into the kitchen and rummage through the fridge for a yogurt when someone rings the doorbell.

"Want me to get that?" Dean asks, but I wave him off.

A black sedan is parked at the curb, and two men are standing on the opposite side of the threshold. One's in a suit, the other in slacks and a polo shirt. They look . . . official.

"Mr. Harris?" the taller one asks. "I'm Detective Patel. And this is Detective Shaw." They show identification from the San Mateo County Sheriff's Office. "Okay if we come in and talk to you for a minute?"

Patel's tone makes me nervous—the last time I'd been questioned by the police was my final night with Joanna, and I hadn't been in my right mind.

"Of course, come in." My voice booms, sounding too enthusiastic.

They stand in the center of the living room, scrutinizing the ceiling, the tapestries, the fixtures. Finally both sit down on the same side of the room, where they have an unobstructed view of the kitchen. The taller one eyes Dean curiously and makes a note before leaning over and whispering something to the other. Unsure of what to do, I stand across from them, arms folded over my chest.

The detectives look comfortable, as if they're staying awhile.

"Can I get you something to drink?" I offer. "Coffee? Tea?"

"No, thank you," Detective Shaw responds, linking his fingers together between his knees. He cranes around to eye the stairs. "Who else is in the home this morning, Mr. Harris?"

"My chef, Dean Lewis." I point into the kitchen. "My housekeeper Samara is upstairs. And my girlfriend Colleen as well. What's this about?"

Patel clears his throat. "Mr. Harris, when was the last time you spoke with your wife?" Shaw's staring at me skeptically.

"Dean, come here for a moment," I call. When he rounds the granite island and enters the living room, he looks nervous. "You don't have anything cooking at the moment, do you?"

He shakes his head slowly.

"Good. Give us a few minutes to talk in private, will you?"

He doesn't say a word as he grabs his things, but his movements radiate irritation. He bangs the door on his way out. When I turn my attention back to the detectives, they're both looking at me like I'm some sort of weird bug they've just discovered.

"It's been a while since I've spoken with Joanna," I say steadily. "July, I believe."

But I know the exact day. How could I forget?

"Do you happen to remember your last conversation?" Patel asks serenely.

I shake my head. I feel like I'm going to vomit.

"Not exactly." I hear footsteps upstairs. Colleen must be out of the shower. "I'm confused as to why you're here. Did Joanna request an escort to pick up her property or something?"

Detective Patel leans back in the chair. "What property do you have of Mrs. Harris's?"

I don't like to think of Joanna as Mrs. Harris. The irritation sounds in my voice. "Everything. As far as I know, she left with nothing but the clothes on her back."

I boxed up a few impersonal things right away—candles, blankets, her favorite set of china, small appliances I wouldn't use—and moved them out into the garage. But her most intimate possessions—clothes and perfume and pictures—have all remained in her room. It was one of the reasons I never told Colleen about Ravenwood. Joanna left in July, and Colleen got pregnant in August. How could I tell her I was still holding on to those memories?

When the doctor advised Colleen to stay somewhere she could rest for the sake of her pregnancy, I knew this solution could benefit both of us.

She'd already filled the void Joanna left in my heart.

Soon she'd do the same for my home.

And maybe one day soon, I would finally clear out the east wing.

Detective Shaw looks up from his notebook. "Mr. Harris, when did your wife leave the marital home?"

"July." My attention flickers between them. "July sixteenth, to be specific."

"And, just to be clear, you're stating that Mrs. Harris didn't take anything with her when she left?"

I shake my head. "Nothing."

"Didn't that strike you as strange?"

Chewing on the inside of my lip, I wonder how they expect me to answer such a question. "I suppose so."

"Why do you think she left everything behind?"

"Why does a wife leave her husband of five years? I have no idea. I can only assume she left everything here because she wanted to start a new life—one without me, or anything that would remind her of me, in it."

The words carve a hole right through the center of me because I know they're true.

"What about her wedding ring?" Shaw asks nonchalantly. "Did she leave that behind too?"

I pause, thinking back to the last day I saw her. It was the morning of our anniversary. She'd had her diamond on, I'm sure of it. The only reason I remember is because I'd taken her hand that morning and kissed it. The angles of her diamond had pressed into my lips. I'd wished her a happy anniversary and told her I'd see her at dinner that evening.

She never showed.

I'd received a goodbye text instead. I don't blame her really. Not after the blowup we'd had the night before.

"As far as I know she took her wedding ring with her." And then it clicks. "She's missing her ring, isn't she? That's why you're here. She thinks I took it. She's reported it stolen."

"She is missing her ring, but that's not the whole story." Shaw's eyes drift over my shoulder. "You must be Colleen."

I turn. She's wearing black leggings and an oversized sweater, her hair damp and falling loose across her shoulders. Even from where I stand, I can smell the sweet scent of her conditioner.

"What's going on?" she asks.

Going over to her, I drape my arm around her shoulders and tug her against me. "They're here looking for Joanna's wedding ring."

She frowns and opens her mouth, but before she can say anything, Patel says, "Maybe you two should sit down."

I glare at him, then release Colleen and plop onto the couch. I get the bizarre feeling that my legs aren't a part of the rest of my body. Colleen sits beside me, her hand clutching my knee.

"I'm sorry to tell you this, Mr. Harris," Patel continues, "but your wife, Joanna Harris, is dead. We believe her body was the one we recovered in the grove across the street."

"I'm sorry," I muster, rubbing my eyes in an attempt to

wipe away the blur. "I—I can't believe—That has to be wrong. You must be mistaken."

"I'm afraid we're not," Shaw says. I'm really starting to dislike him. "Partial DNA came back an hour ago. Her sister called after being notified by a friend about last night's news broadcast. She'd been out of the country since June, and hadn't thought much about the lack of contact with her sister . . . until she learned that a woman's body was discovered across the street from Joanna's home."

"My home," I correct.

"Your home." Shaw eyes me carefully. "Working with law enforcement in L.A., Heather—Joanna's sister—came in and volunteered to have her cheek swabbed. There were a significant number of shared markers between her DNA and that of the woman we found."

"How long has she been out there?" I say, though the words are rough, more like a croak.

"Approximately six months, according to the coroner."

Six months.

I have walked on that path a hundred times since then. Walked right over her.

The thought is more than I can take.

A pair of hands grip my hand. "Are you okay, sweetheart? God, I'm so sorry."

Me too.

I wish I could tell Joanna how sorry I am for everything. What I wouldn't give to go back and replay the last night we were together. I said such terrible things. Christ, I was awful. A demon, she'd said. For the last six months, I damned her for leaving, for saying the things she did, for walking out without looking back, and all this time, she was out there. Buried beneath the dark umbrella of cypresses.

"The baby." I can't breathe. Nausea rises in my throat. "What about the baby?"

"I'm sorry." That bastard Shaw looks smug. "We can't reveal much at this point, but as of mid-July, and the day we believe she was buried out there, Joanna Harris wasn't pregnant."

"I don't—I can't . . . I hear what you're saying, but the words aren't coming together."

"To put it plainly, Mr. Harris, your wife wasn't pregnant when she died."

I retch onto the hardwood.

DETECTIVE SHAW

Once Michael Harris recovered, and their housekeeper cleaned up the mess he'd made on the floor, we asked if they would allow us to escort them to the station. Informally, of course. We read them both their rights, but made sure they knew they were not under arrest and could leave at any time they pleased. Patel also informed them of their right to have a lawyer present. Both declined, which is what we were hoping for.

Keep it light. Keep it informal. Lock them into a story they can't escape from.

On the surface, it may appear as if I know very little. I ask questions about small, seemingly insignificant things. Behind the scenes, however, our investigation is moving fast.

There are many things we already know for certain.

Michael Harris took out a $25 million life insurance policy on his wife last year. She also took one out on him. His business, Harris Financial, is in trouble, and has been for some time. Late in the evening on July fifteenth, Joanna fought with her husband. Uniforms were called to their home for a domestic dispute, but in the end, she didn't press charges, so her husband wasn't arrested. According to Michael Harris, she left him the following day.

Some time soon thereafter, Joanna Harris was murdered.

Cause of death? Blunt force trauma to the back of the skull. The murder weapon was most likely a shovel or other garden tool, considering that the back of her skull was smashed in the shape of a spade. We haven't found the weapon yet, but we're hopeful something will come up in the search of Michael Harris's shed. Toxicology hasn't come back yet, but we expect a report in the next few days. It's standard procedure to order the report, but we're curious to know whether the victim had any drugs or toxicants in her system when she was killed.

After identifying the victim as Joanna Harris, Patel obtained a search warrant for the Harris home. He's working on a search warrant for Harris's phone and for his call records as well as those of his wife. One detective on the team is digging into Harris's financial dealings. Another is contacting Joanna's doctors.

We're painting a picture, and it's not looking good for Harris. Patel thinks all signs point to him as our killer. A crime of passion, perhaps? Or a continuation of the fight that led the neighbors to call 911 on July fifteenth? But there are snags in his otherwise smooth line of thinking.

A gold medallion with the Virgin Mary etched into the front was around Joanna's neck, a topaz gemstone cradled in the Virgin Mother's hands. The gem is the birthstone for November, but Joanna's birthday was in August, which makes her gemstone a lime green peridot.

She's also missing her wedding ring.

It's true, I might be overthinking both things. Someone could have given her the necklace, and maybe she kept it for sentimental reasons.

And it's quite possible she removed her diamond wedding ring after leaving her husband. But where is it now? It wasn't on her corpse when we dug it up.

Since there aren't any pawnshops in Point Reina, I make a note to check ones located between Ravenwood and the city.

Our investigation is far from finished. I'm just digging my hooks in.

I've fired off calls to Dean Lewis, the Harris's chef, and Samara Graves, their housekeeper, along with the grounds-keeper. We need to get formal statements from them as soon as possible. In all my years on the force, I've learned one thing from hired help: they know more about what's going on in a home than the people who live within its walls. And some-times, if we're lucky, they know about marital troubles, too. I'm banking on the fact that the staff will be able to shed some light on the dynamic between Harris and his late wife.

Especially considering the most troubling puzzle piece in the case.

Joanna wasn't pregnant at the time of her death.

We're assuming she was pregnant at some point, since Harris seems to adamantly believe that she was, but we don't even know that for certain. Dates given by her doctor—who refuses to say much, citing patient privacy under the HIPAA laws—reveal she was due in for her next appointment at the beginning of June, the start of her second trimester. She never showed. If she'd had a late-term miscarriage, there should be a record of Joanna Harris checking into a hospital to give birth, even if the fetus was stillborn. We're looking into hos-pitals and doctors' offices in the area, though thus far, no luck.

We've also considered the possibility that Joanna might have gone back to using Buchanan, her maiden name. No luck there, either.

Had Joanna miscarried much earlier in the pregnancy and not said anything to her husband? If that's the case, how had he not noticed that her stomach wasn't growing?

"What do you think?" Patel asks me in the break room at the station, when we stop to get some coffee.

"About Harris? I think he looked genuinely shocked."

"He could be acting," he says. Michael is sitting at Patel's desk, his long body slumped and miserable. "Or the trauma could've blocked the murder from his mind. We've dealt with dissociative amnesia before."

"We'll find out soon enough."

Damn, I wish I could pick Karen's brain. Every so often, I'd consult her on difficult cases. She always had a gift for separating the guilty from the innocent. I relied on the cut-and-dried facts—sometimes to a fault—but she would follow her gut, and it never led her astray.

"What do you make of the new girlfriend?" Patel fills two mugs of coffee.

"Not sure." I take one of the mugs from his hand. "I'll take her. You take the grieving husband."

I escort Colleen through to the room in back, while Patel keeps Harris at his desk near the front. Closing the door behind her, I motion for her to take a seat at a table, and she obeys, thanking me as I offer her the coffee. She's very pretty. Without makeup, she's very pale.

"Do you have decaf?" she asks, and my attention instinctively shifts to her stomach. Baggy sweater. Stretch pants.

I wonder if she's pregnant.

"Sure," I say, and get her what she's requested.

And then, as is routine, I click on the recorder to document our conversation. Patel will be recording the one with Harris. First, I note the time and date. "What's your full name?" I ask, getting the basics out of the way.

"Colleen Leigh Roper."

"Where are you from?"

"Arcata, California, originally. But I've lived in San Francisco since I was eighteen."

"How old are you now?"

"Twenty-seven."

Quite the age difference. Harris is thirty-eight. You can't help judging a wealthy businessman who dates a much younger woman—his secretary, no less. Is it because those men are searching for someone who is inherently inferior, someone who won't challenge them? Joanna was approaching her thirty-fifth birthday. Something tells me she was more headstrong than the pretty, nervous young woman in front of me.

"How long have you and Mr. Harris been dating?"

"Since August." Her voice is soft.

Five months, I note.

"How'd you meet?"

"I heard his company was hiring. At the end of July I came in to apply for a secretarial position, and by the end of August, we were dating. Then, out of the blue"—she caresses her stomach, and smiles—"we were pregnant."

"I had no idea," I lie. "Congratulations."

"Thank you." Her cheeks warm with a pink blush. "We're very excited."

The fact that Harris had impregnated another woman while still married to Joanna strikes me as intriguing. Why not file for divorce? Maybe because he knew his wife was buried four feet under in the grove across the street.

"Did you know Joanna Harris?" I ask, keeping my tone light.

"No. When I applied for the position, she'd already been gone for a couple of weeks. People at the company talked about her of course, and I'm living in her home now, so I guess I feel like I know her in a sense." She fiddles with the handle of her mug. She hasn't touched the decaf. "But in person, no."

"When you say, 'she'd already been gone,' what does that mean to you?"

Her gaze flips up to mine. "She went to Los Angeles to be with her sister."

"You're certain?"

She nods.

I take a note on the pad lying on the table in front of me. "How do you know that's where Joanna went?"

"Michael told me."

"Mmm." I make a note of that too. "Do you know her sister?"

"No, not at all," she says, and I believe her. "Do you think she might've had something to do with Joanna's murder?"

"Right now we're looking into every possible scenario."

It's my standard answer, but in fact the sister has already been ruled out as a suspect. When she came in for the DNA swab, she'd been out of the country since June. So if Joanna went to L.A. at all, it wasn't to see her sister.

Colleen glances over her shoulder, in the direction of the room we'd just left. "But you don't think Michael had anything to do with it, do you?"

I wait before replying, making sure my next words are the right ones. "We're gathering as much information as we can to make sure Joanna's killer is brought to justice. That's why you two are here. To assist us in the investigation."

At this, she seems to relax a little. "I'll help any way I can."

"Thank you, Colleen," I tell her. "We're counting on it. I just have a few more questions, if you wouldn't mind."

She nods.

"We're assuming you know all of Mr. Harris's staff. But has he introduced you to his neighbors, the Martins, yet?"

MICHAEL

I wonder what they're talking about in there.

I can't make out what Colleen is saying, but I hope that bastard Shaw isn't making her too uncomfortable. Moving to Point Reina was supposed to alleviate her stress.

And now this.

Christ, what a mess.

"Mr. Harris?" Patel asks, drawing my attention back to him. "Are you all right?"

Patel's eyes are black as night. I have trouble looking directly at him.

"Yes, sorry, I was distracted." I clear my throat by downing the crap they call coffee. "To answer your question, it was to cover our mortgage in case one of us passed away. We decided twenty-five million would do it."

They're preoccupied with the life insurance Joanna and I had on each other, but there isn't anything wrong with having life insurance on my wife.

And now that she's gone, a small part of me—the darkest part I'd never share with anyone—is relieved. A few of my investments haven't been paying out the way I thought they would. For the last three quarters, my expenses have been higher than my income. I haven't told anyone—especially Colleen. She's got enough on her plate. I wouldn't want to burden her with it—but now, thanks to Joanna's death, everything will work out. With the life insurance, I'll be able to pay off everything.

It's a horrible thought, but there it is, lingering in the back of my head.

You're a monster, Joanna had said that last night. Maybe she was right.

"Do you know if your wife had any religious affiliations?" Patel asks.

"Not that I know of."

"Do you remember Joanna owning a gold necklace?" He pauses, gauging my reaction. "A medallion?"

"No, I don't think so. I didn't pay much attention to her jewelry."

Patel leans back in his chair and temples his fingers together. "Mr. Harris, I need you to really try to remember any talks you may have had with your wife about religion. The medallion had the image of the Virgin Mary on it. Did you or Joanna attend any church? Were there any childhood friends or family who may have influenced her? Anything, no matter how insignificant it may seem, will help us."

My thoughts reel as I talk. "All the years I've known Joanna—the years I *knew* her," I correct with a pang in my gut, "we never once went to church. Neither of us wanted to, really. I don't know about her childhood, or whether her parents were religious, but we were married at the courthouse by a judge, not in a church by a priest. I'm sorry, Detective, but I have no idea why my wife would've had something like that."

Patel makes a low sound in his throat, as if he's thinking.

I seize this time to get some of my own questions answered. "What the other detective said earlier—he said Joanna wasn't pregnant when she died . . ."

I can't finish.

"Yes," Patel says quickly.

"In July, she should've been five months along." I feel like I'm going to be sick. "What happened to the baby? Did she lose it? Or did she—was it something else?"

His lips twist, though his stare is dead-on. "We're not sure about the details yet, but we're talking with her doctors, and the autopsy will shed light on the state of her body when she was killed."

Should I tell them now? My secret is too big to keep for long. But if I reveal the way Joanna left me, they'll think I killed her. They'll say I spiraled into a jealous rage . . . and God forgive me, I did.

I should tell them. It might lead their investigation in the right direction. But I can't formulate the words. Horror and fear and something that feels like guilt spike in my gut.

"Do you . . . know how she died?"

"Nothing is conclusive yet. Again, we should have a clear idea once we receive the autopsy and toxicology reports."

The bastard's not going to tell me. *Why?* Joanna and I may have been estranged, and we may have had our fair share of knockdown drag-out fights, but I still care about her. Why won't he tell me what they've discovered about my wife's death?

Like a camera lens suddenly shifting into focus, realization strikes. I'm a suspect. I see what they see—the whole gritty picture in one horrifying snapshot.

I'm the murdered woman's husband.

I slept with my secretary immediately after my wife disappeared.

I'm the sole recipient of a $25 million insurance policy.

Do they know about the downturn in my investments? If they do, this picture is looking worse than I thought.

"Mr. Harris," Patel goes on grimly, "we'd like to ask you about the event on July fifteenth, when the police were called to your residence. Could you give us the rundown of what happened that night?"

I think I'm going to vomit again.

"That was all a big misunderstanding," I say, swallowing the bile in my mouth. "To be honest, I don't even remember what it was about." *Lies piled on top of lies.* "The Martins called the police as mediators. So they wouldn't have to put themselves in the middle of our marital problems."

"What kind of marital problems?" Patel presses.

I lift my gaze to his, and answer honestly. "The usual kind that come from two people living in the same space, dealing with the stresses of everyday life."

Every fiber of my being wants to demand a lawyer, right here and right now, before they try to trap me into something or twist my words to make me sound guilty. But asking for representation is an admission of guilt in its own way, isn't it? I'll appear as if I have something to hide.

So I pretend my insides aren't churning. Calmly, taking

shallow breaths, I retell the story as best I can. I'm not under arrest. They're not charging me. No, they're *baiting* me. I'm a pawn in their game.

But so is Colleen.

From here on out, we'll have to watch what we say very, very carefully.

What is she telling Shaw behind closed doors?

COLLEEN

On the drive back from the station, Michael doesn't say much. He stares out the windshield, eyes narrowed against the glare of the mid-morning sun. His fingers grip the steering wheel tight. We haven't had any time alone to discuss what happened with Joanna, or the fact that I discovered the nursery and her private bedroom. He must be distraught, and I don't want to upset him further. I can't imagine what he must be feeling—what it must feel like to know someone you once loved has been dragged out of the mud outside your home. I mean, even if they didn't get along and split last summer, he loved her once.

Clearly some part of him was still clinging to her memory. The perfectly preserved bedroom waiting for her return is evidence of that. In the midst of all the commotion, I *have* to find time to confess to him that I know about those hidden rooms.

I glance at him out of the corner of my eye, checking for tears. Nothing. His jaw is relaxed, his lips soft. His expression gives away no hint of emotion. He has to feel something—no doubt he's in shock or still processing. Maybe he's angry and suppressing it. Lord knows how I'd deal with such a blow.

I only want to make this better for him. If I don't know how he's feeling, I don't know how to help him.

"You talked to the detectives for a long time," he says finally, turning west, toward home. "What'd they want to know?"

"Just the basics. My name, where I'm from, when and how we met." I pause. "What about you?"

"They wanted to know about our relationship."

"Yours and mine?"

"No." His voice lacks any kind of emotion. "Mine and Joanna's."

"Oh. Right."

I should've known. Until the detectives finish their investigation, everything is going to be about Joanna and Michael. For the last two days all I've wanted to do is fit into Ravenwood, to carve my own place there, and I've already felt like Joanna is driving a wedge between us. The only comfort in all this—if there's any to be had at all—is the fact that Michael can now put a period on that part of his life. He won't be holding on to any hope that Joanna's going to walk through the door.

Surely he won't want to maintain that yellow-and-white nursery now. Wait . . . does he expect *me* to move in there, and for *our* baby to fill that crib? Like we're some kind of plug-and-play family?

I repress a shudder.

"Colleen, there's something I need to tell you," he says, turning onto the east end of Cypress Street. "The detectives have a warrant to search Ravenwood. They're probably already there. We have to grab a couple bags, let the police search through them, and then leave right away."

"This is ridiculous! You didn't have anything to do with Joanna's death! What do they think they're going to find?"

At that, he weaves his fingers through mine, lifts my hand to his lips, and plants the softest kiss there. "Thank you for your trust in me, darling. I haven't had a chance to talk to you alone since they showed up, and I wasn't sure what you thought—if you were thinking I had something to do with—"

"Michael," I interrupt fiercely, "you are not a killer. You are the kindest, sweetest, most thoughtful man I've ever met. I love you more than anything in this world. We're going to get through this together. Everything is going to be perfect. You said it yourself."

"The fact that you've never questioned me about anything—not even my past with her—means more than you know. You're my angel." He gives my hand a squeeze, and as we drive over a hill, the ocean comes into view on the horizon, vast and dazzling blue, melting into the sky. "I love you, Coll."

His angel. My heart flutters. And just like that, smack dab in the messy middle of a murder investigation, all is right in the world again.

"Where are we going to stay?" I ask, watching houses fly by out the passenger window. "A hotel in the city, maybe?"

He drops his hand from mine and rests his elbow on the door. "You're not going to like it." His eyes are on the road. His voice scares me, just a little. What now?

"Where?"

"Rachael extended an invitation to—"

"Oh, Michael, please don't tell me we're staying with them!"

"It's one night." He exhales heavily. "Maybe two. Only until the cops are done searching Ravenwood. Then we can go back."

I don't know if I can keep up the charade another night, let alone two. I can't keep pretending Rachael is wonderful when I can't shake the feeling she's going to stab me in the back the instant I turn around. And there's something about Travis . . . There's nothing I'd like more than to put distance between us. Instead, we're sleeping over. Talk about torture.

"I'm sure you don't want to hear about this either, sweetheart, but I have to start planning her funeral," he continues. "Heather Chapman, Joanna's sister, came in to confirm

DNA, but she's already gone back to L.A. She's making a quick trip up Thursday to help with the details."

"When will the funeral be?" I try to keep my voice steady. I can't believe Joanna's sister is making Michael responsible for this.

"Don't know. Detective Patel says they won't release Joanna's"—he clears his throat—"body . . . until the county coroner's report is finished, but that all depends on how busy their office is. He said he'd let us know."

"That's not very helpful," I say, trying to keep my frustration in check. "How are you supposed to plan a funeral when you don't know when they'll release her?"

And how is he supposed to get any kind of closure? Or move on with his life, when everything remains up in the air?

"Heather and I will go over all the details, but we'll have to wait to finalize the date until we hear back from the detectives. There's nothing more we can do."

I'm about to rant about the ineptitude of the county coroner's office when Michael makes the final turn onto our street.

"Oh my God," I breathe.

"You've got to be kidding," Michael mutters.

The news vans are back, and they're everywhere. Cluttering the street on both sides. Blocking driveways. And now, instead of reporters gathering on the grassy area in front of the grove, they're lining the curb in front of our house. The police officers are back too, except now they're tramping around the grounds and in the house, invading our personal space. My stomach tightens. I need to stay calm for Michael's sake.

"Just keep going. Drive past the Martins' house. Don't pull in."

"Where are we supposed to go, Colleen?" he snaps.

I ignore the nastiness of his tone. "We can stay at a hotel and disappear for a while."

We pass Ravenwood, and he pulls into Travis and Rachael's driveway, parking behind Travis's black BMW and

Rachael's cherry-red Porsche. "I didn't do anything wrong, Colleen. I'm not running. We're going to stay here and wait this out."

The moment we exit the car, we're swarmed with reporters. Cameras and questions blur together into one loud roar. I stagger back from the force of it as strangers jog up the driveway.

"There he is!"

"Mr. Harris, what was your reaction upon hearing of your wife's death?"

"How soon after your wife left did you begin dating Miss Roper?"

"Hey, Mike!"

At my side in a flash, Michael curves his arm protectively over my shoulder and escorts me toward the glass house.

"Mr. Harris!"

"We'll get our bags later," Michael says, over the onslaught of questions. "After it's died down. They can't stay here forever."

I nod, agreeing. There's no way I'm weaving through the crowd, being analyzed by the deputies. I'm done being questioned for the day.

As Rachael opens the door and whisks us inside, the reporters cluster between Ravenwood and their home. It only then occurs to me that we're staying in a see-through house. Like monkeys on display in the zoo.

How could Michael possibly think this was a good plan?

"Thanks for letting us stay," Michael tells Travis, releasing me to shake his hand. "It's a circus out there."

"Don't mention it. Drink?"

"God, yes."

My hand rests against my stomach as I stare past the reporters, to Ravenwood. The house is buzzing with excitement. The massive entrance door has been propped open, to allow easier access for officers to trudge in and out. They wrap plastic covers over their boots and shove their hands into latex gloves before heading inside.

What are they expecting to find? I realize they're covering their bases, crossing every *t* and dotting every *i,* but they're wasting their time. Over the years, I've read more thrillers than I can count. Reading about an investigation on the page is interesting. But living it, watching it unfold from the window next door, makes me feel . . . *violated.*

Something strikes me with the force of a mallet on a drum. They're going to search the master bedrooms. They'll know one belonged to Joanna. They're going to assume Joanna and Michael were having marital problems. Oh, God. No matter what we do now, the investigation is going to paint a poor picture of Michael.

Another patrol car pulls up to the curb, and the two detectives from the station step out, the short redheaded one twisting something in his hand.

"Damn reporters were knocking down our door earlier," Rachael says, coming to stand beside me. "They had questions about our friendship with Michael and Joanna."

"What'd you tell them?" I ask, keeping my gaze on the chaos unfolding out the window.

"Nothing. Travis chased them away. Said it was none of their business."

"Thank you for that. And for letting us stay. Michael didn't want to get a hotel. He said it'd make it look like we were running away."

"He's right, you know." Staring out across the sea of press, she frowns. "They're going to be watching him closely from now on. He has to be extremely careful what he does." She adds darkly, "And what he says."

"He doesn't deserve this. He didn't do anything wrong, I know it. Michael's not capable of something like that."

Rachael makes a small noise of agreement.

"Can I ask you something?" I whisper, leaning closer.

She turns, facing me. "Sure."

"When was the last time you talked to Joanna?"

Her expression changes, just a flash of something dark, and then it's gone. "I can't remember exactly. Sometime in July, I think."

Hmm, that's interesting. Right around the time Joanna died, according to the dates the police gave.

I repress a shudder.

Rachael could've been the one who killed Joanna. Something about the way she's acting doesn't sit right with me. The first day I met Rachael, when she stopped by for a visit, she'd said she and Joanna used to be best friends. And then something happened. They'd drifted apart. Hadn't Rachael said she was glad Joanna dropped off the face of the earth? Now I can't remember exactly, but it was something along those lines.

"Listen," Rachael says firmly, pivoting away from the window, "it's probably best that everyone minds his or her own business this week. We're already going to feel like ants under a microscope, thanks to the detectives questioning everyone and everything all the time. We don't need our friends doing it too."

"The detectives are questioning you?"

"Oh, I'm sure they'll want to interview us at some point, since I was Joanna's friend, and Travis works for Michael's company. It's exciting, isn't it?"

And then, with a smile that would challenge the brightness of the sun, she's gone, joining Michael and Travis at the bar.

DETECTIVE SHAW

Ravenwood.

Scrawled on a massive beam above the front door, its letters are deeply etched into the wood. In the living room, a wood carving of some kind of bird—a crow or raven?—watches over the room. It's positioned like a trophy, perched on the mantel with its tiny black head tilted up in defiance. I wonder if the bird came with the place, passed along from owner to owner, or if the Harrises purchased it to spotlight the name the house had been given.

Karen loved to decorate, but her tastes veered more toward soft and floral than stark and modern. For nine years she'd created a warm home that I was happy to return to each night. She'd be disappointed if she could see that home now, stripped bare and kept dark. She'd grab me by the shoulders and shake me. Tell me to wake from whatever funk I'm in.

But that's just it. I'm not in a funk at all.

I've simply been shown, in the harshest way possible, that none of these things—the expensive homes, elaborate furnishings, and luxury cars that the people of Point Reina seem to worship—matter. Not in the least. And definitely not in the end, when you'd happily throw all of that junk into the sea if it meant you could have more time. Even if it was one fleeting second to tell someone you loved them for the millionth time.

Out the Harrises' windows, rich green grass leads down to a roiling, turbulent sea. Wispy clouds mark the charcoal-gray sky. By midafternoon, hard gusts of wind rip over the sea and whiz around the house, creating a low whistle that seems to vibrate the very air we're breathing. No one else seems to notice.

But I pay attention to everything.

Windows without curtains. Books lined up like soldiers

on the shelves in the living room. Clean dishes in the dishwasher. The lingering scent of a woman's perfume—powdery and flowery—in the big downstairs bathroom. Upstairs, the hall veers right and left. East and west.

"Shaw," Patel calls from the darker of the two wings, and I follow the sound of his voice. "These doors are locked."

"We'll get the key."

I round the corner and count the doors quickly, testing each one as I pass. Judging from the pattern of windows on the outside of the house, I bet the setup is the same on this side as it is on the opposite side. Many more rooms than two people need. Patel is standing in front of the door at the end of the hall. Unlike the others, this door is cracked open, allowing a pale stream of light to escape onto the hardwood.

"You should see this," he says, and disappears inside.

As I push the door open wide, I log mental notes. Four-poster bed. Bedding that resembles a cloud. Oversize furniture. Pristine and white with a feminine touch. Furry rug. Dark flooring. Strangely sweet-smelling air.

Something tells me this was Joanna's personal space. Somewhere she could be herself, away from her husband. Why did she feel the need to be alone? Had she been afraid of him?

Taking a framed photo from the bureau, I stare at the stunning woman. Long, dark, wavy hair. Heart-shaped face. Pale skin. Big blue eyes that pierce through to anyone who looks at the picture. Michael Harris has his arms around her, and he looks bewitched.

"Shaw," Patel calls once more.

I replace the frame, and when I turn, he's opened a small door beside the bathroom.

"It just gets weirder and weirder," he says, gesturing for me to go through first.

"Wow." I imagine the hopes and dreams that must've flowed through this space, once upon a time. A crib fitted with a yellow sheet and colorful quilt is an eerie reminder of what those dreams must have been. "Doesn't seem like he changed a thing."

Patel stands near the changing table shaking his head. A Gucci diaper bag hangs against the wall behind him, and he reaches up to adjust it on its hook.

"This makes me think he's telling the truth," I offer. "He must not have known what happened to their baby. That she lost it. How else could he bear looking at this?"

"Maybe he never wanted that baby. It's too soon to make any assumptions. We don't know anything yet."

Michael could be innocent. A brokenhearted husband and father waiting for his wayward wife to return home against all odds. Or he could be hiding much more.

Yet, as I charge down the hall, eyeing the locked doors, I can't get the image of that yellow nursery out of my mind. He kept it up. Cleaned it. There was no dust clinging to the dresser or the crib rails. We have a team dusting for finger-prints, although I doubt we'll discover anything but proof that Michael, Colleen, and maybe Joanna have lived here. I'm sure we'll find prints from their staff as well.

Every detail, no matter how minuscule, paints a picture of the life Michael and Colleen live. And if I dig deep enough, I'll discover the kind of life Joanna lived here, too. When I reach the bottom of the stairs, I head out the back door, thankful for the blast of cold air. I felt like I was suffocating in that house.

"Think we have something," a young deputy says when he spots me. "In here."

Hands on my hips, I follow him to the six-bay garage. It's larger than it seems from the outside, if that's possible. Two stories high. Cement floors. Bright lighting. Cabinets stretch-ing along the entire back wall. Exotic sports cars rest in front of each garage bay—a canary-yellow Ferrari, black Bugatti, and silver Aston Martin—and at the far end of the garage, a car covered in a tarp. If Michael leaves *these* beauties exposed, what kind of car has he concealed?

I make a beeline for the car at the far end and lift the cover.

"Surprise," I say with a laugh. "Wouldn't have thought it."

I was expecting a Lamborghini, or maybe a one-of-a-kind classic American muscle car. Not an ordinary Lexus.

"This way," the deputy says, his voice echoing in the big space. "I was searching through the cabinets and found these."

He steps aside so I can study the contents of the nearest cabinet. One side is full of boxes. The deputies have already opened a few, revealing old blankets, candles, some small kitchen appliances, and a set of china with an ugly pattern.

"There," the deputy says, pointing to the opposite side of the cabinet. "Behind the tarp."

I push the tarp aside. Garden tools lean against the back wall. Two shovels, a rake, Weedwacker, a hoe.

"Take these in and have them checked for traces of DNA."

"Yes, sir."

I head back inside to continue peeling back the layers of their lives. I start downstairs, in the guest bathroom, and open the medicine cabinet first. Advil and Theraflu, DayQuil, and two boxes of Q-tips. A near-empty prescription bottle for Restoril. I'm not familiar with it, but a quick Google search on my phone reveals the medication is used to combat insomnia. It's also highly addictive. This particular bottle dates back to July. Prescribed to Michael Harris by Dr. Priscilla Smith.

I bag it.

Kneeling in front of the cupboard, I start sifting, pulling out boxes filled with tissues, feminine products, and first aid essentials. I slide a plastic organizer filled with bathroom cleaners to the side, and—

Bingo.

In the far back corner, behind bottles of Clorox and bathroom cleaner, a silver cosmetic bag catches my eye. I pick it up carefully, unzip it, and shake two large prescription bottles into my palm. Valium and Vicodin. It appears the bottles have gotten wet at some point. The labels are blurred, and lifting at the corners, and the dates have faded away. Both are approximately half full.

I roll them into a bag, seal it shut, and then hold the labels up to the light to get a better look.

They were both prescribed by Dr. Cameron Garcia, who works on Valencia Street in San Francisco. More intriguingly, neither is prescribed to Michael, Colleen, or Joanna.

The prescription is for someone named Mandy McKnight.

It's a crime to be in possession of a controlled substance prescribed to someone else. Had Michael or Colleen bought the medication illegally? Or perhaps Joanna and Michael didn't bother to throw the pills out when they moved in five years ago. Either way, I'm going to find out.

Pulling out my phone, I do a quick Google search for "Dr. Cameron Garcia, San Francisco." One listing hits the mark. He's been a doctor for ten years. Women's clinic. Great reviews. Once I'm satisfied I've found the right doctor, I google: "Mandy McKnight, Point Reina." Too many hits to go through one by one. I open Facebook and do a search. Three Mandy McKnights show up. One is local to San Mateo County. Her profile image is a zoomed-in picture of a Chihuahua's face, and the damn dog is wearing a blue hooded jacket. Private profile. Under "employment," it lists her as the owner of Studio Balance Pilates in Half Moon Bay.

Tomorrow's shaping up to be a busy day.

I'll be heading to the real estate agency where Rachael works, a women's clinic, and a Pilates studio. And maybe, if there's time, Harris Financial.

Fifteen minutes later, after I've checked the recorder in my pocket to ensure it's on and working, I go upstairs to face Michael and Colleen. They're seated on the big leather couch practically on top of each other, holding hands, their eyes shifting to the deputies roaming the room. Two bags rest at their feet, and a quick glance at the deputy standing behind the couch—who gives a thumbs-up—tells me he's already gone through them.

"Sorry to keep you waiting. We should be finished tomorrow morning," I say, "but whatever time we end here, rest assured there'll be an officer on the scene all hours of the night, until we return the keys to you."

I say this for two reasons. One, I want them to know their home is safe. I won't leave it unsecured. We've all seen the hungry journalists outside, greedy for some clue, some insight into Joanna. Two, and perhaps more important, I want Michael to know that he can't come back and tamper with the scene.

"Thank you," Colleen says, trying to smile at me. "We really appreciate that."

Harris clenches his jaw, saying nothing.

"Mr. Harris, we found these in your medicine cabinet," I say, holding up the bag with the prescription bottles. "Could you explain them for me, please?"

"Sure." He shakes his head as if he's in some kind of daze. "I was having trouble sleeping after my wife left." Beside him, Colleen Roper stiffens. "I went to see Dr. Smith to ask if she could prescribe something to help. Since when is it a crime to take something to combat insomnia?"

"No crime," I say mildly. "Do either of you know someone by the name of Mandy McKnight?"

"No." Colleen says. The hand Harris isn't gripping now curves against her belly. "I'm not the best with names, but I don't think so."

As I watch her hand, it strikes me that she's almost showing, maybe at the same point in her pregnancy Joanna was said to have been when she vanished. Something clicks. How had her husband not known that Joanna lost the baby *before* July, when she disappeared? Were they truly that estranged? Or is the guy playing us for fools?

"Mr. Harris?" I prod, when I realize he hasn't answered my question.

"I don't know anyone named Mandy." He glances at a deputy as she leaves his home. "But what does that have to do with my wife's murder?"

"We're not sure just yet," I answer, sitting down in the leather chair opposite them. And I wonder just how much information to divulge. "But we found two other prescription bottles in your bathroom cabinet. These were made out to someone by that name."

I watch for their reactions. Colleen appears confused, her eyebrows pinching together as she turns to her boyfriend. Harris looks straight ahead, stoic, his lips pressed tight. He's handling this well, I note. Too well? After Karen passed away, I was unable to function for weeks. But after learning a few hours ago that his wife was murdered, Michael appears only mildly irritated.

"You found them in our bathroom?" Colleen asks.

I nod. "They were tucked behind the cleaning products."

"I don't know anyone by that name," Harris insists. "I don't know what those bottles would be doing in my bathroom. I've never seen them before."

Deny everything.

It's a normal part of this process, and he's falling in line with most other suspects when they realize the predicament they're in. They clam up, afraid to reveal too much, and deny knowing anything at all. Next will be anger, and judging from the way he's glaring at me, that's coming soon.

"What about Dr. Cameron Garcia?" I ask. "Ever visit a doctor by that name?"

"Never."

"What about your wife?" Poor Colleen always flinches when I call the dead woman his wife—kid's really got it bad for Harris. "Might he have been a doctor who treated her at some point?"

Michael's nostrils flare slightly. "Might have been, but I wouldn't know. The name isn't familiar and Joanna's not here to ask."

He's pissed, and I can't blame him. We're in his home, challenging everything he tells us.

"How long have you owned this home?" I ask, pretending I haven't noticed his mounting anger.

"Five years," he fires back. "I already told you this. Joanna and I bought it right after we got married."

But I need to hear some answers again, to make sure they don't change.

Colleen perks up. "Any chance," she asks me, "that those pills belong to the person who lived here before them?"

"Could be." But that's not what I'm thinking. "We'll look into that."

My guess? Someone—probably Joanna—bought the drugs illegally. It may not lead to anything, but it's a thread to start pulling. If nothing else, it allows me to follow the trail to Mandy McKnight, and opens up the possibility of another cube sliding into place.

"Anything else?" Michael asks flatly.

"We're taking in some of your garden tools. We'll bring them back as soon as we clear them."

"Garden tools?" Colleen parrots. "What for?"

"From what we can tell, Joanna was struck in the back of the head with something."

"Detective Shaw, don't take this the wrong way," Colleen says sweetly, "but do you really think Michael would strike Joanna with something, and then keep the shovel in his cupboard?"

I almost laugh at her candor, or arguably, her naïveté. And

I hadn't said *shovel*. So what made her think the murder weapon was a shovel?

"Honey," Michael says, releasing her hand to squeeze her knee. "You're not helping."

"It just doesn't make any sense." Her eyes go wide. "Why would he leave the murder weapon lying around with—"

"Coll," he soothes, rubbing his hand over her thigh. "Stop."

Clamping her mouth shut, she leans back into the cushions and again rests her hands protectively over the small swell of her belly.

"Mr. Harris, I notice your housekeeper stepped out some time ago. Did she leave for the day?"

"No, she's been outside, waiting for us to finish."

Perfect. "Could you please send her in? Tell her I'll be upstairs. In the east wing."

I watch him carefully as he processes what I've said, and what it means. That we've found his wife's room—the one set up for her to sleep in alone. And we've found the nursery for their child, eerily preserved after that child disappeared. I study the slow tensing of his jaw. The hard, steeliness of his eyes. He doesn't even need to say a word.

I've got him.

"Of course," he answers through gritted teeth. "I'll send her right up. Anything else, Detective?"

"One more thing," I say, standing. "Do either of you have any trips coming up? Anything that might take you out of the area?"

Harris doesn't answer. Standing quickly, he slings their bags over his shoulder and extends his hand to help Colleen up. She has a petite frame, but her pregnancy makes her a little awkward in rising.

"No, I don't think we'll go anywhere," she says, following him to the door. "We're staying close to my doctor in the city. Just in case, for our baby."

As the front door opens, reporters swarm from their cars and vans. Cameras roll. Microphones wave toward Michael. Questions whiz through the air like rapid gunfire.

"Staying close is a good idea," I say, stepping up behind them. "We need to be able to get ahold of you quickly in case we have other questions."

Or want to make an arrest.

....

"You asked to see me?"

I'm going through Joanna's bedroom, sifting through the drawers of her nightstand, when the stern voice pierces the stillness. I crane my neck around. A very fat, very short woman is standing in the doorway, eyeing me skeptically. Her skin is a smooth caramel, and her eyes a rich brown. Guessing from the gray streaks over her ears, and the slight wrinkles around her eyes and mouth, I'd say she's about to hit sixty.

"I'm Detective Shaw," I say, getting to my feet and extending my hand. "You must be Samara Graves."

She walks into the room and gives my hand a limp shake. "Mr. Harris said you wanted a word with me? Would you like to talk downstairs in the library?"

"No, here will do," I reply, then watch a shadow flit across her eyes. "I just needed to ask you a few questions about Joanna Harris."

Folding her hands in front of her, she stares grimly at the drawer I'd just been sorting through. "What would you like to know, Detective?"

"Do you happen to remember where you were in July of last year?"

"I was in Aruba."

"The whole month?"

"From the end of June through the end of July."

"Long vacation."

"It wasn't one," she says crisply. "I'm from Aruba originally. My mother was in the hospital. She needed care for a few weeks until my brother could take over full-time."

"Is she all right?"

"She broke her hip going down some stairs. She'll be walking again soon. I appreciate your asking." She removes her phone from her back pocket and begins swiping her finger over the screen. And then, finding the thing she was searching for, Samara Graves spins the screen around for me to see. "Here's my flight itinerary. I know it doesn't show that I actually took the trip, but I can send you time-stamped pictures of me and my mother in her hospital room to prove I was out of the country, if you'd like."

"That would be great. Email them here, thanks." I hand her my business card and point to my email address listed at the bottom. "Were you close with Mrs. Harris?"

"Detective Shaw," she says, dropping my card into her pocket without glancing at it, "I worked for Joanna Harris for nearly five years, since the day they bought Ravenwood. Joanna is—was—not only one of my favorite employers, but one of my greatest friends. My whole family is back in Aruba, so I appreciated the closeness we shared, probably more than she ever knew. I want to find the person who did this to her as much as you do. You can count on me to help any way I can."

An ally. Great. Or, I correct myself, someone who wants me to *believe* they're willing to be an ally.

I watch as Samara Graves pushes the nightstand drawer closed, and wonder if it's her habit to follow someone and fix what he or she had left in disorder.

"When did she begin sleeping in here?" I ask.

"Last May. Joanna was three months pregnant at the time."

"Had her relationship with Mr. Harris deteriorated that badly?"

"You'd have to ask Mr. Harris about that."

"But you said you were close with Mrs. Harris. Like best friends. Surely she told you something? Women talk about their relationships with their friends."

She didn't blink. "I know she needed space. There were times Mr. Harris could be overbearing."

Now we're getting somewhere. "Any specifics you can recall?"

"It was just a general feeling that she wanted more freedom, which made him hold on to her tighter. A dynamic like that can be a vicious circle."

"And this room," I say, spreading my arms, "was a way to hold on to her memory?"

"I suppose you could say that. I've asked Mr. Harris many times about remodeling or redecorating, and each time he insisted I drop the topic. He wanted to make sure it was kept exactly the way it was when she lived here."

If he's innocent, and had no idea Joanna had been murdered, perhaps he was simply keeping her room for the day she returned. But if he killed her, and had been keeping the room as a shrine to her memory . . .

"Did Joanna have any other close friends we should be talking to? Or any enemies who'd want to hurt her?"

"As far as close friends, no. Joanna didn't have any. I know Rachael Martin from next door would like to think they were best friends, but that wasn't exactly the case. Rachael got on Joanna's nerves." She shakes her head. "And Joanna had no enemies. None."

"At least none that you know of."

The look she shoots me could cut glass. "Joanna was extremely generous with her time and money, witty, beautiful, and usually the most intelligent person in the room. Who could hate someone like that?"

I refrain from pointing out that this witty, beautiful, generous woman was murdered. Obviously there was someone who didn't think as highly of her as her maid.

"Does Rachael Martin have any idea that Joanna wasn't particularly fond of her?" I ask instead.

"Of course not."

"What about Joanna's pregnancy?" I probe deeper. "Was there anything unusual about it? Especially as the summer drew near?"

Samara Graves swipes her hand over the comforter as if smoothing out a wrinkle from where Joanna Harris had sat moments before. "I took Joanna to every prenatal appointment she scheduled. I don't believe a woman should be going to those appointments alone, and Mr. Harris wouldn't accompany her. It was a special time . . . until she lost the baby."

It's what we've suspected, but hearing it spoken so plainly nearly causes me to startle in excitement. "When was that?"

"Mid-May."

"Are you absolutely certain of that timing?"

She looks me square in the eye. "Yes. It was a dreadful time—one I will never forget. I was the only one here to console her through her grief."

"What about Mr. Harris?" Because he certainly seemed surprised to learn that his wife wasn't pregnant when we discovered her. "Did he know about the miscarriage?"

"He didn't at the time." She folds her hands in front of her. "Joanna didn't know how to tell him, and I don't blame her. How do you tell your husband that you've lost his child? That can't be something that slides easily off the lips. But I'm sure he knows now." Her gaze darts over my shoulder. "Are we finished, Detective Shaw? Because now that Mr. Harris has brought a new mistress into the house, I've got double the work to do."

"Nearly finished," I say, because now she's brought up something else. "What are your thoughts on Colleen Roper?"

To my astonishment, a wide smile brightens her face. "I'm very happy with my job, Detective."

"But that's not what I—"

"Good afternoon, Miss Roper." Samara Graves stands ramrod straight, her eyes locked on mine. "How can I help you?"

I follow her line of sight over my shoulder. Colleen Roper steps into the room, treading carefully, her gaze skipping nervously from me to Samara Graves.

"I'm sorry," she says, her voice low. "I don't mean to interrupt. . . . I was just checking to make sure that you'd found the detective up here. Michael said—"

"I've been cleaning this wing for five years," the housekeeper interrupts. "I'm sure I can find my way. Good day, miss. Detective Shaw, I'll email you the required information on my break."

I thank her for her cooperation as she leaves, and before I can take advantage of the chance to speak with Colleen again, Harris charges into the room.

"Colleen?" He's barreling toward us as if the four-poster bed is on fire. "Are you in here?"

He stops when he sees me, then acknowledges my presence with a quick nod. Colleen spins around to meet his stare head-on, and waves of tension heat the room to stifling in seconds.

"I didn't"—he starts, and then quiets—"I didn't mean for you to see this. Not yet."

"Then when?" she whispers, her lower lip quivering.

"Detective Shaw," Harris says, his eyes locked on his lover's, "would you give us a few minutes alone, please? We'll leave after that, I promise. Just . . . one minute."

"I'm sorry," I say, shaking my head. "We really need you to make your way out so we can continue the search. I'm sure you can understand the importance of what we're doing here—"

"Michael?" Colleen cuts in.

Harris exhales noisily. "Of course. Let's go, Colleen."

MICHAEL

The moment we step out of Ravenwood and the salty sea air hits me, I feel more at ease, despite the fact that the reporters are still hovering. I take Colleen's hand to guide her toward the Martins', but she doesn't curl her fingers around mine. It's as if she's turned to stone.

"I should've shown you that earlier." I wish she'd never seen it. "I'm sure you've figured it out by now, but that was Joanna's bedroom. If nothing else, it should show you how strained we were near the end. She moved out of our bedroom in May. I hardly saw her after that."

"You haven't told the police this, have you?"

God bless her for having my back. "Of course not." Glancing up, I scan the second-story windows, certain Detective Shaw is there, spying on us. But there's no sign of his stout figure. "Do you have any idea how bad that would seem? They don't need any more encouragement to think we were fighting. They're only going to make the leap that I killed her. They'll probably think I did it because she was going to leave me and take half of everything."

Someone shouts my name, and, as if the reporters have just now noticed our exit, they swell onto the sidewalk, hitting us with a roar of questions. I push through the crowd, shielding Colleen under my arm, and give a hard yank on the Martins' doorknob. It turns—thank God they left it open for us—and we nearly fall into their foyer. I slam the door, and listen to the grumble of reporters as they draw back to the street. My head is pounding.

"Michael?" Rachael calls from somewhere upstairs. "Is that you?"

"Yeah," I holler. "Give us a minute alone, would you?"

Rachael doesn't respond, but I know she received the message when she doesn't race down the stairs to greet us. I help Colleen to her feet. She's clutching her belly protectively, and her eyes are cloudy with questions. She just won't let it go.

"Why would you keep everything the same?" she whispers. "If I'm being honest, Michael, it's a little creepy."

I shove my hands in my pockets and shrug. My heart turns to stone as I remember installing the tiny mobile over the crib, and watching Joanna fit sheets to the mattress where our baby would've slept.

"I wanted to change it, so many times," I say. "But each time, Samara would talk me out of it. She'd talk about the possibility of Joanna coming back, about building our family. She was so determined to keep the rooms that way. Any time I pushed back, I'd feel guilty about gutting the place."

"I thought—" She is so pale that I worry about her. "Do you want our baby to sleep in there?"

"God, Colleen, no. That wasn't my plan at all." I pull her against me, and feel the softness of her body yielding to mine. "Unless that's what *you* want."

She tilts her head to look up at me, and I can't read her expression. It's a bizarre mixture of confusion and—I'm not sure, but it seems to be—*knowledge*. She's quiet for so long, I'm not sure she's going to respond at all. When she does, I'm relieved; her voice is confident.

"I want to put the past behind us," she says, defiantly. "I want to move on with you and our baby. But if you're still holding on to something you can't get back, how can we possibly be happy with our future? Do you understand?"

"I do." That damn detective had to come in here and rattle our cages, didn't he? Bastard. I could've gotten rid of those rooms in my own time, without upsetting Colleen. "But you have to understand: even a past that's dead and buried can rise up. I wish it were easier to put it all to bed, darling. You know I do."

As Rachael clatters down the stairs, announcing her entrance with some obnoxious pleasantry, Colleen pulls out of my arms to greet her. And I'm left standing alone, my back to the door.

What the hell was I thinking, saying those things to her? Why can't I be like every other guy and promise her the moon and stars with no exceptions? I know what she wants: for me to say I'm completely over Joanna. It'd be easy to say, to give her all the reassurance she needs—but I can't lie.

RACHAEL

It's strange having another couple around. They throw off our routine.

I'm usually curled up on the couch at night watching my favorite shows. Reality television mostly. Housewives from any county. Athletic wives. Celebrity wives. Wives and mistresses. Court television. Dating shows with more roses than morals. Baking cook-offs. Surviving in the wild, nude or otherwise. Doesn't matter what it's about. Show me real people with real problems, however sensational. Let me peek behind the curtain into their homes and their messy lives, and I'm hooked.

It makes me feel better to know I'm not the only one with issues, not the only one barely keeping things afloat.

It's exhausting trying to keep up the façade sometimes.

Travis doesn't watch much television—he despises "reality TV garbage"—so when I'm on the couch Netflix and chilling by myself, he's upstairs in one of the spare bedrooms playing his guitar or writing music.

It gets lonely sometimes, but it's how we make it work. I get what I need, and so does he.

But tonight, we had to entertain Michael and Colleen. All

smiles and stupid games and expensive bottles of the finest liquor. Anything to keep things upbeat and happy and, most important, surface-level.

Because we can't afford for Michael and Colleen to look any deeper.

Especially not now.

As I prop my leg up on the stool in the bathroom and slather vanilla and coconut lotion over it, the bedroom door clicks shut. It's nearly midnight. I've been up here for an hour, showering and getting ready for bed. Travis has been making sure our guests are settled in the guest room.

When I glance up, he's standing in the doorway, staring at the lights above the mirror. One is flickering.

"Michael doesn't look good," he says. "It's like he's falling apart."

"Wouldn't you be if the police pulled me out of the mud across the street?"

"Absolutely." But he doesn't sound like it would trouble him much. "Don't get me wrong, I'm sure he's really torn up about Joanna. But I think the stress of the investigation is taking a major toll. He doesn't like being questioned."

I don't mention that Travis doesn't like being questioned either. They're alike in that way. Instead, I rub lotion on my arms as the sweet scent fills the bathroom.

I glance up at Travis. I'm standing in front of him spreading lotion all over my naked body, exposing the most intimate parts of me, and he *still* won't drag his attention away from that bulb. He's so fixated on the one problem, he doesn't notice anything else. Not even me.

The guy's a perfectionist. One of the reasons I love him. And hate him.

"I'll be right back," he says.

He disappears for a few minutes and returns with not one bulb, but an entire box. Kneeling on the counter, he goes to work unscrewing each one and replacing it. I don't need to ask why. I have before, and the answer is always the same. If one is about to go out, the others are too. This way, they'll all be new. They'll all be perfect. And then he'll be able to sleep at night without brooding about one ultra-bright bulb among the dimming ones.

"Colleen is nice," he says, as he reaches for another bulb.

My gaze snaps to his. "You think so?"

"Yeah." He drops the dead one in the box. "Kind of a goody two-shoes though."

I massage the lotion into my skin a little harder. "They don't seem like a good match to me."

"What makes you say that?"

"I don't know," I say. I can't really put it into words. But I get the feeling she's easily manipulated by men. "She's naïve, I guess."

"Well, yeah. She's green. Much younger than Michael."

"Exactly."

"Exactly what?" He pulls out a new bulb and spins it into place. "Why does that make them a poor match? You're younger than I am."

I hesitate, shooting him a sideways glance as I move on to lathering my breasts. "By a year. Come on. There's an entire generation between those two. What do you think he sees in her?"

Travis laughs. "What every guy sees in a younger woman. A tight piece of ass."

Now Colleen is nice *and* a tight piece.

I ignore the clench in my gut. "What do you think that detective wants to talk to us about tomorrow?"

"I'm sure they're going to want to know more about Michael."

I follow Travis out of the room as we begin our routine. He undresses down to his boxers as I change into a silk chemise. Before sliding into bed, he arranges the pillows behind his back, puts on his reading glasses, and drags a book into his lap. He doesn't say a word as I settle in beside him.

"And Michael doesn't want to hear it," he says, "but he's a major suspect. I assume they're going to ask about what kind of boss he is, what it's like living next to him, how he and Joanna treated each other. Things like that."

I turn on my side to face him and pull the covers over my shoulder. The sheets are icy, sending waves of gooseflesh scattering across my skin. Travis doesn't like to talk after he gets into bed, but after the excitement of the past hours—the headlines about Joanna, the reporters and cops everywhere— I'm not going to be able to sleep. It doesn't help when I remember that Michael and Colleen are in the room down the hall. It feels like Joanna's murder is everywhere I turn.

"What do you think they want to know from me?" I ask, tracing my fingers around the intricate tattoos swirling around his forearm.

Sighing, he turns a page. "You were her friend for a long time."

"I know, but not near the end."

He doesn't reply. Did he even hear what I said?

"That big blowup was the last time I saw her," I go on. "Do you think they're going to ask me about that?"

He's so immersed in his book, he doesn't answer. I worry my lip between my teeth as the memories come flooding back. I'd confronted Joanna that day. I'd said things I shouldn't have said, especially under the circumstances. Am I going to have to tell the detectives everything? God, how will that make me look? Like a murderer, that's how. Everyone will think *I* murdered Joanna.

"Travis," I whisper. "When was the last time you saw Joanna?"

He drops the book to his lap with a huff. "Do you need attention? Is that what this is about?"

"No, I just wanted to know . . ."

I can't finish.

Tossing the book and his glasses onto the bedside table, he climbs on top of me, pressing his body over mine. Tattoos of women and dragons flex over his arms with each movement.

"You don't think I had anything to do with what happened to Joanna, do you?" he asks, hovering over me.

"Of course not." I shake my head.

"Trust is important in a relationship." He nuzzles my neck, then bites my earlobe playfully. "Especially now, when we're faced with something like this."

With the ghosts of the past still haunting us, how can he possibly think I'd trust him now?

"You're the only good, decent thing in my life, Rachael." He takes my hands and pins them over my head before lowering his mouth over mine. "That's why, no matter what happens, we're in this together. To the very end."

WEDNESDAY

Four Days Until Colleen's Murder

DETECTIVE SHAW

"It's your lucky day," Patel says.

"Great." I look up from my computer and rub my eyes. "Remind me which day it is? I can't remember. They're all blending together."

That's what happens when I've been up for two days straight, researching and putting together pieces of the case. Split screens might as well be seared into my retinas. I can almost recite the information without staring at it. Michael Harris's depleted bank accounts. Sketchy investments. Hefty insurance policy. Still, I'll gladly take blurred vision and sleepless nights over ones spent tossing and turning, dreaming of Karen and times I can never have back again.

"It's Wednesday," Patel answers, slouching into the chair on the opposite side of my desk. "Best day this week."

"Why? Did you get the autopsy date moved up?"

"Nope, it's still scheduled for Sunday. Coroner is swamped. Can't get her in before then. But this is better." He drops a stack of papers on my desk and grabs my Rubik's Cube. "I got the go-ahead from the lieutenant to arrest Michael Harris for the murder of his wife. The commissioner wants this thing wrapped up quickly."

"But how? We don't have the autopsy, the toxicology results, or the murder weapon, for Christ's sake. What are you bringing him in on?"

"Everything else, Shaw." He grins wildly. "Rather than focusing on each square, try looking at the whole cube."

But even *that* analogy is off in this case. Something isn't right. I feel it deep in my bones. This isn't like me, to look beyond what I can prove. I wish Karen were here. She would tell me to follow my gut, even if it defies logic and the solution seems far-fetched. She was the best sounding board. My go-to for advice.

Would she peg Michael Harris as a murderous husband?

He's violent; we already know that for certain. The incident report from the July fifteenth 911 call states that Joanna had discoloration on her collarbone and over her right eye, consistent with early signs of bruising. The caller, Rachael Martin, stated that her neighbor, Joanna Harris, had run over to her house screaming, claiming her husband had beaten her. And the photos in the file testify to that.

"But the garden tools in his garage came up negative on the DNA tests," I say, determined to fight him on this. "We need a murder weapon."

"We really don't," he says smugly, crossing his legs so one ankle rests over the opposite knee, "because we have those pills hidden in the back of their bathroom cabinet."

"But we don't know if the pills had anything to do with her murder."

"*Yet,*" he says. "We'll get confirmation on what was flowing through her bloodstream when toxicology comes in. I'm betting he fed her enough pills to kill her."

"That doesn't make any sense. Think about it, Patel. If Michael Harris was going to drug his wife and make her death seem like an overdose, why hit her in the back of the head with a blunt object?"

"Maybe something went wrong," he argues, "and he had to really get his hands dirty. Maybe she discovered he'd drugged her and she confronted him about it—who knows? But the bottom line is that her body was buried across the street from their home. Police were called out for domestic violence just days before her murder. His business is going under, and the insurance windfall is about the only thing that could save it."

"Still not enough."

"Didn't your wife tell you to follow your gut, Shaw? Well, I'm taking her advice. Those pills had something to do with Joanna's murder. I *feel* it."

"My wife used to say that, yes." My stomach clenches from his low-blow shot. "But to close this case, we need evidence, not instincts."

"Shaw, you know the guy is shady."

"Oh, absolutely." I glance back at the screen, at his bank statements. "But a cold-blooded murderer? I'm not sure."

"With a half-competent D.A., the jury will convict him."

"Maybe. But if I'm a juror, I see reasonable doubt everywhere. The biggest problem being that those medications were prescribed to someone else. That'll be enough for an acquittal."

"As soon as we talk to Mandy McKnight, we'll get that straightened out," he says. "It's obvious Michael Harris is our guy."

I play devil's advocate. "Likely, but not obvious. We have other suspects. What about the neighbors? The guy next door reports to Harris. What happens to his job if Harris's business goes under? Perhaps there's more going on with them than we know. Crooked business deals? Jealousy?"

"You want me to let Michael Harris roam free because the neighbor *might've* been a crook and *might've* killed her?"

Patel shakes his head. "Sorry, that's not enough, Shaw. We haven't found a scrap of evidence pointing to them."

"What about that cook? Dean Lewis? He seemed to be pretty tight with Joanna. Maybe they had something going on."

"You think the chef cooked this one up?" He laughs at his own joke. "One problem with your theory: if he kills her, he can't be with her. No one wins in that case. Besides, there's nothing concrete linking them. Next?"

"Colleen Roper," I say.

I'd looked into her immediately after we brought her and Michael in for questioning. But she's clean. Her parents died in a car accident when she was fifteen, leaving her in the foster system for a few years. Graduated from San Francisco State University with a degree in Liberal Studies and worked at Saint Francis Memorial Hospital as a receptionist two years back. She's rented the same apartment for the last year—a tiny place in a questionable neighborhood. She has no criminal record, not even so much as a traffic ticket, and no fingerprints in our system. She's never been married and doesn't have any children other than the one she's currently carrying.

"Come on, Shaw, you can do better than that." Patel smirks. "She didn't even *know* the Harrises until after Joanna was murdered."

What would Karen think? Where would she look next?

"What about the wild card, Mandy McKnight?" I get up and take my Rubik's Cube away from him. "Her pills, her murder."

Patel shakes his head. "We gotta find McKnight, if you're going to make that link."

I sigh. Without a murder weapon, reasonable doubt is shooting holes in the investigation. There are too many ways a defense attorney could spin this to put doubt in jurors' heads. And with the powerful friends Harris has, the lawyers are going to be heavy hitters.

If we bring this to court, our case will be demolished before we've even had a chance to build it.

"It's him, Shaw," Patel insists. "Michael Harris killed his wife. You and I both know it."

I won't agree with him, at least not aloud. "If you bring him in now, and we can't charge him on the evidence within forty-eight hours, he walks. He'll lawyer up so heavy and so hard, we'll never get him talking to us again."

Patel blows out a thin stream of air between his lips. "We can't wait too much longer. He could run."

"He's not running with a pregnant girlfriend."

"If we wait too much longer," Patel says, taking back my Rubik's Cube, "that pregnant girlfriend of his might end up just like his wife."

"Autopsy is Sunday," I say, running through the timeline in my head, "and we can get a fast turnaround on toxicology. Let's wait until Friday. That's only two days from now. He can sit in custody for forty-eight hours, and by that time, we'll have concrete results."

As he's considering my proposal, his phone bleeps with an incoming text.

"It's Mandy McKnight," he tells me. "About damn time."

After a quick call to arrange a meeting, we hop in the car and head toward Half Moon Bay. There's been a break in the bad weather, and it feels like everyone's trying to take advantage of the sunshine between storms. Traffic jams the coastal highway. Surfers flock to the state beach to catch big waves. The sidewalks are filled with people window-shopping and dining on patios. Half Moon Bay has come alive.

Studio Balance Pilates is in a fading shopping center off the main highway, tucked between a car rental place and a hair salon.

"Ever been to one of these places?" Patel asks as we step out of the car.

"Do I look like the bendy type to you?"

He laughs at that and holds the door open for me to pass through. The place is filled wall-to-wall with exercise mats, ropes, and machines that look more like torture devices than workout equipment. A group of women on the far side of the building arrange the mats, while a petite redhead turns and smiles. She's wearing black stretch pants, a tight tank top, and can't weigh more than a hundred and ten pounds. Green eyes. Freckles on her nose. Slightly sunburnt cheeks. She's very pretty, in a fresh-faced, athletic way.

"I'm Mandy," she tells us, extending her hand. "Which one of you did I speak with over the phone?"

"That would be me." Patel shakes her hand as we show our identification. "Thank you for agreeing to meet with us. This won't take long."

"That's good. I have a class starting in ten minutes."

"As I told you," he goes on, "we have some questions about Joanna Harris."

Her eyes fill with tears. "I can't believe someone would do that to her. It's devastating."

"So you and Joanna were close?" I ask.

"She took classes here Monday, Wednesday, and Friday for the last three years. I guess you could say we were acquaintances more than friends."

"And do you know Mr. Harris, too?" Patel's attracted to her, I can tell.

She shrugs. "I've never met him, but sometimes Joanna would mention him in class."

"What would she say?" I ask, careful to tread lightly.

"Just casual stuff. One morning she'd talk about how he'd taken her out to Gary Danko's—you know, the fine dining restaurant in the city? Another morning she'd say he bought her bouquets of her favorite flower. Once, I remember, she

called him a workaholic, but said he supported her in anything she wanted to do." She smiles. "Their marriage seemed
great."

At least that's what she wanted you to think.

"Have you ever been to their home?" I ask.

"She invited me over last Christmas for a party or something, but I didn't go. Went to L.A. for a concert instead. She
lives—lived—in Point Reina, right?"

Patel nods, giving too much away for my taste.

"I've been there, hiking through the grove, and to the tide
pools, but never to her house. It's a gorgeous neighborhood.
Maybe someday I'll be able to afford it."

As Patel and I avoid making eye contact, I'm sure we're
debating the same thing. Should we show our hand and ask
outright about the pills? Or continue, hoping she'll offer up
something that explains them?

"Do you take any medications?" I ask finally, when the
silence becomes awkward.

"Well, that's a personal question." She frowns. "I can't see
what that has to do with poor Joanna. Why would you want
to know?"

We aren't getting anywhere by playing coy. Without nudg-
ing Patel for approval, I take over. "Our investigation needs to
be very thorough," I say. "We're looking for anything that'll
help solve this case and bring Joanna's murderer to justice.
While we were searching the Harrises' home, we discovered
two prescription bottles in the back of a bathroom cabinet.
They were from Dr. Garcia's office."

I pause, waiting for her to signal some kind of recognition,
but she doesn't. She stares politely, waiting for me to go on.

"Have you ever seen a Dr. Garcia?" I ask.

"No."

"Cameron Garcia—have you ever met anyone by that
name?"

"No, doesn't sound familiar. I don't think I've ever met her."

There's our answer: Mandy doesn't even know Dr. Garcia is a man. Or is she playing us?

Two women enter the studio and stare curiously. Class must be close to starting. We don't have long.

I pull out my cellphone and open the photo app. "Do you have any explanation why these two medications would be prescribed to you?"

Confusion flares in her eyes as I show her the image I'd snapped of the bottles. "I—I don't know how to explain that. I don't even use that pharmacy. I get my medications from the CVS on Cabrillo Highway. Maybe it's another Mandy McKnight?"

Not likely. We searched. The woman in front of us is the only one with ties to Joanna Harris. Her shock appears genuine.

"Ms. McKnight—"

"Mandy, please," she interjects.

"Mandy, we believe Joanna was killed sometime in the middle of July. I realize it was a while ago, but if you think back, do you recall anything happening out of the ordinary around that time? Anything that might have struck you as odd?"

"Like what?"

"Did she seem lethargic during workout sessions? Stressed? Venting about her husband or other problems at work, perhaps? She was pregnant while attending classes here, so I assume some of the moves were difficult for her—did that bother her at some point?" I'm reaching, and I know it.

"When Joanna first told me she was pregnant, I told her to take it easy, listen to her body and her doctor's recommendations. As far as I know, she wasn't bothered by anything we did. I'm sorry," she says, shaking her head again. "I wish I could help. . . ."

"What about Rachael Martin?" Patel breaks in. "Did she take the same classes?"

Mandy opens her mouth to speak, then clamps it shut, her attention flipping between us. "I'd completely forgotten about it until now. Rachael and Joanna really got into it one day, right out front. I couldn't help but overhear—oh my God, how could I have forgotten?"

"Forgotten what?"

"Joanna was sleeping with Rachael's husband. They had quite the blowout."

Here we go. "Mandy, tell us what you remember."

JULY SIXTEENTH OF LAST YEAR

RACHAEL

"Knock, knock." My friend Lora pushes the front door open and strides inside. She's wearing black yoga pants and a caramel-colored tank the same shade as her hair. Today, that's pulled back into a sloppy bun, yet she's still somehow rocking it. "You ready?"

"Give me five minutes."

"I already gave you ten." She shields her eyes from the glare reflecting off the living room window. "I told you morning-after workouts were a bad idea."

After Joanna stood me up at the distillery last night, I'd called up Lora and taken an Uber to the city to meet her. I wasn't about to throw away a girls' night simply because Joanna was sick. No way. Girls' night was my night. Time away from Travis. By now, he's fully aware of the way it works. Whether I'm with Joanna, drinking and painting into the night, or partying with Lora in the city, I never make it home before three. Hell, I don't even mind going out alone. I've watched movies Travis would hate. Spent hours in a quiet corner of a late-night coffee shop reading a book I can't pull my nose out of. Or, other nights, I've occupied the end of a bar and waited for a handsome stranger to catch my eye. I've gone home with men who made me feel wanted and beautiful and perfect. Men who simply filled a void that a fight with Travis had caused. Truth is, I don't care what I'm doing. As long as I feel like myself again at the end of the night, it's a success.

Last night, Lora and I hit a comedy club and two Irish pubs and shut down a third. It was a blast, and closing time came fast.

I had no idea the real excitement was waiting for me at home.

"Damn, that's hot." I nearly scald my tongue on my coffee. "I'll drive."

Giving the cup a quick wash, I swipe it dry with the towel hanging on the oven door, then set it back in the cupboard. Can't leave anything in the sink. Drives Travis nuts.

"I'm almost done," I say, rushing toward the bedroom. "Promise."

Because Travis wanted a quickie before work, my morning has been a scramble I'm still recovering from. I missed the morning news and only had one cup of coffee instead of my usual two. It doesn't help that Travis and I had to do major damage control with Joanna last night, so I barely got any sleep.

I wouldn't normally have a problem being late for Pilates, or skipping at all, especially since today is a special two-hour Saturday session. But I've been raving about Studio Balance and Mandy's skills for so long, Lora finally agreed to come with me.

Snatching my Nikes from their cubby in the closet, I shove one on my foot and hop into it, then switch to the other. I'm annoyed that I couldn't find my favorite tank—the cute black one with cutouts on each side and straps in back. I had to settle for my pink one, but it doesn't go as well with these pants. After tying my hair back, I turn my attention to our bed. Sometime this morning, Travis and I must've kicked the duvet and top sheet to the floor and yanked the fitted sheet from each of the corners. I can't leave it like that. I get to work making the bed, tucking the fitted sheet around the bottom of the mattress.

"Oh, for the love of God." Groaning, Lora peers into the room. "Do you really have to do this now?"

"It'll only take a second."

She sighs. "Must've had a rough night."

"Actually, it was. I still can't believe what happened with Michael and Joanna. That was insane."

Lora nods as I run through all the details again.

"The worst part of it is that she lied to me, all this time," I say, smoothing the sheet at the foot of the bed. "I get lying to Michael about her affair, but I was supposed to be her best *friend*. Last night, she said she was feeling sick and dizzy, so she called off our plans. No biggie, you know? I don't want to catch something nasty if she's passing it around. But I guess she was never sick at all. Lying comes second nature to her now."

"This is like something out of a bad reality show," Lora agrees. "She's insane to cheat on Michael and throw all that away. I mean, look at her *house*."

"Right?" I go on. "I can't believe she ditched me to go out with a guy. Never pegged Joanna for a cheater, but you never can tell these days, can you?"

"Who called the cops?" Lora asks. "Did she?"

"Well, I'd just gotten home after leaving you, so I was in the shower when she ran over. She was crying and banging on our door. Travis had called by the time I came downstairs. You should have seen him jump into action, Lora. He was so chivalrous, taking care of Joanna until the police came, making sure she was comfortable. She couldn't stop crying."

"Are you sure Michael *actually* beat her?" Lora frowns. "Or is she lying again?"

"She had marks on her throat and swelling over one eye. Who knows, though? She could've done those things to herself. Hard to filter the truth from lies these days. The people on the shows I watch go through the same thing."

"Did she press charges?"

"No, and she went back to him right after the police left. We offered for her to stay with us, but she wouldn't listen."

Lora takes a slow, dramatic blink. "Well, there's your answer."

"You should've seen her, Lora. She was a mess. And who wouldn't be, after a fight like that?" I prop the pillows against the headboard. "I didn't get a chance to really talk to her, to ask about who she's sleeping with, but you better believe I'll find out sooner or later."

"Do you think she'll show for Pilates this morning?"

"I don't know," I say, making a firm crease on the edges, just the way Travis likes it. "Last night she said she was, but plans might've changed. Travis was really worried about her. He's already called from work, wanted to know if I'd talked to her yet, if I knew how she was holding up. He loves a damsel in distress."

"Well, I guess we know one thing for sure." Lora's poking around the perfume bottles and makeup on my vanity. "You're the luckiest woman on the block. If you figure out a way to clone your husband, let me know. I'd like to order four copies."

Laughing, I shove the sheet between the mattress and the headboard, and my fingers catch something hard.

A ring.

"Whoa," Lora says with a gasp as I hold it up to the light. "Only thing I find when I make my bed is a dryer sheet."

It's not just any ring. It's a platinum Tacori. The princess-cut three-stone beauty is at least six carats, with a crown of diamonds intensifying the center diamond.

"I've never seen *that* one before." Lora sets a perfume bottle down and comes closer. "That's gorgeous. Why haven't you been wearing it?"

"It's not—" Heart drumming, I twist the ring in my fingers so the diamonds catch the morning rays. "It's not mine."

"Then whose?"

I know instantly, without doubt. It's one of a kind. This flawless bauble has been flaunted in my face, waved around at cocktail parties, its outrageous price tag bragged about more times than I could count.

"Joanna's."

"Figures she'd have a ring like that, but what's it doing in your—" Lora stops. Covers her mouth with her hand. "Oh no . . . Rach, you don't think . . ."

I can't speak. Not a word. Her ring is in my *house*. In my *bed*.

If it was in our living room, anywhere downstairs, I could explain it away. I'd concoct excuses in my head about how she must've lost it when they came over for dinner last Friday. But last night in particular, when I came home around two A.M., I swore I picked up the scent of Joanna's perfume in our room. *Joy*. It's an unmistakable scent, and one she's worn since I've known her. When I mentioned it, Travis had brushed me off, telling me how ridiculous I was being. *He'd never break our rules and cheat on me with a friend.* I'd believed him. Not an hour later, Joanna raced over, claiming Michael had beaten her.

My skin crawls with a memory of the company anniversary party in February. Travis and Joanna disappeared for the better part of an hour. He'd said they were out smoking, and even though they'd returned to the party, cheeks flushed, unable to take their eyes off each other, I'd believed him then, too. He'd said it was biting cold outside—that was the reason her cheeks were pink. His hair looked as though he'd tried to style it in a rush with his fingers.

That was nothing but an inkling, hunch, possible female intuition rationalized down to stupid jealous thoughts.

But this—*this*—is concrete proof in the form of diamonds and platinum.

"I'm sure—they couldn't," Lora whispers. "Travis wouldn't . . . He loves you. You guys are the perfect couple."

I'm gripping the ring, scraping my nails along its grooves as anger flares up inside me. He can't explain this away—I'd like to see him try. Lora's eyes are full of pity. When her hand touches my back, I flinch.

"Rachael," she says, "I'm so sorry. I can't believe they would do this to you."

The pity in her voice makes me want to vomit.

I refuse to be this woman—the one my friends whisper about when they get together for brunch. The one they feel sorry for. Poor Rachael couldn't keep her husband happy. Poor Rachael, did you hear he slept with her best friend while she was partying in the city? Poor stupid, ugly Rachael who can't do anything right. I hear the voice I've had ringing in my head since childhood telling me I'm not good enough. No matter what I do, no matter how hard I try, I'll *never* be good enough . . . and now everyone's going to know it.

"Lora." My voice is shaking with rage. "What time is it?"

"A few minutes before nine. Why?"

"We need to get going. Don't want to be late for Pilates."

On the way outside, I slide Joanna's ring onto my finger, up against my own wedding band. Her fingers are impossibly slender; the ring barely slides over my knuckle. It's heavy, its cut brilliant. Michael must've spent a fortune on it.

"Are you sure you feel up to working out?" Lora asks.

"Joanna will be there. She never misses."

"You really think she'll show? Even after what happened last night?"

I don't answer.

An eerie calm settles over me as I drive to Half Moon Bay, Lora blabbering in the seat beside me. She rambles the whole way there without leaving much room for me to respond. Her tone is pacifying and sympathetic. She's trying to calm me down by offering explanations of how Joanna's ring could've ended up in my bed. It's not helping because deep down in my gut, I know there's only one explanation.

Joanna canceled our plans last night so she could sleep with my husband, in my bed.

Bitch.

Travis knew I wouldn't come home early to catch them. I always manage to go out and have my fun one way or another. And he used that to his advantage, to have his own fun. With my closest friend.

He's gone too far.

He'll feel my wrath later, but for now, my hands are trembling as I turn onto Cabrillo Highway and pull into the parking lot. Joanna's brand-new Lexus convertible is there, spit-shiny clean and parked up front, in her usual space. Leaving my engine running, I jump out, slam the door, and hear another door close behind me as I charge into the studio. My cheeks are on fire, my skin burning, prickling.

Mandy's at the front, chatting with the half-dozen women who've gathered for her class. I recognize two of them, but where's the home-wrecker?

There.

Standing on the far side of the studio, Joanna's wearing white leggings and a purple sports bra. Even five months pregnant, she's lean and barely showing. As usual, she's put on a faceful of makeup to work out, with cherry-red lips and a hint of shadow over her eyes. Her dark hair is pulled back into a sleek ponytail with not a single flyaway.

I want to clutch that silky rein of hair in my fist and yank it right out of her skull. I want to gouge my fingers into the soft flesh of her eyeballs, and dig them in so deeply that she cries tears of blood. I want—God, I want the perfect contours of her cheekbones busted and cracked, her lips split open. I want her so mangled, bloodied, and bruised, no man will ever look at her with lustful thoughts again.

"Joanna," I call, out of breath, as I struggle for air. "Can I talk to you outside for a second?"

She peeks around the women who've begun to stretch. When she sees me, she smiles. "Rachael? Sure thing."

I step outside and wait for her to exit behind me.

"Do you want me to go?" Lora sounds worried. "I can wait in the car. . . ."

"I don't care what you do," I snap, and then spin around as the studio door opens behind me. "As long as you don't say a word."

"Hey," Joanna says, a smile spreading across her gorgeous face. Not a single bruise mars her throat or her cheek. Those marks couldn't have healed overnight. How much makeup did it take to cover them? "What's up?"

I've never had such a burning hatred for anyone in my whole life, and I swear, if she weren't carrying a child, I'd drag her down to the concrete and bash her head on the parking block.

"I just wanted to ask you something," I say, spinning her ring around my finger. "How long have you been sleeping with my husband?"

Her smile falters. It's only then I notice a slight discoloring on her throat, where Michael must have tried to strangle her. The bitch deserved it.

"How. Long."

"Rachael . . ." Her gaze flips to Lora, and back again. "Don't be absurd. You're going to cause a scene for no reason.

Come on, let's get back inside before they start to think we're fighting."

She didn't answer my question. She's patronizing and a smart-ass, and I'm not going to let her get away with it.

"Were you together at the company party?" I ask. "In February—were you sleeping with him even then?"

"Rachael—"

"What about last night? After you canceled on me because you were 'sick as a dog'? How many nights, when I had to work late, did you run over to my house to sleep with my husband?"

"Rachael, have you talked to Travis about this?" she asks, planting her hands on her hips. "Maybe you should call him."

"I'm not talking to Travis. I'm talking to *you*. And I want to know how long it's been going on."

Sighing, she leans closer and murmurs, "I don't think you want to do this here. Go home. We'll talk later."

I hold up my hand so that her beautiful, glimmering wedding ring stares her in the face. "Missing something?"

She exhales slowly. "I had a feeling I left it at your place."

She reaches for it, but I pull my hand back. The fact that she hadn't been concerned about losing something so valuable—not only in cost, but in the meaning of her marriage—is astounding. She couldn't love Michael. Not really. Not if she was so careless with her wedding ring. Joanna's features seem to morph right in front of me. Gone is the friend with the kind eyes, the woman we saved from a violent husband last night. Her features harden, and the swelling above her eye becomes more pronounced. But Joanna is no victim. I don't know why it took me until now to see it. I was deceived like the rest of them. Tricked into believing someone so beautiful could never be so evil.

"So you're not even going to deny it." I'm fighting back tears.

"Just give it back, Rachael," she spits out. "I'm not playing games."

"Aren't you?"

Joanna glares, thrusting out her hand. "I won't ask you for it again."

I shake my head, dizzy. "How long have you been sleeping with my husband?"

"Why are you doing this? Seriously, Rachael, I don't know why you're so upset. He told me about the way your relationship works. What's the problem?"

"*You,* Joanna. The problem is you. We were never supposed to sleep with people we knew. It was never supposed to be personal. You were my *friend.*"

"Were?" Her thinly plucked eyebrows rise. "You're going to throw away our friendship over meaningless *sex*?"

"It's only meaningless sex to you. But it means something to me. To my marriage." Her ring burns on my finger, and I ache to get it off.

She folds her arms over her chest as if she's a child ready to throw a temper tantrum. "Don't worry, we haven't been sleeping together long enough for it to be Travis's baby. That's what you really want to know, isn't it?"

"You're sick!"

"Oh, for Christ's sake! Don't blow this up into something it isn't." She raises her hands and studies her manicured nails.

All the nights I'd come home and smell an unfamiliar perfume, the dinner parties when their gazes would linger just a heartbeat too long . . . all this time. I'd been right, and he'd dismissed my doubts. Made me feel as if I were delusional and stupid with jealousy.

This is not what I agreed to.

"You should try having a little perspective," Joanna adds. "Might make you feel better. Travis and I have had fun. A few trysts, that's all. As my friend, I thought you might understand what it's been like for me, going through all of this."

"All of what, exactly?"

"The pregnancy and everything that's happened after. Michael's gone all the time because he thinks he has to work double time to make enough money for us, and meanwhile I'm stuck in that big house by myself, with nothing to occupy my time. I'm lonely, Rachael, and I've been depressed thinking about how much this baby is going to change my life." Her expression turns tender as she shakes her head. "Travis has made me remember who I am. He's made me feel sexy and smart, something I haven't felt in years."

Behind me, Lora makes a mocking sound as if she can't believe a word of what she's just heard. Until this moment, I had forgotten we had an audience.

"Do you love him?" I can feel my heart race as I wait for the answer I don't want to hear.

Joanna's grin flashes. "Of course not. Don't be absurd."

"Good," I snap. "Then you shouldn't have a problem leaving us the hell alone."

At that, she tips her head back and laughs. "You say that as if I'm the one pursuing him. Have you thought about the possibility that it's the other way around?"

"Stay away from him." I yank the ring off my finger, ball it into my fist, and chuck it across the parking lot as she squeals. "I'm not kidding, Joanna. It's over."

"It's over when Travis says it's over. Come on, Rachael, what are you going to do?" she jeers. "Spread rumors through our little town? Tell Michael? Good. Tell everyone. Maybe then we can all stop pretending that our marriages are happy ones."

"If you try anything with Travis again," I cry out, jabbing my finger into her belly, pushing her back, "I swear to God I'll kill you."

DETECTIVE SHAW

Patel seems shocked to learn of Travis and Joanna's affair, but at this point, nothing would surprise me. I always knew there was something rotten lurking beneath this case. As soon as we get back to the station, I'm running through everyone's details forwards and backwards.

If Travis has blood on his hands, I'll find out.

On the drive to Dr. Garcia's office in the city, I shift sides of the cube in new directions. *Left. Right for two. Back side once. Left again, the other direction this time.* Noting what happens, I change my approach. Adapt to the new formation. I'm thinking of Karen more and more these days, and I'm wondering what it is about Joanna Harris's case that's dredging up these feelings again. I'd rather liked my state of numbness, where I didn't have to feel anything too sharply.

"Hope you solve this case faster than that cube." I was toying with the cube even as Patel and I headed into Garcia's office. "You don't look any closer to figuring it out than you were yesterday."

"Looks can be deceiving, Patel."

That's why we're here, after all. On the surface, it doesn't appear Joanna or Michael Harris are connected to Dr. Garcia's office or to the drugs found prescribed to Mandy McKnight. Yet here we are in the waiting room of the San Francisco Women's Health Clinic, because of those mismatched prescriptions hidden in their bathroom cabinet.

Chasing the unknown is one of the reasons I love this job so much. The lack of sleep during the chase? Not so much, but I've gotten used to it. A solid night's sleep has eluded me since Joanna Harris's body was dug out of the grove. I've spent countless hours going over Michael and Colleen's initial interview recordings, studying the wobble in their voices when they get uncomfortable. I'm so absorbed in sifting truth from the lies that I hear their voices in my brain.

Closing my eyes and ignoring the drone of Michael Bolton over the waiting room speakers, I tip my head back until it rests against the wall and let my thoughts run through the Harrises' home. In my mind's eye, I drift past the massive dining room table, through the sun-flooded kitchen and living room. I skate around the couches and up the stairs, taking in details. Absorbing things I might've missed before. Turning right at the stairs, I head into the rooms we've now unlocked. The theater-like screening room with its rows of leather reclining seats. The billiards room with a table set up for a game. Balls racked in the center. Cue ball at the end. Sticks lined up on the wall. I let my mind float into the gym, over the elliptical machine, rowing machine, and yoga mats.

And then I drift through the walls straight into the nursery. It's too quiet in there. Too sterile. Absent a child's cry, a tub of diapers. Will that baby Colleen is carrying sleep there someday?

Patel's phone pings with an incoming text, derailing my thoughts. He swipes his finger over the screen. "Got the search warrant for the Harrises' phones," he tells me. "The office is sending over the call logs now."

"About time," I say. I can't wait to dig in. "Tell them to send over the text messages, too. And I want more than time stamps." I need to know what these people were saying to each other. "We'll dissect them tonight."

As the receptionist calls for another woman to make her way into the back, I glance up, attempting to remind her we're still waiting. But her eyes are downcast, her attention fixed on her computer screen. Three women sit separately, hands clasped in their laps as they ignore the muted television on the wall in the corner. One woman, a pregnant brunette, weeps quietly. Another, an attractive thirty-something blonde in a business suit, crosses her legs and taps her high-heeled foot in the air as if she's got somewhere to be. The third woman, with deeply sunken, tired eyes, stares into space as if there's something there, just out of our line of sight.

"Hear back from the maid yet?" Patel asks, pocketing his phone.

I nod. "She's got an alibi. Took a family trip to Aruba from June until late July. She wasn't anywhere near Point Reina. Checks out."

"We haven't had any more luck with the doctors," Patel says. "Dr. Smith—the guy who prescribed Michael Harris something for his insomnia—won't give any details that'll violate the HIPAA laws. Dr. Souza—the ob-gyn Colleen is seeing—won't give anything either. Dr. Garcia's going to throw up the same roadblocks."

"I know." I twist the blocks on the right side of the cube around and move to the ones in back, giving them a hard spin. "Like you always say, we'll have to think outside the box."

After each woman in the waiting area is called back to see the doctor, we're finally escorted down one blindingly white hallway that leads to another, and then up a narrow set of stairs. The office smells of disinfectant and coffee. A desk, two chairs, and a short bookshelf cram the small space. The clutter on the desk includes a computer, a clunky telephone, stacks of papers, and a lime-green coffee tumbler. Nothing out of the ordinary. Framed diplomas hang on the walls between patents for medical tools. On the bookshelves, pictures of a tall Hispanic man, a very pregnant woman, and two gap-toothed, beaming children showcase the perfect little family. Husband. Wife. A boy and a girl.

Does Cameron Garcia know how lucky he is?

We take our seats in front of the desk as the door clicks shut behind us. I try to steady my breathing. I hate hospitals; never have been able to stand them since Karen died.

"Sorry to keep you waiting, gentlemen. I'm Dr. Garcia." He moves around the table, hand extended, and we stand to greet him. "What can I do for you?"

Towering over six feet tall, with a thick band of fat around his middle, Cameron Garcia has black hair buzzed close to his scalp. Wide-set eyes, intelligent, hidden behind square, black-rimmed glasses. Neatly trimmed beard. His handshake is firm, but his skin is soft.

"Thank you for agreeing to meet with us," Patel says. "We won't take up too much of your time."

"My assistant tells me you have a question about some prescriptions?" Garcia sits behind his desk and studies us impassively.

I nod. "We're conducting a homicide investigation and recovered two bottles of medications prescribed by this office. One was for Valium, the other for Vicodin. The prescriptions are for Mandy McKnight. A patient of yours?"

Narrowing his eyes, Garcia scoots to the edge of his leather chair and leans over the desk toward us. "If you're here about the victim of a homicide, I'm sorry I won't be of much help. As I'm sure you know, HIPAA laws extend fifty years postmortem. I won't be able to give you any insight into the patient—if Mandy McKnight was my patient—until the year 2067. I suggest you come back then."

A real comedian, this guy.

"Mandy McKnight isn't the victim," Patel corrects.

"Has she granted you permission to unseal her medical records?"

Ms. McKnight wasn't exactly forthcoming with her personal information. "Not yet."

Garcia's expression doesn't change. "Then I *really* don't know what you think I'm going to be able to tell you, Detectives. Anything I relate to you today wouldn't be admissible in court."

He's going to be a difficult one to crack.

I've looked him up, and I know his is one of the few clinics in the area that performs late-term abortions. It's not the sole procedure they offer, of course. From what I've read, they also perform tubal ligations and assist in cases of late-term miscarriage and fetal demise. They offer counseling to aid in their patients' mental and emotional well-being. They've received stellar reviews.

"We don't believe Ms. McKnight committed the murder we're investigating," I say, switching up the approach. "We're in the middle of our investigation, and Ms. McKnight's name has been brought into it through these pills. She could be in danger, so time is of the essence. We simply want to know more about Ms. McKnight to keep her safe and to maybe shed some light on details in this homicide."

The doc eyes us thoughtfully. But he doesn't budge.

"You have a beautiful family." I gesture toward the pictures on the shelf beside us. "How old are your children?"

"Five and three." He instantly relaxes back into the chair. "Maria and Martin. That's my wife, Kendra."

"You are very blessed. And I see congratulations are in order," I remark. "How far along is your wife?"

"Eight months. It's a girl."

"I don't have any children myself," I offer, picking up the frame to study the picture of his smiling family. "I hope you don't mind my saying so, but I envy you."

"Well," the doctor says, "you're still young. It's not too late to start a family, if you want one."

"Oh, it's much too late for me," I bite out, aware of the plain gold band still on my finger. "But thank you anyway."

"His wife died last year," Patel interjects, always the blabbermouth. "Cancer."

And with that word, the air seems to be sucked out of the room with a vacuum. I wince.

"I'm sorry for your loss, Detective," Garcia says sincerely. He studies me a moment and I'm certain we're going to get nothing from him. Then he surprises me by saying, "I may not be able to give specifics, but I'll answer what I can. What do you want to know?"

"Mandy McKnight was a patient of yours, correct?"

He nods.

Interesting. Either he or Mandy is a bold-faced liar. "Can you tell me what you treated her for?"

He shakes his head, his face still unreadable.

"When did she first become your patient?"

He pushes out a thin stream of air, adjusts a sheet of paper on his tidy desk. "As I said before, Detectives, I won't give specifics, but I imagine it *might* have been sometime last June."

"When was the last time she visited your office?"

He pauses, measuring me with guarded eyes. "The last time? July, I would say. Around the first of the month."

"Do you remember if she came to her appointments alone?"

Again, his lips purse. "It's hard to say. Many women in her position want the matter to be handled privately. Others prefer to have someone with them, for comfort."

But why did she come to see you?

I can't ask him. At least not outright. Because he won't tell me.

"How many times did you see her?" Patel butts in.

Garcia's razor-sharp focus shifts to my partner. "Not speaking to this case specifically, there are some services we offer that require more in-depth counseling. Sometimes we recommend our patients speak with one of our in-house counselors for four or five sessions before procedures are cleared. We pride ourselves on being a clinic that provides top-notch emotional and medical support."

"Which of your procedures require counseling?" I ask.

"Abortion, late-term miscarriage, and tubal ligation, to name a few."

I nod. "Taking into account this information, and speaking theoretically, you might have seen Mandy McKnight approximately once for her procedure"—whatever it was—"and four times for counseling afterward."

"Not necessarily in that order, but yes. Theoretically it would've been something like that."

"And—still speaking theoretically—what kind of medications might be offered after procedures like the ones you mentioned before?"

"There could be many," he replies. "Ibuprofen or Motrin would be given to relieve minor discomfort. Antibiotics might be prescribed to prevent infection, and other medications might be added to the list as well, depending on whether or not the mother exhibits signs of depression. Also, not that it necessarily pertains to this hypothetical case, but women experiencing more severe pain may be prescribed a combination of Valium and Vicodin to make them more comfortable."

There we go. It's all coming together now.

Mandy McKnight sought some kind of services from Dr. Garcia's clinic in June or July. She was either pregnant and lost the child, chose to abort it, or decided to have a sterilization procedure. She visited this clinic and received counseling here. She was in extreme pain and filled prescriptions for Vicodin and Valium, which she never finished taking, since fifty-two pills remain in each bottle.

But how did her medication end up in the back of the Harrises' medicine cabinet? And what, if anything, does that have to do with Joanna? It could be nothing. Mandy might've been friends with Joanna. She might've come to stay the night and accidentally left her prescriptions behind. Yes, the pills could lead nowhere. But something keeps telling me Mandy McKnight will be the missing piece to finding Joanna's killer.

"Thank you for that information, Dr. Garcia," I say, rising. Patel sends me a surprised look: he has other questions he wants to ask. "It's extremely helpful. I have one more question, if you wouldn't mind."

"Go on," he nods.

"Could you confirm whether Mandy McKnight was pregnant at the time of her first visit?"

I'm not taking a shot in the dark, not at all. I'm studying his reaction, analyzing his response, and measuring those against everything I've heard thus far.

"In your line of work, Detective Shaw, privacy may not be important," he says evenly, his face a blank slate, "but to us, it's paramount to the safety of the women who visit our clinic."

Someone raps on his door, and a second later, the receptionist peers into the room. She's taller than I realized. Glossy blond hair with hot pink streaks in it. Cornflower blue eyes. Round face and high cheekbones. She's attractive in a sweet, innocent kind of way.

"Dr. Garcia," she whispers, "your twelve-thirty is here."

"Thank you, Tiffany," he says, holding her gaze just a little long. He stands. "If you'll excuse me, gentlemen, I have business to attend to."

Just like that, our time is up.

"What about the name Joanna Harris?" I stop in the doorway. "Has she ever been a patient here?"

He stares me down before replying. "As I said, Detective, I'm afraid I can't be of much help."

It doesn't sit right with me that he didn't actually answer my question one way or the other. But nothing about this case does.

"Sun is setting fast," I tell Patel as we walk back to the car. The sky is turning dark, and I'm desperate to make something of this day before it's gone. "I really want to dig into those call logs . . . but do you think we could make it to Pacifica by nightfall?"

"Depends on commuter traffic. It's close to six." Patel frowns at me. "Why?"

"Dean Lewis still hasn't returned my calls." I slide into the unmarked cruiser, and when Patel joins me, I point straight ahead, toward Point Reina. "It's time to pay the Harrises' chef a visit."

....

The town of Pacifica is a gem. Tucked on the coast between San Francisco and Point Reina, it's a short jog off Highway 1, a six-mile stretch of picturesque beaches and sprawling hills twenty minutes south of the city. Although it's larger than Point Reina, Pacifica is still relatively quiet—an oasis for surfers and hikers and those seeking refuge from the daily grind.

I could see why someone like Dean—someone who spends his workday shuffling meals between Point Reina and San Francisco—would like it here.

Patel's GPS sparks to life, informing us that Dean's residence, Seascape Apartments, is ahead on the right. Painted brown and muted green, the complex fades into the landscape and looks as though it hasn't been remodeled in the last few decades. The lawns are mowed short, the trees trimmed back. It's the view at the end of the street that sells the place. A brisk, two-minute walk to the west and I'd be standing in the surf.

"What does Dean drive?" Patel asks, frowning at the line of parked cars at the curb. "A Camaro?"

"2012 Mustang Convertible. Kona blue. Bought it three years ago. According to DMV records, he's the second owner."

"Did I tell you about my wife's new car?" Patel kills the engine. "She's in love. Better be, considering they asked for one of my kidneys as collateral. If I thought I was broke before, I had no idea. You should hear the plans she has for our new pool."

I make a sound of agreement as he goes on about the infinity pool they're putting in.

"The promotion's going to be perfect timing," Patel rambles on.

"Promotion?" I hadn't heard anything about it.

"Didn't I mention my meeting with the lieutenant? Sure I did. He said the Harris case is getting national attention now. Said it wouldn't look good for the department if the case stalled. They want us to wrap it up quickly. Might be a promotion in it for me if we do."

It all makes sense. The promotion *is* perfect timing. Especially if he and his wife have already spent the money he'd earn from the raise. No wonder he wants a reckless pursuit of Joanna Harris's killer, leading to a quick arrest.

But that's not how I work. He should know that by now.

"Let me be the first to congratulate you then," I say, without bothering to keep the cynicism from my tone. "Can we get back to work now?"

Without waiting for an answer, I exit the cruiser, slamming the door behind me. He follows and meets me at the curb as a surfer passes by, lugging a board. The breeze carries a scent of sand and salt. I breathe in deeply and take in my surroundings. Run-down duplexes across the street. Dead-end road. Seagulls swooping in the distance. No traffic. Not much beach parking. Actually, there's hardly enough street parking for Seascape's tenants. There must be a private lot, or—*there it is*. Up ahead, past the complex, a driveway turns off the main road.

"I'm going to check out the tenant garages," I tell Patel. "I want a quick look before we head in."

"All right," Patel says, "but I'm going up. See if I can get him talking. Meet me up there. 3B."

"I know," I call over my shoulder. "I remember."

Flanked by ruthlessly groomed hedges, the driveway leads behind the complex to a large lot edged by three rows of garages. Beside each single-car garage is a covered stall for a second vehicle. I stride down the nearest row, scanning. Honda Civic with expired plates. Dodge pickup truck with blacked-out windows. Electric company work truck. No sign of Dean's blue Mustang.

My gaze lifts to the small metal placards posted above each garage door. 6A, 5A . . .

The stall beside 3B's garage bay is empty. Oil stain on the concrete. Naked lightbulb overhead. There's nothing to find here.

But I'm not about to leave any stone unturned, so I enter the covered stall and search for a side entrance.

"Hey," someone calls from behind me. "That's my garage. Can I help you find something?"

Dean.

I've already run his record, and feel like we've met before, even though we haven't. He's Caucasian, six foot one, thirty-four years old, and has lived in San Mateo County his whole life. Graduate of the California Culinary Academy. Top honors. Never married. Doesn't receive government assistance or pay child support. I put his plates through the system, too. Three speeding tickets in the last two years for going over ninety miles per hour. Not surprising considering his choice of vehicle. Other than the speed infractions, and one night spent in jail after a nasty bar fight—in which I figure he earned that gnarly scar on the side of his neck—he's clean. Tonight, he's carrying two gym bags, one dangling at the end of each arm.

"I'm Detective Shaw from the San Mateo County Sheriff's Office," I say as I approach him. "I left you several messages."

"I've been busy." I can tell from his tone that Dean's not

going to be too talkative today. "Forgive me if I don't shake your hand. I'm late for an appointment in the city."

"I get the feeling you're dodging my calls," I say, keeping my tone light, "but you wouldn't have any reason to do that, would you?"

"I'm not dodging your calls, Detective Shaw. I merely have nothing to add to your investigation. I thought I'd serve Joanna better if I stayed out of the way so you can do your job."

I have to tread carefully with this guy. I want him on my side.

He drops his bags to the asphalt, crouches, and with one swift move, lifts the garage door. It rolls back with an obnoxious whinny and settles on its track overhead. Inside, the garage space is tidy. No garden tools, I note immediately. Not a speck of dirt on the concrete floor.

"No lock?" I ask, pointing to the door resting on the track overhead.

"The lock busted last spring. It's not a big deal." Dean reaches into his pocket, pulls out his car keys, and presses a button on the fob. The Mustang's trunk jerks open with a loud thud. "I don't keep anything valuable in here anyway."

His garage is barely wide enough for the Mustang's doors to open. Against the back wall, a narrow cabinet reaches from floor to ceiling.

Wonder what he keeps in there?

"Listen," Dean says, picking up his bags and tossing them in the trunk. "I don't want any trouble." He slams the lid closed.

I put up my hands as if to surrender, smiling. "I just want to talk about Michael and Joanna Harris. Two minutes."

Maybe ten.

"I like my job, Detective."

"What does that have to do with anything?"

He steps closer. He's wearing cologne, something peppery. "You think Mr. Harris would be happy if he knew the police were interrogating me about *his* family? If anyone sees me talking to you, the news will make it back to Point Reina faster than I will."

"What's wrong with having a civil conversation?" I counter, still smiling.

Dean rolls his eyes. "I'm going to make this easy on you. I loved Joanna as a friend, and—"

"Only as a friend?" I interrupt. "Never crossed the line?"

"Never."

"Not sure I believe that."

His breathing remains even. His gaze holds mine steady. He's either telling the truth or he's a very skilled liar. He huffs in disgust, charges around to the driver's side of his car, and yanks the door open. "I told you I was late. Have a good evening, Detective."

I move in front of the garage door, so he can't leave unless he plans to run me over. "You like your job, and Point Reina is a tight community. You can't afford a bad name, or you won't work anywhere around there again. You're loyal to the Harrises because you and Joanna were close. I get all that. But if you loved her—as a friend—help us figure out who did this to her."

If he doesn't know already.

He curses under his breath, glaring at me. Then he says, "Okay. I'll answer anything you want about Joanna. But their marriage was none of my business. I don't want to get involved."

"You already are, Dean." I stare him down. "You go in and out of Ravenwood almost every day. You know what goes on inside those walls. Inside that marriage. You knew back then. Do you remember anything strange happening last summer?"

"Strange? No. Nothing."

"Anything, Dean. Did they go anywhere in May, June, or July? Take any trips, or—"

"They didn't go anywhere," he blurts. "Especially in May. Christ! Joanna wouldn't even come out of her room for the last half of the month."

"Do you know why?"

He shrugs. "Said she wasn't feeling well."

"She secluded herself in her room for half of the month, and you don't think that's odd behavior?"

"It's not a crime to be sick, Detective. She had a horrible pregnancy. Nauseous all the time. Couldn't keep food down. It wasn't abnormal to find her in bed half the day."

"So she kept to her room and to her bed. Do you know who took care of her during that time?"

"Samara—the woman wouldn't leave Joanna's side."

"Were she and Mr. Harris arguing at the time? Or any time before or after she secluded herself in her room?"

"Didn't you hear what I said? If I want to keep my job, I can't talk about their marriage."

"Did Mr. Harris give you that ultimatum?"

His jaw twitches as he stares into the Mustang's interior. It's as if Dean's deciding whether or not to bolt. Staying would probably mean disrespecting or even disobeying his employer. But running from an open investigation would immediately throw suspicion on him. If he's not guilty, why would he need to dodge innocent questions?

I've got him pinned, and we both know it.

"All right, Dean," I say, pretending to give a little ground. "I'll keep my questions focused on Joanna." Because it'll loosen him up for the more complicated questions later. "Did she have any enemies?"

"No."

"Can you recall any disagreements between Joanna and Rachael Martin?" I press. "Or anyone else in the neighborhood?"

"*No.*" With a heavy exhale, Dean slams his car door shut. The sound ricochets off the walls of the garage like a thunderclap as he approaches me, fire blazing in his eyes. "That's the thing you're *not* getting. Everyone loved Joanna. *Everyone.* She was the light in any room. The life of the party. She was unbelievably charismatic, and kind, and funny. When she talked, you listened. When she walked away, you watched. Everyone did. Women wanted to be her. Men wanted to be with her."

"Then," I insist, feeling my own pulse jump at his words, "who the hell would do this to her?"

"If I knew of one person who thought poorly of her, who would wish her even the slightest bit of harm, I would tell you. But I can't think of a single person in all of Point Reina because there isn't one."

Quite the speech. But I'm not falling for it. "When was the last time you saw her?"

"Am I a suspect now?" he asks bitterly.

"We haven't ruled anyone out, Mr. Lewis."

"July, I guess."

"I don't want you to guess," I say flatly. "Take a minute to think about it."

Anger flares in his eyes again, then recedes. "I can't remember exactly, but with the exception of that period in May, when she was sick, we met every morning to go over their menu. I couldn't say if that happened the day she was killed or not, but in all likelihood it did."

So he would've seen Joanna on the morning of July sixteenth, before she went to Pilates. It's not concrete, since he can't note anything specific that happened that day, but at least he's giving me something.

"Did you see Joanna outside of work?" I ask. "Did you go shopping together? Movies? Dinner?"

He levels his humorless stare at me. "All of the above. Anything else?"

Aha. "You must've been devastated when she left Mr. Harris in July."

His jaw clenches. "I was."

"Anything strike you as odd about the way she left?"

He blinks, then stares me down for so long, I fear I've pushed too far. "If you're asking my opinion, Joanna wouldn't have just vanished without at least saying goodbye. It wasn't like her. She was always thoughtful and kind."

"If you thought her disappearance was strange, why didn't you ever go to the police?"

"Mr. Harris insisted she was fine." He glances at the cabinets at the back wall of the garage, though I'm not sure if he's mentally searching for something hidden there or just desperate to avoid eye contact. "He said she was with her sister. I left message after message on her cell, but there was never any reply. It was strange."

"It was strange," I agree. "And yet you never filed a missing person's report."

"I thought about that," he says bitterly, bringing his gaze back to mine, "and I even mentioned it in passing to Mr. Harris one morning. He said it was absurd. He explained that Joanna wasn't in danger, that she chose to leave, and any effort to bring her back would be useless."

Interesting. Harris hadn't mentioned any of this. "Would you consider Mr. Harris a decent boss?"

"I would say so, yes," he says. "He's reasonable when it comes to days off, allowing vacation time, and even offers me benefits. Some people pay more for silence on certain issues, and—"

"No, you're not skipping over that," I interrupt. "Did Michael Harris offer a *bribe* to keep you quiet?"

His lips press together tightly, giving away nothing.

"What kinds of issues might *someone* pay to keep quiet?" I prod.

"I told you. I won't answer any questions about my boss's marriage."

Dean's acting like he doesn't want to play this game,

but I'll get the information I need one way or another. "Abuse?"

Again, he stares me down, then lowers and lifts his chin. It's the smallest of affirmative movements. If I hadn't been looking right at him, waiting for a sign, I would've missed it.

"Mr. Harris loved his wife, Detective. I don't think that's what you want to hear, but it's the truth. In fact, he probably loved her too much, and held on too tightly when she wanted more freedom."

Fascinating. "Did she ever mention having an affair?"

He laughs.

"More than one affair?"

"For a detective, you sure don't seem to be digging too deep." He shakes his head. "I told you. She was loved by everyone who knew her. *Everyone,* Detective."

He loved her, too.

There's no doubting the nature of their relationship now. Dean Lewis and Joanna Harris had an affair. But he won't divulge the truth to me because he knows it'll make him a prime suspect.

Too late.

"Anyway," he goes on, glancing at his watch, "I know she and Mr. Harris had their problems, but who am I to say what I would or wouldn't do in a certain situation? Everyone has issues."

I get the feeling that I'm teetering on the edge of something dark with Dean Lewis—valuable information that'll turn this case around. I gamble, taking advantage of the answers flowing freely from him now.

"Does Mr. Harris know you and Joanna were having an affair?"

"You think he would keep me on his staff if he suspected I was sleeping with his wife?" With a curse, he jerks open the Mustang's door, and slides inside. "Clearly you don't know a thing about Mr. Harris's character. The man would've carved me in two if he thought for one second that we were sleeping together."

"Were you?"

I need to hear him say the words, if for no other reason than to prove my suspicions about him were right.

"If you want to know about their marriage," he says grimly, "ask Mr. Harris. Be sure to tell him that I wouldn't give you squat."

I barely have time to scramble out of the garage before he reverses, barely missing my toes. Quickly, as if he nearly forgot, he rushes out of the car and yanks on the garage door until it slams against the asphalt.

"I left my number on the voicemails. Call if you think of anything that might help with the case."

He flops into the driver's seat and bangs the door shut again. He doesn't even glance in my direction when he cranks the wheel and peels out of the lot.

"Was that Dean Lewis?" Patel hollers, charging along the stretch of garage doors. He's out of breath. "Flag him down so we can talk to him!"

I'm still shaking my head, watching the taillights of Dean's Mustang fade into the twilight. When Patel reaches my side, he doubles up to rest his hands on his knees.

"You didn't stop him," he wheezes.

"I didn't need to. Our conversation was over."

"Damn it. Took a two-minute phone call and missed him."

"He refuses to bad-mouth his boss. Doesn't want to lose his job. He was probably paid off to keep quiet." My thoughts reel as I recall our conversation. If Dean loved Joanna and believed Michael killed her, would he keep working for him? Not likely. "Apparently Joanna had multiple lovers, and I'm convinced the list includes Dean Lewis."

"I'm not surprised, considering how much time they had alone at Ravenwood. But you figure Michael Harris paid him off to stay away from us?" Making a shocked, whistle-like sound, Patel plants his hands on his hips and eyes the door. "You're thinking what I'm thinking, aren't you?"

It'd be easy to lift up the door and search through those cabinets. Easy, but also illegal. Would I find a shovel—the one that shattered Joanna's skull? Her missing wedding ring? Or a bunch of useless old cooking utensils? I start the short walk back to the cruiser.

Patel follows. "Maybe Harris and his chef were in it together."

"Why would you say that?"

"Love triangles never work out well in the end. Maybe they were *both* jealous of Travis Martin?"

THURSDAY

Three Days Until Colleen's Murder

MICHAEL

I've always hated funerals.

Hands shoved deep in my pockets, I stand on the sidewalk under the awning of Morrigan's Funeral Home, shielding my face from the steady drizzle of morning rain, and wait for Joanna's sister to meet me. Heather flew in from Los Angeles last night and chose to stay at a hotel rather than at Ravenwood with Colleen and me. It's probably best. The walls feel like they're closing in as it is.

We were allowed back into our home yesterday—having stayed only one night at the Martins'—but now the place has a completely different vibe. It feels violated, destroyed, as if its guts have spilled out for everyone to see. I don't feel comfortable there. Not anymore.

It might have something to do with the fact that they opened the locked rooms, making me confront things I wasn't ready to. It still feels too soon. I don't expect anyone, including Colleen, to understand.

Or maybe it's just that I can't live across the street from the place where they found Joanna's body.

The reporters camping outside Ravenwood don't appear to be leaving anytime soon. They're attacking Colleen with questions every time she steps outside. It's as if I'm a serial killer, and they're trying to save my pregnant girlfriend from being my next victim.

If I'm honest with myself, I know in the five years Joanna and I were married, I thought about killing her on more than one occasion. That's normal, isn't it? For married couples to hate as passionately as they love? Man alive, I hated Joanna, especially that final night. I wanted to wrap my hands around her neck and squeeze. I could even imagine the way her windpipe would collapse under my fingers, the way her blue eyes would pop out of their sockets as she looked at me one last time with the realization that she might've struck first, but I'd gotten her in the end.

"Michael," a small voice says behind me, and I whirl around.

I was so lost in thought, I hadn't heard anyone approach. Now, I force a smile as I greet Joanna's only living relative with a tight embrace. Heather's tiny in my arms, narrow and bony, just like Joanna, but on the inside I know she's tough as nails. Just the way Joanna used to be. They were a lot alike, shared a close bond, and frequently talked on the phone.

But last winter, something happened.

Heather stopped calling, and Joanna stopped mentioning her. I supposed the sisters had gotten into some kind of squabble, and after some time had passed, they'd get over it the way they always did. A few months later though—probably around the time we found out we were pregnant—Joanna mentioned that Heather and her husband had taken an extended vacation in Spain. Joanna found out on social media, and wasn't thrilled about it. From Heather's pictures, it appeared she was having the time of her life. Joanna kept making snide remarks about how Heather's taste in beachwear was pretty gruesome. Deep down, I think she was jealous. Even though I'd always given Joanna everything she could've ever wanted, she never understood why we couldn't get up and leave whenever we wanted. The way Heather and her husband had. But managing a successful business meant I was tied to it. *Married* to it. I guess it wasn't in Joanna's makeup to understand that level of loyalty.

"It's good to see you," I say, stepping back to look into Heather's eyes.

They're bright blue like Joanna's, with the same almond shape, lined with the same thick fans of black eyelashes. Heather's irises are shadowed, her eyes rimmed with red as if she's been crying, yet I still see Joanna in them. My gut clenches into a solid fist at the resemblance.

I haven't seen her in years, since Christmas before last, when we drove down to L.A. to spend the holidays together. Those were different times. Feels like decades have passed since then.

"Wish it wasn't under these circumstances," I force out.

And I wish Joanna hadn't confided in her sister all the years we were married. For better or worse, the details of our marriage should've stayed inside Ravenwood's four walls. Heather was never given the opportunity to make up her own mind about me. Her opinion was tainted from the start—her sister saw to that—and she's never let me forget it.

Heather doesn't even try to smile. Her face stays sullen, her color as flat gray as the sky overhead. "You look well rested."

"Don't be nasty. This is hard for all of us."

"How's your new girlfriend?"

"Fine."

"And the baby?"

"Healthy, as far as we know," I say, ignoring the bitterness of her tone. I open the door for her to walk inside. "She's coming up on six months. What about you and Al?"

"We're good. Al got a promotion at work, so we're moving back. We're buying a new house in Corona. Should close at the end of the month."

"Congratulations."

The word rebounds off the deeply Victorian walls. This place is like a tomb—the air musty, the lights dim.

We're greeted by a forty-something woman in a pantsuit who steps out of the shadows. She's much too chipper for her working atmosphere. Heather and I take the seat across from her desk and pick out a casket, followed by a funeral schedule and music. I let Heather decide everything, deferring to her taste and her beliefs in what Joanna would want. I know better than to toss my hat into the ring. Joanna and Heather shared headstrong, stubborn personalities. Which was probably what kept them from swallowing their pride and calling each other after their fight—whatever it was about.

Heather chooses a rose-tinted casket, simple satin, programs, classical background music.

"I'm thinking we should have her funeral at a Catholic church," Heather states. And then she turns to me. "Don't you agree?"

"Heather, you know Joanna was an atheist."

"But the detective said she was found wearing a necklace with the Virgin Mary on it. Maybe she changed her mind in the end, and this was what she would've wanted. Don't you think?"

I don't totally agree with Heather, but I'm the last person who would know what Joanna wanted. She'd changed so much in the last few months of her life. We both had.

In the silence before I answer, realization creeps in. Whoever murdered Joanna could have given her the necklace *after* she was killed, like a token. Or maybe it was from her lover, our baby's father—*her* baby's father, I correct. I'd wanted a family with her so damn bad. . . .

I sigh. "Catholic church it is."

As the woman helping us disappears into the back to tally up the fee, Heather turns to me.

"You're on the news down there," she says flatly.

"In L.A.?"

She nods.

"Christ." I scrub my hands through my hair. My face is plastered on every local news station. I can't go anywhere without people glaring, suspecting I've killed my wife. Now I'm making national news? The thought revolts me. People are too eager to gossip, to sink their teeth into this case. I'm guilty before the cops even have the facts. "What are they saying?"

"Officially? Nothing. But everyone thinks you murdered my sister. And I might believe it too, to be honest."

Her resemblance to Joanna strikes me again. Their candor is nothing if not cunning.

"Knocking up your girlfriend right after your wife was murdered doesn't exactly help your case," she goes on, keeping her sour gaze locked on mine. "Honestly Michael, it looks like you killed Joanna to get her out of the way so you could whore around with your secretary."

"Jesus, Heather, I know how it looks! It's all I can think about." Knives pierce my temples. I attempt to rub the pain away. It doesn't help. "But Joanna left *me,* not the other way around. I'm sure she told you."

She shakes her head. "You know the thing I don't understand, Michael?"

Here she goes.

"I know the kind of hot-cold relationship you and Joanna had. I remember how thrilled she was to marry you—I'd never seen her so happy. But then she'd call late at night, sobbing, locked in the second master bedroom because she couldn't stand to lie next to you."

"I remember those things too."

With ugly, painful clarity.

I couldn't sleep those nights, when the sound of her weeping seemed to fill our home. When I let my anger get the best of me and said things I didn't mean. But Joanna could push my buttons so easily, flirting with men right in front of me. Spending outrageous amounts on bags or shoes or dresses she'd never wear, just to wave the bill in my face. She'd go out partying with Rachael or Lora and stay out until dawn, and then confront me as if I were the one in the wrong. Like clockwork, I'd lose control first. She'd forgive me in the morning of course, when tempers simmered down, but I never deserved her mercy. She would push me to say horrible, unforgiveable things that no husband should ever say to his wife, no matter the circumstances. On the surface, to everyone around us, we had everything. We were so much in love, with the perfect house, the perfect life. The perfect marriage. But hatred and bitterness simmered beneath the surface.

"Tell me something, then." Heather's voice is getting a little shrill, and I flinch. "If you loved my sister so much, why would you let her walk away without making the slightest attempt to get her back? She was carrying your *child*, Michael. The last time you talked to her was in July, when she left you? The baby would've been born in November, and you—not one time in the months since then—never thought about getting in touch with her? About calling her up and asking how she and your child were doing? Even if you didn't kill her, you have to understand that makes you a different kind of monster, but a monster just the same."

"You don't know anything," I bite out. "I wanted her to come back. I waited for months."

"All that waiting must've been *so* difficult while you were banging your secretary."

"That's not fair."

"Fair?" she seethes, stabbing a finger into my chest. "I'm about to bury *my* sister, and you don't think I'm being fair to *you*? You probably did kill her, you narcissistic bastard!"

"I'm sorry," a voice calls from the door. It's the woman in the suit. She stands in the doorway, a fat binder cradled in her arms. "I'll give you two another minute. . . ."

"Thank you," I manage, but I feel sore, beat up, my insides pulverized.

I don't even give a damn what she overheard. What does it matter if one more person believes I killed my wife?

Without saying another word, I fish my cell out of my back pocket and press the messages app on my phone, leading me to a long list of texts. There, near the bottom, is Joanna's final message.

A reminder of what I lost.

"I haven't showed anyone this," I say, handing over the phone. "Not even the police. It was the last text Joanna ever sent me. Maybe you'll understand."

"July sixteenth, 10:04 P.M.," she reads aloud, her voice sounding eerily like Joanna's. "Michael, I don't know how to tell you this, but the baby growing inside me isn't yours. I'm in love with the baby's father, and the only way we can have a future is if I bury you in the past. I'm sorry. Please understand. J x." Heather pauses, and then looks up into my eyes. "She never mentioned any of this to me."

"It doesn't matter. That's the reason I didn't try to win her back, Heather. Right there."

She hands the phone back with a curse.

"She'd been cheating on me," I say. "That baby was his, whoever the hell he was. What good would it have done to call her, or check up on the child that wasn't mine?" A dull numbness blooms through my chest. "It wouldn't have changed anything. I was so hurt. And angry. I'd lost her, Heather. She didn't want to come back."

She stares at me a moment. Then she snatches back the phone and rereads the message. "Wait. According to what the police told me, Joanna should've been five months along at the time she was killed, but she was no longer pregnant. That means she either went into labor before the murder—and the baby wouldn't have survived—or she miscarried."

Suddenly my thoughts come together. Joanna staying in the second master in May, avoiding me for weeks. That could've been when she lost the baby. If only I'd known, I would've been there for her and helped her through it. Things between us could've turned out so differently.

"All of that makes sense. But *this* doesn't." I point to the text. "She had to have been pregnant when she sent this. Look— she says the baby is growing inside her. And this was in *July*."

"The timeline doesn't match up at all! Oh, Michael! Why haven't you shown this text to the police?"

"Because they're going to pin this as my motive. They're going to think I had nothing to lose, that everything was being taken from me. That I killed her because I lost my head in some kind of insane jealous rage."

"Did you?" she blurts, her tone accusing. She's crying now, ugly tears dribbling down her cheeks.

Leaning forward, I take her hands in mine. "Heather, I had nothing to do with what happened to Joanna or the baby. I swear to you I'm innocent. If I show them this, I'll become their number one suspect."

She jerks away and smacks me in the chest with my phone. "You already are! If you showed them her text, it might lead them to another suspect. Maybe it's the guy she left you for. Who was it?"

"I don't know. She never told me."

God forgive me for trying to rip the name from her throat.

Heather's eyes narrow to slits. "And you have no idea?"

"None."

"Were you that neglectful? Did you not pay attention to how she was spending her time at all?" Before I can defend myself, she says, "No wonder she was so unhappy."

I don't argue with her. Because I know I didn't treat Joanna right, and I've been tormented with guilt since the last moment I saw her.

"I'm sorry to rush you," the woman in the suit bleats from the doorway, "but we can nail down the funeral date at another time, and we have an appointment arriving in just a few moments. Which one of you will be paying for the services today?"

"That's me," I say.

As I remove the wallet from my pocket, the woman places a binder on the desk in front of us. Opening it up, Heather peeks at the bill, swiping tears from her eyes with the back of her hand.

"Ouch, that'll make a dent," she says, making a twisted face. "I guess it's a good thing you just came into a bunch of insurance money, isn't it?"

DETECTIVE SHAW

July sixteenth, 10:04 P.M. Michael, I don't know how to tell you this, but the baby growing inside me isn't yours. . . .

Adjusting my laptop screen to eliminate the glare from the sunlight pouring through the windows of the Point Reina Distillery, I reread Joanna's last text: *I'm in love with the baby's father, and the only way we can have a future is if I bury you in the past. . . .*

"Isn't this crazy?" Patel's frowning, stroking his coffee mug. He should lay off the caffeine.

"I know. Joanna wasn't pregnant in July when she died. It doesn't make sense."

"Not that. *This*," he says, pointing to the big-screen television mounted over the bar. "Sixty-footers are rolling in now. Those guys could die just trying to get out there."

He's referring to the surfers participating in the Titans of Mavericks—a big-wave surfing competition held off Point Reina's rocky coastline. Storm surges and monster waves in January and February beckon the most daring and reckless surfers in the world. Today, the distillery has opened early to accommodate spectators who'd rather watch the show on television and benefit from the close-up camera angles than fight the crowds on the beach. At the moment, every seat in the place is filled with a riveted surfing fan, and all eyes are glued to the big screens. All but mine.

"Doesn't look like Joanna contacted anyone after leaving her husband. Not her sister in Los Angeles, or the people at Harris Financial," I say, though I don't know if Patel's really listening. I sip my coffee. "Michael Harris's phone has a record of receiving the text. But he didn't respond."

"At least not through a device," Patel says glumly.

"You think he responded by killing her."

He shrugs. "You know what I think about the guy."

"Joanna's cell service has been left on all this time," I argue. "If Harris killed her, it's strange that he continued paying for service for two lines, don't you think?"

Patel groans as a surfer takes a hard fall, and then he levels a humorless stare at me. "And you don't think it's strange that he continued paying for service for a woman who'd cheated on him, got pregnant by someone else, and broke up with him via text message?"

The man has a point.

After that final text to her husband was sent, Joanna seemed to disappear from the face of the earth.

"They've only had two successful wave rides so far," Patel grumbles. "Unbelievable. I bet they're going to call it. They do that, you know. Cancel the whole thing if the waves are too rough. Don't want another death on their hands."

My thoughts veer straight to Joanna, the way her body was found in the shallow grave. I feel a spike of rage, remembering that her murderer is still at large.

Sifting through the Harrises' call and text logs is a tedious process, and by the time I finish going over the texts from Joanna's phone, Patel is on his third cup of coffee. The distillery erupts in cheers when someone tries to challenge the rising mountain of water. But it's followed closely by a collective moan when the surfer takes too heavy a drop and succumbs to the power of the wave.

"Look at this," I say, drawing Patel's attention from the television to my laptop screen. "There are a number of texts from Travis to Joanna and vice versa between February and the middle of July."

I slide the screen over to him.

Would you and Michael like to come over next weekend?
Are you and Michael planning on attending the
    conference in Seattle?
Has Rachael called you about dinner plans?

Patel finishes his cup and reluctantly declines a refill from the waitress. "We already know Travis and Joanna were having an affair. The fact that they were communicating shouldn't be a surprise."

"But look." I point to Joanna's responses as I scroll through the list. "Each time, she only texted back a single word: yes or no."

"So she wasn't much of a talker."

And just like that, he's sucked back into the competition.

But there has to be something more, something beneath their informal conversations. After each initial question was asked and answered, it appears they went radio silent for a few days. But they'd always chat again, repeating impersonal questions followed by terse replies.

"On July fifteenth," I go on, "Travis texted, 'Has Michael talked to you about the Lennox account?' Joanna responded quickly with 'yes.' That was the second to last communication she had with anyone."

"So what does the Lennox account have to do with—oh, look, here he goes!" Patel is enthralled, pointing at the screen. "You know, it's crucial that these surfers focus not only on the wave they choose, but on the ones after it. They have to keep their eyes on the lineup because it's the ones *behind* them that might be fatal."

Keep their eyes on the lineup.

Frowning, I scan the texts again.

"He's going to make it." Patel lets out a loud whooping sound as the surfer—a professional from Santa Cruz—pops up on his board and drops into what the announcer calls "the barrel." "That's amazing."

It truly is. I look up and watch in awe, captivated, as the surfer seems to glide effortlessly through the curling wall of water. And then, as the colossal wave begins to break behind him, something happens. He tumbles headfirst into the sea. His board shoots into the air behind him, flipping and twisting over the swell of water. A hush falls over the distillery. It's as if everyone's trying to hold his or her breath as long as the surfer. One-one-thousand, two-one-thousand, three—he's still underwater—four-one-thousand, five—another powerful wave follows on the heels of the first. Jet Skis can't come to the rescue while waves this massive are breaking. They have to wait for a lull.

"See," Patel says, justified, "they're pummeling him down there. He can't catch a break to come to the surface."

"The surfers have to wait for a break between swells," I put in, as something shifts in my brain. "They have to wait until the time is right before taking the risk."

As the surfer's head pops up a few seconds later, the people in the distillery applaud, toasting him with house-special mimosas. And I think I might know why there was always a few days' break between texts.

Travis and Joanna had to wait for the coast to be clear to set up their secret rendezvous. But none of those texts had anything indicating an affair.

"Come on," I say, downing what's left of my coffee. "You've seen enough of the competition. Let's head over to the city and get to our appointment with Rachael Martin early. I've got a few questions for her."

RACHAEL

What do you wear for an interview with a detective?

Stiletto heels and a pencil skirt. Narrow, rectangular fashion glasses that sit on the end of my nose. A tight coat that doesn't quite button in front. Yeah, that'll do. I'm channeling Jackie O. and that curly-haired woman from *CSI,* and it's perfect.

As I parade along the sidewalk in the Marina district, my hair blowing in the breeze sweeping over the bay, I catch a glimpse of myself in the reflection of a passing window. Professional and classy, with a sexy edge. *Exactly* what I was going for. Checking the time on my phone, I speed my pace so I'm not late.

When I open the door to my office, two strangers stand to greet me.

"Good morning," the taller one says, reaching into his pocket to pull out identification. "I'm Detective Patel, and this is Detective Shaw. Could we talk with you for a few minutes, Mrs. Martin?"

"Yes. Of course." Smoothing my skirt, I escort them beyond the front desk area, where I get a sideways glance from our receptionist, to my private office in back. "You're Amanda's husband, right?" I ask Detective Patel as I glance over my shoulder. "I see her around the neighborhood from time to time."

"Oh, right," he says. "I think she might've mentioned you before. We love the area. Before this week, we would've called it a haven."

"I agree. But it's tainted now, isn't it? Our home values will probably plummet. No one wants to move to a murderer's playground." Gesturing to the chairs in front of my desk, I offer them comfortable seats and coffee, but both refuse. "What can I help you with?"

"I wouldn't go around saying Point Reina is a murderer's playground, Mrs. Martin," Detective Shaw says, adjusting the suit jacket over his chest as he sits back. If he weren't questioning me about a murder, I might find him marginally attractive. He's a little burly, with a strong, defined profile. Slightly wide-set green eyes, square jaw, and a sloping Roman nose. "It's one murder. At the present moment we don't have reason to think there'll be another. Anyway, that's not what we came here about today. We wanted to speak with you in private. To get your thoughts on a few things."

"Of course." I sit on the edge of my leather-backed chair and try to calm my nerves. My heart is beginning to race, and I think I know why.

"Would you mind if I recorded this?" Patel asks, removing a small device from the inside pocket of his coat. "For reference purposes?"

"Oh, no, not at all. Record away."

The anxiety that'd been tying me up in knots moments before vanishes. A weird kind of exhilaration fizzes through me at the thought of being recorded, of my words being so important that these men will be listening to them later. I feel like Sharon Stone in *Basic Instinct*. Only there's a desk between us, and I'm wearing underwear.

"How close were you to Joanna Harris?" Patel asks, setting the device on my desk.

"We were friends and neighbors. Our husbands worked together in the city."

"What about in July? Were you close with her then as well?"

They know.

My skin crawls, going cold, as if someone just walked over my grave. If they know my husband was having an affair with Joanna, they're going to inquire about it. Upon discovering his infidelity, it's true I was angry beyond anything I'd ever felt before. As any woman would be in my situation.

It's true I'd wished Joanna dead.

But I'd taken it so much further, hadn't I?

If I tell them the truth about Travis and Joanna, about my hatred near the end, I'm going to be a suspect. Her body was found across the street from my house, for Christ's sake. They're going to assume I killed her.

I don't know why, but I hadn't thought about this angle until now. I hadn't seen things from their point of view.

"Of course we were close with both the Harrises," I lie, forcing a smile. But when they don't smile back, mine falters. "I mean, once I started working here, Joanna and I didn't see each other as much, but that's not because we didn't want to. I was simply so busy, my priorities refocused."

For a split second, I wonder if I should come clean about their affair, before the detectives ask. That way it won't look like I'm hiding something, as if I'm guilty.

While I'm still contemplating which is better, Shaw speaks, his voice a low rumble that's oddly comforting. "When was the last time you saw Joanna?"

"Sometime in early summer. July, I think. At Pilates."

"An exercise class? Where?"

My heart starts to race. "Studio Balance. In Half Moon Bay."

Something flickers in Shaw's eyes. "So the two of you took classes together?"

I nod. "Every Monday, Wednesday, and Friday morning. Nine o'clock."

"Do you still attend classes?" Shaw asks after a pause.

"Not anymore."

"Any particular reason?"

I can't tell him the truth. Not about this. I've already said too much. If I go any further, he's going to leave here and head straight to Studio Balance and talk to Mandy. And then life as I know it will end.

"I switched to Bikram Yoga. I take afternoon classes at the place on Polk Street." And they can look into *that* as much as they want because it's the most honest thing I've said so far, aside from my cell number. "Is this what you really wanted to talk to me about? My exercise regimen? Because I can give you any details you want, but I must say I'm confused as to why this is relevant to your investigation."

"Do you know Mandy McKnight?" Detective Patel asks. I'm starting to dislike him.

"Yeah, of course. She's the owner of the Pilates studio, and one of the instructors."

"How well do you know Ms. McKnight? Were you friends outside of Pilates?"

Where are they going with this? "No—I mean, we never hung out. I don't know her well at all, but I can tell you her swan dive is amazing." When they stare blankly, I say, "You know, the Pilates move? The—oh, never mind. The only times I've ever seen Mandy were at the studio. Is she a suspect or something?"

"We're merely compiling information, Mrs. Martin." Shaw pulls out a notebook from his jacket pocket, flips open to a page somewhere in the middle. "Do you happen to recall if she was pregnant last spring?"

"Mandy? No, I don't think so."

"Thank you," Shaw says. "This is extremely helpful, Mrs. Martin."

"Anything I can do."

"Actually, there might be something more you can do for us." He flips a few more notebook pages. He's making me nervous now. "We've spent some time going over the Harrises' phone records. There were calls made from Joanna Harris's number to yours almost every day until July."

"That sounds about right. We were friends."

Until . . .

I can't even finish the thought without feeling as though every light inside me has dimmed. I pray to God the detectives don't see it.

"Do you know any reason why Joanna would be in close contact with your husband?" Shaw fires, straight to my heart.

A million thoughts stream through my head at once, loud and scattered like firecrackers. If I tell Detective Shaw about Travis and Joanna, I'm going to paint a target on Travis's back. These guys are going to meet with him next and probe him about the relationship, and who knows what their conclusions might be? They might say the affair with Joanna drove him mad. They might even throw around a term like "crime of passion." Michael will find out, too. It's inevitable. Travis will undoubtedly lose his job.

I already thought the dynamic among the three of us was bizarre.

I was wrong. It would have nothing on the coming storm.

"No," I lie. "Not at all."

"So you wouldn't be able to explain phone activity between Joanna Harris and your husband?"

"Well," I falter, "there might've been a few times when he called Michael and didn't get an answer, so Travis would call Joanna instead. But only to relay a business message, you see."

They exchange weary glances, and I know I've made a terrible misstep. Tears burn my eyes.

"So you can't think of any reason Travis would want to talk to Joanna personally?" Shaw asks gently. I wouldn't trust this guy as far as I could throw him. "In matters not concerning business?"

"Well, of course they were friends as well, Detective." I lift my hands palm up, as if to show I have nothing to hide. "We all were. I've called Michael hundreds of times. Would you like to check my phone records to verify that as well?"

A long, hard pause, and then, "We might, yes. Thank you for the offer."

Goddamn it.

I have to watch myself. "Anything else I can help you with?"

"One more thing." Shaw leans forward, resting his elbows on his knees.

Staring into his beady green eyes, I realize he's the shrewd one of the two—the one who scratches beneath the surface, determined to find the thing that's hidden. Patel's the ambitious one, the guy on the lookout for a promotion, the one who buys his wife a flashy Jaguar to parade through our neighborhood. He's probably cheating on her. Wants to keep her happy, so she won't question why he's spending so much time "at the office." That's the way Travis works. I never received prettier flowers or more luxurious jewelry than last summer, when he was sleeping with Joanna behind my back. But Shaw . . . I can't pinpoint his motives. I can't get a read on him. He's the one we need to be wary of.

"I was hoping you could clarify something for me," he goes on.

"If I can." I smile, to show I'm on their side.

"There were times when you and Joanna seemed to speak via text or phone every day, and other periods when activity was sparse. Especially in July, around her approximate date of death. Your phone interactions seemed to shorten, if they occurred at all."

"I'll have to take your word for it," I say, suddenly feeling tired of this whole charade. "I can't remember exact dates and times."

Sweat forms on my brow as Shaw looks up from his notebook and stares, unwavering.

"Mrs. Martin, when I said we'd discovered 'phone activity' between your husband and Joanna Harris, I didn't specify that they were phone *calls*. That was a jump you made. As it happens, we can't find a record of any calls between them. What we *have* discovered are frequent text messages between Joanna and your husband from February through July."

My head spins. They texted *frequently*? The lying, cheating—

"Can you give any other explanation as to why they might've been in such close and constant contact?" Shaw asks mildly.

"There are only two people who could answer that question, Detective." I'm fuming inside, struggling to formulate words that aren't vulgar. "And you know where to find both of them. Are we finished?"

COLLEEN

It's been two days, but I'm still thinking about how Michael said we could use the nursery for our baby if *I* wanted to. As if I would ever want to put our child in the crib he'd planned to use for his child with *Joanna*. The more I think about it, the more disturbing that thought is, and I know I need to voice my feelings about it. The stress of all this is really getting to me. I felt jittery for most of yesterday, probably because I haven't eaten much. I simply can't force myself to eat from a menu chosen by his dead wife.

But I can't keep quiet any longer about the nursery.

He has to get rid of it. Clear everything out. Keeping Joanna's and the baby's room that way—like it's some kind of shrine to the both of them—is sick. Seriously disturbed. He has to understand how it's making me feel, like I'm second rate compared to what he had before. Nothing but a stand-in.

Joanna's dead. We know that now. It's time to clear out her room and the baby's room and put all of that behind us. It's time to focus on *us,* on our future. And I'm so sick and tired of feeling like I have to fight to be seen in his home, and in his life.

I'm done.

After paying my cab fare, I approach Harris Financial, tightening the belt of my trench coat around my waist. The weather is wicked, rainy and cold, and there's no sign of its letting up. Wind catches the door, holding it open as I squeeze inside. Using all my strength, I pull the door closed, but a rogue blast of frigid air sweeps up my bare legs, instantly freezing me. I would've worn pants, or something more comfortable, but this is the first time I've gone back to the office since quitting. I want to show Michael that I understand what it takes to be the wife of a successful business owner. And I won't embarrass him by coming into the office looking anything less than professional.

The heels are killing me, though. Either the shoes have shrunk since I put them on last, or my feet are swelling. I don't want to acknowledge the obvious reason, so I pretend I'm not in pain, and strut into the building.

Although I only worked for Harris Financial five months, the lobby feels like home, with its off-white walls, glossy floor, and bold splashes of abstract artwork. I don't notice anyone familiar, but most people are tuned in to their phones as they whiz in and out of the front doors.

I get a nod from the receptionist—she always used to eye me warily—and make my way to the elevators. I'm dreaming of the day when I'll be surprising Michael with our baby in tow when the elevator whisks open on the top floor. Stepping out, I reknot the sash around my waist and try to walk as quietly as I can. Each step in these heels is an announcement, the *clack-clack-clack*ing rebounding off the walls. As I pass a balding young man clutching a stack of folders, I smile in acknowledgment, and am completely ignored. Suddenly I remember why Michael was always the highlight of this place for me. He truly saw the value in me, even when I doubted myself. And now he has to realize that he needs to place that same value on our relationship and our family.

Turning right, I pass a maze of cubicles, a small galley kitchen, and then, after another right turn, I see my old desk, positioned in front of Michael's closed office door. I have a dark thrill at the thought that he hasn't found a new personal secretary yet. He swears no one can replace me.

I secretly hope the position stays open indefinitely.

"What are you doing here?" someone calls.

Spinning, I repress a gasp. "Travis."

His hair is greased and swept to the side, in that cool and casual way he seems to have nailed down. He's wearing a tight-fitting black dress shirt that completely covers his tats, along with black slacks and blue Converse sneakers.

"I wanted to talk to Michael," I answer.

"Simple phone call wouldn't cut it?" His tone is teasing.

"Not today."

"Couldn't you talk to him after work?"

"I could, yes."

I leave it at that because he doesn't understand. How could he? He's not the one being watched in Ravenwood every second of every day. He's not the one being held under the microscope by Dean and Samara. I can't talk to Michael the same way when they're there, hanging on our every word.

And there are things I really need to discuss with him.

He hasn't made a single effort to address my concerns about the second master and nursery. Not even a mention of it.

He's not taking me seriously. He doesn't know how much it's bothering me. At home, he's been able to blow me off, and I've been too timid to push the issue, too conscious of prying eyes and ears. But here, at work, he means business. And today, I do too.

"You might be waiting here awhile." Travis leans back against my old desk, toys with the paper clip holder. "You just missed him."

"You're kidding."

"Afraid not." He eyes me curiously. "I've been meaning to talk to you, though. Do you know if the detectives are any closer to—you know . . ."

"No, I don't think so. Or, at least, they're not telling us that they are. They ask the strangest things. Sometimes I think they're asking over and over again to make sure the story doesn't change, or we don't accidentally reveal some new piece of information. It's as if they've already made up their minds that Michael's guilty."

"How awful," Travis says, though his tone doesn't match his words. He sounds almost . . . relieved.

"I wish they'd leave us alone so we can go back to focusing on our family." When my own words echo and come back to me, I gasp, covering my heart with my hand. "I'm sorry, that was rude of me. I should be more sensitive about Joanna."

"It's not rude, it's honest." He twists a paper clip until it breaks in his fingers, and then tosses it on the desk. "And you don't need the added stress. You shouldn't have worked here as long as you did. Joanna never held a real job, so I don't see why you'd have to either."

"I think I'd like to volunteer somewhere eventually," I say, recalling the conversation with Rachael my first day at Ravenwood. "I'll look into it after our baby's born."

"Joanna volunteered at a healthcare foundation—I'm sure you know that already—but it was basic charity work. Nothing too demanding. Everything was on her terms, but that's no surprise. Listen, I was heading to lunch." He pushes off the desk and walks so close beside me that he touches my shoulder. "Why don't you join me?"

"I—I don't know." Going to lunch with one of Michael's employees doesn't seem like a good idea. "I should probably stay and wait for Michael to come back."

"He won't be back for at least an hour. Probably longer."

"Really?"

Travis shrugs. "He's been disappearing a lot lately. I think he walks through Presidio park after lunch to clear his head."

"Oh." I can't help but feel completely deflated. I'd so carefully planned what I needed to say. "That's too bad."

"Why don't you text him? Tell him you stopped by and that you'll be back later, so he won't disappear again. And in the meantime, we'll go somewhere nice—my treat—and then you can meet up with him when we're finished." He shoots me a friendly smile. "Come on. You've got to be hungry."

"A little," I admit.

"Then text him while I grab my wallet." He moves toward the glass-walled offices on the opposite side of the cubicles. "And then we'll head out."

I shouldn't be doing this. It's not a good idea, is it? To be going out with someone who works for Michael. But it's really just an innocent lunch with one of his colleagues—who is also our neighbor—so why do I feel guilty? I'm warring with myself as I fish my phone out of my bag.

Hey honey. I type fast. *Stopped by the office to talk to you about something. Kind of important. Ran into Travis instead. Going to lunch. Will be back to see you within the hr.*

I hesitate, taking a deep breath before I hit SEND.

Travis and I walk to a Greek restaurant on Jackson Street, not far from Michael's building. I always wanted to try the place when I worked in the city. People rave about the octopus salad, but I could never justify spending upward of thirty dollars on a single meal. Not with what I was earning, anyway.

On the way there, I shoot Michael another text letting him know where we're headed, and steal a glance at Travis out of the corner of my eye. I should've declined the lunch invitation; I don't want to do anything that could anger Michael, especially when I feel like I'm already walking on eggshells. But I can't help myself. Even though I shouldn't be, I'm *intrigued* by Travis. He's one of the only people I know who knew Michael when he was with Joanna.

After we enter the restaurant, the host escorts us to a table near the windows and reaches for my shoulder. "Can I take your coat, miss?"

"Sure." I slip out of it, then smooth down my dress. It's a new one, one I bought hoping to please Michael.

"Your waitress will be with you momentarily."

The restaurant is super elegant and cozy with white linen-covered tables, chandeliers, and the robust smell of something rich and buttery wafting through the air. It's lunchtime and it's busy, with only a few tables open, and the clinking sound of forks on plates mixes with chattering voices. Dean would probably blow a gasket if he knew I was dining somewhere like this, rather than eating his food, and that thought thrills me more than I can express.

"This is Joanna's favorite restaurant," Travis says, reaching for the wine list. "Have you ever eaten here?"

Joanna's favorite restaurant. Did Michael bring her here for special occasions? Did they sit at a candlelit table in the shadows and talk quietly together? Or perhaps share a drink after work at the bar, leaning close and whispering in each other's ears?

"No, never," I tell Travis, opening the menu and skimming the prices. There's nothing under forty dollars unless I want to pick an appetizer for my main meal. "But everything looks delicious."

After the waitress approaches and introduces herself, Travis orders a wine I couldn't pronounce if I tried, a baked feta appetizer, and a halibut steak. When she turns to me, I draw a blank, hitting some kind of mental wall. It's something that's been happening a lot lately. I'm misplacing things. Forgetting things. I'm fidgety and nervous, and it's driving me crazy.

"Colleen?" Travis asks, with the waitress looking on. "Did you need more time?"

"No, it's fine. I'm bouncing between the octopus salad and the moussaka." I hope I pronounced that correctly, though I'm sure I didn't. I'm so out of my element. "Do you have a recommendation?"

"She'll have the salad," Travis answers with authority. And then he winks at me, smiling, and I smile back. "It's Joanna's favorite."

Swallowing hard, I smile politely at the waitress, who takes my menu and disappears behind a faux brick wall.

I don't know what's throwing me off more: the fact that I'd almost ordered Joanna's favorite dish without knowing it, or that Travis keeps bringing her up as if she's still alive. Does he do this when he's with Michael? Or with Rachael? How does she tolerate her husband constantly bringing up another woman?

"Did Joanna come here a lot?" I ask, sipping my water.

"Almost every day for lunch."

"Wow," I say, recalling the prices on the menu. "Michael must've spent a fortune here over the years."

"She never came with Michael."

Travis takes a long, slow drink of wine. Who would Joanna have come here with, then? I don't know how to respond—if I should probe deeper, or drop it completely. I suppose I didn't expect him to be so . . . honest.

For the next thirty minutes, we make small talk over the mouthwatering appetizer and avoid the topic of Joanna completely. Travis is surprisingly attentive, inquiring about my pregnancy and actively listening, which I find rare for a man these days. By the time the meal arrives, he's three glasses down, his smile is widening, and he's digging into his meal without hesitation.

"How is it?" he asks, stabbing his fork in the air toward my salad. "Amazing, right?"

I nod, my mouth exploding with flavor. "Truly is."

"Want to try mine?"

I shake my head to refuse, but he's already loading a fork and lifting it my way. Leaning over the table, he commands, "Here. Give it a try."

Warning bells go off in the back of my brain. I shouldn't be doing this. I shouldn't be here, dining in Joanna's favorite place with Michael's best friend, letting him feed me off his fork. This is wrong.

"Come on," he says, his eyes glinting with kindness. "One taste won't kill you."

On a wild stupid-stupid-stupid impulse, I open my mouth and close my lips around his fork. The taste of broccoli, Kalamata olives, lemon, and spices hits me first, followed by the juicy halibut.

A moan slips out of me. His eyes widen as he quickly pulls back his fork. My body tingles from heat. Or maybe that's shame.

"Thank you," I manage, cheeks burning.

"Best you've ever had?"

"Mm-hmm." My eyes meet his, and I have to look away. "So, how did you and Rachael meet?"

"Mutual friends." He goes back to his plate, pushing chunks of halibut around the china before shoving them in his mouth. "We were in our early twenties and didn't know what the hell we were going to do with the rest of our lives. But we knew we wanted to do it together."

"That's sweet."

"No, it's dumb." After finishing another glass of wine, he goes on. "We were broke with no plans to get us out of debt. This was before I met Michael and Joanna of course, before Harris Financial really took off. Rachael was in school to become a marriage and family therapist, but that didn't pan out. Student loans piled up, and she only did it for a year or so before she bailed, leaving her unemployed and bored out of her mind."

"Why?" I ask, completely riveted by their history. "I mean, why'd she quit? It seems like the perfect career choice for someone so—"

"Nosy?" he finishes with a laugh. "Don't worry, you won't offend me. I know my wife's flaws better than most."

"I was going to say *curious*, but, yes."

And then we're both laughing, and I'm picturing Rachael in her jogging gear, trotting over to the reporters on the day Joanna's body was dragged out of the mud.

"I think she initially chose that path because she wanted to help people who were having problems in their marriages," he tells me, the laughter in his dark eyes dying down. "But after a while, the thrill was gone, and she realized she wasn't really making a difference."

"I wish I had those skills," I confess, leaning back and resting my hand on the curve of my stomach. "To learn someone's most intimate problems and insecurities, then help them turn their life around. It must be so rewarding. I wonder if Rachael misses it?"

"Nah," he says, waving his knife around, "don't go feeling sorry for her. She's the top agent in her company, and she still gets to poke her nose into our neighbors' lives. Only downside is she's not getting paid for it anymore."

I chuckle at that too, and my guard begins to drop. There's an honesty simmering beneath the surface of Travis's intricately tattooed skin. It's startling and . . . raw. I get the feeling I could ask him anything and he'd answer truthfully, unflinchingly. It makes me want to press him about Joanna.

"Wait until you see Rachael work the room at the company anniversary party," he goes on, pushing his plate aside and refolding the napkin in his lap. "She can get anyone to talk about anything, and she loves it. By the end of the night, she's peeled back everyone's layers."

"Count me in," I say. Hopefully by then, Michael and I will have put the matter of the nursery behind us. "When is it?"

"This Saturday."

My smile drops. Michael hasn't mentioned it. Not once. "As in, two days from now?"

"He probably forgot to tell you," Travis blurts, as if he's read my mind. "He's juggling a million things right now. With everything going on, you can't really fault him."

"He owns the company," I say. "He didn't forget."

"Well, it's possible. It's not like he planned it himself."

"Then who did? It wasn't me. This is the first I've heard of it."

He shoves a piece of broccoli into his mouth. "Joanna took care of everything last spring. It's done."

Of course she took care of everything. In her perfect way. Perfect Joanna, who could plan the party of the century. Flawless Joanna, with the enviable home and adorable nursery.

"Travis," I say, feeling like this is my only chance to ask what's really been bothering me, "what do *you* think happened to—"

Something flutters inside me, startling me. "Oh my God." A smile tickles my lips. "I think I just felt—I think that was—I think the baby just moved."

"Really?" Travis grins. "Is this the first time?"

I nod, tears welling in my eyes, as something stirs inside

me again. It's the tiniest movement, a butterfly's wings beating against the walls of my stomach. A slight rolling sensation that happens again . . . and then again. It almost feels like indigestion, but I know it's not. *There*—I feel it again.

"Our baby's moving."

"Can I feel?" Before I can respond, Travis gets up and comes around the table to rest his hand on my stomach. His touch is featherlight, and strangely comforting. "I don't feel anything yet."

"I don't think you'll be able to." Giggling, I glance up, meeting his eyes. "This is—it's, God, I'm so happy! I've been waiting for this moment for so long, wondering what it would feel like. I was starting to fear that maybe something was wrong, but it's not." I caress my stomach over and over again, my fingers bumping into his as tears blur my eyes. "Everything's going to be all right."

"Of course it is." Travis rubs my shoulder. "Why wouldn't it be?"

"I don't know," I ramble, not thinking clearly, or maybe not thinking at all, "because of what happened to Joanna, the way Michael has been so detached from the pregnancy, the detectives snooping around for God knows what, and— *everything*. All of it. Because every time I think something beautiful is finally going to happen in my life, it turns rotten."

"You can't mean that."

"Oh, but I do." Tears stream down my cheeks as something inside me breaks free—a dam to hold back the emotions I'd guarded for so long. "My parents died when I was fifteen. I moved around to three different foster homes before I finally found one where the family truly loved me. At least, that's what I thought until I overheard my 'mother' on the phone telling someone she was looking for a way to get rid of me."

"That's awful." Squeezing me against him, Travis pulls me close. "I'm sorry you had to go through that."

"Through college, I clung to boyfriends who treated me like trash. But this time—this time, with Michael and our baby—everything's going to be perfect. It really is."

"Of course it is." He glides his hand over the curve of my stomach with a delicate touch. "And you deserve everything that's coming your way, Colleen."

Hope and love swell within me, drying my tears. It's so silly of me to be so weepy. I burrow my head into his chest as sheer happiness consumes me. Travis stiffens. I glance up.

"What a surprise," he says, his voice taking a strangely formal tone. "Join us for lunch?"

I go cold as Michael approaches the table and eyes the arm Travis has draped over my shoulder. And the one stroking my stomach. "Michael . . ."

"I got your text." His face is very pale.

Travis removes his arm slowly and stands, motioning for Michael to take his place beside me. "Hungry? I'm sure I can find someone to bring us another menu."

"I'm happy you came," I say, looking up at him. "I'm—"

Michael bends and kisses my cheek. His lips are ice-cold. "How's the salad?"

"Good."

He sits, but doesn't take off his coat or look at me. Tension flows off him in steely waves, and without him saying a word I know I was right. He's furious at me. I shouldn't have come here.

"It's like our waitress has disappeared," Travis mumbles to fill the silence, craning around in his chair. "How far could she have gone?"

"You'll never believe what happened," I say to Michael. "I felt our baby move. Just a second ago. It was magical."

"I bet it was."

He doesn't place a hand on my stomach. He doesn't even smile. His gaze never wavers from Travis. It hurts that he isn't eager to join in the excitement.

"Ah, there's the manager," Travis says, grinning broadly, and then, "Patrick, good to see you. Could you bring another place setting? And a menu?"

"Of course, Mr. Martin," Patrick says as he stops at our table. "It's great to have you back, after so long a hiatus." Patrick nods at Travis, and then glances over Michael. When his gaze reaches mine, he sucks in a clipped breath. "Oh, it's been too long! We're happy to see you two back together, miss." He snaps for the waitress. "I'll have her bring over your usual bottle of red."

"Excuse me?" I furrow my eyebrows in confusion. "Have we met?"

"Wrong—it's not—it's the wrong girl," Travis interjects with a stutter, then stops abruptly, as though he's just said something he shouldn't have.

Patrick shakes his head with a nervous laugh. "Oh, my apologies! I was so sure—what an uncanny resemblance to your Joanna."

"You're *mistaken*," Travis bites out again, harsher this time.

But the damage has already been done. Michael sits stoic as a statue, both of us stunned.

Your Joanna.

Not Michael's, but Travis's.

They were lovers.

"Yes, of course. Of course." Patrick squints theatrically. "I left my glasses in the back. That should teach me. Forgive me, miss. Let me find your waitress."

And then he's gone, retreating into the kitchen. Michael and Travis jolt to their feet in some kind of nonverbal stand-off. I tug on the sleeve of Michael's coat, but he bats my hand away. His breath rasps as if he's having trouble getting air.

"You son of a bitch," Michael seethes, hands clenched into fists. "All this time . . ."

Every eye in the restaurant turns our way. My cheeks burn

with shock and embarrassment as I motion for help from the waitress, who has frozen to a stop. Letting out a groan, Travis removes his wallet, flings out a wad of twenties.

"Time for me to go," he says. "This should cover your lunch. Stay and enjoy. It's on me."

"Arrogant bastard—"

"Colleen," Travis says, ignoring Michael, "it was a pleasure." But his eyes won't meet mine.

Michael twitches, clutches the edge of the table, then tips it over. Glass shatters everywhere. His face is flushed red, and fat veins throb in his neck.

I've never seen him this way.

Without another word, Travis charges out of the restaurant. Patrick tries to speak to him at the door, but Travis pushes past, leaving everyone gaping in his wake.

The waitress and a busboy are there, gathering up shards of glass and china. But I'm watching Michael, terrified at the hard clench of his jaw and the fire in his eyes. He looks possessed, a man consumed by rage. He looks—I hate to think it—like he could *kill*. Michael really is capable of snapping, isn't he? No, I correct my thoughts. He'd never do anything that extreme. I *know* the kind of man he is.

But I don't know what to say to calm him down. There'll be no bringing him back from this ledge.

"Grab your coat," he snarls. "We're leaving."

He leaves me in the booth and storms out of the restaurant.

I sit for a moment and then I stand. I apologize for him, avoid eye contact, take my coat from Patrick at the exit, and slip into the chilly afternoon air.

Michael stands waiting for me. "There's something you should know," he says. He's walking so fast, I can barely keep up. He doesn't seem to care. "I've been waiting for a good time to tell you this, Coll, but there hasn't been one. I suppose this afternoon couldn't get much worse. Might as well get it all out now."

I jog to catch up. "Can we slow down?"

"Do you remember when we first got together, and I told you that Joanna broke up with me by texting? I was telling the truth. But I lied about what she said." He crosses the street without looking, earning a honk from a taxi turning at the light. I wave apologetically, stumbling after him. "She didn't go to stay with her sister in Los Angeles. I told you that because I didn't want to admit the truth—not to anyone."

Anxiety pinballs through my gut. "What'd the message say?"

He stops at the door to his building. "She said the baby wasn't mine. She was leaving me for her lover, so they could start their family together. She never told me who she was sleeping with, but now it's clear—it was Travis. The baby was his."

"Oh my God." I cover my mouth with my hand. I can't stop shivering. "Michael, I'm so sorry."

I don't know whether to run to him, wrap him in my arms, and tell him everything's going to be all right, or give him space to blow off steam. I've never seen him so angry.

"When Joanna first told me she was pregnant, I traced back the date of conception. I was in London on business. Gone for twenty days. I confronted her, asked how that was possible. She said doctors can never know the dates exactly— they must've misjudged the timeline. She told me it happens all the time." His tone was brittle with rage. "Travis might not even know the baby was his. All this time, he never said a goddamn word. Invited us to his home for dinner, walked into this office every damn day . . ."

Relief surges through me, followed swiftly by guilt. Joanna wasn't the perfect wife Michael believed her to be, and now he knows the truth. Part of me is *thrilled* at the idea that her pristine image has been tarnished. But that's wrong of me. Michael loved Joanna once, and loved her passionately, and deep down he might have unresolved feelings. Especially considering all that's happened. Isn't that the reason he's kept the nursery as some kind of shrine—because a part of him is desperately clinging to the good memories he had of Joanna? Was he lying to me when he said Samara was the one pushing him to leave the rooms alone?

"Michael . . ."

"I don't want you seeing Travis ever again."

I swallow a nervous chuckle. "But he lives next door. How are we supposed to—"

"I don't want you seeing him!" Michael explodes, turning on me. He charges a few steps closer, his face twisted with fury. "Do you understand? I *forbid* you to see him!"

"I—I'm sorry, I won't—" I flinch instinctively, backing away, hands up. "I'll do whatever you want."

As if a switch flips, his shoulders slump, and the features of his handsome face soften. He scans the people staring at us on the sidewalk and seems to check himself. "Damn it, don't look at me like that. Come here."

He draws me into his arms and hugs me. He's burning up, the heat from his chest radiating into my cheek. I'm holding my breath, waiting for the fury to surge again. Somewhere in the distance, cars honk, wind rustles the trees and the trash, and business carries on as usual.

"I'm sorry, I shouldn't have lost my temper," he says, tipping my chin up so that my eyes meet his, every trace of anger erased from his tone. "I shouldn't have taken it out on you, sweetheart. Please don't look at me that way, like I broke you."

I don't know what to say, so I keep my mouth shut.

"Look at me." His fingertip brushes my cheek. "I'm sorry."

"It's okay. . . ."

"No, it's unforgivable."

"It is," I agree. "But I forgive you anyway."

He kisses me, hard, and as he pulls back, he ghosts his fingers over my hair. "I still don't want you seeing him anymore."

"Then I won't. I'll do anything to make you happy."

"Did he say anything to you before I got there?" He takes my hand in his and leads me into the lobby. "About me . . . or Joanna?"

"Only that she planned the company party this weekend." It's a bit of a jab, and I know it. "But you haven't mentioned it, so I assume we're not going."

"I'm sorry, it's been crazy lately, and I haven't felt like myself."

"I know what you mean. I haven't felt like myself either. And we haven't felt like us."

"No," he whispers as he punches the elevator button. "We haven't. I think once they figure out who killed her, and this whole investigation goes away, we can finally get back to normal."

Normal.

I'm not sure what that looks like anymore.

"Did you ever make an appointment with the doctor?" he asks.

I nod. "They were able to squeeze me in tomorrow at ten. Will you be able to make it?"

"Honey, you know I can't take off work," he says, stepping into the elevator.

For a crazy moment, I wish I were back in the restaurant, tucked against someone who truly cared about the baby fluttering around in my stomach.

The elevator doors close in front of us, and I'm left staring at a glossy reflection of me and Michael, this man I've loved more than life itself. I'd do anything for him. But side by side this way, we don't look like we fit. He's handsome in his pinstripe suit. The figurehead of the company. My complexion is ashen, my eyes are sunken from lack of sleep, and my hair is a mess. The woman I see in that reflection, in her dress and heels, looks like an imposter.

"The party is six o'clock Saturday night at the distillery, Coll. I'm sorry I didn't tell you sooner, but I've been debating canceling the whole thing. Under the circumstances, that might be best."

"No, don't cancel." I look up at him until he meets my eyes. I can't help but wonder if he sees me—*really* sees me— or if he's like Dean, and Rachael and Travis, and everyone else. If he compares me to Joanna every second of every day and is keenly aware that I fall short. "It'll be nice to have a night out."

"If you're sure it's not too much."

No, the party's not too much. It's everything—and everyone—else. Most of all, it's Joanna. *She's* too much, even in death.

But I can't say that, so I kiss her widower instead.

RACHAEL

I pull into the driveway a little after three o'clock, and fight through waves of reporters to get to my front door. The news crews have been relentless, constantly firing questions about our relationships with Joanna, Michael, and Colleen. Under normal circumstances, I would've waved and smiled, turned my cheek to the ideal angle.

But not today.

He texted Joanna from February through July.

If Travis lied to me about that, who knows how long they were having an affair? It might've been—heaven help me— *years.*

Fuming, I charge up the steps, unlock my door, and practically fall inside before the reporters can formulate a single question. I can't think about makeup or proper answers now. Not at a time like this, when I'm bursting out of my skin.

He lied.

He was seeing Joanna. All that time. Right up until she was killed. He didn't slip up and make a mistake. They weren't merely having fun. *A few trysts.* This wasn't uncontrollable lust. Oh no. This was an everyday, emotional affair. She seduced him, lured him away from me.

At least Joanna got what was coming to her in the end. Stupid bitch.

Now, I have to deal with Travis.

The house is still pristinely clean, just the way we left it this morning. But as I fling my purse onto the counter, a blotchy yellow stain on the granite catches my eye. My heart starts to thud as I stare at it.

That wasn't there before, was it?

After a frantic search through the kitchen cabinets, I'm armed with rubber gloves, a steel bristle pad, and three bottles of cleaners. I get to work fast, spraying the whole counter down. Then I clutch the scrub pad and scour until my fingers burn and my hand aches. That stupid stain won't go away. It's blemishing the flawless swirls of colors in the granite. For the life of me, I can't get it out. I press down harder, scrub faster and faster, putting all my strength behind it.

He texted her frequently. I know what else they did frequently.

On a wild impulse, I jerk open the oven door and wipe the whole thing down. Top to bottom. It looks clean at a glance, but there, near the light, I find a discoloration. It's slight, barely noticeable, but I see it. That means Travis will too. And at the bottom, something must've spilled. It was probably from dinner the other night when Colleen used the oven to keep the catering trays warm.

She was so eager—borderline twitchy, even, jumping at the chance to help me with *something*—and now look what she's done.

I clean furiously, scouring until no trace is left.

He kissed me before bed every night . . . after kissing her.

Every night over dinner, Travis and I talk about our day. He never mentioned texting Joanna. He would've if they were innocent business messages.

It was only a few times. I won't see her again. It's over, Rachael. Stop overreacting.

I can't believe anything he says.

I scrub every last corner of the oven, lashing the sides with the pad. I scrub so violently the oven shakes. My eyes blur with tears.

"Rachael?"

I jerk upright, swiping at my eyes with the back of my wrist. The scent of bleach stings my nose, and I blink back more tears. Travis is standing there, briefcase in hand, his eyes wide. His hair looks windblown, as if he drove back from the city with the windows down. I can't remember the last time I felt carefree enough to roll the windows down.

Did Joanna do those things with him? Did she make him feel that way?

I never used to be this person—the jealous one who doubts everything. I used to be confident and self-reliant. I was never jealous of Joanna or in need of reassurance. My friend was gorgeous and whip-smart, but I wasn't threatened by her.

Then she decided she wanted my husband.

"What are you doing?" Half laughing, Travis sets his briefcase on the counter and bends to peer into the oven. "Did you . . . *clean*?"

Biting back a sarcastic remark, I peel the wet gloves from my hands and toss them into the sink. I really can't be irritated at his surprise. I've never cleaned the oven before, but I had to do something or I was going to splinter apart. Now I'm out of breath and sweating, and no more prepared for this confrontation than I was when I slammed through the door.

"How was your day?" I fire back, leaning back against the counter as I fold my arms over my chest. "Did you meet with the detectives?"

"Not yet. Detective Shaw called and rescheduled. They must've gotten tied up somewhere."

I search the angles of his face, the square line of his jaw, the sculpted edge of his cheekbones, for signs of deception. Because now I can't trust even the smallest of statements.

"They stopped by to see me late this morning," I say, my tone sharp.

"So you were free for lunch then?" He moves around the island and pours himself a gin and tonic. He doesn't offer me one. "Why didn't you call?"

"The afternoon filled up with appointments."

But it doesn't matter. Even if I were free during his break, I wouldn't have called the way I usually do when I'm working out of the office. I couldn't have been in public with him, sitting across a table in some swanky restaurant, chatting as if nothing had gone wrong. I couldn't fake wedded bliss. Not today.

"That's too bad," he says, tipping back his drink. "Would've been nice to see you."

"Really?" I hear the bitterness in my voice.

"Of course. Why do you say that?"

"I don't know. Maybe because I'm not sure I can believe anything that comes out of your mouth anymore."

He sets his glass down with such force, I worry it'll shatter on the granite. "Jesus! What the hell's the matter with you today?"

"They have the phone records, Travis." I swallow down the fear rising inside me. "They know you texted her, and she texted you, for months, right up until the time she was killed."

"Rachael . . ." He takes a step toward me.

"No, don't come any closer." Hands out, I slide along the counter to put space between us. I'm not afraid of him hurting me. I'm afraid of the weakness I'll feel if he gets too close. I'm terrified of losing my reserve, of giving in and letting him win before he's been wounded from battle. I want him to hurt the way I've been hurt, to feel like he, too, is shriveling inside. "You were seeing her behind my back for *months*. How could you do that to me?"

"Rachael, you always knew what was going on—"

"With the others, yes. But not with *her*." My voice trembles, betraying me. "Did I complain when you slept with anyone else? No. I didn't say a word. I let you have your fun, and—"

"And you had yours," he interrupts curtly. He splashes more liquor in his glass.

"Yeah, but we agreed *friends* were off-limits."

He sighs, burying his long, burdened exhale in his second drink.

"That was your rule for this game, and now—Jesus-fucking-Christ, I can't believe you put us in this position." I sweep the hair away from my neck, but it doesn't cool the flash of heat blooming there. "I can't breathe."

"Calm down." He rounds the island, drags me into his arms, and caresses my back. "You're getting all worked up over something that happened last year. What Joanna and I had is over. It's done."

"Because she was *killed*, for Christ's sake!" The laugh that bubbles out of me is borderline hysterical. "And now the police suspect us and—"

"Whoa, whoa—what?" He jerks back, nearly pushing me away, his dark eyes wild. "We're *suspects* now? Did the cops tell you that?"

"No, but it doesn't take a genius to figure it out."

"What'd they say?"

"That you talked to Joanna sometime right before she died."

"Is that all they have?" He paces from the back door to the living room windows and back again, clenching and un-clenching his fists and popping his knuckles. The sound makes my skin crawl. "Those messages could've been about business."

"That's what I tried to tell them."

"And they didn't believe you?"

"Travis, it's not that simple. I don't think you realize how bad this looks. You were sleeping with your boss's wife and were talking to her right up until the end. Once they find out about the affair, they're going to know you had motive."

"What motive could I possibly have?" he snarls.

"You're the jealous lover."

His jaw tightens as if I've hit the nail on the head, and something inside me wilts.

"If that's the case," he says, his voice darkening, "you're my vengeful wife. You don't think they'll try to spin that too?"

I hadn't thought of that. "Travis—should we get a law-yer?"

"No." He takes a loud, labored breath. "Not yet."

Outside, Melissa Mendes fluffs her hair in front of the camera and prepares to go live for the six o'clock news. She's standing on the grassy patch between our home and the Har-rises', her back to us. Without saying a word, Travis wraps his arm around my shoulder and guides me in front of our floor-to-ceiling windows. From here, we'll be caught on camera looking like the worried couple next door.

"We need to stay calm, especially now." His voice is low and soothing, vibrating my head where it rests against his chest. "They're just trying to make us panic, to see how we react when they put pressure on us, but they can twist the story as much as they want. There's nothing to find, right? We did nothing wrong."

I nod against his chest, hesitantly.

"Now kiss me," he says. "And let's give them one hell of a show."

FRIDAY

Two Days Until Colleen's Murder

COLLEEN

Settling into the corner of the couch, I glance out the window at the grove before peeling open the book on my lap. It's *A Study in Scarlet,* the very first Sherlock Holmes novel. I've read it a dozen times, and don't know why I felt the need to pull the classic from my shelf this morning. But when I flip through the pages and begin skimming, it comes to me.

The cryptic word *Rache* written in blood. It'd been a clue in the classic Sherlock tale—crimson letters scrawled on the walls of two different crime scenes. Although the police had been stumped, Sherlock deciphered the message. It wasn't short for a woman's name, as officers had rashly presumed.

As Sherlock swiftly pointed out, *Rache* was German for "revenge."

If Rachael knew about Travis's affair with Joanna, she'd have a motive for killing Joanna, too. Rachael might've been enraged, seeking vengeance, and . . .

Dean whistles off-key from the kitchen as he whisks together Joanna's favorite breakfast, distracting me. I've come downstairs early, before my coffee's ready, and it's irked him. He hasn't said as much, but I can tell by the tightness of his whistle. I know the less Dean sees of me the better, but this morning Michael's home, and going into work late, and I wanted the two of us to eat together. He said he would meet me downstairs in a few minutes. That he had to take care of something first.

From my position in the living room, I can clearly see Dean leaning against the kitchen island as he cuts through a handful of greens. He's efficient with that knife, isn't he? And he was close to Joanna.

Suddenly, as if the clouds part in my brain, I'm noticing suspects and motives everywhere. Dean and Joanna. Were *they* having an affair? Clearly they were close. It's possible. If there's one thing I've learned from reading Sherlock Holmes, it's that *anyone* could be the culprit.

Michael leans over and plants a kiss on my forehead. "I have a surprise for you."

I spin around, curling my legs beneath me. "Surprise?"

"I know you never needed a car in the city, but I was thinking it'd be a good idea to get you one," he says, rifling through his briefcase. "Especially since you're alone here most days."

"Wow," I say. A car wouldn't be such a bad idea. It could be nice. On days I feel trapped among Joanna's things, I could take a drive and escape for a while. "What's the surprise? Are we going car shopping after my doctor's appointment?"

"That'd be an awful waste of time." He pulls a single key out of his bag and hands it over. "Considering I already have the perfect car for you."

All goes quiet in the kitchen.

Confused, I turn the key over in my palm. "You bought me a car?"

"Not exactly. You still have your driver's license, don't you?"

"Of course, but—"

"Come on then, follow me." He opens the back door and spreads his arm toward the private, circular drive. "She's yours if you want her."

I follow him onto the limestone steps and stop short, staring at the midnight-blue Lexus coupe parked in the center of the drive. If it's not brand-new, it must've been kept in the garage, because the paint is immaculate. Shiny and perfect. Not a dent on it. Two doors. Sloping hood. It looks exactly like the kind of car all of the women in this neighborhood would drive. It's luxurious and sporty, and probably cost more than I would have made in two years at his company.

"You're not serious," I say, gulping air as my heart races. "Michael . . . is it a—"

"Convertible," he finishes for me. "Thought you might like that feature."

"But I don't understand. You said you didn't buy me a car."

"I didn't. I bought it years ago, for me, but never drove it much. It sat covered in the far garage stall until I hired someone to come out yesterday and tune it up. They detailed it and filled up the tank, too. It's ready to go."

I can hear reporters prattling in the distance, beyond the curving drive and security gate. I'm thankful for the privacy back here; yet something is wrong. The hairs on the back of my neck stand on end.

"Colleen?" He caresses my arm. "You don't like it."

That's the last thing I want him to think. I plaster on a smile. "Of course I do, sweetheart. How could I not? Thank you so much."

"Good. It's yours then." He stoops to kiss my lips. "Don't forget to ask the doctor about the fatigue and mood swings you've been having. We need to make sure everything's on track with you and that baby."

That baby.

"I'm sure everything's fine, but I'll ask anyway so you

don't worry." I lean into him as he envelops me in a goodbye hug. He smells so good, the scent of his cologne a deep, woodsy musk. My heart flutters as I close my eyes. "Michael, I wish you'd come with me to the doctor's."

He drops his hands, and I go cold.

"You know I can't," he says. "If you want the kind of life where you can stay home in Ravenwood and raise this baby, I need to support us. That means I can't skip work for every doctor appointment."

"Not even one?"

"Don't beg."

"But I might be getting an ultrasound today." I keep my voice soft. Light. No pressure, even though I'm dying for him to come with me. The key burns in my hand. "Wouldn't you like to see our baby? Or hear its heartbeat?"

That might make this pregnancy real for him. He might start to think of the baby as his. Then, he could focus on everything we have to look forward to in our future and put Joanna, her affair with Travis, and the loss of their baby behind him.

I wonder if the detectives have come any closer to figuring out the reason Joanna wasn't pregnant when they discovered her body. The thought of the possibilities makes my stomach turn. Maybe I should stop by the station to check in. We're certainly not receiving any updates from the news crews camping outside.

"I would go with you," he says, "but someone has to provide for this family, and nothing gets done at the office if I'm not there. You know that."

"I know." He micromanages the business so obsessively, I often worry about the strain it puts on him. "I'll text when I'm leaving the appointment to let you know what the doctor said."

"I'd like that." Michael kisses me again, this time on the cheek. "Love you, Coll."

"Love you back."

"Enjoy your new car."

I watch as he disappears into the garage. Minutes later, the door opens, and he backs out, waving before disappearing down the drive. As I pocket the key and plop back onto the couch, Dean resumes his whistling of a song I don't recognize. I hold the book in my lap and stroke the cover as my gaze lingers on the scraggly branches of the cypress trees. Out front, the die-hards and cynics still linger, parked across our street twenty-four hours a day, hoping to get the first scoop or prove their sinister hunches right.

"If it makes you feel any better," Dean says from the kitchen, "he didn't go to any of Joanna's doctor appointments either."

I should ignore him and go back to my book, but I'm morbidly curious about Joanna, the constant presence in this house and in Michael's heart.

"How do you know?" I ask nonchalantly, closing the book and setting it aside.

His lips pinch together as if he's just bitten into something sour. "She told me everything. He's not the type to get involved in things like that. Never was. But I'm sure you know that by now."

I'm not going to let Dean drop a bomb like that and then return to scrubbing potatoes for dinner. Sliding off the couch, I move into the kitchen and head straight for the coffeepot.

"No, I've got it," he says, cutting me off. "You sit. Take a load off."

This time, when he reaches for the vanilla creamer, I stop him.

"Just a shake of cinnamon," I say firmly. "No sugar or cream. Please."

He eyes me wearily but fulfills my request. After sliding the mug over, he goes back to prepping. Snatching a handful of fresh herbs from the fridge, he slaps them on the cutting board and chops feverishly. He grates lemon zest, then roughly dices everything together, all with increasing speed and force. Much more of this, and he's going to bend the knife. Or slice a finger off.

I dare not hope.

The boldness of the coffee hits me hard, and I let my thoughts fly. "Why is it such a stretch for you to realize Joanna and I are two completely different people, with completely different relationships, who want completely different things?"

"Oh, believe me, the differences are stark. I notice them every day," he replies through clenched teeth. Removing two salmon fillets from the fridge, he slams them on a second cutting board. "But old habits die hard. Forgive me if I continue to serve you her coffee."

The differences are stark?

Isn't that what I've wanted from the start? To be my own person, living out of Joanna's ever-present shadow? But I don't know whether to take what he said as a compliment or a criticism.

"Take that scowl off your face," he spits, raising the knife. "It's not pretty."

Definitely a criticism.

"Michael and I are happy," I say. "We're so unbelievably in love. I'm sure you've seen it from the short amount of time I've been here. Being different from Joanna must not be so bad after all."

"Mr. Harris is one of the most dedicated men I know. He's thoughtful and charismatic. And he would do anything for his family." Dean slashes through the bodies of the fish. Six equally spaced incisions. "But there's another side to Mr. Harris I don't think you've seen yet. A darker side."

I try to laugh it off. "Are we talking about the same Michael?"

He glares, deadpan. "He's got a switch that flips. Joanna

used to talk to me about what would happen if she questioned his authority. He'd practically lose his mind."

"I don't think you can compare—"

"According to Joanna," he goes on, stuffing seasonings and slices of lemon into the fish's gaping lacerations, "they'd love hard and fight harder. Get into nasty screaming matches, those two. In the mornings, after their big blowouts, he'd send her long-stemmed red roses. One dozen for every year they'd been together. As if that could make her forget what had happened. He never understood her."

"Ahem." The voice sounds behind us, and Dean and I both freeze. "I hardly think Mr. and Mrs. Harris's marriage problems are on this morning's menu." It's Samara, hands on her hips, hair drawn back behind her ears, her thin lips set in a disapproving line. "What would Mr. Harris think if he knew you two were in here gossiping about him?"

"We're not—" I start.

"Oh, don't make excuses to her, Miss Roper. Threats are her thing," Dean retorts, returning his focus to the fish. "I'd forgotten that the words that come out of my mouth are *also* under her scrutiny."

As Samara storms out of the kitchen, mumbling something about people needing to mind their own business, I get up to follow. She can't tell Michael that I was bad-mouthing him and Joanna. It'd make me look awful.

"Samara, wait," I call out, and catch up to her as she enters the library. I shut the heavy doors behind us and watch as she begins straightening papers on Michael's desk, refusing to look at me. "I wasn't bad-mouthing Michael, I swear. Dean was talking about how he would buy Joanna flowers when they—"

"I heard every word of what you were saying in there."

I pause, waiting for some kind of reassurance that she won't say anything to Michael about it. But it never comes, and now I feel like I have to patch things up.

"I was talking about how much I love Michael, that's all."

"And what was Dean saying?"

"He might've mentioned how tumultuous his relationship with Joanna was."

She piles books into a stack at the corner of the desk with a huff. "What no *man* in this house seems to understand is that Joanna was complex. One of a kind. She was lonely. Desperate to talk to someone who understood her. During one of the toughest times of her life, there were only two people who actually took the time to listen—me and her counselor, that's it. 'Tumultuous.' Humph. See if he could go through what she went through and not lose his mind."

I swallow hard. "Go through what?"

She narrows her eyes at me. She's a dumpy woman, burly, and very plain. "You know why there was no baby in the ground when they found her, don't you?" When I shake my head, stunned, she pauses, chewing her lip, as if that'll help her decide how much to trust me. "She miscarried the baby. Back in May. She was three months pregnant at the time. Holed herself up in the second master until she had the strength to face the world again. I'm surprised Mr. Harris didn't tell you."

"It must've slipped his mind." As the words escape me, I want to slap myself. How could he possibly have forgotten to mention that his wife miscarried his child? "We try not to talk about the past," I say, truthfully.

Removing a cloth hanging out of the front pocket of her apron, Samara strides to the bookshelves and begins dusting the spines. "Joanna didn't tell him at first, of course. Mr. Harris wanted a child so badly, the news would've crushed him. And their marriage was already veering off a cliff— Joanna didn't want this bump in their plans to set him off. It was horrible, the way she had to go through all of it alone. Bless the Lord for her counselor, who helped her find God before the end. At least now she won't be alone in death, the way she was in life."

"Counselor?" No one mentioned Joanna had been seeing a shrink.

"Last summer, she was seeing someone at a women's clinic in the city." She swipes the surface of the shelves clean. "She had to attend four counseling sessions before she could be medically cleared."

"What does that mean? Cleared for what?" I sink into the leather chair in front of the hearth. "Was Joanna sick?"

"I'm not sure."

"Come on," I urge. "You were closer to Joanna than anyone. She must've told you."

She glances at me over her shoulder as she continues to wipe down the shelves. "Believe it or not, I have no idea. I asked her many times. But her reason for going to the clinic was one thing she seemed determined to keep private."

"Well, I'm sure the detectives will find out soon enough. They seem to uncover everything."

"They won't find out about the clinic. Not on their own, anyway." With her back still to me, Samara shakes her head emphatically. "I don't know what was going on with her, but she was worried about people finding out. When I suggested seeing someone at a specialized clinic rather than her usual doctor, and using a false name, she was all for it."

My brain begins to swim with the new information. "Does anybody else know? Michael or Dean?"

"No, Joanna made me swear not to tell anyone. Only reason she told me was because she needed someone to drive her to the appointments. But I probably should say something now, shouldn't I? Now that she's . . . gone?"

"If you think it'll help them find the murderer, yes," I offer, "because if you know something and keep it to yourself, they might think you had something to do with her death."

And now that Samara has told me, I should go to the police with the information, too.

"I'll consider it," Samara says. "Anyway, all that matters is that God was with Joanna in the end."

"From what Michael tells me—I mean, what I heard him tell the police—Joanna was an atheist."

"She was. But the counselor changed her." She removes a few books and, scowling, replaces them somewhere a few shelves lower. "By the end, Joanna was starting to believe in religion. It helped her heal."

Yes, it's nice that God forgives everyone. Including liars and adulterers.

I keep that nugget to myself.

"How are you holding up in all of this?" I ask, trying to show Samara I'm compassionate and caring—and that maybe I can be as close to her as Joanna was.

"This whole tragedy has been terribly rough on me," she admits, softening slightly. "And there are times when I'm overwhelmed with grief, like Mr. Harris."

Is Michael truly overwhelmed with grief? The blowout with Travis was the first time I'd seen him lose control since we heard the news—but that was anger, not sadness.

"There's only one thought that gets me through each day," she continues, standing on a chair to reach the highest shelf. "One thing that keeps me going."

"What's that?" I ask, because I know she expects me to.

"Joanna won't be alone long. Everyone dies someday." She glances at me, and the malice in her eyes makes me rest my hand against the swell of my belly. "Everyone—including you."

DETECTIVE SHAW

Friday.

Patel's deadline for arresting Michael Harris.

Thankfully, he's decided to hold off. He can no longer deny that there are too many wild cards in this case. Too many things we need to take into account. Mandy McKnight's revelation about Travis and Joanna's affair. The strange brevity of the texts between them. The possibility that Dean might've been having an affair with Joanna, too. Michael's name should top the suspect list, but there are other moving parts to this puzzle.

"We'll know more Sunday," Patel decided. "After the toxicology report comes back."

He's banking on the fact that a large amount of Vicodin and Valium will show up in Joanna Harris's bloodstream. If that happens, it'll be difficult not to think Harris had something to do with his wife's murder. But if Patel's wrong, and the test shows she's clean, what conclusion will he draw next? Will he still believe Joanna was killed by her husband? I'm not sure.

Personally, I'm not surprised to hear about their extramarital activities. I knew the Harrises were hiding things—doesn't everyone?—and now their secrets are coming to light.

I've spent the last forty-eight hours turning my attention from Joanna's husband to Travis and Dean. Although we don't have concrete evidence showing that Dean and Joanna were having an affair, the tug in my gut warns me that Dean and Joanna's relationship was more than platonic. We've received court orders to release their phone records too. All Patel needed was to prove that their phone records were relevant and material to our investigation. It wasn't difficult to do. And now we've put tails on both of them. It's critical to the investigation that they don't know we're closing in. We want both men to proceed with everything as normal, so when they slip—and eventually, they all do—we've got them.

Rolling my chair closer to my desk, I shake the computer mouse to bring the desktop to life, and open windows that'll reveal the phone carrier information once more. I create one segment for each of the twisted personalities on that street: Michael, Dean, Travis, Rachael, and Joanna.

With a frustrated sigh, I rest my head in my hands and go over the information again. And again.

Phone calls or texts between Dean Lewis and Joanna Harris are nonexistent. All contact with the chef was made through Michael's phone. Looks like Dean was another aspect of Joanna's life Harris controlled—or attempted to. Likewise, there are no calls between Travis and Joanna. But we knew that already.

I must be missing something.

Tapping my fingers against the mouse, I scan the text messages between Joanna and Travis.

> Would you and Michael like to come over next weekend?
> Are you and Michael planning on attending the
>   conference in Seattle?

What was so important about those trivial questions? I double-check the time stamps.

An idea sparks.

Rather than studying texts from Joanna and Travis, I turn my attention to those between Travis and his wife. I note the days Rachael told him she had to work late. At least once a week for the entire length of the spring season, there was some piece of property that needed to be shown in the evening. Pulling up a split screen, I cross-check those against the dates Travis texted Joanna.

They match up perfectly.

On at least a dozen different occasions, Rachael texted her husband telling him she wouldn't be home until late. Minutes—sometimes seconds—later, he'd text Joanna and ask her a seemingly innocent question.

> Has Rachael called you about dinner plans?

Each time, Joanna had texted back a single word: *yes* or *no*.

After that, they didn't communicate until the next day

Rachael had to work late. Not a brilliant code, but one that apparently kept their affair hidden for months.

"Sneaky bastards," I mutter, studying the timeline.

Their final secret rendezvous was on July fifteenth, the night the police were dispatched to Ravenwood. Mandy Mc-Knight claims she heard Rachael threaten to kill Joanna the next morning at Pilates, which was the last known sighting of our victim. Had Rachael caught Joanna and Travis in the act?

"Hell hath no fury like a woman scorned," I murmur, pulling up as much information on Rachael as I can.

I skim through her history at a breakneck pace, sliding screens aside and expanding others. Rachael Mary-Magdalene Martin. Born and raised in Sausalito. Parents separated young. Apartment lease filed in the city when she was eighteen years old. Arrested at nineteen for driving while intoxicated. Warrant for failure to appear in court. License revoked and reinstated twice over the next few years. Married to Travis Martin in St. Patrick's Catholic Church on Mission Street.

Catholic church.

Rachael *Mary-Magdalene* Martin.

Exhausted as I am, I feel my adrenaline starting to spike. I fish my phone out of my pocket and call Patel.

"It may be just a hunch," I say when he picks up on the first ring, "but we need a deputy tailing *both* of the Martins."

COLLEEN

After my talk with Samara in the library, I spend the next twenty minutes putting on a comfortable outfit—leggings with a cute tunic—and styling my hair. I'm hyper-aware of movement in my stomach, but haven't felt anything since my lunch with Travis. I'm sure the baby's fine, but I wish he or she would move more.

As soon as the baby's born, Michael and I will be linked forever, and Joanna should be gone from our lives completely. I won't have to wonder if I'm doing everything as well as she did, because we'll be in new territory. She never got to experience being a mother, after all, so everything I do will be my way. I'm hoping Michael will let us hire a new staff as soon as the investigation is over. Dean and Samara might be the reason Michael can't shake Joanna's memory. I won't have them turn Michael against me.

I grab the car key and exit through the back door. The Lexus is waiting for me in the back driveway, a glittery shade of the most beautiful blue I've ever seen. It's been so long since I've been behind the wheel of a car, I don't even know if I remember how to drive.

"God," I mumble, pressing the unlock button, "please don't let it have a manual transmission."

It's automatic, thank the Lexus Lords. Sliding inside, I'm swaddled in the rich, strong smell of expensive leather. The air is stuffy—definitely not the fresh scent of a new car—but the seat cradles my body comfortably. There isn't much room between the seat and the steering wheel. Whoever sat here last must've been short. Reaching to the floorboard between my legs, I search for the adjustment.

My fingers bump into something small and round, and send it rolling over the floor mat. Without thinking, I pick it up and turn the tube over in my palm. Lipstick. Giorgio Armani Rouge Ecstasy. The color? "Diva."

The air in the car becomes sweltering and too thin to breathe. I pop the top off the lipstick. The color is bright red, as a diva would demand. And the tip is indented from being molded against someone's lip.

Joanna.

Barely breathing, I brush my thumb over the angled tip, and wonder how many times she held this tube in her hand and pressed it against her lips. I smash the waxy film between my forefinger and thumb and smear the color over my skin. Her lipstick wasn't on the passenger seat or hidden away in the console. No, it'd been left on the driver's side.

This car was hers.

And suddenly I don't know whether to cry or scream or beat my head against the steering wheel until I can't think about Joanna anymore. It's too much. She's saturated everything in Michael's life. Even the air in this car is stale because she breathed it first. I shove the lipstick in the glove compartment and close my eyes.

Holding back the impending hysterics, I slam the door closed and crank the key in the ignition. The car whirs to life, purring as I put it into gear, circle the drive, and head out through the tunnel of trees. I can almost envision Joanna's manicured fingers curling over the steering wheel as mine are now. I can picture her glancing into the rearview mirror, checking on the baby that'd be buckled there.

Every minute of the drive into Half Moon Bay is torturous. I keep measuring my movements against how Joanna might've driven this car. When Dr. Souza's building appears in a complex on the right, I almost miss it.

Parked in a spot close to the entrance, I tilt my head back and take a few deep breaths.

Joanna's gone.

It's my time now, to focus on our baby.

Leaning over, I jerk the glove compartment open and steal the lipstick from inside. And as I glance into the sun-visor mirror, I smooth the color over my lips. I won't be afraid of overstepping my boundaries or stepping on her memory. This is *my* life now.

Diva *is* a great shade. I think I'll wear it better.

I pucker at my reflection and toss the lipstick into my purse.

With newfound confidence, I exit Joanna's car and enter the ob-gyn's office. Expectant mothers in all stages of pregnancy fill nearly every chair. I can't wait until I'm like that woman across from me, full-bellied and glowing radiantly. Or that one, in the corner, who looks as if she's about to pop any second. I'm deep in a *Cosmopolitan* article titled "Keeping Your Man Happy" when the television above the reception desk catches my eye.

Melissa Mendes's face fills the screen. "The investigation into the Point Reina murder is in full swing. Detectives have brought in Joanna Harris's husband, Michael, and his new girlfriend, Colleen Roper, for questioning."

"Oh no," I say on an exhale as I lean forward, heart racing.

The footage cuts to Detective Shaw. "We're working closely with Michael Harris," he says dryly, "who is just as eager to discover who killed his wife as we are."

Have they connected the dots yet? Do they know Travis had more than enough motive to kill her? And that Rachael did, too? I should stop by the station after the appointment and tell them what I've learned. The sooner this is put to rest, the better.

The film cuts back to Melissa Mendes. "We're keeping a close eye on the developments in this case as the truth about Michael and Joanna Harris's marriage unfolds."

The chipper reporter summarizes the basics about the case until my name is called and I'm weighed in. It's not long before the doctor knocks on the door and lets himself in.

"Colleen," he says, closing the door behind him. He's forty-something, thin as a rail, glasses perched halfway down his narrow nose. "How are you holding up?"

"Good," I answer immediately, shifting my weight on the exam table. "I felt the baby move on Thursday, and it was amazing."

He frowns. "No, I mean, how are you holding up with everything else? From what I hear, you and your husband have been under a lot of pressure lately."

How does my doctor know Michael? He's never accompanied me to any appointments. And the medical records are under *my* name, not his. It's from the news, I realize with chagrin. Our faces have probably been featured on most news stations around the country.

"Oh," I say, feeling my shoulders slump. But a part of me is pleased he assumes Michael and I are married. "You heard about the investigation."

"Hard not to."

"I suppose everyone knows by now." He stares blankly at me, and I realize he wants me to continue. "We'll be fine. Everything should die down in a few months."

I wince when I hear my words. Poor choice. Stupid of me.

"Have you been sleeping?" he asks, checking my folder.

"It's getting better, but on the whole, not much. I get so tired at night, I can't help but crash on the couch. And I can't seem to find the energy to do, well, anything."

I mean that I don't have energy for sex, but I'm not sure if he picks up my subtlety.

"Fatigue is common in the first trimester, though it can continue through the entire pregnancy." He hugs the folder against his chest and nudges his glasses up his nose. "It's possible that hormonal changes might be responsible for the exhaustion you're feeling. Iron-deficiency anemia can also cause fatigue, but as long as you're still taking your iron supplement, you should be fine there. We'll do a test that'll monitor the level of iron in your blood, along with a handful of others that are routine at this point. Those should give you some answers, though I'm not concerned. If you're feeling anxious or stressed, that can also cause you to be overwhelmed and exhausted at the end of the day."

"I don't know why a murder investigation revolving around my boyfriend would make me anxious or stressed," I say, forcing a smile.

"Ah, your boyfriend. Pardon my mistake earlier. I'm not

sure why I assumed you were married." He doesn't smile back. "Have you talked to him about how you're feeling?"

I pause too long, and I fear he sees through me. "Not much. This is affecting him too. He's having a hard time."

Dr. Souza nods. "I imagine the grief would be unbearable."

Grief. There's that word again. I suppose Michael must be grieving for Joanna, but the only time I saw him shed tears over her was the first day we spoke with the detectives.

"Have you been nauseous?" Dr. Souza asks.

"No, thank heavens. Not since the beginning of the first trimester."

"That's good. Have you had any spotting since your last appointment?"

"Nothing."

"All of that is wonderful news, Colleen." He pulls a rolling cart from the corner and lets it rest beside the bed. A large machine with a screen fills the width of the cart. "Why don't you lie down?"

I do as instructed and pull up my shirt, grinning. This is the moment I've been waiting for. He squeezes a tube filled with cool gel over my stomach, then goes to work smearing it around with the wand.

"Michael have to work today?" he asks. I guess Michael has been in the headlines so much lately, everyone feels they can call him by his first name.

I nod, watching the screen for signs of our baby. I see black-and-white splotches, but no shapes that make sense.

"It's too bad he couldn't make it," Dr. Souza says.

At that, I feel my smile drop. He presses a button on the machine. I hear a muffled *thwump-thwump-thwump,* and my heart leaps.

"Is that it?"

"Your baby's heartbeat. Yes."

Tears well in my eyes. I wish Michael were here to see this, to experience it with me. It's a miracle. It's everything. And he's missing it.

"There is your baby," Dr. Souza says, pressing gently on my stomach with the wand. "It's a good size, growing nicely. There's the heart. Everything looks great so far."

He explains the phases of our baby's development as he presses buttons on the machine, snapping photos and sliding the wand around. But I can't take my eyes off the grainy image—my baby. There's the head and stomach. Is that an arm or leg? A tiny circle—its heart—flutters. My chest blooms with warmth. I'm so happy, so in love with this moment, but still, Michael's missing.

Someone bangs on the door, and a nurse pushes her head inside. "Doctor, there's someone here to see . . ."

Her voice fades as the door swings open.

Michael rushes inside, his eyes wide and worried. "Did I miss it?"

I smile, tears rolling down my cheeks now. "No, you didn't miss anything. You're just in time. But what are you doing here? I thought you had to work."

Commandeering the swiveling stool beside me, he leans over and takes my hand. "I got halfway there before I realized I was being an idiot. I can't miss this, and I'm—is that . . . ?" We listen to the rhythmic pulsing of the baby's heart echo through the room. "That's it, isn't it? That's our baby."

My heart bursts, right then and there, and I rest my hand on his cheek. "Yeah. That's our baby."

"And here is your baby's first picture." Dr. Souza moves the wand over my stomach.

"That's the head," Michael gasps, staring at the screen. "Look at that, Colleen. Look, he's perfect. Is that his hand? Is he sucking his thumb?"

Our tiny baby holds his hand to his mouth. "Looks that way," Dr. Souza tells us.

"He?" I ask Michael. "What if it's a girl?"

He squeezes my hand. "Then she'll wrap me around her little finger the way you have, and I'll love her for it."

This is the first time I've heard him talk about the baby this way, with tenderness in his eyes and a grin on his face, and it's more than my heart can take. The tears keep coming. Michael catches them with his thumb and brushes them away.

"Would you like to know the sex of the baby?" Dr. Souza asks softly.

Before blurting out my answer, I look to Michael. His cheeks are pale, his eyes locked on the blurry image on the screen.

"What do you think?" I ask him. "Do we?"

He nods eagerly, and I'm thrilled we're on the same page.

Dr. Souza maneuvers the wand again. "From the looks of it, you're having a boy."

"I knew it!" Michael exults, and then kisses me. "A boy!"

After letting us ogle the images for another few minutes, Dr. Souza shuts the machine down. He shows us a roll of black-and-white photos printed on thin, glossy paper.

"I'll take those," Michael says, grinning wide, as he holds them up to study them. "The baby's first photo shoot. Unbelievable."

Yes, it is. Just when I thought I was going to be alone in all of this, going solo to my pregnancy appointments and keeping the joys and anxieties to myself, Michael shows up and makes everything right again.

It isn't possible that this man mistreated Joanna the way Dean and Samara suggested. This man is thoughtful, caring, and so deserving of a loving family. This man doesn't have a violent bone in his body.

"Come on." Michael lifts his eyes from the gorgeous photos of our son, and takes my hand again. "Let's go home and find a place for these."

SATURDAY

The Day Before Colleen's Murder

DETECTIVE SHAW

After Patel declined my request to add Rachael Martin to the growing list of suspects to follow, I decided to take matters into my own hands. If he couldn't afford the manpower to tail her, I'd do it myself. Though I'd never tell him, I don't think his decision had anything to do with the number of officers at the station.

He's already made up his mind about this case. He doesn't want to consider another option.

Nevertheless, I was at the station before dawn. I scooped up the keys to an unmarked cruiser, grabbed a quick cup of coffee, and made the short drive to Cypress Street. I parked a few houses down from the Martins', and waited for the excitement of the day to begin.

Despite the news vans still parked along the side streets, Point Reina felt abnormally quiet. Shortly before eight, a Mustang rounded the corner and skidded to a stop in front of Ravenwood. Dean exited the car and removed a few reusable grocery bags from the trunk before making his way inside. I thought the staff had Saturdays off. . . .

Usually, when the sun shows its face between storms, Point Reina is alive with activity. Especially on weekends. Most residents take advantage of the break in the weather and hit the beach. Dog walkers hike through the grove. Housekeepers whisk in and out of front doors, brooms and mops under their arms. Private chefs carry heaping bags of groceries into immaculate homes. Women in leggings strut down the sidewalk, pushing babies in strollers with one hand and chugging Starbucks with the other. But the parade seems to have been called off today, and somehow everyone but me received the memo.

When the clock on the dash clicks over to noon, I tip back my coffee cup and drink the last cold drops of breakfast. I should've brought some food to tide me over. I suppose my eagerness—or frustration, perhaps—overruled my logic. Trying to ignore the growling in my stomach, I scan the street.

Rachael's Porsche Carrera, red as a cherry with the sun beating on it, is parked in her driveway. Travis's car is either in the garage where I can't see it, or he's not home. Dean's Mustang is still parked in front of Ravenwood. Strange . . .

Exiting the cruiser, I head down the sidewalk toward the Martins' glass home. Why they'd want a house where everyone could see what was happening at all hours of the day, even in their most relaxed moments, is beyond me.

Today, though, their transparency suits my needs.

I keep my pace slow as I walk by and peek inside. Rachael is curled up on one of the big couches, blond hair spilling over the edge of a pillow, a white blanket pulled up to her chin. A wine glass rests on the table in front of her, and even from here I can detect the blood-red remnants of her drink pooling at the bottom. A little early to be hitting the bottle, I muse. She must've had a rough Friday night.

Movement near the grove catches my eye. It's Colleen, striding down the steps that lead to the beach. I almost call out to her, but something warns me not to. Another glance into the Martins' home tells me Rachael is still crashed on the couch. I'm here to keep tabs on her, not Colleen, but what are the chances she'll wake up in the next few minutes?

I follow Colleen, and run through all the case's contradictions. Gold necklace with a religious symbol around her neck. *Atheist.* Struck in the back of the head. *No murder weapon.* Everyone loved her. *But someone wanted her dead.*

Perhaps Patel is right. Perhaps I'm looking at the facts too closely to see any of them clearly. Studying the trees instead of the forest.

I let my attention drift into the enormous canopy of the Monterey cypress grove. Killing time while I waited this morning, I did a quick Google search on my cell and learned that there are only two natural Monterey cypress groves in the world. The trees need moist weather and near-constant fog, which makes Point Reina a perfect fit. On days like today, when the sun shines through the tangled green canopy, it's peaceful. Other days, like the day Joanna Harris's body was discovered, dense fog wraps around the spindly branches, and the forest becomes eerie. As if something evil is lurking in it, beyond the line of sight.

Moving toward the edge of the cliff, I peer down onto the narrow stretch of beach below. The sand is empty except for Colleen bending near the water's edge. Her back is to me. She picks up something small and chucks it into the waves. Her blue dress whips around her, catching around her beautiful legs as she repeats the motion again and again. She's barefoot. Her dark hair flies about her face. Her belly is really starting to swell now; it won't be long until she's holding a baby in her arms.

Zigzagging down the wooden stairs, I call her name into the wind.

She turns, her face glowing. Then her shoulders slump as if she's disappointed that I've ruined her alone time. "Detective Shaw! I wasn't expecting to see you here."

"I could say the same for you." I stand firm on the bottom stair, mere inches from the sand. "Are you headed back up?"

Cradling a hand beneath her belly, she picks up a rock, analyzes its curves, then throws it into the sea. "I don't think so. Michael called Dean in today, and he's not finished yet. He's roasting lamb for a late lunch. Joanna's favorite, of course."

There's an unmistakable chill to her tone.

"Can we talk?"

"Sure," she agrees easily. But she strides in the other direction, down the beach toward the tide pools.

"Damn it," I mumble, staring at the sand.

With a groan, I heel off my shoes at the bottom of the stairs, roll off my socks, and shove them into the toes of the shoes. I fold up the bottom of my slacks until they're bunched at the knees. And then I head down, letting my feet sink into the plush mounds of sand. It's warm on my feet, and although the heat feels good, the damn sand has already worked its way between my toes.

I catch up with Colleen minutes later. She doesn't seem bothered by the sand at all. It's covering her feet and ankles, inching up her calves. Hand protectively cupping her stomach, she crouches at the water's edge and picks up another rock. I stay quiet, watching her roll it in her palm. It's white and smooth, with a faint purple marking around its edge.

"Purple is a strange color to find out here," she says, looking up at me. I keep forgetting how very pretty she is. "What do you think caused it?"

"The algae. That rock was most likely chipped off a boulder, and it banged against another rock covered in the stuff. It's smooth because of the beating it's taken." I'd learned that fact from Karen—she loved the beach. She found the ocean calming and peaceful. I've always found the sand a pain and the water too cold, too turbulent.

Colleen makes a small, satisfied sound. "Its beauty comes from its struggle."

"I suppose you could look at it like that."

Karen used to say the flattest, smoothest rocks skipped the best. I find a rock of my own to throw into the water.

"I can relate to this little guy." She holds the purple-stained rock in her hand, stroking her fingers over its curves. She doesn't look at me. "You've looked into my background, haven't you? You know what I'm talking about."

"I know you grew up in a series of foster homes. That's about all."

Even though I know a little bit more, I don't divulge it now. I'd rather hear what she has to say about her past. People reveal the skeletons in their closets when they feel trusting and unguarded.

"It was hard without my parents," she says. "It's hard to explain to someone how important it is to feel wanted, to feel loved unconditionally, unless that person has felt the same void."

"I'm sorry," I offer, because I know too well the void she's talking about.

I pick up another rock. This time, I hand it to her. A peace offering of sorts.

She smiles sweetly as the wind sweeps tendrils of hair back from her face. She's definitely a beauty—I can see what Michael sees in her. There's lightness to her. A spark gleaming in her eyes.

"Adversity must've taught you to be strong," I say.

"You would think so, wouldn't you?" She pauses, and then, "But I was never strong enough to tell the difference between a good guy and one who wanted to hurt me." She flings the rock I'd given her into the water. "I walked an awful, broken road to get to Ravenwood."

"Does Mr. Harris know about your past?"

"Michael knows the basics, and that's enough. From the start, we made a conscious decision to keep the past behind us and only focus on the present."

If Michael beat his wife to death and buried her across the street, he happened upon the perfect woman to replace her—one who didn't want anyone digging into her past, either.

"Are you happy?" I ask without thinking. The personal nature of the question surprises me. I'm equally surprised by my desire to know the answer.

"I am." She eyes me carefully before stooping down to pluck another rock from the sand. "I've known from the moment I met Michael that his heart rules him. Morally, he's solid, right to his core. He treats me like I'm special, and I've never felt that, not once in my life. And I can offer him things he's always wanted, things no one has been able to give him before."

"Like what?"

"Our child." She smiles when my eyes go to her growing belly. "Listen, Detective, I heard something yesterday—something you should know that might help you with your investigation." She turns, stepping through wet sand as her dress billows behind her. "I'm not sure how to say it, exactly."

For the first time since we've been talking, Colleen seems fidgety. She drops the rock into the waves and clasps her hands in front of her. Her eyes shift from the surf to me and back again. What could possibly have her more on edge than talking about the demons from her childhood?

"Take all the time you need," I say.

She blows out a shaky breath and starts to walk. I keep pace beside her. "Samara told me that Joanna miscarried her child in May, and then went to a women's clinic in June or July, though she didn't know the reason for the visits. Joanna didn't want to tell anyone—not even Michael, if you can believe it. To keep the secret, Samara told her to choose a different name, so she could be treated under complete anonymity. I just thought—I knew you'd figure it out eventually, and I— well, I thought you should know as soon as I did."

My skin prickles. "It was her."

Mandy McKnight. *Joanna.*

"Samara said she was the one who took Joanna to her appointments. Michael doesn't know about the clinic visits at all," Colleen continues. "If you think about it, he's the true victim in all this."

I hear the pleading in her voice, but I can't agree with her. Not yet.

MICHAEL

"You almost ready, Coll?" I check my watch. "I don't mind being fashionably late, but this is pushing it. I need to make sure the staff is handling everything properly."

Tonight's the five-year anniversary of Harris Financial. We've come a long way, hustled until our feet hurt, worked until our eyes burned, and we've created a successful company. At least on the outside. If any of my employees knew the truth about our declining accounts and bad investments, it'd be a different story.

If it weren't for the insurance money I'm about to receive from Joanna's death, I'd probably be giving layoff notices rather than hosting a party at the Point Reina Distillery.

I'm equally relieved and disgusted by the thought.

I hear Colleen fussing with something in the bathroom and call out to her a second time.

"One more minute," she says. "I promise I'll be worth the wait."

"You always are."

Things have turned around between us since yesterday's ultrasound. Overall, the mood in Ravenwood has shifted.

Colleen seems happier, and from the way she snored last night, I'd say she's sleeping better too.

I understand why she's worried about my reluctance to attach to her or the baby—she's afraid I'll pull away in the end—but I simply needed time. When Joanna left me, I was devastated. But what made my world crumble to the ground was the fact that I'd invested so much time, energy, and hope in our baby. And it wasn't even mine. I simply couldn't let myself get wrapped up so easily this time. I had to protect myself.

The investigation and media circus have been the greatest tests of all. All this week, I expected Colleen to doubt me, or just walk out. But she's stuck by my side. Through thick and thin.

"I'm ready," she calls, and emerges from the master bathroom, hands raised from her sides. "What do you think?"

The breath catches in my throat. She's wearing a black, old-fashioned dress, like something from the twenties, covered in beading and tassels. Some kind of sheer material barely conceals her shoulders. Her hair is sleek in front, parted on the side, and pinned into a feminine roll near the bottom of her hairline. Her lips are glossy red, her eyes smoky, her eyelashes thick and black. As she spins, I get a clear look at her growing belly stretching the dress's slinky material.

"Well?" she demands, beaming at me. She's as delighted as a child.

I can't formulate a single word. Does she know? She couldn't. . . . How could she? There are no pictures of Joanna at last year's anniversary party. Who would put her up to this? Samara? Travis? Dean?

The dress could be the exact same one Joanna wore that night.

Black and beaded, yes. Knee-length, I'm sure of it. Joanna had decided on a twenties vibe, her hair drawn up, her lips blood-red. She'd insisted I wear a pinstripe tux, with a red rose on the lapel, to match her.

"Why are you looking at me like that?" Colleen's smile falters.

"Did you get that from—never mind." I must be mistaken.

"What?" Her face scrunches in confusion. "Is it bad? Should I change?"

"No," I force out, my voice suddenly hoarse. "You're stunning. You took my breath away, that's all."

It's not a lie. My chest is tight, my heart is pounding. Should I ask her to change? We don't have time—we're already late—and I fear telling her to pick another outfit would dampen her spirits and ruin the whole night.

Shaking my head to clear away images of Joanna, I step forward and wrap Colleen in my arms. "You were right. Absolutely worth the wait."

But then I breathe in, and—*Joanna*. Joy again. Is she doing this on purpose? The perfume makes Colleen smell powdery, fresh, and sweet as a rose. But the scent is disturbingly familiar. Did she raid Joanna's bedroom, taking the dress from her closet, just the way she took the perfume from her vanity?

"You look handsome." Pulling away, she gives a short tug on my lapels. She's smiling again, pleased. "Are you ready?"

For a second, I think she's going to suggest I pin a flower there, right where Joanna had insisted I wear one. And suddenly I'm feeling like I've slipped into an episode of *The Twilight Zone*.

I need a drink.

"Let's go," I say, a little too harshly, and Colleen glances up at me, surprised.

The reporters are there, as always, snapping pictures as we step out front. Microphones are shoved at us as we face a barrage of questions about Joanna, about the investigation.

Tonight, we elbow through without a word, and by the time we turn the corner onto Beach Street, miraculously, we're alone again.

It's quiet tonight, I notice as we walk to the Point Reina Distillery. All I can hear is the soft rush of waves hitting sand and Colleen's heels striking the sidewalk. It's nearly eight and pitch-dark, with only the glare of the crescent moon and the dim glow of the streetlamps to light our way. The air is crisp and cool on my skin.

"I wanted to talk to you before we went in," I say as we move together through the parking lot. "Travis and Rachael were formally disinvited from the party tonight."

"I think that was a good call."

"But that doesn't mean they aren't going to show up."

She glances up at me. "Do you really think they would?"

"They might. I've hired security so no reporters or un-wanted guests can get in, but I wanted you to be aware, just in case."

"Thanks for the heads-up," she says after a beat, and then, "Michael, this is the first time most of your employees will see us together. Are you worried about that at all?"

I hadn't thought about it, but she's right. We'd kept our relationship secret for the few months Colleen still worked for me—up until she could no longer hide her baby bump—and then she quit, before anyone could ask questions.

"No," I say finally. "Unless they've been in a cave, they've seen the news reports. They know we're together, and I really don't care what they have to say about it at this point. If that's what you're worried about."

She shivers, squeezing her eyes closed. "I'm not worried. Just nervous, I guess."

"There's no reason to be, sweetheart."

Right before we go inside, she stops me and tugs me down to her. As her lips press against mine, a draft of cool sea air sweeps up the cliff, carrying Joanna's scent straight to my nose. I could be kissing *her*. I've been in this exact place, on this exact night, kissing my wife, who happened to look exactly the way my pregnant girlfriend does now.

I pull away with a curse. "Come on, we're late."

Because if I don't get whiskey flowing through my system within the next few seconds, I'm going to combust.

COLLEEN

Dinner goes so smoothly, I'm almost shocked.

No one mentions Joanna or her murder. There's not one awkward silence or uncomfortable situation. Conversation is flowing. Music is playing. And Don is working overtime, keeping the distillery open late for us. As the hours roll by, I'm thankful for security at the door. Three reporters posing as employees tried to sneak inside, and it wasn't until they were asked to show proper identification that they gave up and left.

There's been no sign of Rachael or Travis, which is a blessing considering that I wouldn't know what to say to either of them.

After dinner, I break away from my conversation with the head of Harris Financial's marketing department and search for Michael. Instinctively, I head toward the bar. He's been hovering there most of the night, talking with Don rather than his employees.

"Hey," I say, kissing him on the cheek before taking the stool next to him. "Hope I'm not interrupting."

"No, not at all." He flinches as if he's suddenly disgusted by something, then turns toward the bar. "Have you ever had déjà vu, Don?"

He shakes a martini. "I have."

"Me too." Michael buries his chuckle in a long drink. "Seems like every time I turn around—*wham*! I've been here before, in this exact moment." Slamming his palm on the bar, he whirls toward me, eyes wide, as if he just now realized I'm sitting next to him. "Colleen, sweetheart, have you met Don?"

"I don't think so." I take his hand. "I'm Colleen Roper, Michael's girlfriend."

"Mother of my son," Michael slurs, lifting his drink to toast himself. "She's a special one."

"I'm sure she is." Don smiles shyly and goes back to mixing a fruity drink. "Nice to meet you, Colleen."

As I order another virgin daiquiri, a security guard approaches Michael and rests a hand on his shoulder. They talk briefly, though the music is so loud I can't hear what's being said. Michael slides off the barstool.

"I'll be back in a flash," he says, patting my thigh. "Need to step outside for a moment. Order me another?"

And then he follows the security guard to the main room where the rest of his employees are enjoying dessert.

"He's had a lot to drink tonight," Don remarks, sliding to my side of the bar. "More than usual. Make sure he gets home safely?"

"Of course."

"I've seen you, out and about." He starts washing a line of dirty glasses one of the waitresses has set on the bar. "You go for a walk through the grove and down to the beach every morning."

"Yeah, I do." I've been going down to the trails first thing every day to think, and try to relax. "Have you been following me?" I tease.

"Nah." He punches buttons on the register to clear a tab. "You know the bench near the cliff? The one overlooking the tide pools?"

I nod. It's black wrought iron and sits off the beaten path, a few feet from the groomed part of the trail.

"I like to go there to clear my head before work. It's peaceful. Stay there long enough, right in the thick of the grove, and you become a part of nature." He mixes vodka and tomato juice. "You wouldn't believe the things I see and hear. It's like people don't even know I'm there."

I swivel on my stool and scan the room. I hardly know anyone here. After all, I only worked for Michael's company a few months. I mostly kept to myself. Even now, I prefer Don's company to anyone in the main party room, especially now that Michael has stepped outside.

I think about the bench Don likes. It's not far from where Joanna's body was found.

I wonder . . .

"Did you know Joanna?" I ask, keeping my voice as casual as I can.

He slides the Bloody Mary down the bar to the waitress waiting to fulfill an order. "Oh yeah. Everyone knew Joanna. Came in all the time."

"With Michael?"

"Michael. Rachael. Travis. That woman might've been friends with everyone in town."

"Well, not everyone," I blurt, and instantly regret saying it. "It's a terrible thing that happened to her."

Don bends beneath the counter and comes up with another shaker. "Seems to have worked out for you in the end, though."

I frown. "What do you mean by that?'

"Just that you seemed to benefit from her loss, that's all." He puts his hands up in surrender. "Hey, that came out wrong. I don't mean to imply—all I mean is, I see the way you and Michael look at each other. You're happy, and now you're starting a family. If Joanna hadn't been killed, you two would've never gotten together. You wouldn't have had any of this, including your baby."

I suddenly feel very uncomfortable. I shouldn't have brought up Joanna.

"It is a strange thing, though," Don says, after he takes another order.

"What?" I ask.

"You look just like her." He meets my gaze head on. "Especially tonight."

I force a tight smile as my skin shrinks over my bones. "It was great meeting you, Don. Please excuse me."

I find Michael outside, talking to the security guards.

"I want the police here. Now," Michael rasps. His finger comes so close to the guard's nose, he nearly flicks it. "Pick up your little walkie-talkie and call Detective Patel. He'll come by, ask them all kinds of questions, and then *they'll* be the ones on the news. Travis is the one they should be investigating anyway. That bastard could've been the one who killed Joanna. Do you hear me? He could've killed my wife! They should be looking into him!"

My wife.

A part of me dies inside.

He stumbles, and the guard next to him steadies him. Michael jerks away. He doesn't even realize how drunk he is.

"Hey, honey," I say, brushing my hand up and down his back. "Everything okay out here?"

Spinning around, he struggles to focus on my face. "No, Coll, everything is *not* okay. Travis and Rachael came by, but these idiots didn't call the police like I instructed them to, so now I have to do it myself."

"Did something happen? Did they cause a scene?"

"No, but Travis could be a cold-blooded killer, Colleen! Can't have someone like that roaming around. We need to make it clear they're not welcome anywhere around us. All eyes need to be on *them*."

He's out of control. As he removes his phone from his jacket pocket, punching random buttons, he starts to sway again.

"You're right," I say, sliding the phone from his fingers. "Here, let me call for you, honey." While I pretend to dial, I turn to the guard. "Did they damage anything? Cause trouble of any kind?"

He shakes his head.

I put the phone to my ear and make a fake call to the station. Looking rather pleased, a tight-lipped smile stretched across his face, Michael folds his arms across his chest and waits for me to explain the results of the call.

"There," I say. "The detectives got the message. What do you say we head home? That way, if the police show up, we're out of their way."

"But the party." He tries to point toward the door, but loses his balance and points to the parking lot instead. "I should tell everyone I'm leaving. They'll want to know. I should say goodbye—"

"They'll be fine. As long as you're picking up the bar tab, no one really cares if you're there."

As he scoffs, the guards laugh, and one of them says, "True story."

"So come on." I link my arm through his and nuzzle into his shoulder. "Take me to bed."

At that, Michael salutes the guards military-style and marches home, leaning heavily on my arm to steady himself. The second the front door shuts behind us, Michael pins me against the wall. He's all sloppy lips and fumbling hands, but my heart leaps when he kisses me. He hasn't made a move like this since I came to Ravenwood. We stumble up the stairs and down the hall, kicking the bedroom door open and laughing like teenagers as he pushes me onto the bed. I land with a squeal, undressing fast, flinging the beaded dress to the floor. But when he tries to take off his pants, he falls face-first, right on top of me, and laughs into a snort.

He's a wreck.

It's not going to happen tonight. As he fumbles with his shoes and pants, my heart sinks. He's going to pass out the second his head hits the pillow.

With a groan, he crawls onto his side of the bed and collapses. "I'mso—sorry," he slurs, his face mashed against the pillow. "Ihadtoomany."

"Shh." I run my fingers through his hair and earn a deep, satisfied sigh in response. "It's all right, darling. Sleep now."

A pleasant realization hits me. We don't pretend to be perfect like Travis and Rachael, but that's okay. We don't have to. I can be paranoid, self-conscious, and stick my foot in my mouth more often than I'd like to admit. Michael can work too hard, drink too much, and be a little possessive. In the end, we're perfect for each other.

"You looked beautiful tonight," he whispers, his breath slow. "So beautiful."

"Thank you."

"This time was better than last time. No Travis, that's why." He yawns, loud and obnoxious, like a big bear. "You smelled good too. And your dress." He makes a pleasant moaning sound. "Nice."

"Thank you," I whisper, nestling into the crook between his shoulder and his chest. "Now get some sleep."

He's quiet for a few minutes, his chest rising and falling. I listen to the soft thumping of his heart beneath my cheek.

"Good night, Joanna," he murmurs. "I love you."

SUNDAY

The Day of Colleen's Murder

DETECTIVE SHAW

Thanks to Colleen, we've finally had a breakthrough in the case. We now know Joanna Harris walked into the women's clinic in June posing as Mandy McKnight. Considering she'd miscarried a month earlier, it shouldn't have had anything to do with her pregnancy, but then, why?

I stare at my screen and realize I'm still searching for a needle in a haystack. And I don't know even know what the needle looks like. It keeps pricking the edges of my mind, so I know it's there . . . somewhere. I have to keep digging.

Why am I finding it so much harder to do my work without Karen at my side? Is it this case in particular—the first high-profile homicide since she was taken from me—or is every case going to be this way from now on?

We need to know who last saw Joanna alive. Clearing my throat, I push papers across my desk and straighten out the notes I've taken regarding the month of July last year. I create a timeline and work my way through it.

On July sixteenth, Michael and Joanna's wedding anniversary and the day she went missing, Michael claims he only saw her in the morning. He'd worked long hours that day and made dinner plans for them that night, but she never showed. He'd received her final text instead.

His story is clear-cut and hasn't changed.

"All right," I think aloud, sifting through my notes. "You went to Pilates that morning and had a blowout with Rachael. Let's assume you were killed on the evening of July sixteenth, after you sent that text to your husband. Where were you between those times, Joanna? Who were you with?"

I run through everything backward.

The last call Joanna made was to Gary Danko's restaurant at six o'clock in the evening. I already called. Asked them to check their reservation log. There was nothing listed under Michael's or Joanna's name. The Harrises' bank account doesn't reflect a charge from the restaurant, either. We checked under the name Mandy McKnight too, in case Joanna had gotten into the habit of using that alias. Again, nothing.

"Why," I mumble, snatching the Rubik's Cube from my desk, "would you call the restaurant in the first place?"

To make a future reservation she ultimately decided against? To check if someone was there?

I quickly shift sides of the cube around as my thoughts race.

Maybe someone else picked up the bill. . . .

"You had a date," I whisper, fingers curling around the toy. "You went with someone. Someone who wasn't your husband."

On instinct alone, I search the number for the restaurant online and make the call.

"Good morning," a woman says cheerfully. "Thank you for calling Gary Danko, this is Lisa, how can I help you?"

"Good morning, Lisa." I'm about to introduce myself properly when, mid-breath, I flip my approach. If I admit I'm a detective, she's going to be wary about revealing sensitive information, especially when I can't show her proper ID. She'll be guarded and give away little or nothing, and then I'll have to drive into the city. But Patel's on his way over to meet with me. I can't leave the station now. "I have an odd question, and I was hoping you could help me."

"I'll try," she says. But her voice has turned wary.

"Last July, I took my wife to dinner for our wedding anniversary. The food was amazing, the staff exceptional, and we had a terrific time. The night was really special to her, but you see, I can't remember the name of the restaurant. It's near Ghirardelli Square, I know that much, but other than that, I'm at a loss. I've been searching online, but haven't had much luck. If I ask her, I'm afraid she'll suspect that I'm planning something for her. Do you understand?"

"I think so, sir."

"Her birthday is coming up," I go on, "and I'd love to surprise her with another fabulous night at her favorite restaurant. Do your reservation logs go back to July?"

I already know they do.

"Yes, sir. Would you like me to check whether you made reservations with us?"

Gotcha. "That'd be great. The name is Dean Lewis."

"Hold on, please. July of last year, correct?"

"That's right." I shift a few more slides of the cube.

"I'm sorry, sir. You said Lewis? Nothing under that name."

"What about Martin? Travis Martin?"

The line goes quiet. "Yes, sir. Reservation for July sixteenth. Seven o'clock, quiet table for two."

Jackpot. "All right, thank you, Lisa, you've been so helpful."

"Would you like to make another reservation for your wife at this time?"

"No, thank you," I say as Patel strides through the door. "Have a great day."

Yanking at his tie, Patel heads straight for the coffee machine and fills the largest mug we have. "Michael Harris is on his way. Should be here any minute."

"You called him in?"

"No, this was on him." He reaches for the sugar. "He says he has something to tell us."

"What time is the autopsy?"

"Four." He checks the time on his phone. "I put a rush on the toxicology, too. Should be ready shortly after. I'll let you know as soon as we have the results. What've you been working on?"

"Well," I say, clutching the half-finished cube in one hand as I give my arms a stretch. "Although Joanna's final text was to her husband, her final phone call was to Gary Danko's, to confirm a dinner reservation that *Travis* made sometime earlier for July sixteenth."

"Wow—Travis texted her the night before, too." Patel slouches into the seat across from me and slurps his coffee. "Those two really couldn't get enough of each other—on her wedding anniversary, no less."

I tell him about my conversation with the hostess, and then we review the phone records, the matching dates and times of the texts, and Joanna's short, coded answers.

"I know you've got your heart set on Michael Harris," I say, chewing on my pen cap. "It's a convenient conclusion to draw since the police were called to Ravenwood on a domestic violence call the evening of July fifteenth. But if Joanna and Travis went to Gary Danko's the following night, he had to have been the last one to see her alive."

Patel shakes his head in disagreement. "I gave the Travis angle some thought yesterday, but the answer's been in front of us the whole time. It's Harris, Shaw. The thing that was holding you up before about the prescriptions being in Mandy's name doesn't matter anymore. Those pills belonged to Joanna, and Harris had access to them. Once toxicology comes back and proves large amounts were in her blood-stream, we'll have a slam-dunk case. Won't get clearer than that."

"But Joanna could've taken those pills herself. Maybe she was still recovering from the procedure and—"

"If she was taking the pills on a regular schedule, why would there be so many left in the bottles? Why would she tuck them away in a place that's hard to access?"

"But if what you're saying is true, that means Michael Harris had to have known those pills were there, in the back of that cabinet."

"Harris is a control freak. Of course he knew."

"And you don't think he questioned why those pills were in someone else's name?"

At that, Patel scowls. "He might've, but it doesn't matter. We'll have enough. Big picture, Shaw, remember?"

"It's not about that," I argue. "It's about making sure *all* the pieces add up."

"That's where you're confused," Patel says, hitching his chin at the cube in my hand. "This case isn't like that toy you're messing with. It doesn't need to be finished, with every single thing lining up. That's practically impossible for a case like this. As long as we have the outer edges done, the frame of it, the district attorney will handle the rest."

I'm thinking of the best way to argue with Patel when the door opens and Michael Harris strides in. He heads straight for my desk, a desperate gleam in his eye.

"Mr. Harris, thanks for coming in," Patel says, his long fingers gripping his coffee mug. "What'd you bring us?"

"Proof that Travis killed my wife."

I shoot Patel a knowing look, but he doesn't bite.

"Well . . ." Patel says blandly. "Where is it?"

"Here." Harris points to his chest. "*I'm* the proof. I was with Travis and Colleen when he slipped up."

"Who slipped?" I ask, confused. "Travis?"

"No, a waiter," Michael insists, his eyes shifting from me to Patel and back again. "We were having lunch in the city together. The waiter thought he recognized Colleen. He thought she was Joanna because they went there together as a couple. Travis and my wife. They were having an affair. He's your killer."

"This is the proof?" Patel asks mildly.

"Well, yeah. I thought it'd be more convincing if I came in here and told you myself. So you could look in my eyes and see that I'm not making this up—it's not in my head." Harris's face reddens. "Don't you see? It's him."

"We appreciate your input on the matter, and we'll look into it." Careful not to spill his coffee, Patel raps the bottom rim of his mug against the table, as a judge would strike a gavel. "But I'm glad you came in today. Because there's something I've been meaning to talk to you about. By now we're sure you've realized that the child your wife was carrying couldn't have passed the age of viability before she was killed."

"Yes." He's staring at Patel. "I figured that."

"According to one of our sources," Patel continues, "Joanna sought services from a women's clinic in June. Were you aware of that?"

"June? No. I had no idea. Do you know what kind of . . . service she received?"

"We're still investigating, Mr. Harris," I say. "But we're hopeful that the coroner's report will shed light on that."

"When will it come in?" he asks. "When will you know?"

"Soon," Patel assures him. "You'll be one of the first people to receive an update on our findings."

Does Harris have any idea what that means for him?

"Thank you. I appreciate that. But before I go there's something else—something I've been hesitant to show you, but I—I can't keep it to myself any longer."

He slides his phone across my desk, and I quickly skim Joanna's last text message.

"Her sister and I put the timeline together and suspect she lost the baby in May. If that's true, why'd she send me a text in July saying the baby wasn't mine? Why'd she tell me that she was leaving to raise the baby with her lover? Why bother if she'd miscarried months before?"

"We've already seen this," I tell him. "And we came up with a few possibilities."

"She wanted to torture me?"

"If she hated you that much, sure." I go on, "Or it might've been to keep you from trying to win her back. Judging from her actions, Joanna was a woman who, when she made up her mind, didn't want to hear others' opinions. Maybe she decided she didn't want to be with you any longer, and this was the nail in the coffin."

He massages his temples. "You have no idea."

"She wanted to end things on her terms. Clean break. No carnage. Maybe she felt you needed that kind of closure to move on."

"No carnage . . ." He shakes his head.

"Or, there's another option," I offer, watching his expression carefully.

Patel clears this throat loudly, and I know that the sound is meant to silence me. He's giving a signal that I'm offering too much of my own opinion. If Harris is a possible murder suspect, I should keep these next suggestions to myself. But I've gone by the book with this investigation, and although we've had a few leads, I'm no closer to finding Joanna's killer than I was the day we pulled her out of the mud. Karen would tell me that I need to trust my gut. So I'm ignoring the sound coming from Patel's throat, and I'm taking my wife's advice.

"Joanna's murderer could've sent the text from her phone so you wouldn't try to contact her." My gut jumps as if it knows I've just spoken the truth. "If you thought she had moved on and didn't want to see you again, you wouldn't file a missing person's report. If no one thinks there's been foul play, no one searches for the killer. He or she goes free. Might've been an excellent diversion technique."

"You've got quite an assortment of theories there," Harris snaps. "Which one do you think is the truth?" His eyes are locked on mine.

"Mr. Harris, at this moment, it's impossible to know for certain."

"But what do you *think*?" he insists.

"The final one," I say, eyeing Patel. "I think those were the words of her killer."

He groans.

"You're going to look into Travis, aren't you?" He looks up, his eyes glossed with tears. "I think—no, I *know*—he killed my wife. Please don't rule him out."

"We're not, Mr. Harris," Patel says, getting to his feet. "We're not ruling anyone out yet."

Including you. Those are the unspoken words, and I get the feeling Michael Harris knows it.

"He's paranoid," Patel says as soon as Harris leaves the station.

"Of course he is," I say. "He thinks we're closing in on him."

"We are," Patel says. "He's sick, if you ask me. I don't like that he's getting shifty, telling us who we need to be looking at, what we need to be doing. We should've had him come in, put more pressure on him. We might've been able to crack him. I worry about that girlfriend of his—he could take it out on her."

"I'm telling you, Patel, there's something else going on here. Something that doesn't fit. Let me look into the neighbors a bit more. The chef, too. I don't know that I trust a word out of his mouth."

Patel narrows his eyes over the rim of his giant mug. "When we get toxicology back, we'll know for certain. But I'll bet you a week's salary that we'll be arresting Michael Harris for murder before day's end. For his new girlfriend's sake, we can't afford to waste any more time."

RACHAEL

I'm sitting up in bed reading an entertainment magazine when Travis slams into the room and heads straight for the closet. He doesn't say a word, but that's not surprising. We haven't talked much since last night, when he insisted on making a regal entrance at the Harris Financial party. It was tacky as hell to walk in like that. After all, we'd been disinvited. But Travis insisted we shouldn't hide. We should show our faces *proudly* because we didn't do anything wrong. Give me a break. What do we have to be proud of lately?

"Where've you been?" I ask, flipping a page of my magazine. I try to keep my tone calm, but I hear its edge anyway.

"I went for a drive. To clear my head."

I'm not buying any of his excuses. Not anymore. I can't believe a word he says. If he lied to me about his affair with Joanna, he could be keeping anything from me. What else is lurking in the dark, waiting to rise up and ruin my life? Other affairs? Murder? I don't want to think he had something to do with Joanna's death, but he's been odd lately. Jumpy and tense. He's hiding things, like the lunch on Thursday with God-knows-who. And he's too concerned about what I'm telling the police. Staying up later than usual to clean his gun, and rising earlier to head into the city.

Things shift in the closet. Something thumps onto the floor. Hangers slide on the rod. More thumping. Now I've completely lost my place, damn it. Which celebrity wore the red carpet dress best? Oh, there it is. Sixty-two percent say she did. I disagree—I wouldn't be caught dead in those gaudy shoes—but whatever.

Travis groans, and then the sounds start over again. Shifting, thumping, sliding.

I drop the magazine in my lap. "Travis, what are you doing?"

"Packing bags." He peers out from the closet. He looks tired, his eyes red and strained. "I was thinking we could get out of here for a week or two. You know, just the two of us. Escape all this madness and disappear. Put everything behind us for a while."

"Disappear? What about work?"

"I was let go."

"What?" My voice kicks up an octave. "What do you mean you were let go?"

"Michael fired me. Well, he didn't. Bastard was too much of a coward to say it to my face. He had someone else relay the message." He ducks back into the closet and comes out with two pieces of luggage: his black duffel and my Louis Vuitton. He throws them on the bed. "It's fine, Rachael. I'll find another job and take his clients with me when I go. It's good timing, actually. Let's just go."

"You know I can't do that. I'd have to reschedule all of my appointments."

"Do it. I'll drive, and you can make calls on the way."

I frown, slap the magazine closed. "On the way to where, exactly?"

"I was thinking Napa." Fishing his key ring out of his back pocket, he heads to the closet once more. The clink of the safe opening hits my ears. He emerges with his modified Glock and shoves it into his bag. "You enjoyed yourself the last time we visited. Remember that great bed-and-breakfast with a spa? You can drink wine, take a mud bath, read as many of those trashy magazines as you want."

"Why do we need a gun in Napa?"

He jerks upright. "I come home to tell you that I'm whisking you away for a week of wine and pampering—what every woman dreams of—and you sound put out by it. Would it kill you to be thankful for once?"

"I am—I guess a weekend in Napa sounds great—but what about the cost? If you don't have a job, how are we going to afford a trip?"

"Oh, here we go," he says spitefully.

I hover on the brink of saying what's really on my mind. *You're running.* It doesn't look good. In fact, it makes him look guilty.

"I just don't know why you're in such a rush," I say instead.

He stands at the foot of the bed, and his eyes go dark. "Have you been talking to the cops?"

"What?" A chill creeps over my legs despite the blankets covering them. "No. Well, except for when they came to see me at work."

He measures me carefully, and when he speaks again, it's nearly a whisper. "Have you noticed anyone following you?"

I roll my eyes. "Travis—"

"I'm being serious, Rachael. Look."

He stalks around the bed, snatches my arm, and drags me down the hall. I protest the entire way, trying to shake off his fierce grip. But he doesn't stop. He's gone mad. He charges down the stairs, and I stumble behind him, struggling not to fall and break my neck. The house is dark, thanks to the clouds that moved in this afternoon. Rain batters the glass. At least the terrible weather has driven away the reporters. No one occupies our lawn tonight.

Downstairs, he pushes me against a window. From here, it looks as if we're standing behind a waterfall. Heavy streams of water sluice down the glass, and the sound echoes through the house.

Mouth against my ear, he says, "What do you see?"

"Travis, I—"

"What do you see?" he roars. His hands bite into me and I wince. "Look, damn it!"

"I see Ravenwood with a few lights on inside. Michael's car. Two news vans. The cypress grove."

"There," he hisses, grinding his fingers into my hips. "Where the street bends by the trail, where Cypress intersects Beach, what do you see?"

I squint, and barely make out the shape through the rush of water. "A car?"

"It's been following me all day." Finally, he releases me. "It's a blacked-out Lincoln. I've been paying attention. They're not tailing Michael anymore. They're on *me*."

"Are you sure? Why—why would they be following you?"

"Because they must've discovered my relationship with Joanna went deeper than a few pointless texts."

Relationship. Not tryst, or stupid, regrettable fling. *Relationship*. Why does he talk about the affair so casually, as if it's not a big deal, as if I've forgiven him? God, it burns me inside. I think about him cheating on me with her every day, yet if I bring it up, he'll say I'm holding a grudge and destroying our marriage. He's under the impression he can do whatever the hell he wants, and from one simple apology I'm supposed to forgive and forget.

But it's not that easy. I thought I could forgive him, but now I'm not so sure. I've never believed a confession erases all the sins someone has committed, even if that's what my parents taught me.

Maybe he doesn't deserve my forgiveness.

"Are you going to get a lawyer?" I ask, as I slip out of his embrace and head upstairs.

"No. We're going to leave." He's on my heels, one step behind me. "Finish packing. We'll be out in thirty."

Cheeks flushing hot, I storm into the bedroom and peel

open the flap of my bag. He's packed it with enough clothes for the weekend: a couple of shirts, a skirt, a pair of flats, and a few pairs of underwear.

"If you're innocent, you probably shouldn't go anywhere," I can't resist saying.

"What do you mean 'if I'm innocent'? You think I killed Joanna?"

"No, of course not," I say, backing away from him. His face scares me. "It'll look bad, that's all. Murderers run when they're guilty. You see it all the time on TV. It's what tips the cops off that you're the main suspect. Haven't you ever watched a detective show?"

"Damn it, Rachael, this isn't a television show, this is our life." He shoves a stack of underwear into his bag, followed by two pairs of shorts and a handful of socks. "We're not running because we're guilty. We're an *innocent* married couple being victimized by the crazy amount of hype on our street, who desperately need a vacation to recharge our batteries. There's absolutely nothing wrong with that."

But I've never known him to pack his gun when we take a vacation.

"You're right," I answer, feeling myself become angry. "Of course you're right. You always are."

"We're going to Napa," he snaps, chucking his shaving kit into the bag, "and that's it. End of discussion."

A thought strikes me, sudden and conclusive: *I can't do this anymore. I can't stay with him.*

A flare of contempt rises in my gut. "What if I don't want to go with you?"

"Jesus, we're going on *vacation,* Rachael! It's not like I'm dragging you to the desert. It's fucking *Napa.* Why do you always make everything so damn difficult?" As he adjusts the sides of his bag, he mumbles, "Joanna wasn't so difficult to please."

"What was that?"

He glances up, his expression flat. "I said you couldn't be more difficult to please."

But that wasn't what he said. If I challenge him on it further, he'll only deny it. We've been through this ritual so many times before. We'll fight. The ruined evening will somehow end up being my fault. Then, by tomorrow morning, I'll question whether I actually heard him say that bitch's name in the first place.

"Now shut up," he says, jamming a finger through the air in my general direction, "and pack your shit."

I feel it again, sharp as a whip. *I can't stay here.*

Travis has betrayed me time and time again, and if I'm honest with myself, I know I've thought about packing my own bag on more than one occasion. Everyone wants to live here, on the coast, in this lavish neighborhood, where it's nice and quiet, the perfect place to raise a family.

But I don't want to be in these glass walls anymore, on display for the world to see.

Now that I think about it, I don't think I ever really did. Travis picked this house. One day out of the blue, he'd pulled up in the driveway, dropped the keys in my lap, and said it was ours. It'd been the surprise of a lifetime, and everyone had said I was the luckiest woman in the world to be gifted a home like this.

But it's not mine. I'm simply one of Travis's possessions in it, no more important than his piano, his bar, or his gun.

Maybe, just maybe, I deserve something better.

"What happens when we come back?" I ask as I fiddle with the zipper.

He turns in the bathroom doorway. "What do you mean?"

"Our problems are going to be waiting for us. The lack of trust, your constant need for control. Nothing is ever going to change, and I'm tired of it."

Closing the distance between us, Travis strides up to me

and cups my chin in his hands. The gesture should be tender and soft, but fury brews in his eyes, and it scares me to death. I shake, swallow down the fear welling up inside me, and meet his gaze.

"If I were you, Rachael," he whispers, "I'd choose your next words wisely."

A ragged breath escapes from my lungs as I shy away from his touch. "I think you and I should—"

"Careful," he warns.

"I think we should spend some time apart."

There, I said it. But I don't feel free or relieved. I have the distinct sensation of jumping off a cliff and free-falling, my pulse skyrocketing as the ground beneath me closes in much too fast.

"You think I killed her." His upper lip curls in disgust. "You do. I see it in your eyes. You think those cops are following me because they know something you don't."

"The only thing I know is what you tell me, and so far, you've told me nothing but lies. We've built this beautiful house on them, Travis, and the walls are cracking beneath the weight." I clutch at my nightshirt and gasp for what little air is left in this room. "I can't take it anymore. I can't stay up at night wondering about how many times you slept with Joanna behind my back, how many times you wished you were with her when you were next to me." I'm steamrolling now, and there's no coming back from this. "I can't stop thinking about how many times you kissed me with the same mouth that kissed her, how many times you slept with her in the afternoon and me in the evening. I wish I were numb to all of this, Travis. But I—I can't—it's eating me away inside. I won't live like this anymore, and I—"

"Shh, you don't know what you're saying." He drags me against him, burying my head in his chest despite my resistance. "Stop, Rachael. Just stop. I hate seeing you this way. Tell me what you want. I'll give you anything."

I break away and stifle a laugh. Because he still doesn't get it. "How about something you've never given me before?"

"Name it."

"Loyalty and honesty."

I don't look at him when I hitch my Louis Vuitton over my shoulder and strut out the bedroom door. I can't. Because if I look at him now, I won't have the strength to leave him.

DETECTIVE SHAW

It's after dark when I turn in to Skyview Cemetery. I haven't heard from Patel yet, which means the autopsy must be more complicated than we originally thought. He's eager to rub my nose in the findings, so I'm sure he'll call the instant he knows something conclusive. I've kept my phone's volume on high all day to ensure I don't miss his call.

But it's getting late. Surely he's heard something by now. . . .

The cemetery grounds sit at the base of Montara Mountain with an unobstructed view of San Francisco Bay to the west, which is especially stunning with a blanket of stars draped overhead. I drive past the main office building and wind through the cemetery, zoning out, hating where this road leads. Manicured lawns. Fake flowers filling cement vases next to the headstones. Mausoleums housing flat-faced tombs. The grounds are beautiful, but I doubt anyone who visits gets much joy out of the landscaping.

Inching along in first gear, I make a wide right turn and then a left, climbing toward the section with the newer graves. I've turned off my radio because it doesn't feel right to be listening to upbeat music right now. I need to bask in the silence, to give myself the space to remember.

Karen was healthy. Training for the Bay to Breakers foot-race in the city. We'd recently bought her dream home in Half

Moon Bay, and we were planning to start our family when she received the diagnosis. Our plans came crashing down.

I don't realize I've been parked until my dashboard lights up with a reminder that my headlights are still on. Switching them off, I sit still as stone, hands gripping the wheel.

I haven't visited Karen's grave since we laid her in the ground last year, but time hasn't dulled the stabbing pain in my chest. I'd thought, foolishly, that I'd come back daily. I'd gotten close a few times. Turned off the main road and driven along the path to where I sit now. But thinking about striding over the grass that covers her cold body has kept me from taking one step out of my car.

Tonight, though, I need to do this. I need *her*.

With a one-two-three count, I shove the door open and step out into the cold night air. The scent of freshly cut grass hits me, and I almost duck back into the car. There's no one out here. It's so quiet, every one of my thoughts feels like a scream in my brain.

It would've been so much easier to stay in my car, the way I always have before.

I weave around stones and nameplates smashed into the ground. My feet somehow know their way through the plush grass.

There.

A gray marker with an angel perched on top, its granite wings arched protectively around the sides of the stone. At the sight of it, I nearly break into a run in the other direction. My heart stings with grief and I don't think I can do it.

I crumple to my knees at the foot of her grave. I sit on the lawn for God knows how long, blinking back tears. My legs go stiff, and I think the grass is damp, soaking through my pants, but I couldn't move if I tried.

It feels as if I've been on a journey from hell for an entire year, and have just now returned home.

"I'm sorry," I say, pinching my eyes shut. "I'm not doing well without you. I know I said I would try to find a routine and get things back to normal, but I can't. I need you more than I ever thought I would."

My thoughts tangle and unwind, and my throat aches.

Because the silence is too heavy to bear, I talk about the case.

"This one's got me in knots, Karen. I wish you were here to help me, to show me where to look next. It's one of those investigations you loved so much, where the answers aren't black-and-white. There are all kinds of gray areas, questions that are still unresolved, and I don't know what to do."

I begin to whisper the details of Joanna's murder. I tell her about the Martins, Ravenwood's staff, Michael, and Colleen, and the web of lies they've spun. I don't hold back.

"We had it all, didn't we?" Plucking a handful of grass, I rub the blades around in my palm. "We didn't need a million-dollar home or an expensive car to be happy. It was always me and you. Us against the world."

And we lost.

I hang my head in defeat, overcome with pain.

"Give me a sign," I beg. "Tell me what to do, and I'll do it."

I wait for an answer, and then laugh bitterly because I realize it'll never come. The temperature seems to have dropped a few degrees suddenly. I brace myself against the wind as I say a silent prayer. Brushing grass off my pants, I rise unsteadily. Clouds have moved in, covering the moon, drenching the cemetery in darkness. The coughing call of a raven splits the night air. I look up. I think I'm alone until I see the figure of a woman standing close to a headstone under the nearest oak.

I hadn't even heard her approach.

She too is speaking to her deceased loved one. I don't want

to disturb the woman, but I'm going to have to pass by to get back to the car.

Bowing my head, I stride through the grass, giving her a wide berth.

The raven calls again, mockingly. I glance up at the sound. The bird has perched on top of the tombstone the woman is facing.

And etched on the stone is the name Joanna Harris.

Shock throttles me—Joanna's not in the ground yet. I freeze, adjusting my eyes to the letters shadowed in the dark. Michael's name is beside Joanna's. There are no dates. The Harrises must've reserved their plot and purchased the head-stone already. But when, exactly? Had Michael bought it last summer, around the time he claims she left him? That action alone would scream guilt.

If I could only remember if the Harrises' headstone had been there when Karen was buried. But I'd been so consumed by my grief, there's no chance I would've noticed anything else.

"Excuse me, who—" I stop. "Samara. What are you doing here?"

It's all I can muster under the circumstances. I hadn't ex-pected to run into anyone here, and I get the feeling Samara Graves feels the same way.

"Detective Shaw." She turns toward me slightly, the forced smile on her face betraying her lack of desire to speak with me. "I didn't see you. What are you doing here?"

"Seeking clarity." My gaze skips to Karen's headstone. "But I'm not sure I'll ever find it." I want to ask what she's doing here, since Joanna isn't in the ground yet, but at the last second, I think better of it. Grief defies reason. If this is where she feels closest to Joanna, so be it. It's not the time or the place for questioning. "Have a good night."

As I walk away, Samara calls, "Are you close to figuring out who killed my friend?"

I turn. "We're taking our time," I say. "We need to make sure we're arresting the right person. Murder cases are serious. We have to be sure."

"You're taking too long." She rubs her hands together briskly. "If you still have questions for me, Detective, fire away. I'm an open book."

I look at the tombstone, searching for the raven that had first called my attention to Joanna's grave, but it must've flown away. "I'm assuming this is where Joanna will be buried?"

"It's a beautiful spot, don't you think?" Her eyes glitter at me.

"It is." That's why I'd chosen it for Karen. "Do you know when the Harrises purchased this plot?"

"Years ago." Her gaze flickers to the stone, then back. "It's not what you think. He didn't purchase it alone. They chose their place together." She's much more observant than she lets on. "I've been thinking more about the conversation you and I had, when you asked if she had any enemies."

"You said that everyone loved her."

"Yes, that's what got me thinking," she begins, but stops. Her brittle voice softens. "Have you looked into the women's clinic in the city? The one she visited last summer?"

"We have."

"At first, Joanna hated going," she says softly. "Despised the drive, the wait time, the fact that the woman would pray over her at the end of each session. But along the way something changed. She suddenly thought the world of her, couldn't wait to go in again. 'She'll fix everything,' she'd say, and then she'd laugh, as if she was the only one aware of some strange joke."

Had the sessions been grief counseling after her miscarriage? Or was she being treated for something else?

"I think the counselor knows more than anyone what was

going on with Joanna in her final few months—why she went to the clinic, who she may have been having problems with."

"I appreciate the tip," I say. "Do you happen to have her name?"

"She never told me the woman's name. Just called her 'my counselor.'"

My brain races. I've already tried to look into employees at the women's clinic, but Dr. Garcia resisted, threatening to call his lawyer. And Patel's already flipped the hourglass, dropping sand faster than I can catch it. Unless I get something more concrete on this counselor, whoever she is, Patel isn't likely to stall Michael's arrest for another interrogation that may go nowhere.

"Joanna was attached to anyone who gave her attention," Samara continues, resting her hand on the headstone, caressing it with her fingertips. "She was desperate to be noticed, to be cared for, wanted, and envied by everyone around her. I think the counselor gave her those things. Joanna was the loneliest woman I've ever met."

"Even though she had Mr. Harris?"

Samara stares me down. "Mr. Harris was working such long hours, he wasn't paying attention to her. When he was around, he was dismissive of her. He didn't care about how she spent her days as long as she was the trophy on his arm. And she liked that, while it suited her. Eventually though, she wanted to be more. She didn't want to be trapped in Ravenwood by herself, with nothing to occupy her time. She didn't have many people she felt she could talk to."

"But she talked to you," I point out.

She nods. "And to that counselor. The odd thing is that Joanna didn't even want children in the first place," Samara says, rubbing her fingers over the rough granite. "Mr. Harris conveniently forgets that. He was the one who wanted the family, not her. Joanna never wanted children. She was still taking birth control, even though they argued all the time about it. Mr. Harris was furious when she started another pill cycle each month. And then, like a miracle, she was pregnant."

"She told you that?"

Samara looks up at me, but her eyes seem dazed. I wonder if she's taking medication. Or recreational drugs. "She finally compromised and told him she'd have one child. One, no more. When she lost that child, she really pulled back from him. I don't believe that their marriage ever fully recovered."

"Did she happen to tell you who the—"

"Father of the baby was?" she interrupts, smirking as if she's enjoying the taste of the secret in her mouth. "Let's just say the timeline didn't match up for it to be Mr. Harris's." The raven calls out again, a single raspy bleat that draws our attention to the tree overhead. When Samara brings her gaze back down to me, her expression has softened.

"But you didn't answer my question, Samara."

"Joanna was almost certain it was Dean's."

I want to believe her, but can I? Does she want me to suspect Dean Lewis, so I don't look elsewhere? I was almost ready to close in on one of the Martins. Or does she want me to think Michael killed Joanna when he found out the child wasn't his? I don't understand her motivations—or what she's gaining from this.

"Does Dean Lewis know?" I ask.

"Of course." She gazes at the ground that'll soon be Joanna's final resting place. "He knew Joanna wouldn't leave Mr. Harris unless he had something in his corner to persuade her. That baby was his bargaining chip. He believed he had a chance. He was wretched when she miscarried."

"I'm sure they both were."

"Oh, Joanna didn't grieve, not for a second. She was physically ill for a week, and used the next to process her feelings, to make her plan. You might not believe me if I told you, but she was thrilled when she lost the baby. *Thrilled*. The counselor told Joanna it was strange to be excited about losing a child. But then they realized it showed how she truly felt about having a baby in the first place. It was like she was given a second chance at life."

Her soft voice goes on relentlessly, and I feel as if, for the first time, I've glimpsed the real Joanna Harris.

"Why did she keep the miscarriage a secret from her husband?"

"To understand the answer to that question, you had to have known Joanna, and the type of woman she was. She got a strange thrill out of keeping things from the men in her life." Samara crosses her arms in front of her, as if she were suddenly chilled to the bone. "The men she brought into her bed—they were pawns in her little game. And they loved her so much, they didn't even care how they were being used. They gave her fancy cars, designer clothes, the perfect house, and in return, she made them feel powerful. As if they *could* control her."

She laughs sourly. "No matter what she made Dean or Travis believe, she was never going to divorce Mr. Harris. She was desperate to live the kind of life his money could offer and was willing to accept his controlling ways in exchange. He *managed* her the way he did his business. And having children was the one thing he desperately wanted from her. The *only thing* she had ultimate control over." She waits two beats, and then: "Joanna believed that miscarriage was the best thing to ever happen to her. A gift from God. And whatever happened at the clinic in June, I think it had something to do with taking back control of her body. I don't know if that's helpful, but there you have it."

As she looks directly at me and purses her lips, my phone rings too loud in the darkness.

"Enjoy the rest of your night, Detective," she says.

"Wait," I call out, fishing my phone out of my pocket. "Samara, don't go."

But she disappears into the night, as mysterious as she'd come. I check my phone's screen. It's Patel.

"Shaw here," I say into the cell.

"Toxicology results are in." He's out of breath, and talking fast. "Joanna had Hydrocodone and Diazepam in her system. Shaw, we got him."

Valium and Vicodin—the ones we found in the back of her medicine cabinet. Had Joanna taken those pills herself, of her own volition, before she was killed? Or had the murderer drugged her before taking her life?

"Overdose?" I ask, staring at Joanna's tombstone.

"It's not conclusive, but we're going after Michael Harris anyway."

Why the hell is he rushing this? As I take a second to curse his urgency, a large bird rustles and takes flight from a nearby tree. My conversation with Samara echoes through my head. Losing her baby. Control over the men in her life. Her religious counselor. How does it all fit?

'She'll fix everything,' she'd say, and then she'd laugh.

"Anything else?" I ask Patel. "What about the autopsy?"

"It's finished. I'm on my way back to the station now. Shaw, we know why Joanna went to the women's clinic. You're not going to believe this, but Joanna's tubes were tied. . . ."

In the distance, the raven cries out again.

TWO HOURS BEFORE COLLEEN'S MURDER

MICHAEL

Colleen and I haven't said much to each other since I called her by Joanna's name, and there's only so many times I can apologize. I was drunk, for Christ's sake. She can't hold my feet to the fire for every single word that comes out of my mouth when I'm in that state. Still, it was a terrible slip, and I'm tired of the tension between us.

Anxious to get home and talk things over with her, I leave work early. I turn in to the drive. A single light is on in the living room—she's probably curled up on the couch reading one of her thrillers. I can almost see her, blanket wrapped around her, hair loose around her shoulders, and my pulse jumps at the thought.

If only we could get back to the way things were.

The back porch is dark this moonless night, making it difficult to find my keys. The bulb must've gone out. I'll have to remember to ask Samara to replace it in the morning. Walking beneath the fixture, I glance up.

Wait . . .

The bulb hasn't burned out. It's missing entirely.

I unlock the door and push it open. A blast of cold air wafts out, followed by Joanna's scent, raising the hair on my arms.

Colleen's books are gone. Her framed pictures are gone from the shelves. Not a single blanket drapes over the back of the couch. I might as well have walked into the house the way it was last summer.

And then I see her.

"Joanna?" I can't stop myself. I walk closer to the figure crouched on the couch. "What—are you all right?"

Dark wet strands of hair drape over a ghostly pale face. A sheer white nightgown sags down her naked shoulders. In her lap, a large book has fallen open. A dark smear of blood mars her lap. It hits me all at once. Colleen and Joanna. How similar their appearances are—*were*.

Confusion warps the air around me. "Colleen?" I whisper, my voice shaking with strain.

I breathe her in—that sickly sweet floral scent I both hate and love—as my heart pulses in an unnatural rhythm. And then she looks up at me with wide, innocent eyes.

Joanna, gorgeous and perfect. The way everyone remembers her. The way she was at the beginning, when things were fresh and new and we were happy.

"You're home." Joanna pats the cushion next to her. She smiles, and I greedily study her features. Soft and supple lips. Bright eyes. Smooth skin. So much like Colleen. "Come. Sit. I have something to show you."

Seconds later, I'm sitting beside her, my thigh touching hers. I can't explain how I lost track of my movements. Don't even try to make sense of it.

"What are you doing here?" My voice sounds strange. As if I'm not the one speaking, or not in control of the words coming out of my mouth. "I thought you were—they said you were—"

Dead.

"Shh," she says, sweeping the back of her hand down my cheek. "I've made everything better. We're finally going to be happy."

Chills settle deep in my bones as she pulls back her hand, and I realize it's covered in mud. It hadn't been a moment before, had it? I swipe the filth away from my cheek. What's happening? Where's Colleen? Nothing makes sense. I shouldn't be here. Not with her. Not anymore.

"We're going to start over." She whirls on me then, but only her head turns. The rest of her body remains still as stone. "Don't you think that's what we should do? Go back to when we were happy? You could go back to being you and I could go back to being me."

"I am me." I cover my heart with a shaking hand. "And you're you."

She stares me down as if it's the first time she's ever laid eyes on me. I hadn't noticed before, but she's wearing a necklace. It's gleaming against the thin, filmy fabric of the nightgown. A gold chain with a tiny medallion of a woman's figure embossed in the center. The figure cradles a topaz gem—the birthstone for November, the month our baby was going to be born.

"Do you like it?" Joanna asks, clutching the medallion in her dirty fist. "It was a present."

"I—I think it suits you. Who gave it to you?"

Lights flicker. Her hands drop to her sides. She's sitting cross-legged, blood pooling from between her legs. My gut sours, and panic strikes through me like a lightning bolt.

"Help me." Tears gloss her eyes as she looks down at the blood in her lap for the first time. "Michael, don't you know what I've done? I need help. I'm hurt."

I jump to my feet, frantic, searching for a phone. "I'll call 911—"

"They can't help me."

She shakes her head slowly, calmly, then raises the arm that's been resting at her side. A pair of scissors is clutched in her muddy fist. Blood glimmers wetly on the blades.

"Joanna," I whisper, shaken to the core. "What'd you do?"

"I already told you, Michael. Weren't you listening?" Her voice is strong. Determined. Not a trace of weakness or indecision. Without warning, the icy Joanna I knew in the end has returned. "I'm making things right, sweetheart. Getting back to the way we were in the beginning. Doesn't a fresh start sound perfect?"

My vision swims again, and I swear I see her smile.

"But you're bleeding, Joanna," I protest. "We need to get you to a doctor."

Blood soaks her white gown and drips on the hardwood with sickening *tap-tap-tap* sounds. Too much blood . . .

"No, no more doctors. I did this for us, *honey*. It was worth it, to make us perfect again." She spins the bloody scissors. "Don't you see? Losing the baby was the best thing to ever happen to us. It wasn't going to make us happy. You don't want a family. You never did."

"Joanna. I did want a family with you. I never wanted anything more—"

"No," she interrupts firmly. "You wanted someone to control. And when you realized I wasn't going to let you, you wanted a child to take my place. You wanted a stupid little puppet. Well, I took the control back, Michael. I fixed us from the inside out."

"What are you talking about? What'd you do?"

"I fixed me." She uses that fake singsong voice she perfected over five years of a terrible marriage.

Tap-tap . . .

"Joanna, what—" I stop as it hits me. "What have you done?" Vomit rises in my throat as I kneel at her feet and shake the scissors from her hands. They fall to her lap. "Joanna, I'll get you the help you need."

She reaches for the scissors again. The blades gleam silver and crimson red. Her scent washes over me, flowers mixing with the scent of blood and metal, and I'm about to throw up.

"Michael? Michael, wake up."

The room is flooding with blood.

Tap-tap-tap . . .

"Michael, are you okay?" Colleen's voice. I can't place where it's coming from.

Nausea sours my stomach. Joanna laughs as I back away from her, from the blood pooling on the floor.

"Michael? Michael, wake up."

I open my eyes. I'm on the couch, where Joanna had been moments before. No blood, but I swear I can smell the metallic tang. No mud. I rub my eyes and struggle to focus. Colleen is standing in front of me, the light from the kitchen bathing her in an aura of gold. She's dressed in white, and as a draft of air sweeps through the house, the familiar aroma of Joy hits me. She's built exactly like Joanna, I realize suddenly, having just seen Joanna's figure so vividly. A petite little thing, with a narrow waist and heart-shaped face. Long hair. Nice smile. Scissors clutched in her hand. No, wait . . .

Digging the heels of my hands into my eyes, I feel like I'm going to break. Snap clean in two like a twig. Swinging my legs to the floor and sitting upright, I lower my head and try to force my heart to calm. The dream felt so real. I could've sworn Joanna was here, blood everywhere, laughing.

"Are you okay?" Colleen asks, her hand suddenly on my back.

"Don't." I jump up from her touch and circle the coffee table as the scent of Joanna's perfume heightens my nausea again. "Don't come any closer."

"Michael—why? What's wrong?"

Because anger and resentment and pain are building to a violent crest inside me, and because I can't push them down any longer.

"Just stay there." I put up my hands. "Please. Give me a second to clear my head. I'm not seeing straight."

"Why don't you sit back down?" She frowns, confused. "Come on, sweetheart, let's get you onto the couch."

But I won't sit. My gaze lingers on the grove across the street. All those smooth trunks and crooked branches. Torrential rain rushes over everything, flooding the street and the grassy area in front of the grove.

Joanna was buried right there, just out of my line of sight.

A car passes by, then slows. It stops in front of Ravenwood, and the doors fly open. Detectives Shaw and Patel emerge from either side, their heads bowed to protect their faces from the barrage of rain.

Colleen opens the door wide before they can knock. They're dressed alike in black shoes, black pants, and white collared shirts, shoulders drenched from even the short time they were exposed to the storm. They smile at Colleen as they pass by, but when their eyes turn to me, their faces turn stony.

"Make yourself at home," Colleen says, oblivious to the tension in the air. "Can I get you an espresso? Tea?"

Shaw lifts his hand dismissively as Detective Patel takes handcuffs from his pocket.

"Mr. Harris," Patel says, "you're under arrest for the murder of your wife, Joanna Harris."

"Wait," Colleen interrupts, shocked. "What?"

Detective Patel goes on with the formal statement, but I can't make out anything through the static buzzing in my brain. The walls close in, and the floor disappears beneath my feet. Colleen starts to cry, and her frenzied voice drones in and out as she tugs on Shaw's shirt. She's begging. Dropping to her knees. Wind and rain blast through the gaping front door, howling through Ravenwood. Joanna's scent swirls in the torrent of air.

"Please, no, he didn't kill her," Colleen pleads, attempting to block the doorway. "You can't do this. You can't take him from me—"

"Step aside, Miss Roper," Patel snaps.

Shaw lifts me off the couch and twists my arms behind my back. The cold prick of metal slaps against my wrists.

"It's okay, Colleen," I say, grasping for a moment of lucidity. "Contact my lawyer. You can get the number in my office. Can you do that for me?"

She nods, tears streaming down her cheeks. "I know you didn't do this. They won't be able to keep you for long. I'll do whatever I can to get you out, I promise, darling. Whatever it takes."

"I know," I say, and lean to plant a kiss on her lips, but the detectives pull me back. "I'll see you soon."

"Soon," she swears. "We're going to be a family, Michael. It's going to be all right. You'll see."

I want to believe her, but I don't dare hope. Not now.

As Shaw escorts me to the car, I lower my head to shield my face against the slashing rain. I glance back at Ravenwood, blinking through the drops gathering on my eyelashes. The house appears ghostly and dark. Shrouded in secrets and lies. The door and two huge windows at the front of the house look like evil, all-seeing eyes and a gaping mouth. Something moves behind one of those eyes. Colleen stands there, biting her nails. When her eyes meet mine, she blows a kiss and crosses her arms over her belly.

And I get the strange skin-crawling feeling it's the last time I'm going to see her.

ONE HOUR BEFORE COLLEEN'S MURDER

COLLEEN

I have to do something—anything—to get Michael out.

Do I need to figure out how to pay bail? I realize I don't have access to Michael's accounts—and there certainly isn't enough money in mine. I start to panic. Wait, Michael told me to call his lawyer first, so he must be able to help. But it's nearly eight o'clock at night on a Sunday. No one will be at Michael's office at this hour. I'd drive over if I had keys to his office, but he's never given me a set. Not even when I was his assistant. I won't be able to get his lawyer's name and number until morning.

I try to find one on my own. A quick Google search pulls up more lawyers' offices in the San Francisco Bay Area than I could possibly imagine. I skim through reviews and testimonies, but my eyes blur before long. Choosing one who looks the most professional—and the most expensive—I dial the number and get sent straight to voicemail. Of course. Who's going to take a case at this hour? I leave a panicked message, hating the tremor in my voice as I ramble through the details of Michael and Joanna's story.

When I hang up, I'm so filled with adrenaline and anxiety, I'm trembling. Waves of nausea rise up, but I can't lose control.

Michael needs me at my best. He needs me more than he's ever needed me before.

I haven't come this far to lose it now.

Ravenwood is too quiet, echoing with the drumming sound of rain on every window. I wish there was someone I could talk to. Someone composed and put together, who would tell me everything's going to be okay in the end.

Because I just don't know anymore. This was never supposed to happen.

I pace through the house, though I haven't the foggiest idea what to do. It makes me heartsick to think of him locked up. I can't raise our baby without him. There has to be a solution.

In order to get Michael out, I'll need to take matters into my own hands and prove the killer is someone else.

I know who that person is.

Throwing on my trench coat, rain boots, and a pair of gloves, I snatch the spare keys off the hook in the kitchen and head outside. Bracing myself against the howling wind and icy rain, I run to unlock the garage. Against the far wall, Joanna's Lexus—my Lexus, now—rests beneath a black cover, which Michael had insisted I use. I search frantically through the cabinets on the back wall as rain hammers against the roof.

There.

Hidden in the Keurig reservoir, where I'd left it when I'd packed up a few kitchen items and replaced them with my own. I'd banked on the fact that no one would think to search a kitchen appliance for something this valuable.

The one thing that can save me, save us.

Feeling as though live wires are pulsing through my arms, I charge through the storm to the Martins'. The path is soggy, and I stumble and nearly sink to my ankles in mud. Rather than head toward the front door, I trudge around back, behind their garden shed, and move a tarp covering a pile of firewood. I find what I'm looking for quickly; after all, I'm the one who put it there.

There's no going back now.

I'm going to prove that Dean killed Joanna.

....

Rounding the corner into the Seascape parking lot, I double-check the address on Dean's business card and squint through the rain-smeared windshield. I scan the garage numbers as I roll by.

1A . . . 1B . . .

Accelerating the Lexus slowly, listening to the scrape of wipers against glass, I count aloud until I reach 3B, Dean's garage. The stall reserved for his Mustang is empty. Does he park inside the garage? Or is he gone? I hesitate for a moment. There's only one way to find out.

Leaving the car idling, I cradle my stomach and step outside. I'm drenched in the seconds it takes to reach the covered carport. Fat raindrops smack against the roof and drown out the rumble of my car's engine as I fumble for the handle on the bottom of the garage door.

Even though I doubt it'll be unlocked, I give the knob a hard yank and gasp as it rolls up. I duck inside, peeling strands of wet hair from my cheeks and eyes. The space is empty and dark, the only light coming from the Lexus's headlights. It reeks of oil. Cabinets on the back wall reach from floor to ceiling. A single lock threads through the handles. No car.

Dean's not home.

Where could he be?

I can't let Michael down now. I run back and climb into the warm interior of Joanna's car. It smells strangely familiar tonight, the way her bedroom had when I'd first gone in, and I realize I never gave much thought to ghosts before.

But I believe in them now.

And I believe they can be exterminated.

When I get Michael out of jail, and we're together with our baby, he'll understand what lengths I went through to be with him. To give him the future he's always wanted.

When this is over, I'll overshadow Joanna completely.

After rummaging through my purse for my cell, I check the business card lying on the seat and dial Dean's number. It goes straight to voicemail.

"Hey, Dean, this is Colleen," I say, a tremor in my voice. "God, I don't know what to do. They arrested Michael for Joanna's murder, but I—I think I know how she was killed, and Michael didn't do it. Can you meet me at Ravenwood in an hour? Please? I really need to talk to you in person. One hour, all right?"

And then, necessities in hand, I scurry into Dean's garage before I lose the courage to follow through with this.

....

As I wait for Dean at Ravenwood, I put the kettle on the stove and think about what I've learned this past week. Michael's lifestyle seemed so enticing from the outside—luxurious cars, a beautiful home, a successful business—but now, I couldn't care less about how glamorous my life could be. Without Michael, those things aren't worth the dirt that'll cover Joanna's grave.

Pulling two mugs from the cabinet, I watch for the headlights of Dean's car to sweep across the windows. A part of me fears he won't show, but I know what Dean cares most about—*who* he cares most about. Dean needs to keep everything perfectly on schedule and consistent: his sacred breakfast routine, his carefully prepared dishes. But he couldn't place Joanna in the neat, orderly box of his life, especially when their affair didn't go as he'd planned. So she paid for it.

Soon, everyone will know how vile Dean truly is, how deep his obsession with Joanna ran.

It's time to prove he's not only skilled with a knife, but with a shovel.

When lights beam into the kitchen, I take a shaky breath. I press the record button on my phone. This is what I have to do. Sliding my phone into my back pocket, I return to my position behind the counter and fill the two mugs with boiling water.

I hear his car door slam shut, and when I don't see his form cross the window, I realize he's planning on entering through the back, as he always does.

Moving fast, I drop a tea bag into each mug and then doctor them to my liking. *See if he enjoys being served without being asked.* A splash of milk and a teaspoon of honey. And then, I fish the tiny, rolled-up Ziploc bag out of the drawer beside the sink. I tip the white, ground-up contents into his tea, rinse out the bag in the sink, and toss it in the trash. Dean won't taste the Restoril, but the drug will hit his system soon.

I only hope I spiked it enough to finish the job.

Michael will never know the lengths I've gone to secure a happy future for us, but if he ever finds out, I'd like to think he'd thank me for this. For freeing him, in every sense of the word.

"Hello?" Dean storms inside, bringing the wind and rain with him into the kitchen. "Colleen?"

"Oh, Dean, I'm so glad you came!" I lay it on thick and embrace him in a tight hug. It's the first time I've made such a gesture, and he registers the strangeness by stiffening in my arms. His raincoat is spattered with rain. "They arrested Michael—he's gone."

"I got your message and came as fast as I could," he says, patting my back awkwardly. "They think he killed Joanna? I have to admit, the thought had crossed my mind that he'd—"

"This whole situation has just gotten so far out of control," I interrupt as a shudder rolls through me. I can't let him finish what he was about to say. Not when I'm recording his every word. "I don't know what I'm going to do. They came and handcuffed him, and everything."

Gripping me by the shoulders, Dean holds me at arm's length. "You said you know how Joanna was killed." His voice is raw with worry.

"Can we sit down—would that be all right? I think my body's pumping too much adrenaline or something, and I'm suddenly not feeling well. I made tea. Would you mind sitting with me, just for a minute? Once my head stops spinning, I'll tell you everything. Here," I say, and quickly push the tea laced with something extra special toward him. "I took the liberty of making yours. Hope you don't mind."

"No, that's fine."

He removes his wet coat and hangs it on the rack, as I take a seat on the opposite side of the island.

"I just want to know what's going on." He takes a sip of the tea, and grimaces. "You added honey?" he asks skeptically.

"Mmm." I drink my own tea heartily, watching him over the lip of the mug. The milk and honey add the perfect hint of sweetness, but the sour look on Dean's face is even sweeter. "It's the way I've always taken my tea. Thought you'd like it."

He frowns, but takes another sip. "I assume Mr. Harris will be out of jail by tomorrow morning?"

I shake my head and stare into my drink for answers that aren't there. "I have no idea," I say weakly.

"Didn't you call a lawyer?"

"I left a message."

"Surely Mr. Harris has enough in your accounts to cover the bail to get him out—oh, wait," he says with a grin. "Let me guess. . . . Mr. Harris wanted complete control over the finances, too? Some things never change. This time it came back to bite him. I assume if you had the money on your own, he'd already be out by now."

"I'm doing all I can under the circumstances," I whimper. "I feel like I'm rattling apart. I haven't eaten anything all day, and—"

"You haven't eaten?" He glares. "Are you completely incapable of caring for yourself? Ugh. I'll cook while you talk."

"I'm sorry I'm not more prepared," I say. "I appreciate your help so much. . . ." I choke back a sob.

With a disgusted huff, he searches the refrigerator and cupboards. "Spaghetti will have to do. It's the fastest thing I can make with what we have here."

He opens the wine cellar door and flips on the light.

"Wait," I say. "Where are you going?"

"The recipe calls for red wine." He points down the stairs. "Is that a problem?"

"I'm pregnant." I caress the curves of my stomach. "I can't have wine."

"It's for flavor. The alcohol burns off in the cooking. Besides, a little wine wouldn't hurt you."

He finishes his tea and sets down the mug. Then he disappears down the stairs and returns a few minutes later with a bottle. Pulling zucchini, onion, and tomato from the fridge, he sets everything on the counter next to the stove and pours oil in the pan. He spins the burner dial to high, checks the flame, and then waits for the oil to bubble.

"All right, you said you knew how Joanna was killed." Sliding a knife from the block, he chops the vegetables with rapid, erratic slices. "Let's hear it."

"You and Joanna were close near the end, weren't you?"

He nods. But he's frowning now, rubbing his hand over his eyes as if the big, gleaming kitchen were suddenly enveloped in fog. "I was one of the only people she trusted."

"Well, then I'm sure you know about her visits to the women's clinic in June, and what happened to her near the end."

"What did that *maid* tell you?" he grunts. "Because you can't believe half of it."

As the oil spits, he slides toward the sink to wash his hands. Reaching for the soap, he grasps nothing but air. He chuckles darkly before trying to pump out the suds again. The Restoril is working fast. He'll be out on the couch in twenty minutes, maybe less.

"Joanna was happy when she lost the baby, Dean."

He wags a spatula at me. "You're trying to get a rise out of me." He's starting to slur his words.

"I'm not." My heartbeat strums in my ears. "It wasn't a rumor Samara told me, either. It's the truth. The detectives have probably figured it out by now too. Joanna didn't even want the baby in the first place."

"The detectives didn't know her, and you didn't either, for that matter. How could *any* of you determine how she felt about the baby?" Dropping the dish towel on the counter beside the stove, he spins toward me, staggering a little. "She wanted that child because it was *ours*—hers and mine."

He pauses, eyeing me for some kind of shocked reaction. When I don't respond, he continues, "The baby was our future, and she was distraught when she lost it. Distraught!" He swipes sweat from his forehead. "Christ, I can't see straight."

"You're wrong, Dean." I take a deep breath and steady myself for the final blow. "What happened at the clinic explains everything, and shows her true feelings about the pregnancy."

"What?" The word explodes out of him. "What the devil are you talking about?"

"She had her tubes tied in July. So she couldn't get pregnant again."

Squeezing his eyes shut, Dean sways into the counter. "But I don't—why would—you're wrong. You don't know *anything*."

"Once you see the autopsy results, you'll see that I'm right. She lied to you, Dean. She didn't want your baby, and she took matters into her own hands to ensure she'd never get pregnant again. You were never going to have a family with her."

"*Noooo*. She was going to run away with me, and leave him and—it wasn't supposed to end this way."

I need to bait him further. "Don't you see? After everything that'd happened, she was going to stay with Michael. She chose Michael over you."

"No," he seethes. "She chose *wealth*, and where did that get her? Buried in the mud in the goddamn grove. She should've stayed with *me*, married *me*, had *my* child. If she'd done that, she would still be alive. Oh, Joanna," he moans.

I slide off the stool so I'm able to run if he charges. There's no telling what he'll do in his dazed state. I glance around the room for something I can use to defend myself if he comes after me. A wine opener? Whiskey glasses? If I could get past him, I could make a run for the knives in the block near the stove.

"I get why you lost control," I say, stepping slowly away from the island. "Michael wins for beating his wife. And you lose for loving her."

Clutching his head, he sways back, back, back, and bumps into the stove. Behind him, oil simmers in the blistering-hot pan. "She was supposed to leave with me—the sixteenth, that was the day we'd planned. She was going to leave that bastard on their anniversary. But then she said she couldn't do it. I went numb, and I can't remember, but I thought that I— I thought I might've . . ."

"What, Dean?" I ask, hanging on his every word. "What'd you do?"

"I drank myself stupid. Crawled back begging, but Joanna wouldn't listen. Said it was over for good. I don't remember the rest of that day, but honestly I'm—I'm glad she's dead. I'm glad it happened, Lord forgive me. I'm *glad*."

Bingo. I've nailed him. The police will see that Dean, drunk and in a blind rage, murdered Joanna on the day they were supposed to run away together.

His legs buckle, and he stumbles, grasping at the counter for balance. "What's happening . . ."

At that, I race for the knives. He pitches forward, blocking my path. "Stay away from me, Dean. I won't tell anyone what you've done, I swear. Please don't hurt me."

"What are you talking about? What's happ—" His eyes open abnormally wide, as if he's having trouble focusing. He snatches the mug, stares into the bottom, and swipes his thumb over the rim. "Colleen, you crazy bitch, what'd you put in here?"

"Dean, you're ill, and—"

"Tell me!"

I put my hands up in defense as he lurches toward me. This is bad—he was supposed to pass out after the confession. "Stop, Dean, you're scaring me. It was only tea. You need to leave, okay? You're ill. Just go home, and we'll sort this all out tomorrow morning."

"I'm not going anywhere." He stops before he reaches me, gasping as if he can't breathe. "Not until you tell me what's happening."

He lunges at me again and staggers when our bodies collide. He loses his balance as our arms tangle. He's heavy, hanging on my shoulders and clawing at my arms as he struggles to regain his footing. I'm not strong enough to hold up his weight.

"Get off, Dean, you're hurting me! Let me go, or I'll—"

"Tell me what you did! I swear to God I'll beat you un-til—"

"I tell you what you want to hear?" Fear sears through me. "Is that right? Just the way it happened with Joanna."

It's worked so perfectly: my plan, and his confession. But as I squirm, he only holds tighter. I want to call for help, but we're alone in Ravenwood, and no one will hear me anyway over the deafening storm. My feet skid against the tile as we grapple. We're too close to the stairs, to the wine cellar. His face is close to mine, his pupils shrunken and nostrils flaring. Sweat beads at his temples. I've pushed him too far, and now there's no going back. I hadn't planned for him to become so violent. Who knows what Dean could do to me in this state?

A pop sounds from the stove. Dean doesn't seem to hear. He doesn't see the sparks fly from the burner and catch on the dish towel.

I gasp as flames engulf the cloth. Writhing against him, twisting in his hold, I fight for air and space and with one hard push, I jerk out of his embrace. I expect my body to slam against wood, but there's only air. My feet slip down the stairs, into the depths of the wine cellar. I land with a sickening crack. Pain explodes through my chest. My head snaps back against the floor. Numbness spreads from my legs into the upper half of my body. My vision blurs, then refocuses on the orange haze blazing through the kitchen.

RACHAEL

I should be long gone from Point Reina right now, but I forgot my Louis Vuitton clutch at home—the one that matches my bag—and I'd stuffed some important banking papers inside. God, I hope Travis isn't home. I can't handle seeing him again. As hard as it is, I'm ready to close that chapter of my life. We haven't been happy for some time, and it's taken Joanna's death—and all his dirty secrets that have tumbled out because of it—for me to realize that. Hopefully, if I know him like I think I do, he'll be at the distillery, drinking his sorrows away.

Smoke plumes into the sky as I round the corner on Cypress, cutting off any thoughts of Travis, my papers, or my clutch.

"Oh my God," I whisper, leaning across the seat to get a better view. Thank God Michael isn't home. Jail isn't the ideal place to be, but under the circumstances . . .

Ravenwood is burning.

The wind rages, fanning the flames of the fire faster than the rain can quell it. And Dean's car sits at the curb.

Oh, God . . . Dean . . .

Colleen may be trapped inside, too.

I slam the car into park and dig my phone out of my purse to call 911. What else can I do?

"Fire," I blurt out when someone answers. "Hurry, it looks bad."

As I'm giving the address, a media van turns the corner of Beach and Cypress. Through the windshield, I can see them pointing at Ravenwood, gawking, yelling. They're going to cover the story. And I'm sitting in the car on my phone.

This is my chance.

Screw the six o'clock local news. My face will earn national attention. I'll be a hero.

Pushing away all hesitations, I race out of the car. I pretend not to see the van and cower as the rain pummels down, flattening my hair. I'm crossing the yard when flames shoot out the kitchen window, shattering the glass. Whimpering, I duck and burst inside the front door.

"Dean! Colleen!"

I've stepped straight into hell.

Dark, thick smoke clings to my lungs like tar when I attempt to take a breath. Eerie rippling sounds emanate from the kitchen and I hear an earsplitting crack. The wood beams holding Ravenwood together are fracturing under the flames. Yanking a blanket off the back of the couch, I wrap it around my face, leaving only my eyes exposed. They burn and tear as I scramble down the hall, coughing.

"Dean!"

I can't find him.

"Colleen!" Bending low to escape the greasy billows of smoke, I scan the living room and kitchen in a flurry of stumbling movements. Panic sets in. "Colleen!"

No one's here.

But the Mustang out front . . .

Flames engulf the kitchen counters and burn through the cabinets, which churn out even more horrid black smoke. I choke on it as I call out their names over and over again.

And suddenly, I catch sight of movement. It's the door to the cellar, wavering on its hinge.

They wouldn't be downstairs . . . would they?

Shooting a glance at the still-open door, I envision the warm, safe confines of my car where I could wait for help to arrive, but—*no.* I can't leave until I'm sure everyone is out. Crawling—the only way to escape the smoke pluming through the kitchen—I scramble into the cellar doorway.

"Dean!"

I see him, crumpled at the bottom of the stairs.

"I'm coming!"

In a rush of adrenaline, I clamber down the stairs. The air is cleaner down here, but not by much. My lungs ache, and tears stream from the smoke as I descend.

At the base of the stairs, I see Colleen. She's draped over Dean, her head resting on his chest as if she's listening for a heartbeat.

"He fell!" she cries out. Her cheeks are filthy with smoke and tears. "He hit his head, and I—I can't find a pulse!"

Shock freezes the blood in my veins. Dean's . . . *dead?* He's flat on his back, mouth gaping open like a fish, his eyes rolled back. His chest isn't rising and falling, and his lips have taken on a sick purple tint. I crouch to check his pulse for myself, but Colleen shrieks in pain and throws her arms around my legs.

"I need help," she wails, gazing up at me in horror. "I think I broke my leg."

The sound of something exploding ricochets off the walls upstairs and reverberates over the arched beams above our heads.

This ceiling might not hold.

Gaze shifting from Dean to Colleen, and to her belly, I make the choice, knowing it'll haunt me for the rest of my life. I sling my arm around Colleen's back and help her up the stairs, staggering, supporting her weight, praying the stairs hold long enough for us to escape. I'm not going to be able to carry her far. The flames are hellish in the kitchen. Wheezing and tightening the blanket around my mouth with one hand, I guide Colleen into the living room with the other. She grips my shoulder painfully tight and hobbles through the scorching heat.

Once we've burst out into the clean, sweet, fresh air, sirens wail in the distance. Ice-cold rain carried by wind gusts smack into my face and soothe the heat that's burrowed into my skin. A safe distance away, the media van sits at the curb, and someone jumps from its sliding door, camera in hand. I hope they were already recording; I would hate to have done all that for nothing.

As I hear parts of the house splinter and collapse behind us, I realize we need to get far away, fast.

"Come on," I say, holding most of Colleen's weight. "We're almost there."

"Thank you . . ." She doubles over, coughing. "You saved me. You're an angel."

"Thanks." If I wasn't coughing myself, I would laugh. The sirens are closer now. "Real help is on the way."

We reach the edge of the grove, and the acrid scent of mud stings my nose. As we collapse to the ground, soaked and stunned, I realize we're on top of Joanna's grave.

I wonder if any of us will ever be free from the series of lies and tragedies that led us here. As I watch Ravenwood burn with a blood-red glow, I think I know.

TWENTY-FOUR HOURS AFTER COLLEEN'S MURDER

DETECTIVE SHAW

Sipping my coffee outside Colleen's hospital room, I watch Michael scoot his chair closer to her bed and cling to her hand while she sleeps. I hate this place—Karen and I spent too much time here. The sterile aroma of bleach and latex gives me the creeps and dredges up my worst memories.

Michael was released this morning, all charges dropped, and we've spent the last day waiting for Colleen to recover enough to give us all the details about what happened.

"I'm surprised you haven't rubbed my nose in it," Patel says from beside me. He's blowing on a cup of steaming cafeteria sludge. "I guess I'll say it first: you were right, and I was wrong. Michael Harris was innocent."

"We're too old for told-you-so games, but . . ." I bury my smile in a drink. "Told you so."

I check the time. A little after four in the afternoon. Colleen's only woken up for a few brief moments, just long enough to smile each time she gets a look at Michael.

"He's been asking what happened," I say. "It's time we tell him."

Patel nods and rises. He tosses his coffee cup and strides into the room without an invite. "Knock, knock," he says.

"Please don't wake her." Michael looks up, the purple smudges beneath his eyes indicating he hasn't slept. "It's good for the baby that she rests as much as possible."

"Let's step outside, then." I motion toward the hallway outside her room. "We won't take up too much of your time."

He lowers his head to her hand and plants a kiss on her pale knuckles, then follows us into the hall.

"Did your lawyer inform you of what's been going on?" Patel asks.

"Not really." Michael shoves his hands in his jeans. "He just said I was free to go, and Colleen was here. I came as fast as I could."

"Your girlfriend suffered a traumatic incident," Patel says dryly. "She's lucky to be alive."

At the mention of her name, we all look into Colleen's room.

"Although she's been in and out of consciousness since she arrived here," my partner goes on, "the recording she had on her phone, along with Rachael's testimony, gave us a good picture of what happened. I'm sure she'll share all the details when she's feeling stronger, but from what we can piece together, Dean Lewis murdered your wife. It sounds like jealousy drove him to it. Apparently he and Joanna were having an affair, and he couldn't handle the fact that she wouldn't run away with him."

"Dean killed Joanna?" Michael shakes his head. "No. Not possible."

"Afraid it's true," I respond. "Your wife's wedding ring was found in one of the cabinets in his parking garage. There were a few shovels in there as well. We're waiting on DNA results, but we're fairly certain we've found the murder weapon."

Michael blinks at me, disbelieving.

"We still have to fill in some holes," Patel continues. "Dean Lewis's body was discovered in the wine cellar of your home. There was a near-lethal dose of sedatives in his veins. Looks like he and your girlfriend got into some kind of scuffle. Maybe she confronted him with what she suspected and he knew he had to silence her. The gist of it is that he had some kind of a psychotic break and fell down the stairs. Cracked his head on the tile. Knocked him out cold. When Rachael saw the smoke and came in to rescue your wife—"

"Rachael?" Michael repeats, seemingly having trouble catching his breath. "Rachael pulled Colleen from the fire?"

Patel's eyes shift to mine, as if to ask which one of us should handle this part.

"That's right. Rachael said she was on her way to San Francisco when she realized she'd forgotten something at home. She turned around, drove back, and noticed the smoke. It's too bad she didn't arrive sooner. Another few minutes might've made the difference in saving your home."

"My lawyer told me about Ravenwood," Michael says grimly.

"You can always rebuild," I offer, though I know it's not helpful. Patel and I had visited the smoking ruins that morning. There wasn't much left. "We're still waiting for the fire department to determine the cause, but they're pretty sure it started in the kitchen."

"None of that matters now," Michael says, and I believe him. "I don't give a damn about Ravenwood, or the property, and I don't give a damn about Dean—not if he did what you say he did. The doctors say Colleen has some bruising, and her leg is broken, but other than that, she and the baby are going to be fine. That's the most important thing." He pauses, and then asks, "How's Rachael? Is she okay?"

"They admitted her overnight, as a precaution," I answer. "She left earlier today. No major injuries, but she's spooked."

"Pulling your friend out of a fire—and having to leave somebody else behind—might do that to you," Patel interjects.

"She gave us a number for us to reach her if we had any questions," I add. "From what I understand, she's left her husband. She'll be staying in the city for now."

Michael blows out a shaky breath. I swear he appears twenty years older than the day we met.

"So, what now?" he asks, staring into her room.

"We'll finish our investigation, tie up any loose ends," I say. "They'll keep Colleen here for observation, to make sure the baby is safe. Then you both can get out of the spotlight for a while."

He glances up at me, then smiles. His whole face seems to light up. "Then if we're all settled here, I'm going back to my girlfriend."

He shakes our hands—mine first, then Patel's—and walks away.

"Murderer overdoses, takes a spill down the stairs, knocks himself out, and a fire takes care of the rest," Patel grumbles. "Can't get much cleaner than that."

"Well," I begin.

"What?"

"There's still the question of why Joanna got her tubes tied. Why do something that drastic and not tell her husband? Or her lovers?"

"Why do women do anything?" Patel laughs. "Who cares, anyway? That has nothing to do with why she was killed."

"Maybe. But what about that necklace? Where'd it come from? Why'd Joanna have it around her neck if she wasn't the religious type?"

"That again?" Patel groans. "Maybe the counselor gave it to her, maybe she stole it. Doesn't matter. There aren't many cases that tie up as neatly as this one did. Let this necklace thing go or it'll drive you crazy." He pats me on the back and heads down the hall toward the exit. "Speaking of crazy, did you ever finish that Rubik's Cube?"

"No, not yet," I admit, keeping pace with him through the lobby. "Every side is finished except for one, and no matter what I do, one square in the corner won't line up."

Patel breaks into another laugh. "Maybe one day you'll figure it out. But today, buddy, you're buying lunch to celebrate my new promotion."

FORTY-EIGHT HOURS AFTER COLLEEN'S MURDER

MICHAEL

As Colleen's eyelids flutter, and then finally open, I slide to the edge of my chair and squeeze her hand.

"Hey," I whisper. "How are you feeling?"

She licks her lips and bats her eyes as if she's having trouble keeping them open. "Better. Are the detectives gone?"

"Yeah, it's just you and me now." I kiss her cheek, her nose, and wish I could hold her in my arms. "You were so brave, baby. So brave."

Swallowing hard, she tries to sit upright. I arrange the pillows behind her and use the remote to tilt the bed. She winces, holding on to her side. "How long have I been here?" she asks, her voice so weak that my heart aches.

"Long enough. I'm ready to go home." I squeeze her hand again. "What about you?"

She nods. Her eyelids droop, and for a moment I think she is going to sleep again. "But they said . . . Ravenwood . . . we don't have a home to go back to."

"Shh," I say, stroking her cheek. "Home is anywhere we

say it is. For now, it'll be a hotel in the city, but soon we'll find a new home—one that fits our new family perfectly." I had been stunned and hurt to read about Joanna's procedure in the autopsy report, but it proved that I never would've had a family with her. She'd deliberately robbed me of that. Now, with Colleen, I can change everything. "I don't want you worrying about anything anymore. All that matters is that you and our baby are safe."

She smiles faintly, closing her eyes. "Say that again."

"All that matters is that you and our baby are safe."

A tear rolls down her cheek. "You have no idea how much I've done—how much I've hoped and prayed that we'd be able to move forward. I love you so much, Michael. . . ."

Wiping the tear away with my thumb, I swallow down the ache forming in my own throat. "I love you, Coll. Everything's going to be all right."

"It's going to be better than all right," she murmurs. "Our story will have the perfect ending."

"It's our beginning," I agree, and kiss her. When I finally pull away, she's smiling at me with more happiness than I could possibly deserve.

But when she reaches up to touch my cheek, she winces. "The doctors told me I'm going to have to take it easy for a while," she says. "I've been thinking—I know I wasn't keen on the stay-at-home-mom role before, but I think I'd like to give it a try. I think that I'd like to raise our baby full-time. Would that be okay, Michael?"

"Nothing would make me happier," I assure her. "I'm so glad we're on the same page."

"What do you mean?"

As I brush my fingers over her hand, I perch on the edge of her bed. "I assumed you wouldn't want to come back to work once we had the little one, so I hired someone to take your place."

At that, she frowns. "What—you mean at the office?"

"I have a new personal secretary. She said she knows you, actually. Recognized you from a picture on my desk. She said she worked with you at your previous job, and that last summer, my company was all you talked about."

All the color drains from Colleen's face. "Who?"

"A girl named Tiffany. I think she's going to be a perfect fit." I pause. "But, sweetheart, why didn't you ever tell me you worked at a women's clinic?"

ONE WEEK AFTER COLLEEN'S MURDER

COLLEEN

"In the name of the Father, and of the Son, and of the Holy Spirit." I dab two fingers to my forehead. Center of my chest. My left shoulder. My right. "My last confession was in July, six months ago. Before I begin, I need to ask you something, Father."

He lowers his head toward the screen dividing us. "Of course."

Outside the confessional, the church is filled with attendees for Joanna's funeral. I can hear people speaking in low, grieving voices. A few seconds ago, I slipped out of the pew, telling Michael I needed a moment to myself, and my heart hasn't stopped pounding since.

"Is it true that you are bound, as a man of the cloth, to keep my confession secret, no matter the sins I've committed?"

"I am," he says.

"Even if they're mortal sins?"

"Mortal sins are a deadly offense against God, but He will

forgive every sinner who is truly sorrowful. The sinner must confess, complete penance, and set a firm resolution not to commit the sin again."

"I see."

"If you are ready to repent, rest assured the sacramental seal is inviolable. Sins confessed to me still remain between you and the Lord—I am merely the vessel you will use to cleanse your spirit. Now, what sins have you committed that you would like to share with the Lord?"

I take a deep breath, inhaling the scent of oil and candles, and try to meet the gaze of the priest sheltered behind the screen. I can't see his face, only the wispy white hair that falls down the sides of his head, and the deep crease lines etched around the corners of his eyes and mouth. Outside the confessional, another priest begins a prayer for Joanna to comfort everyone who loved her. I cringe at hearing her name.

"Lord forgive me, I have committed three sins," I confess softly. "The first way I've displeased God is by lying. During the application process at my job at a clinic, I used my mother's maiden name rather than my own. It was a rash attempt at reinvention, to forge a new identity after running from a man who didn't treat me well. I didn't want him to find me, and I thought—well, I thought it'd be easy to become someone else. Like shedding one skin and trying on another."

"And what consequences came from executing this sin?"

"I never heard from him again," I say, satisfied. "I'd done what I set out to do: eliminate him from my life. But after a couple months, my boss at the clinic started asking questions. I hadn't thought the details through. By the time he confronted me, though, I'd already committed my second sin."

As the priest crosses one leg over the other, the wooden bench groans beneath his weight. "Which was?"

I wring my hands together in my lap. "Coveting my neighbor's wife. Only she wasn't technically my neighbor, and it wasn't she that I coveted, but her husband. She was my very first patient when I was training to be a therapist. This woman had everything I'd ever wanted, right in the palm of her hand: wealth, beauty, a perfect husband. But she didn't appreciate any of it."

The mourners mumble "Amen" as one voice.

"Envy is one of the seven deadly sins," the priest whispers, "but it's not a mortal one."

"Yes, Father, but I haven't finished." I pause, glaring at the screen. "She lied to her husband, cheated on him, took him and the lifestyle he gave her for granted. Then she deceived him in the worst imaginable way: she made certain she could never get pregnant again. She committed these sins without remorse, and acted against my advice. It wasn't just envy that drove me to take action—Father, she deserved it."

"Oh, my child—"

"That's my third sin, Father. I took from her what she took from him: God's precious gift of *life*."

"Let me make sure I understand," the priest whispers, after a stunned silence. "Are you saying the mortal sin was—"

"Murder." I refrain from smiling as our baby tumbles inside me. "And now I'm giving her husband what he deserved all along—a perfect wife and a perfect child."

He mumbles something—a sick, hoarse sound—and then squirms in his seat and clears his throat. "My child, taking a life is the most grievous of sins. God takes these offenses very seriously."

Someone is speaking at the podium about Joanna, and the voice echoes off the walls of the church. I hear Joanna's name again and again, and I can't wait for the day when they stop celebrating her.

"I understand, Father, but it had to be done, and God made it easy to execute. The woman trusted me. I advised her at the clinic for weeks. On the day of her last appointment, July sixteenth, I stole two bottles of medication from her purse while she went to the restroom. When she returned, I asked her to meet me to talk outside of the clinic. As friends. Of course, I had other plans."

Someone begins playing "Amazing Grace" on guitar, and everyone sings along. I swear I hear Michael's voice rising above the rest.

"She suggested an evening stroll through a cypress grove in Point Reina, and I told her I'd bring coffee. I spiked hers with enough Valium and Vicodin to kill her—because that was what had been prescribed to her, you see. Everyone would believe she overdosed, and that'd be the end of it. I took an Uber to meet her. We walked at dusk, winding through the trees along the dirt trails. She'd given the clinic a false name, but that night, she told me the truth about her identity, her real name, and Michael's too. We sipped our coffee together on the trail overlooking the ocean. At the time, I had no idea I'd been standing mere feet away from the place I would lovingly call *home*.

"As we continued talking, though, I started to worry. The drugs weren't working. Or perhaps I hadn't given her enough. I thought I'd lost my chance." I hang my head. "If God had wanted me to spare her, He certainly could've swayed me in another direction. Instead, He gave me the necessary tools. We stopped near a bench at the cliff's edge, and there it was, just sitting there as if it'd been meant for me to find: a shovel. God only knows who had left it there. It was exactly what I needed, at precisely the right moment."

The memory of Joanna's final evening rears its head, and I can almost imagine myself back there. The sun had just dipped below the horizon, blanketing the grove in a burnt-orange glow. Joanna was blabbing on and on about her dinner plans that evening with her lover—Travis, I know now—when I raised the shovel and struck her. I stripped the wedding ring from her finger before burying her. Did she deserve to keep in death what she didn't cherish in life?

And then I exchanged her ring for the necklace I wore

around my neck every day—I wanted it to burn through her sinful, selfish flesh. I kept her ring until I found the perfect place to hide it. I stashed the shovel in the nearest yard—how serendipitous that it had been the Martins'! I didn't know what to do with her prescription bottles, so I kept them, and ultimately replaced them inside the bathroom cabinet at Ravenwood. I assumed that's where Joanna kept them hidden away from Michael when she was alive. In hindsight, I should've gotten rid of them immediately. I sent a final text from Joanna's phone to give Michael a clean end to his marriage. His lie that she'd run away to Los Angeles to be with her sister kept my secret safe. Until that stupid dog dug her up six months later, of course.

"It was as if God had illuminated the path before I'd even walked it," I continue. "Yes, I committed a series of sins, but it was all so simple—like it was meant to happen."

The priest makes another muffled sound, but I don't let it distract me from continuing to the most righteous part of the story.

"I dug up all the information I could on Michael and fell for him before I even applied for a job at his company. It was an intense and pure kind of love, Father, and I knew God always meant for us to be together. He was so different from any other man I'd been with—I finally felt someone truly cared for me. But his wife's shoes were harder to fill than I'd realized, and for a long while, I didn't know if I was going to be able to do it. I went into her bedroom and stole her clothes and perfume so I could rekindle some of the feelings he must have had for her—and have him transfer those feelings to me. Along the way, I stole her husband's heart, and no matter what has happened, I'm not sorry for that."

The mourners go silent for a moment. I hear the priest take a ragged breath, but I have one more thing to say. "Funny thing is, I learned that balancing the scales gets easier as you go. Just last week, I was forced to do it again."

"What do you mean, my child?"

"I had to eradicate a sinner from the earth in order to save an innocent man from a death sentence." Michael's life for Dean's. An easy trade. "And now God's work is done. I'm sorry for my sins, Father, and any other sins I may have committed in my life. Lord, please forgive me."

There is a long silence on the other side of the screen. Then he says, "You have confessed grave sins, my child, but God will grant forgiveness if there is true remorse in your heart. Are you ready to receive penance and live a life of grace?"

"Yes, Father. Thank you."

"Give thanks to the Lord." His voice falters for a moment, as if he's not sure what he is going to say next. "For He is good." I listen intently as the priest assigns penance—a small price to pay for what I've done—and bask in the sacramental absolution of the Church. The weight has been lifted from my shoulders; I can breathe again. I'm cleansed. Even though I can't distinguish the movements exactly, I know the priest is making the sign of the cross over me. I wonder if he's ever heard such an honest confession before.

"One more thing, my child," he says as I'm about to leave. "If I may?" He pauses, and through the screen I think I glimpse him lowering his head into his hands. "Some sicknesses can't be cured with a simple confession. Sometimes the body and mind must be treated by earthly means. Would you mind if I referred you to someone, so you can extinguish any evil lingering in your heart?"

"Oh, Father, there is no evil within me anymore! Not one drop." I smile. "Besides, there isn't any reason for me to sin again. My life is going to be perfect from here on out. Absolutely, blissfully perfect."

With a conscience as clear and bright as the sun, I step out of the confessional and wait at the back of the church for Joanna's service to end. The nave is dark and smells like well-oiled wood and incense, a mixture that reminds me of my childhood, when my parents would take me to Mass. A gorgeous brunette sits near the altar, next to Michael. Decked out in black, she has narrow shoulders and dark, glossy hair swept back and pinned on the side of her head. When she turns to glance at the man beside her, I can see a heart-shaped chin and a narrow, sloping nose. Even though I haven't seen Joanna since last summer, I know instantly that the woman is Heather, her sister. They look so much alike; my heart hitches at the sight.

In the second row, behind Michael, Travis sits with his arm casually resting on the back of the pew. Rachael is a solid yard away, dressed in black with her pale golden hair falling down her back. It looks like he's trying to mend things between them, but she's keeping her distance. Before the ceremony, I caught up with her for a few minutes. She said she's done keeping secrets in her glass house, and has already signed a lease for a new apartment in the city.

The service goes on for the next ten minutes, honoring Joanna's glory days with a video montage Heather must've put together. The moment the priest concludes the service, Michael stands and searches for me through the crowd. Everyone moves toward him, hands outstretched, eager to hug his grief away. But when Michael catches my gaze, he strides down the main aisle with purpose, ignoring those around him.

Suddenly, he stops in the middle of the aisle. Something distracts him. He reaches into his coat pocket and pulls out his phone. The corner of his lips twitch as he reads a text.

Was he holding back a smile?

When he glances up, his expression changes again. A warm blush rises to his cheeks, and a glimmer of something mischievous flits across his eyes. I wonder what that text message was about. . . .

"What is it?" I ask when he's closed the distance between us.

"Just the office." He grips me gently by the shoulders. "They can't seem to finish this proposal without me. I'm going to have to pull another all-nighter. You'll be all right if I leave once we get home, won't you?"

"Yes, of course."

I know he's lying. This is the third "all-nighter" this week. I clasp my hands in front of me and squeeze until my fingers go numb. He's going to be spending time with *her* again. My replacement, Tiffany. The eager secretary sitting right outside his office door, willing to do *anything* for him. I know she's trying to seduce him—because I did it myself not too long ago.

Only she's made one grave mistake. She's underestimated me.

As Michael escorts me outside, a black-and-white patrol car drives past the church. It brakes suddenly before swerving against the curb, only a few car-lengths away. My heart leaps into my throat when I see the silhouettes of Detective Shaw and Detective Patel. And now I can't breathe.

"Are you all right, Coll?" Michael rubs his hand up and down my back reassuringly. "What's the matter?"

"Nothing." Detective Shaw's beady eyes are watching me through the rearview mirror, I'm certain of it. "Let's get out of here."

I fold my arms over my stomach and brace for the coming of another storm. I will do what I need to secure my future, and all will be forgiven in the end.

For His mercy endures forever.

SIX MONTHS UNTIL COLLEEN'S *NEXT* MURDER

AUTHOR'S NOTE

Several years ago, my husband and I took a leisurely drive along Northern California's coast and discovered the Moss Beach Distillery perched on the edge of a cliff just north of Half Moon Bay. We ducked inside, seeking reprieve from the rainy weather, and were illuminated by tales of the Blue Lady: a ghost that haunts the restaurant. As the story goes, over seventy-five years ago, the woman (who always dressed in blue) fell in love and had an affair with the distillery's piano player. But she was already married to another. She was allegedly murdered while walking along the beach below the distillery, and the case has never been solved. It is said that the Blue Lady haunts the distillery because she is searching for her lost lover. The restaurant still reserves her favorite table.

I immediately fell in love with the story, the mystery of it all, and was inspired by the affair and the lies. As I visited the area more frequently, book ideas began to stir. The Monterey cypress grove exists as it does in the novel, tucked between a quiet suburban area and the rocky coast. Hiking trails lead to tide pools, sheltered beaches, and a marine life sanctuary. The ocean in this area can be tumultuous and angry, the weather overcast and dreary. I tried to honor the area as much as I could while still satisfying the needs of the plot.

While I've taken creative liberty and changed even the core of the story, a hint of the Blue Lady remains in these pages. I humbly thank her spirit for the inspiration, and the Moss Beach Distillery for holding a candle to her memory.

ACKNOWLEDGMENTS

First and foremost, I'd like to thank God, who has blessed my life in unimaginable ways. Nothing would be possible without His grace.

Thank you to my wonderful agent, Jill Marsal of Marsal Lyon Literary, who makes my wildest dreams come true. To my editors, Kate Miciak and Alyssa Matesic, for having the foresight to see what this book could become and believing in my ability to make it happen.

To Tina Klinesmith, Deb Lee, Jennie Marts, and Vanessa Kier. Not only are you talented writers, but you are incredible friends. Thank you for your advice when it came to the development of this book.

Love and thanks to Monica Wunderlich, Gary and Giuliana Martin, Heather and James McKenzie, Justin Smith, Laurie and Manish Patel, Lora and Donald Walker, and Sarah and Steve Rhyne for years of friendship and inspiration. Thank you to my Spartan family for your support and enthusiasm. Heartfelt thanks to Aggie Smith for reading every word I've written. I wouldn't have gotten from "Joliet" to this place without you, and certainly not in "nine days."

I would like to give special thanks to Ann and Al Brocchini, whose wisdom and generosity were gifts when researching this novel. Thank you for taking time out of your busy schedules to assist in making this book as accurate as possible. Any mistakes on the police procedural side of things are mine alone.

I'd like to thank my amazing family and support system: Larry, Charlene, Donny, Nora, Cameron, Kendra, Chris, Laura, Juliann, Willow, Steve, Ashlee, and Kaley. Loving thanks to my parents, Don and Marie, for your unwavering faith in me. To my husband, Justin, and children, Kelli and Gavin: I love you with my whole heart.

Read on for an exclusive look at
Kristin Miller's next riveting novel

The Sinful Lives
of Trophy Wives

Available in 2021 from Ballantine Books

CHAPTER ONE

GEORGIA

PRESENT DAY

ST. MARY'S MEDICAL CENTER, SAN FRANCISCO

Pain is the first thing I remember. One moment I'm sleeping the soundest sleep anyone has ever slept. In the next, pain blooms through the tips of my toes. It crawls up my body, slinking over my skin, torturing every nerve ending, until it fills my chest like a giant, throbbing balloon. I try to suck in a jagged breath, but lead sheets crush my chest. I'm flattened against a firm mattress. I'm cold. So unbelievably cold.

Panic lashes through my veins.

I can't open my eyes or my lips. I can't speak. I'm lifeless. Immobile. My strength is gone, completely sapped from my muscles. I can't move, can't shift my weight. I'm pinned.

Beep.

Knives piece my eardrums as the sound goes off again. Swallowing is an effort. A jagged rock has taken up residence in the back of my throat. I'm so thirsty. My lips are unbelievably chapped.

Beep.

Without warning, the nightmare floods back in violent, vivid color. Flashing lights and blood and screams create a chaotic painting against the back of my eyelids. Agony follows, and grief, too.

The accident.

Something terrible happened. I—I didn't stop it. I could have—God, I should have—but I didn't. What have I done?

It strikes again—that cold, wretched feeling that sours my gut. Guilt. I could've done something, opened my mouth and changed the sequence of events that catapulted me into this dark place. I could've changed everything. I held the future in the palm of my hand. But I didn't act, didn't try hard enough.

This is my fault.

Beep.

The annoying bleat morphs from something intrusive and foreign into something familiar. A machine I've heard before, when my first husband, Jake, slipped and cartwheeled down our spiral staircase. He landed on the bottom, arms and legs broken in awkward angles, like a demented starfish. His head hit the tile hard and oozed blood from the crack in his skull all over our Grecian tile. An ambulance rushed him to St. Mary's Medical Center. He was dead on arrival, much like Andrew, my second husband, who swallowed a bullet the following year. I found *him* in our office, his brains staining the back of an Italian leather chair I'd given him for Christmas.

Beep.

I know that noise. I'm in the hospital. The knowledge only increases the adrenaline surging hot through me.

"Open those curtains, would you?" someone says from beside me.

I'm here! I can hear you! I want to scream. But I can't. My lips might as well be stapled shut.

"There, that's better," the nurse says after another shrill chirp from the machine. "She's still really pale, though."

"Do you think her color is off because of blood loss?" someone answers from the other side of me. This voice is softer. Sweeter. "Or lack of sunlight from being stuck indoors? Look at those nails—she's definitely not the outdoorsy type. Maybe she's always this pasty white."

Pasty? My complexion has never been ashen before. Have I truly lost that much blood? My pulse races at the thought.

Beep . . . beep . . . beep.

Something tugs on my arm. I only vaguely remember the feeling from when I was eighteen and put under for my nose job. It's an IV. They're upping my medication.

How long have I been here? It could be a couple of hours after my fortieth birthday party, or a month later. In this state, I wouldn't know. It feels as if I've been sleeping my entire life. Consciousness slips away as blobs of inky darkness threaten to pull me under. My thoughts knock together clumsily like shapes in a kaleidoscope, changing and smearing until time and dream and reality are inconsequential. Is my husband here too? Tucked away in the room next door in the same situation? Too many questions swirl through my brain at once and I can't make sense of any of them.

"You know," the nastier of the two says, "she kind of looks like that woman."

"Which one?"

"The woman all over the news," she says, the IV jerking in my vein. "The one who killed her husband, married another guy right after, and then killed him, too. I think it's her."

Beep.

"Oh, I'd almost forgotten about her," the louder one says. "They say she pushed one down the stairs and shot the other one while he was working in his office." She's beside me now. The side of my bed slumps as if she's leaning over to get a closer look at me. "Yeah, she kind of does look like her, doesn't she? What where they calling her?"

"The Black Widow."

"That's right.

"Hard to tell what she looks like with those bandages on her face."

Oh, for the love of all that is holy, please don't let my face be covered with scars. I wouldn't want to live if I've become disfigured.

"Did you hear if the other woman made it?" the louder one asks. "The one they hit with the car?"

"There was no way that poor woman could've survived. They had to have been going fast." The woman's voice lowers. "When they brought her in, she was really messed up. Did you see her? The officer said she flew thirty feet. Cracked her head open on the asphalt."

"What was she doing in the middle of the road?"

"No one knows."

The woman sighs heavily, as if whatever she's thinking has taken a physical toll on her. "But that's not the worst of it. This woman's husband—the one driving—was ejected through the windshield of their car when they veered into a tree."

Denial flares in my gut. That's not right—they're mistaken. My husband couldn't have been ejected from the car. That's not possible. . . .

"He was killed on impact," one of the nurses whispers.

Beepbeep . . . beepbeep.

"Oh my God," the sweet one says as she pats my hand. "She's going to be devastated when she finds out."

"It gets worse," the other retorts. "I overheard the officer outside her door talking to a detective last night. They're going to have a lot of questions for her when she wakes up. They're going to try to arrest her for murder."

Murder? No—this can't be happening. As a heavy dose of medication deluges my blood, I fall into a deep, comalike sleep—one plagued with nightmares of shattered glass and blood-soaked skin and screams bubbling from the pit of hell.

CHAPTER TWO

BROOKE

ONE MONTH BEFORE THE ACCIDENT

"The area is an architectural dream, with Italian Renaissance, Elizabethan, and Mediterranean influences," the real estate agent says. "There are only forty homes in Presidio Terrace, all located around one street that makes the shape of a lasso."

Or a noose, I think, though I don't dare speak.

"There is a twenty-four-hour guard at the front gate, and anyone using the pedestrian entrance must show proper identification." The agent leads us through the formal dining room, featuring a table that could easily seat thirty. "Not even Google Earth can get in here. The community association negotiated for this area to remain unseen from all maps. There is a security system on the home as well, of course. It features cameras for every door, sensors on every window, and a panic button in each bedroom. It was created by the Secret Service."

"Really?" Jack says, finally acknowledging the agent's

presence. It's as if she'd been beneath him all this time and not worth speaking to. "Interesting."

She nods excitedly. "The level of security here is quite extraordinary."

Jack lets his arm fall heavily around my shoulder, and I'm not sure why but it feels fatherly. As if I'm a child he's trying to shield from something heinous. At fifty years old, Jack is only fifteen years older than I am, though he's aged incredibly well. I gaze up at him, admiring how smooth and tight his skin is, even though he doesn't have a nightly facial routine. He's clean-shaven, with one of those hardened jaw lines that must've manifested after years of clenching his back teeth. He takes care of his body, too. I've dated twenty-year-olds who don't have the muscles he's got. But his hair and eyes give his true age away. We've only been together a year—and married for ten of those months—so of course I wouldn't know what he looks like with a full head of dark hair, but to me, his silver hair only enhances his sex appeal. And his eyes—they're crisp blue and full of light and vitality, but when he smiles, which he doesn't do often, tiny lines splinter from the corners. I won't think about the size of his—*ahem*—wallet, but that's impressive, too.

"Top-level security is what we're looking for. Isn't it?" He squeezes me against him, indicating that I'm not supposed to answer the last question. *Stand silent and smile.* I do as I've been previously instructed. "My job takes me away so much, I need to make sure my wife is protected. As a newly elected U.S. senator, I anticipate I'll be spending most of my time in Virginia."

"Don't senators have to live where they're elected?" the agent fires.

"My permanent residence will remain in Virginia. This home is for my wife."

"Lucky lady." The agent smiles at me. I return the gesture

without showing my teeth. "This way," she sings, "to the kitchen."

My stilettos click-clack over the tile and echo through the cavernous kitchen. I won't be cooking, so I'm not interested in this room of the house. The counters are quartz and the appliances are all stainless steel. It's pretty, in a simple way. The sink's faucet is hooked like a swan's neck, and the box-thing above the stove is beautifully detailed. Actually, the entire thing resembles the kitchen in Jack's Virginia Beach home.

I've wondered half a dozen times this weekend why we can't simply live there. His home is gorgeous, and it would make more sense. I like being close to him. But he says he's selling it. Reminds him too much of his ex-wife. They've recently divorced after twenty years of marriage. And he doesn't have to live in Virginia to be a senator there. He only had to while he was being elected. Now that it's done, he can live anywhere he wants. Last week I mentioned something about taking a trip to California. Here we are, one private jet ride later, seriously looking at homes.

"All of this will have to be redone. Obviously," Jack adds, skimming his hand along the counters. "The colors aren't to our taste."

Aren't they?

"That's the great thing about this place," the agent says. "There's enough room in your budget for you to make all the changes you want. This way. Follow me."

Jack has already hired a full-time staff for whichever California home we choose and has them on standby. Although he hasn't spoken the words, I know this is the home we'll buy. It's the security and privacy he's after, and nothing rivals this place.

Peeking out the kitchen window over the sink, I steal my first glimpse of the backyard. It's landscaped beautifully, with a pool, a spa, a cabana on either end, and trees lining the edges for privacy. I can definitely imagine summers spent back there. Alone.

"The community board is active, as you would imagine in a place like this," the agent says, letting her hand drift over the banister as she leads us upstairs. "So there are rules that must be followed if you intend to purchase the home."

"What rules?" He stops dead. "You didn't mention that before."

There's the husband I know, hesitant to follow any kind of orders.

"Nothing too strange. This way to the master. You must see the view."

I stop a few stairs above him and extend my hand. He clenches his jaw and follows reluctantly, taking my hand as he passes.

"These rules are going to be a deal breaker," he says with a groan, and leads me down a hallway wide enough to fit a car through.

As the agent pushes open two oversize doors simultaneously and stands back with the smile, the room washes in light. The bedroom is enormous, with a cathedral-like ceiling, a chandelier in the center, thick crown molding, and a window with a sprawling view of the Pacific Ocean and Golden Gate Bridge.

"Before we go a step further, I need to hear about these rules," Jack presses. He's standing in the center of the room with his arms folded over his chest. He's taken on his booming politician voice. "What are they and who makes them?"

The agent turns, her blond hair falling over her shoulder. "It's about the front of the home, mainly. Grass can't be more than two inches long. Garage doors cannot be left open for longer than five minutes at a time. Cars must be parked in the garage overnight—not in the street or the driveway. No music over seventy decibels. Things like that."

Nodding, Jack seems to chew over her words. "Those aren't too cumbersome. Who makes them?"

"The Presidio Terrace Homeowners Association. It's run by a few of the wives in the community." She checks her phone. "Mrs. Erin King, who lives there, across the street, is the president. Mrs. Georgia St. Claire—I'm sure you've heard of her from the news—lives next door, to your right, though you can't see her home from here. She's the secretary."

"Why would we have heard of Georgia St. Claire?" he asks. Then he repeats the name, thoughtfully. "St. Claire. Is she married to the state governor?"

"No, no, nothing like that." The agent lowers her voice as if telling a delicious secret. "She's the Black Widow." When Jack stares blankly, she prattles on. "Oh, it's just a nickname the press around here has given her. She's had two husbands pass away in the last few years, and some say she's killed them. Her third husband, Robert St. Claire, is still alive, but there are bets as to how long that'll last."

Talk about morbid gossip.

"I don't know that I want my wife associating with a husband-killer." The corners of Jack's mouth kink up in an attempt at a smile. "What if that kind of behavior rubs off?"

"Mr. Davies, I'm sure that's not the way it works, and—"

"That was a joke," he says flatly. "Brooke wouldn't dare associate with someone nicknamed the Black Widow."

But I don't even know her. How could I say who I would or wouldn't hang out with? Surely I could make up my own mind about her man-killing tendencies. And it's not like Jack will be around to police me.

"There's more of the house to show you: the gym, the up-stairs office, a handful of guest bedrooms. Allow me to show you. This way." The agent glances at me out of the corner of her eye, and then continues the tour. "I wouldn't let Mrs. St. Claire's presence sway your decision to purchase the home,

Mr. Davies. I can assure you there are plenty of wholesome housewives on the street for your wife to associate with."

I was wondering how long it would take for them to leave me out of the conversation completely. It's as if I've become invisible, a ghost walking the halls. I'm impressed with the agent, actually. Within my husband's inner circle it usually only takes a few minutes, and she's nearly finished giving the tour. Points for making an attempt.

After showing us everything the magnificent home has to offer, Jack moves the conversation to other couples on the street. He covers the husbands' occupations and the length of time each couple has lived in the community. Listening intently, though pretending not to care, I stand in the backyard near the pool, relishing the warm California sunshine on my cheeks.

"All right, Brooke," Jack says with a tone of finality. "Sounds like you could make some friends in the neighborhood." He's at my side again, though this time he doesn't touch me. Clearly he's interested in the home and ready to negotiate. His demeanor has completely changed, which leaves no room for emotion. It's all business now. "You'll be happy here. You can get involved in the board, too, if you'd like."

Happy. I'm not sure I know what that is anymore.

I smile brightly, playing the part of a politician's wife. He nods decisively in return.

"It's done," he tells the agent. "I just have a few other questions for you, about the security system. Brooke, I'll meet you at the car."

As he takes her by the elbow and leads her back into the house to talk business, I take in my new backyard. Flowering bushes and walkways leading to hidden places and fountains and birdbaths. It's going to be peaceful here. I can already see my future. Following a tiny shaded path on the left side of the house, I tiptoe from one stone to another, beside towering ferns that take my breath away. The path leads me out front, near Jack's and the realtor's cars.

"Good morning! I'm Erin," a woman yells from across the street. She takes a break from unloading groceries from the trunk of her Tesla to enthusiastically whip her arm back and forth over her head. I can't remember if she's the rumored husband-killer or if that's the woman next door, but I like this one already. "Are you looking or buying?"

"Buying," I holler back, and then check over my shoulder for signs of Jack. He's nowhere to be seen. "My husband's inside finishing up the details."

"Oh, how exciting!" The woman strides across the street, platinum-blond hair blowing in the breeze behind her, and extends her hand. "Allow me to introduce myself properly, then. I'm Erin King, president of the Presidio Terrace Home-owners Association."

"I'm Brooke," I say, shaking her hand. "Brooke Davies."

"You must be married to Jack Davies, the senator."

I squint. "How'd you know that?"

"Not many people can afford this neighborhood, and politicians love the privacy it offers. I heard about your husband's win in Virginia. Be sure to give him my congratulations."

"I will."

"It was a mudslinging campaign overall, wasn't it? They kept bringing up his nasty divorce and his hasty marriage to—well, to you. It was all over the news. You'd make the third family in politics on the block. Kids?"

"No, not even on the radar." I try not to sound upset. "You?"

"God, no." She makes a scrunched face as if she's tasted something grotesque. "Mason hates kids. Loathes them. That's why we moved here. No children on the street."

"Is that because people aren't allowed, or—"

She laughs sweetly. "Oh, that's not part of the community's bylaws or anything. God, can you imagine? Limits to procreation." She laughs harder now, and I wonder if she's on a mood-lifter. "Most people who can afford these homes are older, so their kids are already grown and out of the house. Except for me, of course. I'm midthirties. I would assume you're pushing thirty, but I won't dare ask. Have you met her yet?"

"Who?"

"Georgia."

"No, you're the first one I've met on the street."

"Oh, you *have* to meet her." She clasps her hands over her chest. "You're going to *die* when you realize how sweet she is. Not like the media makes her out to be at all. I mean, she probably killed her husbands, let's be honest, but I'd never tell that to her face."

I shake my head. "I haven't heard much about her at all."

"I'm sure the agent told you some things." She moves closer, invading my personal space. I resist the urge to back up. "Well, Georgia's been married three times. The first time was for love, of course, as first marriages often are. He died very shortly after they were married. She was devastated, or at least pretended to be, then rebounded into a second marriage, much like your husband did. You don't mind my talking candidly, do you?"

"No, not at all." I fold my arms over my chest guardedly, though I can't help but smile. I love her fast chatter and the ease of our discussion. I don't feel like I could say anything wrong to Erin. She'd simply eat up any mistakes in the conversation and bury them with beautiful new words. "It's no secret that my husband had a bit of . . . overlap in his relationships."

"Overlap." She nods, grinning ear to diamond-dangling ear. "I like that. Anyway, the second time, Georgia married for money. She was miserable from the start, so when he died she was happy, in a way, if you get what I mean. She felt free to love and marry again, so she found Robert, whom she simply adores. He's really into his yachts, but he treats her like a queen, as I'm sure your husband treats you."

Like a queen. Locked in a palace.

"What about your husband?" I need to turn the tables before tears gather in my eyes. "What does he do?"

"He's a plastic surgeon. He's responsible for these," she says, pointing to her full lips, "and these," she adds, tapping her cheeks, "and getting rid of all of these lines." She traces an imaginary line from one side of her forehead to the other. "I don't like to boast, but my husband is brilliant."

Judging from the perfect roundness of her breasts, I'd wager he took care of those as well, though I don't ask. I had mine done last year, and the doctor went a little fuller than I'd originally wanted, but Jack is happy, which means I am, too.

"Well, you look great," I offer. "Good enough for the movies."

"That's what I do. Not movies, but television" She drags her hair over her shoulders and squares up to me. "Erin King, ABC, five o'clock news."

"You're a news broadcaster? That's amazing. I could never talk in front of a camera, no way."

She tilts her chin to catch the sunlight. "It's taxing at first, having to be perfect all the time, hitting all the right angles and saying all the right things, but I find, with practice, it simply becomes a part of who you are."

"I understand completely." Behind me, the front door closes. "It was great meeting you, Erin. Since we're going to be neighbors soon, I look forward to continuing our conversation another time."

She's across the street before Jack rounds the corner, and for that I let out a huge sigh of relief.

"What do you think?" he says once we're inside the safety of his car. "Do you love it? Is there anything about that community board that strikes you as strange?"

I tilt my chin to catch the sunlight, pull my hair over my

shoulder, and say, "I love it, sweetheart. I wouldn't change a thing about the home or its neighbors."

As he backs out of the driveway and we pass the home next door, where the rumored husband-killer lives, I wonder if she's married to a man who pretends to be strong in public, but desperately requires his wife's opinion in private. A man who finds shame in being equal to his wife. A man who demands his wife to be flawless, yet is wildly flawed himself.

Above all else, I wonder how she got away with murder.

I'll have to bring over a tray of cookies and ask her.

KRISTIN MILLER is the *New York Times* and *USA Today* bestselling author of more than thirty novels. After writing dark and gritty versions of "happily ever after" for more than a decade, she turned her hand to psychological suspense, a genre she has loved since childhood. She lives in Northern California with her husband and two children.

kristinmiller.net

ABOUT THE TYPE

This book was set in Sabon, a typeface designed by the well-known German typographer Jan Tschichold (1902–74). Sabon's design is based upon the original letter forms of sixteenth-century French type designer Claude Garamond and was created specifically to be used for three sources: foundry type for hand composition, Linotype, and Monotype. Tschichold named his typeface for the famous Frankfurt typefounder Jacques Sabon (c. 1520–80).